CHAPTER ONE

KSARA

K sara lingered too long near the shadowed rail of the ship, and a dark tentacle slithered around her boot and up her calf like the fingers of an unwanted lover. She stifled her yelp and stalked up the deck, away from the dangerous shadows.

They weren't dangerous to everyone. For anyone else, shadows were just shadows, innocuous pools of dark. Inert. Static. Harmless. Even a relief on a hot day.

But for Ksara they were a constant reminder that some insidious, unknown thing wanted her, longed for her, and she could not stop it.

On any other day she'd pretend to her crew that she was directing this relentless presence that haunted her. Then, when the crew grew tired or distracted, she'd sidestep around the shadows and hurry to Ulric's side. Her brother would give her a crooked smile, check the deck to be sure all eyes were away from them, then snap his fingers. A burst of light would ignite with the motion, just bright enough to drive the shadows away from Ksara's boots. They'd share a conspiratorial smile and she would take a long, deep breath.

That trick would have served her now, too, except Ulric was lying on the deck, dying from a wound none of them understood.

She moved to Ulric's side and hovered over him. He lay on a bundle of blankets, his eyes squeezed shut tight and his arm cradled to his chest. The wound was only three inches long and he should have just shrugged it off. He hadn't. This superficial slash had driven him to his knees, and seconds later, he'd fallen unconscious with a fever that could fry eggs. The skin around the wound had changed from a smooth, deep brown into a thick, cracked gray that peeled away from the muscle and bone like bark from a tree.

In an instant, Ksara had known this was an injury they could not treat. They needed a healer mage. And that meant returning to the chamber pot of academia and vandals called Nokte Murosa.

More shadows slipped across the deck to swirl and slither around her, as if sensing she had no protector this time. No one could chase them away from her now. The living dark reached up her leg and a chill ran deep through her veins.

She flinched away from the brazen bit of darkness, her sudden movement breaking its hold, and she continued pacing up and down the deck faster than before.

She could have saved Ulric. If she'd been able to push back the shadows, they would have seen the monster lurking there. They would have been able to dodge those scythe-like claws and Ulric would be standing beside her, elbowing her in the ribs and teasing a smile out of her.

But she hadn't been able to control the shadow. Instead, she'd let Ulric take the lead into the darkness. Let him fall because she was afraid. Weak.

And Atlas had seen it all.

He watched her now, his gaze fixed on the shadows chasing her. Suspicion and anger a darkening storm on the man's face.

"Use your power, mage," he said, his voice low. A challenge.

Ksara forced herself to acknowledge the metal-clad man standing at attention at the bow of the ship. He wore full Imprevari armor despite the danger it posed while at sea. The charcoal gray steel as grim as it's wearer. "What did you say?"

"I said use your power, mage," Atlas said again, louder and sharper.

Ksara squared her shoulders.

He shifted his hand to rest on the hilt of his short sword. "You don't seem very comfortable with your little friends there. Why don't you make them go away?"

Ksara kept her gaze even and her voice calm. The Imprevari craved a fight—he always craved a fight—and she wouldn't give it to him. Not here. Not with Ulric dying at their feet. "My power is my own."

"If you say, mage. If you say."

The muscles between her shoulder blades tightened. Her jaw set. She wanted to drive Atlas's face into the deck. She could drop the Imprevari in three hand strikes. One hand strike and a kick if he drew his sword.

More shadows sloshed at Ksara's boots, sending chills up her legs.

To an outside observer, the darkness seemed to rally to her anger. And she let the charade play as though she was summoning her power, matching Atlas's intensity with plenty of her own.

"Nokte Murosa on the port bow!" Coronata called from the helm.

Ksara turned on the heel of her boot, strode right through the shadow, gritting her teeth at the chill, and joined her first mate at the helm.

Coronata maneuvered the ship with relaxed precision and an amused curl to her lips. The sea loved the woman, the wind played with her long black hair, the sunset enhanced the golden tones of her skin, and the *Falco* danced beneath her touch. "Did Atlas lose another dagger up his ass?"

"For this foul mood? A dagger is too small. Might be a rapier."

Coronata laughed. "That is a clenched ass no weapon returns from."

Ksara almost smiled. She almost took a deep breath of sea air. Almost.

"Guide us into port, Captain," Coronata said with a grin and stood to the side of the helm, leaving one hand on it until Ksara took control. "I'll man the sails."

"What's left of them."

"What's an adventure without a little damage?"

Ksara winced and her gaze fell to Ulric on the deck.

Coronata sobered some, too. "Don't worry. He'll be in the hands of the healer by sundown. And the arms of a barmaid by midnight."

Ksara swallowed. "Let's get to it, then."

Coronata smiled wide, leapt down the stairs, and got to work climbing into the rigging.

Mere moments later, a screeching whoop filled the air and something crashed below deck. A voice murmured curses and the next second a creature darted up from the ladder and raced up the mast in a flash of black and white until it found Coronata's shoulder and curled up there.

A giantess of a woman climbed up the ladder after the thing, her face nearly as red as her hair. "Khyven!"

The creature hissed back at the woman.

Ksara spun the helm to port and then held steady. "Merewen, help Coronata at the sails."

The Usaran woman straightened her muscled shoulders and composed her expression. The blue tattoos on her jaw twitched. "Of course, Captain."

"Did he do unmentionable things to your sacred shaving basin?" Coronata called out as she climbed down the rigging.

"No," Merewen said, her placid calm returning. "He did unmentionable things to my scrolls on magic curses."

Coronata stroked the creature on her shoulder. It looked something like a cat with wide fox ears, curved black horns, and tiny dragon claws. "Khyven the kapicat!" She scolded. "I told you to only use Atlas's things for your dirty business."

"I'll kill it," Atlas growled from the bow.

"You've already tried," Coronata said, retying a series of ropes on the deck. "Twice."

"He will taste my sword!"

"Ew."

Ksara slapped her hand to the railing. "Stop!"

The crew quieted.

By Grina's skirts! She'd led them through the mazes of Selvo Pass. Bested bandits and ambassadors in turn. She'd even guided them to the most coveted magical artifacts in Noksonon. They could hold their petty arguments until after Ulric was safe. "All hands to the sails."

The crew complied and the ship slid across the water faster than before, catching a coastal wind and skipping along the waves toward the unfortunate city of Nokte Murosa.

Two noktums hemmed in the city, towering canyons of black air that loomed hundreds of feet over the tallest building.

More reasonable folk would have left that strip of land between the two noktums alone, but the one sure thing obscure academics and desperate criminals had in common was a deficit in reason. And now they also shared the port city where the very wind that bolstered the *Falco*'s sails brought in plenty of trade and even more trouble.

The bay held a dozen different ships, all with their sails low and coasting normally into the docks. The *Falco* crew kept the sails high and hurtled dangerously past the other ships—Ksara whipping the helm back and forth and Coronata angling the sails just so. They cut a wake into the port faster than any ship in history.

Fifty feet from the docks, Ksara's heart thumped in her chest. They were headed right at the harbor near full speed with a crew of three and Ulric's unconscious body sliding about the deck. "All hands prepare for Lotura's Luck."

"We should have died the first time we did this!" Atlas growled into the wind.

Forty feet.

Coronata whooped with delight. Ksara gripped the helm with white knuckles.

Thirty feet.

Merewen lashed Ulric to the mast. Ksara widened her stance and let out a short breath.

Twenty feet.

"Now!"

Ksara whipped the helm to port in three sharp rotations. In the same instant, Coronata and Merewen released five ropes, dropping the sails while Atlas threw the anchor.

The *Falco* jerked hard and spun out around the anchor. The hull groaned. The waves crashed. And the *Falco* slowed for just a moment before it finished its spin and cracked its starboard hull into the Nokte Murosa docks.

The crash flung Ksara to her knees and the *Falco* listed side to side, nearly dumping them all into the angry ocean. Ksara clung to the helm until the ship steadied.

"Everyone still breathing?" she asked.

Atlas moaned. Coronata laughed.

"Ulric's fine," Merewen said.

Ksara leapt to her feet and hurried to the starboard hull. Merewen sat beside Ulric. Atlas vomited over the side of the ship. Coronata calmly joined Ksara to examine the damage.

Splinters of the dock protruded from the *Falco*'s hull like spines from a porcupine.

"That's a new record for holes in the ship," Coronata said.

"It won't sink," Ksara said.

Coronata cocked a brow at her.

"Tonight. It won't sink tonight."

Coronata grinned. "And what's your prediction for the dock, then?"

The dock had all the appearance of a sailor who had just lost a tavern brawl and now couldn't locate several of his teeth. Two poles sticking up out of the water were crushed into oblivion, the missing pieces now wounding the *Falco*'s side. Four sections of planks dipped into the water. And another two-foot section was lost to the sea completely.

And that's when the shouting began.

Nokte Murosa dock workers ran at the *Falco*. Followed by

some fellow sailors. All of them angry. And armed to the teeth.

"Get Ulric," Ksara said. "We slow down for no one."

CHAPTER TWO

KSARA

Seventeen people ran across the docks toward them. They were annoyances. Obstacles between Ksara and the nearest Nokte Murosan street where her crew could disappear into a crowd, find the Life Mage, steal the elixir he made, and dump the stuff down Ulric's throat in an alleyway that smelled of piss and *shkazat* smoke.

Seventeen people. And she probably shouldn't let Atlas kill any of them.

Probably.

Killing the humans would have been mostly acceptable. Nokte Murosa had a good handful of murders a day. Seventeen would make for a record and plenty of enemies, but they'd still be able to get to the healer and back before vengeance found them.

But there were three Shadowvar among the dockworkers. And if you so much as bruised a Shadowvar in Nokte Murosa, you could be watching the next sunrise with a noose around your neck. A Shadowvar Guildmaster ruled this cesspool of a city and he allowed for the violence and villainy as long as it profited the

Shadowvar and left them unharmed so they could enjoy those profits.

In Nokte Murosa, it was almost a given that the Shadowvar would steer clear of a fight. The slight, short race with black skin and bright white horns had a talent for keeping to the cursed shadows and scurrying off to report it all to the Guildmaster and his goons.

But Ksara and her crew had just destroyed a substantial amount of Nokte Murosan property. There was no telling whether the Shadowvar would keep clear of the fight. And when Atlas drew his sword, there would be no restraint. No reason. Just the thrill of new enemies and a zealous desire to end to them all.

The dilapidated dock swayed and groaned beneath her. The footsteps of the approaching mob clapped nearer. She turned to her crew.

Merewen and Coronata had already gotten the unconscious Ulric off the ship on a litter. They held it still, keeping him above the waves lapping at their feet. Khyven the kapicat sat atop the litter, curled up beside Ulric's head.

Atlas crouched at the edge of the *Falco*, ready to jump to the docks.

"Jump or sink, Anchor!" Coronata called.

"Don't taunt him while he jumps," Merewen said. "He'll die in the waves."

"Then he should take off the armor while near them," Coronata said. "Or tie a rope around his waist so he can be a proper anchor when he goes."

With a groan and a thud, Atlas leapt onto the dock. His armor clanked as he scrambled to his feet and away from the water's edge. "Sandrunner whore," he breathed as he straightened.

"You lonely, soldier?"

Atlas bristled. Coronata laughed.

"Atlas, help Merewen with Ulric," Ksara said as she strode down the dock. "Coronata, you're with me."

Atlas grumbled a curse and Coronata glided up beside Ksara in an instant.

"The plan, Captain?" She asked, her long legs taking the missing dock planks with ease.

"Some of your diplomacy."

Coronata grinned. "Let's make 'em swim."

The two women strode to meet the mob and neither of them pulled a weapon—Ksara kept her staff buckled to her back and Coronata her rapier. So when the first four dockworkers staggered up to them, they hesitated for a fraction of a second. Slicing down two unarmed women, no matter how they'd entered the harbor, wasn't what they'd been expecting. In another town, that hesitation would have stayed the whole fight and Ksara could have talked her way out of the violence.

But this was Nokte Murosa, so Ksara used that hesitation to strike first. A punch to the throat, a kick to the knee and the first dockworker plummeted off the side and into the waves with a yelp. Coronata charged right at another dockworker and shoulder checked him off the edge.

Then things got interesting.

The two remaining dockworkers shrugged off their surprise and swung their swords.

Coronata sidestepped the attack and relieved the weapon from the dockworker so fast, he blinked at his empty palm before getting a kick to the groin and tumbling into the water.

Ksara stepped inside the other sword strike, caught the man by the arm, and pivoted her body, using the man's own momentum to propel him off the edge.

Coronata and Ksara advanced on the next group, gaining a dozen more feet down the dock before they had to stop and fight again. This time Coronata used her stolen sword to parry blows. She spun and danced in the fight, the smaller the space the more adept she was at winning. More and more people fell from the dock.

Ksara dealt with the Shadowvar. All three stayed close together. The foremost swiping a dagger at her and the others clutching knives of their own. They weren't quite as brazen as the human attackers had been—it would have been easier if they'd continued their charge right at her and she could have danced around them, adding just the right bits of momentum to their trajectories and sending them into the water. But the static, slashing trio, had more sense than their fellows and far less fighting experience.

She backed up three steps, almost bumping into Atlas carrying Ulric in the litter. There she caught one of the sailors Coronata had just propelled toward the edge. Holding him by his tunic, Ksara twirled the still screaming sailor back onto the docks and right at the Shadowvar.

The Shadowvar trio shouted as the sailor collided with them. The thrashing sailor dealt the necessary blows to the Shadowvar, knocking two of them off and grabbing the third with all of his strength to keep on his feet. One kick to the sailor's back and both fell from the dock.

They were close to the city now. The stench of gutted fish and *shkazat* smoke mingling with the scent of salt and sea.

The last three sailors waited where the dock met the street. They didn't stand on the dock itself, wary after seeing so many of their fellows ejected into the water. All of them brandished cutlasses and scowls.

And the dockmaster wasn't among them.

The dockmaster was the only widely accepted human authority in Nokte Murosa and the heavy man and his rotted smile was never far from the docks.

If they'd had time to pause and consider the strangeness of his absence, Ksara would have. But Ulric was slipping closer to death with each breath, so she sprinted at the armed sailors with Coronata laughing at her heels.

Three feet from the sailors, Ksara launched from the dock, landed a foot atop one of the poles anchoring the dock in the sea, and leapt right on top of the sailors.

The maneuver would have earned Ksara a fleeting advantage and a quick death had Coronata not followed right behind, parrying the quickest swordsman's blade and slamming him to the ground.

Ksara landed atop another sailor, striking him in the throat as they hit the ground and then breaking the wrist of his sword hand. The last sailor staggered toward Ksara, and she rolled to her feet, kicked the side of his knee, crumpling him to the ground with a cry.

"Now it's my turn," Atlas said from behind.

Ksara looked up to find Dockmaster Gid flanked by a contingent of armed Shadowvar. They closed in around them in an instant.

The Shadowvar wore leather armor stamped with the Guildmaster's own crest, each carrying a spear, sword, or crossbow. This was the Guildmaster's Guard. And, unlike the Shadowvar dockworkers Ksara had helped go for a swim, these Shadowvar had more combat experience on the streets of Nokte Murosa than most Imprevari soldiers.

Ksara gritted her teeth, her heart thumping hard from the fight. If she waged combat with the Guildmaster's own guard, she'd wage war on the Guildmaster himself. And Dockmaster Gid knew it. His flabby cheeks spread like a curtain to unveil his *shkazat* rot of a mouth. The few teeth he had left were stained blue-green and the reek of it filled the several feet between them.

"The Demaijos Devils have returned," Gid said.

The litter dropped to the ground and a sword skidded from its sheath behind Ksara. She raised a hand, halting Atlas without glancing back at him. "We have business with the healer mage," she said.

"Only one of the Demaijos Devils still stands?" Gid cackled and the jowls beneath his chin quivered with his mirth.

Ksara's upheld hand closed into a fist. Maybe she should drop her hand completely and signal the attack. Maybe ending up in the Nokte Murosan gallows would have a sort of satisfaction to it. But only if Gid bled out on these cobblestones.

The Shadowvar must have sensed the change in Ksara because six crossbows leveled at her.

Gid smiled wider, showing more wide gaps between his teeth. "Guildmaster Ariston would see you now. And your invitation is about to expire."

"Guildmaster Ariston can wait until we attend to our business with the healer mage."

"The healer mage is with the Guildmaster now. So is every other person of consequence in Nokte Murosa." Gid gave Ksara a slow once-over. "With a few exceptions."

"He's leading us right to the gallows," Atlas murmured. "Fight and die now or die later."

"To the gallows?" Gid asked in a coy voice. "Have you a crime to pay for?"

Ksara kept her expression neutral. They'd left Nokte Murosa last time not intending to return. Mostly because they'd also stolen a magical family heirloom from the Guildmaster's own home.

"We cannot linger," Merewen said. "His breathing is slower."

Ksara glanced at Ulric in the litter and then up to Coronata. She shrugged. "We need to get to the healer fast. This will take us there."

She was right. But if the Guildmaster wanted to exact justice for their theft, he could clap them all in irons and make her watch Ulric die before hanging her.

Ksara considered the group standing between her and the city and calculated their odds. The four of them could beat the guards. They'd likely take a crossbow bolt or two, but they were headed to a healer anyway, and she was sure they could at least get there.

But could they get back?

Taking out that many Shadowvar would send the whole city into an uproar. They'd have to fight every single Shadowvar citizen on their way back from the healer, only to get to a ship that may or may not be able to stay afloat long enough to get to another port.

And, after all that, what if they didn't grab the right elixir to heal Ulric?

Without the healer mage in his shop, they'd just have to guess which elixir might bring Ulric back from death. They'd be able to grab a dozen different vials. A dozen out of thousands. To cure, not just a typical flesh wound, but something much worse.

Could she risk Ulric's life on that chance?

Ksara swallowed her revulsion at the thought of walking side-by-side with the dockmaster. "Take us to Ariston and the healer mage."

"Your weapons first," Gid said.

"No."

"Then your brother dies here," Gid said with a smile. "One less devil in the world. A pity."

She gritted her teeth, unbuckled her staff from her back, and dropped it to the cobblestone. Atlas spat a dozen curses, but soon all the weapons clattered to the ground.

Gid leaned closer, breathing his sour breath right in Ksara's face. "Ahh. So a devil can be tamed."

Ksara punched him in the nose.

CHAPTER THREE

GENOVE

Genove LeGrande sat poised in his office chair, boots up on his desk, back to a roaring hearth—waiting for just the right moment to lead the young student before him up the stairs and to his bed.

"You believe me, don't you Master LeGrande?"

It was the question that troubled students always asked Genove. It's why they found him in the hallways of the Nokte Murosan Academy. It's why those hushed conversations always led right here to his office, just below his residence.

The students claimed to be seeing monsters. Nightmares of the noktum come to haunt them. And no one else could see them. They'd tell their friends and family. Their instructors and sometimes healers. People on the street and even the Guildmaster's own guard. But none of them believed them. None of them had answers.

So, eventually, they'd come to the scholar of all things in the noktum—Genove LeGrande. They'd beg for validation. For that one person to believe them when no one else did.

Of course he believed them. He's the one who crafted the monsters and warped their minds to see them.

The monsters weren't real, unfortunately. Just hallucinations caused by Genove's own magic infused into ink and then painted onto parchment. Sometimes the victims were coincidental— Genove would paint a monster and leave the parchment stashed in a book at a library or he'd slip it beneath a random door at the academy. He'd bedded merchants, masters, and maids that way. And also sat just so at his table, watching the most powerful crime lords of Nokte Murosa weep.

Sometimes, like in the case with the girl sitting opposite him now, Genove deployed his magic carefully. He hunted for the perfect victim and painted the perfect nightmare just for them. That was a more satisfying task because then you knew the thing you were breaking and you got to watch it pull apart, inch by inch.

You got to see their desperation morph into a twisted desire. They needed him in the end. He was their savior. That was power worth the patience.

The girl fidgeted in the chair. She wore her honey-blonde hair in a ringlet of braids and loose, gray academy robes hid her figure. She had one of those bright minds all of the instructors at the academy hummed about. An aptitude for learning. A memory for history. A quick wit and a strong rhetoric. Everything that an academy master, such as himself, should dream of having in his school.

And Genove did dream. He dreamt of all the terrible monsters he could inflict upon her mind. He dreamt of the moment her mind broke and she collapsed into his arms. He dreamt about all he would take from her in that moment of vulnerability.

That moment was soon.

"I'm not lying, Master LeGrande," the girl said. She had to be just over eighteen years old. Half his own age. "I know it sounds false, but I saw it. And I know it was a Zekroach, not some trick of the shadows. It had faces on its antenna. Faces that moved. Eyes that watched me."

The girl stifled a shudder and glanced about the room as if waiting for that Zekroach to crawl down the stairs and sink its pincer jaws into her side. Her hands began to quiver and she clutched them together. She had some strength to her. Resolve.

Oh, she would be a delightful distraction.

"You have to believe me," she said in a hoarse whisper. "It's real. I think it's going to …" She swallowed hard. "I don't think I have much time left."

There. That was the moment.

Genove removed his boots from his desk and got to his feet. His back was sweaty from the fire spitting and crackling behind him. And his skin tingled with desire.

He glided around his desk, his sapphire-blue scholar robes sweeping around him with the movement. He knelt in front of the girl and locked eyes with her. She did have beauty about her. But more intoxicating than any lip or hip or curve was the fear in her eyes. The glistening terror.

Genove suppressed his own shudder. This one of anticipation.

"I believe you," he said with that warm charm he'd practiced for decades now.

Tears sprung to the girl's eyes and her voice quivered. "You … believe me?"

Genove reached out and grabbed the girl's soft, cold hands and wrapped them in his own. "I believe you. And you're safe here. With me."

Two tears tumbled down the girl's cheeks. "Thank you."

Genove pulled the girl toward him and she collapsed into his shoulder. She wept into him and while she did, he kissed her neck. Explored the curves of her body with his hands. She stiffened at first and then, like all of the others, she let that barrier break, too. Fear had that power. He had that power.

He led her up the stairs and she followed.

Hours later, the girl slept beside him. Naked and curled up into him like a child. He traced a finger along that sharp jaw, down her long neck and across her collar bone. She looked so peaceful. So content.

Much too content.

He leaned away from the girl's young, warm body and pulled a book from the table. Cradling the book in his hands, careful only to touch the cover, he turned it over and shook it over the sheets. Out fell a single, loose parchment the size of his hand. On it was one of his paintings, this one of a Manticore crafted in thick, black strokes of Genove's own magical ink with a blot of red wax on one edge of the paper.

Clasping only the wax between two fingers, he picked up the paper and placed it on the girl's back. She shivered. Genove's gut tingled and the magic activated.

Her brow furrowed. Her breathing quickened. In another moment she kicked and thrashed and moaned. By the time he put the book back on the table, the girl startled awake, her eyes wide and sweat glistening on her face, neck, and back.

"A different monster?"

She nodded, her eyes tracking something unseen as it stalked closer and closer and closer.

"I foresaw as much," he said, slipping an arm around her bare shoulders and drawing her close. He smelled her fear, and it intoxicated him as completely as the purest *shkazat*.

"You saw this?" She asked, her voice a bare whisper. "You knew it would come?"

"I can see many things," he said. "And I can protect you from all of them."

She leaned into Genove, her heart beating so fast he could feel it pumping against him. "Don't let it get me," she whispered. "Please."

"In my arms you are safe." He smiled a little at that lie, breathing in the virile scent of her fear and letting his hands quest about her bare skin.

A door smacked open downstairs. The girl screamed and cowered. "Don't let it get me. Please. Master LeGrande. Please!"

Genove's body hummed with desire. Gritting his teeth, he removed himself from the blubbering child, dressed, and hurried down the stairs.

There he found Guildmaster Ariston himself standing in the doorway, the captain of the guard at his side. The two Shadowvar nearly blended into the growing dark of dusk, their horns a glaring white.

Genove tidied his hair. "Ariston! Any word on Eshe?"

"What manner of mage are you, Genove LeGrande?"

Genove's breath caught in his throat, then he covered his surprise with a perplexed smile. "Ariston. What's wrong?"

"What manner of mage are you, Genove LeGrande?" the Guildmaster repeated, emphasizing each word like a strike of a whip.

Genove worked a little moisture into his mouth. "I am your mage, Ariston. I would use all of my power to help you. Are we not friends?"

The Guildmaster's gaze hardened, water freezing to ice. "Tell me you're a Lore Mage."

Genove rallied all of his charm and lied, "I have seen glimpses of your future dozens of times. You know this to be true. I am a Lore Mage!"

Ariston raised a hand from his side and the captain put a satchel in it. Genove recognized the satchel, but maintained his false innocence. Best to commit to the lie than concede. "What have you found? I can try my lore magic on it, but if Eshe hasn't touched it in a while, my visions could be incomplete."

Ariston tipped the satchel upside down and dumped vials of ink, bundles of parchment, and a handful of brushes to the floorboards. One of the vials broke and spilled the precious ink across the floor.

Genove hid his irritation. "What is this?"

Ariston glared at Genove for a long moment. The girl upstairs wept, her cries the only sound. "I showed it to Lyshan."

The words crumbled Genove's facade and a scowl gathered on his face like a summer thunderstorm. Lyshan was the only other mage in Nokte Murosa. And a talented Life Mage, at that. He would have been able to sense the Love Magic in Genove's tools. In the ink he used to craft his monsters.

"I have stood at your side all these years," Genove said. He didn't pretend at charm. The words carried all of his strength. All of his fury at being caught in his decades-old lie. "Do not make an enemy of me."

Ariston shook his head, the silver chains draped between his horns jingled with the movement. "If you had made a fool of me alone, I would forgive you. I would see you for the greedy, power-thirsty mage that you are and call it a lesson learned. But Eshe has been taken. For six days he has been gone."

This time Genove didn't need to lie. "I had nothing to do with that."

"But you advised me," Ariston said, his voice cold. "You told my guard where to look. And we trusted you. We trusted the Lore Mage above all other leads. I trusted you."

Genove reached into his robes. He kept one of his drawings in a pocket there. If he could grab the drawing by the bit of wax on the top edge and touch it to Ariston, a new nightmare would occupy the Shadowvar and Genove would be able to slip away.

"Seize him."

The captain was on Genove in an instant. Genove had four inches on the Shadowvar, but none of the training and in a flash of black, the Shadowvar had Genove's hands behind his back and his face shoved into a wall.

"Do not make an enemy of me," Genove spat into the wall.

"You were my enemy all the while," Ariston said and he turned from Genove. "Purge him."

Genove thrashed in the Shadowvar's grip and bellowed his own scream and the girl wailed louder upstairs.

CHAPTER FOUR

KSARA

Ksara led her crew into the Assembly Hall with her hands shackled and blood dripping from her bottom lip.

Gid hobbled a few feet ahead, marking each step across the polished stone with a groan.

After she'd punched Gid, the guards had reacted instantly—but so had Atlas. The Imprevari had bought her time for a few extra blows against the screaming, pudgy dockmaster. And she'd used them all to mangle the man's left leg.

She could have dealt fiercer pain to softer spots, but she'd decided on the leg in an instant. And now every step the man took reminded him of just how dangerous a Demaijos Devil could be.

The Assembly Hall's antechamber was big enough to swallow a modest home and had all the comforts of a grave. Long slender windows cut through the walls like wounds. Tapestries hung in silent homage to bloody wars Ksara didn't even know the names of. And the shadows—the shadows reached for her. Waited for her to slow so that they could claw at her feet and legs and body.

Ksara strode faster, catching up to the dockmaster. He

scowled at her, his broken, bloody nose still oozing. His red-stained lips parted to speak, but before he could do more than wheeze his diseased breath at her, the guards reached the doors to the next room and swung them open wide.

If the antechamber was a graveyard, the meeting room was a lavish tomb. Five pillars leafed in gold stood sentry, with pedestals of art and artifacts crowded between. A domed ceiling loomed above it all, painted in a grisly depiction of Shadowvar battling a noktum.

A raised dais sat at the center of the room and stone benches circled it like ripples in a pond of red stone.

Guildmaster Ariston stood on the dais, commanding the room with the force of his gaze.

Ksara paused for a fraction of a second, feeling for any sensation coming from the black, metal band on her arm. Not so much as a shiver came from the thing, which meant that none of the artifacts so proudly presented about the room were even marginally magical.

A pity. Khyven could use some training stealing in a room like this with so many eyes on him.

Gid hesitated beside Ksara, and he tried to stand tall on his swollen leg. "I've brought the *Falco* crew."

Ksara stepped around the dockmaster and glided down an aisle, right toward the dais.

Town officials, merchants, and crime lords shuffled out of her way. "Where is the Life Mage," Ksara said, loud and firm. This wasn't the first dignitary she'd charged right up to, bound and bleeding. Her aunt was Queen of Demaijos. Her mother the Queen's own guard. And she the youngest, and most stubborn, of seven children.

"Where is my Ring of Salgimore?" Guildmaster Ariston countered coolly.

Ksara kept her expression firm. They'd stolen the Ring of Salgimore from the Guildmaster's own house several months before—and sold it to a Luminent ambassador hours after the theft. The artifact was halfway to Laria by now and the coin long since spent.

She stopped at the dais and the shadows drew toward her. The crowd gasped and backpedaled away. Ksara broadened her stance and beckoned the dark toward her—pretending at control until the dark was at her boots and licking up her legs. The touch sent chills up her spine, but she kept the discomfort—the fear—far from her face. Instead, she stared down Ariston with the shadows writhing all around her. "The Life Mage," Ksara repeated. "Now."

Guildmaster Ariston took in the exhibition with calculating eyes. "Your brother is dying."

The words struck Ksara to her core. In all the tense hours since they'd fled the nuraghi to come here, none of them had said those words out loud.

"I will not waste more time with words," Ksara said. The shadows swelled around her, stinging her skin like a bitter wind. But she didn't move. She didn't even lean away. She just stared right back at the Guildmaster and used all of her grit to keep her panic from showing in her face.

Guildmaster Ariston turned his gaze to a short, balding man in a cloak with a dappling of stains on the sleeves. "Can you save her brother's life, Lyshan?"

The Life Mage hurried around the dais to Ksara and her crew. Khyven the kapicat hissed and chittered at the mage as he approached, but Coronata pulled the creature up into her arms and settled him.

All of them watched the mage for a breathless moment as he prodded Ulric's wounded arm, listened to his breathing, and pressed a palm to his face. "He is dire. But I can save him yet. Shall I take him to my shop, Guildmaster?"

"No."

"Yes."

Ariston and Ksara spoke at the same time.

Ksara exchanged a brief glance with her crew. Atlas shifted his stance, Merewen scanned the room, and Coronata winked. They'd fight their way out of here with the Life Mage in tow, if they had to.

"The Ring of Salgimore," Ariston said.

"We don't have your ring."

"The ring is nothing. Not now. But its double—could you find its double? Same as you found the first?"

"You lose an heirloom?" Coronata asked with a hint of a smile.

The shadows pawed at Ksara and she fought back a shudder. "No. He lost a person. No one else has been able to find them. Now you're hoping that we can find them because they're wearing the twin to the ring you *think* we stole."

Ariston's cool facade cracked. His brow furrowed and the grief shone in his dark eyes. "It's my son. The Dorumai took my son. Six days ago."

"Dorumai?" Atlas asked.

"A cult," Merewen said, adjusting her grip on the litter. "Old and violent. They have a fascination with the Giants. Worship them. And want to prepare the world for their return."

"So the average kind of crazy," Atlas said. "That's easy enough to kill."

Ksara's gaze fell to Ulric and the worried Life Mage beside him. Then she turned back to Ariston. "And if we don't find your son?"

Ariston's face changed. The grieving parent was gone and in his place was something colder. A husk of a man. The fragments of a leader. The makings of a tyrant. "Then we both lose family."

Ksara considered the crowd of people already in the meeting room. Some of the most savvy criminals she'd met sat among scholars and merchants. And all of their eyes were on her and her crew. None of them had a hope of finding the boy. They'd tried and failed for six days already.

"He has the ring on him?" Ksara asked.

"Yes."

"Just like the Ring of Salgimore?"

"A matched pair," Ariston said.

"It wasn't here last time."

"And neither was my son," Ariston said. "He was away to Nokte Shaddark."

"You're sure he had it on when he was taken?"

"He never takes it off."

"And these Dorumai," Coronata interjected. "They were after your son, not the ring?"

"They thrive on terror, not treasure," Ariston said, eyeing Coronata with disdain. "Some criminals specialize, pirate."

Coronata chuckled, then gave the Guildmaster a sultry gaze. "Oh, I specialize."

"Grina's ass!" Atlas groaned. "Can we not do this now?"

Coronata shrugged. "Do what?"

"The actual flirting with danger," Merewen said. "You're literally flirting with danger."

Coronata grinned and eyed the Guildmaster. "Of cou—"

"Enough," Ksara said and her crew silenced. She glanced at each of them. They'd banded together in a Triadan prison to steal and sell magical artifacts. Two mages, a retired pirate queen, a barbarian historian, and a disgraced calvary captain. They weren't here to save the Guildmaster's son from a cult she'd never heard of. They weren't in the hero business.

But, this was finding treasure, of sorts. A sister ring to one they'd already stolen before on the finger of an abducted Shadowvar. That presented some challenge, but at its core, this was a find and sell mission. The buyer of the artifact just happened to be a city official with every inclination to hang them by their necks if they failed.

"We'll do it," she said. "We'll find your son."

"You have two days."

Atlas spat a curse.

The shadows inched higher on Ksara, she grit her teeth to keep from shivering. "Two days to do what none in this room could do in six?"

Ariston motioned at Ulric. "He has hours. I give you days."

"Fine," she said. "Two days."

Atlas swore louder.

Ariston held Ksara's gaze. "Find my son."

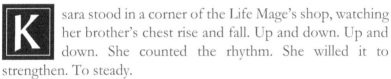

CHAPTER FIVE

KSARA

K sara stood in a corner of the Life Mage's shop, watching her brother's chest rise and fall. Up and down. Up and down. She counted the rhythm. She willed it to strengthen. To steady.

Ulric wheezed and the middle-aged Life Mage mixed two elixirs together, swirled them until they changed color to a turquoise blue, and then placed three droplets of the liquid onto Ulric's tongue.

Ulric rasped and the mage abandoned the first elixir, gathered five more, and nursed a little of each into Ulric's mouth.

Ulric groaned, his voice hoarse, and the mage retrieved a whole shelf full of elixirs and applied them, seemingly at random, to patches of Ulric's skin. Sometimes near the wound and sometimes on his head and hands. Neck and chest.

And when Ulric went silent, his breathing soft, and the rise and fall of his chest strong, the mage leaned against the worktable where Ulric lie and wilted. He grabbed one of the half-used elixirs from the table and drowned it himself.

"That curse should have killed him," the bald man said. "Hours before you even reached Nokte Murosa."

"He's hard to kill," Ksara said, her voice tight. She'd known that they had had very little time to get Ulric to the healer. She'd felt the dire countdown in her soul. But hearing another say it out loud made her want to weep at what might have happened and pump her fist to the sky in defiance of that universe, those gods, who tried to take her brother from her.

"Did another mage do this to him?"

"No."

"An artifact, then?"

"A wound from a beast."

"Oh," the bald mage said, wiping his sweaty face on his sleeve. "How long until he wakes?"

"That's a matter of spirit," the Life Mage said. "Some patients take days and weeks. With your brother? I suspect less. Much less."

Ksara breathed a little deeper. "He's healed, then? He'll recover?"

The Life Mage gave her a weary smile. "Healing. He's on his way back to life. But whatever beast inflicted this wound is not done with your brother yet."

Tightness returned to Ksara's ribcage. "He's still ... he could still ..."

"Life is fleeting, but he's out of danger for now," the mage said. "Curses, like this one, don't let go easily. They stay in the mind."

"What does that mean?"

"It means I make a call to the Nokte Mursoan Academy Library in the morning," the Life Mage said with a smile. "And you rest yourself before I find you on my table in need of elixir."

Ksara assessed the mage. He'd seemed like a subservient tool around the Guildmaster, but here, in his own shop, he had a brightness to his eyes. A calm. He wasn't a politician; he was a healer. This was his domain. And he seemed entirely intent on keeping Ulric alive while under this roof.

If Ariston came and stole Ulric away, however, Ksara doubted the meek man would stop him.

"What do you know of the Guildmaster's son?" Ksara asked.

The mage sighed and began returning elixirs to their shelves. "I cannot find him, if that's what you're asking. I already tried. My powers reside in these elixirs and healing. Nothing more."

"But you knew him?"

"I've known Eshe since he was born," the mage said. "I tried to save his mother on this very table after the birth." His gaze grew distant. "Not every patient has your brother's strength."

"Do you think the boy's still alive?"

The mage focused back on Ksara and his brow furrowed. "By Lotura, I hope he is. For all of us. I hope he is."

"And if he's not?"

"The Dorumai won't need to tear Nokte Murosa apart," he said. "The Guildmaster will do it for them."

"He'd destroy a city for one boy?"

The mage's eyes softened. "Grief pushes a person. Bursts them at the seams."

She felt her own seam, the weak places in her soul that had felt the strain of Ulric's impending death the keenest. It throbbed inside her still, warning her of the pain she'd just escaped.

She moved to Ulric now, grabbing hold of his hand and pressing it between both of hers. His skin had cooled to a normal temperature. And the pain had eased from his face. She yearned for his eyes to open. And she knew, even as she stared at him, that she could not stay here to watch over him. No matter how desperately she wanted to.

She had a Shadowvar to find. And fast.

"You won't be resting."

She glanced up at the mage and there was compassion on the round man's face.

"You have the same strength."

She shook her head. "If he wakes—"

"I'll find you. Now go. Find Eshe and all of Nokte Murosa will thank you."

CHAPTER SIX

KSARA

Two streets down from the Life Mage, Ksara found *The Saunter Inn*. It looked like the upside-down hull of a ship smashed between two respectable houses—and it leaked blue smoke from the collision.

Sucking in one last breath of untainted air, Ksara pushed past the dilapidated door and into the tavern. There she was met with a rowdy chorus of Coronata's favorite sea shanty. Shouldering through the crowd of enthralled sailors, Ksara arrived at the epicenter of the joviality to find the retired pirate queen lounged on the top of the bar, her long legs draped over a chair.

She winked when she saw Ksara and led the sailors in the last verse the shanty: "And a night with Lady Ariciyane! … Will make a Shadowvar shine!"

Cheers and laughter rocked the tavern and Coronata whooped and hollered right along with them. Someone handed her a tankard and she emptied it with gusto, then slid off the bar and into the crowd. In another moment she stood at Ksara's side, eyes bright.

"Ulric's well?"

"He's on his way there." Ksara glanced at the quieter tavern patrons sucking down blue *shkazat* smoke from communal pipes at the tables. "Is Merewen back?"

"Just came in," Coronata replied.

"And a room?"

"The room isn't available for another few hours."

"Few hours?"

Coronata smiled. "You can't hurry love."

Ksara made a face. "They get half an hour and then I send Atlas in."

"That's a little cruel," Coronata said. "No tavern tumble should end with Atlas."

"Stop," Ksara said, a hint of a smile on her face.

"Stop speaking truth?" Coronata gasped with feigned alarm.

"Stop trying to make me laugh. There's work to be done." Ksara spotted Merewen bent over a table and started toward her. Coronata follows beside.

"Work doesn't mean you don't laugh," she said. "Else we may become like sir armor stand right there, who looks for all the world like he stashed his side dagger up his arse."

Ksara cracked a quiet smile, but smoothed it away before they reached the table.

"Captain," Merewen said, sparing the briefest glance from her study of four scrolls unfurled on the table.

"What do we know about the ring?" Ksara asked.

"The Ring of Salgimore does have a sister ring," Merewen said. "Both were crafted by the same smith and mage duo—Azure and Cirrus—in 1722."

"Sounds like we could have charged that diplomat double for the first one," Coronata said.

Merewen sighed. "If we hadn't been running to the *Falco* after the grab, I could have done more research on it. And we could have asked more." She tapped the scroll. "With the documentation to prove it."

"The kapicat gave us away," Atlas grumbled from the wall.

Coronata whistled, short and low. In a flash of black and white, Khyven the kapicat darted out from the crowd of sailors and leapt to Coronata's shoulder, a dozen coins clutched in its dragon claws. Coronata whistled again and the kapicat bared its tiny teeth at her.

"Khyven," Coronata scolded.

The kapicat's ears drooped and it released its fistfuls of coin into Coronata's palm. She pocketed the money, gave the creature a nut, and shrugged. "Still knows more tricks than Atlas."

Atlas reached for his sword. "I'll show you a trick, Sandrunner."

"I keep telling you—no one wants to see your sword," Coronata said.

"Whore," Atlas growled.

"Jealous?" Coronata countered with an arched brow.

Ksara raised a hand. "Do we know what the second ring can do?"

Merewen pointed to a place in the scrolls, though it was written in a dialect only the Usaran fully understood. "Both were Love Magic. The first influenced fame. The second fortune."

"It was a weak spell," Ksara said.

"The ruins showed some wear," Merewen said. "But paired with the second ring, the affect would have been greater."

"The first ring made people inclined to like you," Ksara said. "And the second made them, what? Want to give you money?"

"Simply put, yes," Merewen said. "The rings were made for Salgimore, a notorious trader of the day. Salgimore and these rings shaped the Triadan trading routes."

Coronata leaned back in her chair and pulled a nut out of her pocket, nibbling around its edges. "Why didn't Ariston wear both of them? Why give a ring to the kid at all?"

"Tradition," Merewen said.

Coronata blinked at the Usaran. "So, not a good reason at all."

Merewen stiffened. "You're teasing me."

"Yes," Coronata said with a grin.

Ksara pointed back at the scroll. "Alone, the second ring is as weak as the first?"

"Yes."

"The first one was hard for you to feel," Coronata said, stroking the kapicat between its twisted, black horns. "That's not great news for the Shadowvar kid."

"Or the rest of us," Ksara said with a sigh. "If I'm within a dozen feet, I'll be able to feel it."

Atlas fully turned to the group now, his gaze even darker than before and his hand on the hilt of his sword. "You can feel magical objects and manipulate shadow? What manner of mage are you, Ksara Sajra?"

Merewen unfurled her height, her head nearly brushing the rafters. "Captain Sajra. You mean Captain Sajra."

"What do you know about Captain Sajra, Usaran? What do we really know about her?"

"She came back for me," Coronata said, her voice suddenly void of mirth. "She guided your ungrateful arse through the Selvo pass. She doesn't give up. Not on a mission. Not on us."

Atlas stepped back to the wall, his hand still on the hilt of his sword and gaze burrowing into Ksara.

The Imprevari sensed the deception and, for a moment, Ksara considered telling them all about the properties of the black ring on her arm. That it had been a broken shard of a larger magical artifact that her father had had reforged into an inconspicuous ornamentation. He'd intended for the thing to inhibit Ksara's unseemly power, to keep the dark away from his daughter. It hadn't worked as planned. But it did vibrate when she was near another magical artifact—something any treasure hunter with a knife would try to kill her for. And she certainly didn't need more enemies. Least of all in Nokte Murosa.

"Merewen," Coronata said, "How long has it been since Atlas has gotten into a fight?"

Merewen frowned. "Does the nuraghi count?"

"No, I mean one of those senseless alley fights."

"Ten days."

Coronata spread her arms wide. "There you have it. Atlas needs to get knocked on his ass once every week. It's keeps him cheerful."

"And here I thought I was about to ruin your day," a new voice interrupted, "Not improve it."

Ksara knew that voice. And the stench that came with it. She turned to find Dockmaster Gid and five sailors with the thickest necks she'd ever seen gathered around him. Gid's nose still had a swollen bend to it, but he'd cleaned up the blood and changed tunics.

Coronata rose and hung an arm around Ksara's shoulders while her free hand fell to her rapier. "Has anyone told you you smell terrifically foul?"

Gid eyed Coronata up and down and he wet his amphibious lips.

"Ariston wants us alive," Ksara said.

Gid wrenched his gaze back to Ksara and her skin crawled under his hungry scrutiny. "Alive. I have plenty of ways I can help you feel alive, Demaijos. And we can even let the little Imprevari watch if you want."

Ksara sensed the shadows around her. Felt them lapping closer to her. Always closer to her. But in this crowded tavern, few would notice an errant curl of shadow at their feet. Shadows and charades wouldn't help her now.

Gid hobbled closer. The reek from his rotting teeth permeated the air and his eyes sparkled. "Come now. I like a rough girl."

"How about you limp out of here," Ksara said. "While you still have one good leg."

Coronata unbuckled the staff on Ksara's back, and, in the same instant, Ksara ducked and twisted, catching the weapon in her palm and striking hard at Gid's good leg before he had even seen it leave her back.

Atlas bellowed, drew his sword, and charged at the biggest brute of a sailor; drawing three of the sailors to him immediately. Coronata drew her rapier and parried a cutlass aimed at Ksara. And Merewen whipped a chair out and cracked it over another sailor's head, raining debris down on them all.

The tavern erupted into chaos.

Some of the sailors sided with the *Falco* crew, due in no small part to Coronata's charm, and they ambushed Gid and his sailors.

But the majority, out of fear or loyalty to the dockmaster, rallied to the opposite side.

Tables broke. Bodies crunched against walls. Fists pounded flesh and bones broke. And Coronata sang her sea shanty again, using the thump of the violence as the beat to the song.

"Some things are well worth the hanging," Coronata called out, clapping another sailor's head into a table. "Some things are well worth the crime."

A sword rang through the air, missing Ksara's head by inches. She pivoted backward, pulling her staff high to block the next blow. But before the attacker could rally another strike, Coronata slashed and the sailor fell as she sang, "And a night with Lady Ariciyane! ... Will make a Shadowvar shine!"

Ksara grabbed the tavern door, threw it open, and moved through it. A beat after Ksara and Coronata staggered out onto the cobblestone, Atlas growled a curse and tumbled through the door, Merewen just behind.

"Don't put your hands on me, Usaran," Atlas growled, panting and bleeding from a dozen different shallow knife wounds.

Ksara glanced about the dark street and the shadows immediately crawled toward her, as eager an attacker as the ones she'd left in the tavern.

"We stay at the healer's tonight," she said.

"There's no room for sleeping there, Captain," Merewen said.

"We won't be sleeping long," Ksara said. "We have another ring of Salgimore to find."

CHAPTER SEVEN

GENOVE

G enove LeGrande watched all of his possessions burn on the street outside his home. All of his research. All of the implements he needed to wield his magic. Everything he thought his life would be dissipated into the night sky in a malicious plume of smoke.

The girl stood beside him for a while. Naked and wrapped in a bed sheet. She sobbed and the sound made him grind his teeth.

The weak wallowed in their defeat. The strong learned from it.

He didn't speak to the girl. When she tried to lean into him for some modicum of comfort, he stepped away from her and let her stand on her own. Eventually a gawker on the street took pity on her and escorted the blubbering girl back to the academy where more of the weak could coddle their own.

The academy—he'd rather walk into the flames right now than follow the girl there. The place had always been a nest of sniveling, worthless scavengers who pecked and squabbled over the corpses of history. Never brave enough to look power in the face.

Now the scavengers would circle him, like a Kyolar without a pack. But, as he watched the embers fade to black, he realized that the best predators had no need of a pack.

Most assumed that the Kyolars, Sleeths, and Zekroaches were the top predators of the noktum. That because they hunted efficiently and viciously in numbers that that could defeat all.

But in a balanced ecosystem, there was always an apex predator. A monster that could best a pack of lower creatures on its own. A bear among wolves.

As best as he could tell, the noktums had lost their apex predators when the Giants vanished and the noktums had suffered for it. The Kyolars, Sleeths, Zekroaches, and a dozen other pack-oriented monsters all competed for the same prey. The same territory. With no apex predator to curb their populations. To add order to the chaos.

Genove's fingers moved to his left forearm, to the puckered scar beneath his robe. The line stretched the length of his arm, over his shoulder and down his back and it lived as a daily reminder of just how brutal the noktums had become.

And the fire before him marked a similar blow. He'd strode into Nokte Murosa much as he had the noktum so many years ago—eager and certain he could outwit the monsters there.

Now he saw his fundamental mistake and a profound, exquisite joy bubbled up through Genove. His lips twisted into a smile.

Genove's mistake hadn't been to play with his magic in Nokte Murosa. His error hadn't been lying to Ariston about being able to find his son. His fundamental mistake had been subtlety.

He'd carved a placed among scavengers. He'd gained the fickle favor of a city leader. He'd slipped into a city of monsters and used subtlety to try to control them.

Apex predators didn't use subtlety. They struck with decisive, brutal violence.

And now Genove would do the same.

Ariston had thought to destroy him. To punish him for his deceit. But what he'd actually done was point Genove to his true path. Show him his true power.

Genove scooped a handful of ash into his hand and tested the substance between his finger and thumb. It didn't have the elegance of ink, the subtlety of hiding monsters in plain sight.

But the ash warmed to his touch, accepting his magic as readily as any ink had.

Genove scooped up more of the ash and smiled.

CHAPTER EIGHT

KSARA

With all five of the *Falco* crew crammed in the Life Mage's shop, the place took on a distinct odor. That was mostly Atlas's fault; the man never took off his armor around the crew and bathed and cleaned it only when he could do so in privacy. It was some sort of Imprevari military tradition—a soldier only removed his armor when he returned home from a battle. And since the Imprevari Calvary captain had been banished from his homeland, he'd taken to keeping his armor on full-time.

And the stank was terrific. Like sweaty feet and pickled horse manure. The smell alone should have been enough to keep them all awake, but only Ksara remained conscious. Atlas slept with his back leaning against a door. Merewen dozed on a stool, propped up by a cabinet so the moment she opened her eyes, she'd be able to check on Ulric lying on the table. Coronata sprawled on the floor between Ksara and the back door, her fingers laced behind her head and the kapicat sleeping on her stomach. The Sandrunner had been the last to fall asleep and only did so when

Ksara closed her eyes and pretended to sleep first.

Despite the smell, Ksara wanted to sleep. She hadn't rested no more than an hour or two since Ulric's injury. Fatigue pulled at her. Every muscle weighed heavy, sinking her toward unconsciousness. Her breathing quieted. Her eyes slipped closed—

And a biting chill caught hold of her leg. She startled awake and kicked the shadow snaking up her calf, gritting her teeth to keep from yelping.

The shadow retreated a few feet, but no farther. She felt it writhe and slither and wait. Its presence was alive inside her mind—a murmuring thunder at the edges of her thoughts.

And it wasn't for lack of trying. Ksara's parents had used their wealth to hire mages to tutor her. Year after year a new tutor came under the guise of an advisor to the Sajra house, but always to teach her to control her power. To hide their eternal shame.

Ksara was the blight of Demaijos.

The Demaijos were the children of the Lux. They reveled in the light and the bounty that grew in it.

And Ksara and her power were a curse on her house. A bad omen and a danger to both of her parents' prestige—her father a renowned gem merchant and her mother the sister of the queen.

When her father died suddenly, her mother blamed it on the stress of hiding Ksara. Of being one dancing shadow away from all of their trade partners leaving port and the king removing them from his western estate.

The worry took him from me.

That's what her mother had said, but she'd meant Ksara. Ksara had killed her father. Just by existing.

So she'd left. She'd begged Ulric to stay and inherit all of the business and power their father had yearned to give the true child of the light. But Ulric had laughed, as warm and loud as he ever did, and followed her onto a Luminent ship set to return to Laria.

The shadows snaked toward her.

She pressed her back against the wall and assessed the room. She couldn't get to either exit without waking her crew. And there wasn't enough room in the cramped shop for her to pace about and keep a step ahead of the haunting shadows.

But maybe she could muster up just enough control to keep it away from her skin. To let her rest, even if she couldn't sleep.

So she closed her eyes. She steadied her breathing. She quieted her body and stilled her mind.

Then she went to that place in her thoughts where the shadows lived, where she could feel their presence no matter where she looked.

And she hesitated.

All the Land Mages had described a moment of connection of self to element. A rippling of your mind through water. A deepening of yourself through earth. Ulric had explained his own connection to the light as an orb of light in his center that he drew down his arms and into his fingertips.

But she didn't have a bright happy Lux in her heart; she had a hungry noktum in her mind. And touching it, even in her own imagination, seemed like a terrible idea.

But she knew no other way, so she pictured herself standing before the noktum inside her as a tentacle of shadow stretched out of the noktum and snapped at her, grabbing hold of her in an instant and wrenching her inside the black.

Cold consumed her, stealing away her breath before she could scream. She couldn't move. She couldn't see. Her thoughts changed. Her voice was not her own. It was deeper. A whisper with the force of thunder.

Her eyes flashed open and she shouted.

"Ksara!"

"The hell?"

"What's wrong?"

Ksara blinked and her eyes focused on the room. She shivered, glaciers in her veins. Coronata bent over her and Merewen towered behind.

She waved them off, scanning the room to find where the living shadows waited for her and pushing away from them.

Atlas groaned as he got up and stretched in his armor, wafting his stench about the room. "Are we just screaming to wake each other up, now?"

"It could have been your smell," Coronata said. "Gave me nightmares."

"Are you well, Captain?" Merewen asked.

Atlas glared at Ksara. "Our fearless leader was startled?"

Footsteps creaked down the stairs. Ksara pivoted. Atlas drew his sword.

The Life Mage raised his hands above his head. "My apologies!"

Ksara retrieved her staff from the floor, and strapped her it to her back. "You have been a gracious host. We will be gone soon."

The Life Mage frowned, the worry lines traveling high on his balding head. "You haven't seen it."

"Seen what?" Atlas growled.

"Open the door."

Atlas complied, casting the gray of early dawn into the room. He leaned out the opening and uttered a string of curses blaspheming all the gods and goddesses of Noksonon.

Ksara cut across the space and joined the Imprevari at the door to find an upside down pentagon with a triangle in its center painted in red on the cobblestones just outside.

"That's the symbol of the Dorumai," Merewen said.

Coronata leaned against the doorframe. "And drawn in blood. Not a new trick, but a good one."

CHAPTER NINE

KSARA

sara looked up and down the street. Not a soul watched them from window or alley. And yet she felt the eyes of the Dorumai upon them.

This job just got a few turns harder.

Merewen knelt before the symbol, testing the liquid between two fingers. "Coronata's right. This is blood. And it's fresh."

Atlas wrung the hilt of his sword. "Show me where these cowards hide and they'll have enough blood for a damn mural."

"You think they're just waiting in some basement for you to find them?" Coronata asked, resting her hands on her hips. "This cult is older than Imprevar."

"There were rats before Imprevar, too," Atlas growled. "Called them Sandrunners."

Coronata shrugged. "It would explain my uncle's ears."

Ksara shook her head. She wasn't here to cross blades with cults. She just needed to find the Shadowvar kid and get out of this city. "Anything there that will help us find the kid?"

Merewen stayed crouched over the Dorumai's symbol for

another few breaths then she rose from the ground like a giant growing up from cobblestone. "The lines are steady. Practiced. The Dorumai have been plaguing this city for some time, I'd guess."

Ksara glanced at the houses around them and into the dark windows. "They're a cult that loves storybook monsters and now they're abducting kids. How does this connect?"

"Maybe they just hate kids. Like Atlas," Coronata said.

"Fools. I hate fools," Atlas said. "And that includes you."

Coronata grinned.

"The Dorumai believe the Giants are real," Merewen said, ignoring the others. "And that all mortal races are subservient to the Giants. That is the natural order. And the Shadowvar openly defy that order."

Coronata strode in a lazy loop around the bloody patch of cobblestone. "So, they picked the cesspool of Shadowvar cities to flex their ideology on."

"With the help of a self-proclaimed prophet," Merewen said. "The Orator."

Ksara sighed. "The Guildmaster crossed the Orator, the Orator took his kid. And here we are."

"The scrolls seemed fixated on the Night of the Soul," Merewen said.

"Scrolls?" Atlas scoffed. "You have scrolls on obscure murderous cults hidden in your bear-skin bra, Usaran?"

Coronata laughed. "You're looking at her bear-skin bra?"

Merewen didn't break her gaze with Ksara. "I found propaganda scrolls at *The Saunter*. The Dorumai are recruiting all over Nokte Murosa."

Ksara gave the street another look over. "Ariston can't trust his own people. It's why he's sent us."

"A terrible idea," Atlas added.

"So is staring too long at Merewen's bear-skin bra," Coronata said.

Atlas jolted toward Coronata. She reversed directions in a blink of an eye, dodging his would-be charge with a flash of black hair and a laugh.

Atlas growled and pulled his sword halfway out of its sheath.

"Enough," Ksara said. Loud and certain. Atlas backed away from the Sandrunner and her laugh devolved to a soft chuckle. "Nokte Murosa can fall into the ocean, for all I care," Ksara continued. "We just need to be out of here before it does. How bad is the *Falco*?"

"We can't just leave the Shadowvar kid to the Dorumai," Merewen said.

Coronata shrugged, ignoring the Usaran as best as anyone could ignore a woman that size. "The *Falco* needs a good shipyarder."

"You still friendly with Junli?"

Coronata's eyes brightened. "I'm always friendly with Junli."

"Atlas, get this mess cleaned up off the street. No need to bring more attention to ourselves," Ksara said.

Atlas muttered a curse. Khyven the kapicat chittered back at the Imprevari from Coronata's shoulder.

"I'll kill that thing," Atlas said between clenched teeth.

The kapicat screeched louder at the Imprevari, only settling back down when he'd huffed back into the house and shut the door.

"You antagonize him," Merewen said.

Coronata stroked the kapicat. "And *you* invigorate him."

"Merewen's right," Ksara said.

Coronata draped her hands on her hips. "Come on! It's Atlas!"

"Ulric would be dead without Atlas," Ksara said, and the words drained the mirth from Coronata's face. The shadows in the alley tilted toward Ksara, oozing their way across the street toward her. "That's enough for me. Coronata, lead the way to the shipyarder. I could use with some sea between me and this city."

Coronata smiled again, a little more contritely than before. "Yes, Captain."

❦ ❦ ❦

Coronata led them through a sleepy Nokte Murosa. Only a few houses had smoke drifting up from their chimneys and the only residents they saw out and about were rats crawling along rooftops and scurrying into alleyways.

When Coronata stopped at one of the merchant houses near the docks, they stopped alongside her. The pirate nodded at the house. "Merewen, knock that door down."

Merewen's mouth parted, but no words came out.

"Go on," Coronata said. "Show off those Senji muscles."

Merewen looked to Ksara. "Is this necessary?"

Ksara shrugged. "It's efficient."

"We don't have enough coin to get the *Falco* repaired the lawful way," Coronata said, pulling Khyven off her shoulder and handing the creature to Ksara. "And I like a good entrance."

Merewen's brow furrowed, her distress mounting.

Ksara suppressed a smile. "Knock it down."

"Yes, Captain." Merewen lowered her shoulders and rammed the door, bashing it in with a single hit—a feat Ulric might not have managed on the first try.

Coronata entered in an instant. "I'm back, my love."

There was a yelp, a laugh, and another crash.

Ksara stayed outside the door and Merewen shifted her stance awkwardly. "Does she need help?"

Another crash and a groan.

"She's the Bloody Queen of the Western Sea," Ksara said, scratching the kapicat just between the horns as he settled into her arms. "She can handle one of her Nokte Murosan lovers."

"*One* of her lovers?"

"One of her lovers."

"Just in Nokte Murosa?"

"You got it."

Merewen frowned "I was here last time and I didn't see any lovers."

"You had your face buried in a scroll," Coronata said, striding over the broken door and rejoining them on the street. She wore a sultry smile and a new brocade jacket with swirls of burgundy.

"That suits you," Ksara said, giving the kapicat back to Coronata.

"I'm the *former* Bloody Queen of the Western Sea," she said with a smile. "Red's my color."

Merewen sighed. "Did you steal that jacket?"

"Forcefully negotiated."

"And the *Falco*?" Ksara asked.

"It will take a day to repair. Maybe two."

Ksara turned to take in the breadth of the city around her. It didn't compare to the splendor of Triada with its colorful banners nor the somber elegance of Laria. It was a cesspool of incompetent crime lords, unsavory traders, and *shkazat* tents. All shrouded in two noktums that blocked the direct sunlight for all but a few hours of the day.

All of that Ksara had known the first time they'd come to Nokte Murosa. What irritated her now, as never before, was the size of the puss-crust of a city. It sprawled at least ten miles wide and another six deep. Plenty of room to hide a Shadowvar kid in while their time slowly eked away.

CHAPTER TEN

GENOVE

Genove traded his scholar robe—an exquisite sapphire blue brocade with bronze buttons—for a beggar's tattered tunic. It smelled of piss and grime, but it was invisibility that Genove needed most and that was what the foul garment gave him.

Breathing mostly from his mouth to avoid the smell, Genove crossed the courtyard, climbed the stone steps, and stopped before the Assembly Hall's door. For a moment, the beauty of the woodwork gave him pause. Teased into the grain of the wood by a skilled Land Mage was an ornate portrait of a Shadowvar man with patterns carved in his horns and spectacles perched on his nose. Even in gray hours, before the sun could properly light up the courtyard, the door was a masterpiece.

A masterpiece of magic in a city of swine.

Reaching under the putrid tunic to his belt, Genove retrieved a coin purse filled with ash. He dipped two fingers in and smeared the first line on the Assembly Hall's door. He pulled the line slowly, infusing the ash with his hatred. His fingers itched with the magic. His heart raced. And the rage he willed into the ash also thumped through his veins.

Putting his fingers back in the ash, Genove cast another line of vitriol on the door. Then another and another. And another.

When he'd finished, his hands quivered so violently he struggled to tie the string of the empty coin purse and reattach it to his belt. He wasn't accustomed to using this much power in one sitting. But the new masterpiece lay plain before him. A rough, scrawled, smudge befitting swine.

He scurried to the shadows now, eager to rest and hungry to watch his revenge unfold.

CHAPTER ELEVEN

KSARA

The streets of Nokte Murosa woke like a tree of Bazen monkeys, chattering and angry. Merchants shouted at each other from across the way, cursing and throwing gestures at each other. A cart driver turned her horse at a group of kids, whipping the horse faster. The children escaped hoof and wheel only with quick feet and a good bit of luck. Three different men, hazy-eyed on *shkazat*, had staggered over to them and tried to lay clumsy, calloused hands on Ksara, Coronata, and Merewen. Now the men lie in three different alleys nursing bruises in unfortunate places. Atlas seething at being a step too slow to fell two of the three.

"I love this city," Coronata said with a grin and this time Ksara joined Atlas in giving the pirate a sideways glare. She laughed. "Come on, Ksara! You have to agree it has its charm."

Ksara felt the pull of the shadows with every step. She could not escape their chilling presence in any street of this city. She hadn't slept. She couldn't rest. And still the dark air haunted her.

She couldn't say any of that aloud. Not to the crew. Only Ulric knew her struggle with her power and he lay unconscious under the care of the Life Mage. "Nokte Murosa has its charms," she said. "Especially from the sea. Have we searched this one?" Ksara asked nodding at a shop on the street corner.

"We haven't," Merewen said from Ksara's other side, startling her a little. Merewen had a knack for silently, seamlessly moving along with the group for so long you almost forgot she was there. An incredulous skill when considering her physical presence.

Ksara guided the group to the shop door and entered in. A gust of air followed them in and chased a pile of parchment off a desk and stirred up dust and feathers from the floor.

The shopkeeper bent to retrieve the pages with a sigh. "I told you Master LeGrande, I cannot sell you more supplies on credit. Not with the Guildmaster up in arms—"

The shopkeeper snapped upright, beheld Ksara and her crew, clutched the parchment to his chest, his lips frozen mid-word.

"Sorry to disturb you, scribe," Ksara said, waving feathers and dust from her face. Empty pigeon cages sat atop a stack of leather-bound books to her left.

The shopkeeper scrunched his beak-like nose and fussed with the parchment in his hands. "You appear to have lost your way, traveler. The smithy is a street to the north and the closest tavern just beside."

"We're not lost," Ksara said. She began pacing the perimeter of the shop, waiting for the bracer on her arm to so much as hum. They had been searching Nokte Murosa for hours and the bracer on her arm hadn't so much as moved once. Their whole search plan relied on them—her—being able to detect Ariston's second magical ring on the kid, finding him before the night's end tomorrow, and sailing away from here as soon as possible.

She made a show of searching the room, pausing every few steps as if accessing her magic and prodding the room with some invisible sense.

All of this only served to make the shopkeeper visibility agitated. Sweat beaded on his brow and his hands trembled.

Coronata moved to the scribes' desk, leaning against it and

giving the shopkeeper an easy smile. This didn't help. The poor, spindly man didn't look like he'd been away from a desk for the better part of a decade; with a sickly pallor and ink stains at all angles of his tunic. He blushed at Coronata's closeness and swallowed hard.

Merewen immediately took an interest in the scrolls and books stashed about the cramped shop and began skimming through them, opening tomes and reordering stacks to get to more. This disturbance finally teased out the shopkeeper's voice, "Please!"

Merewen looked up. Ksara paused. Atlas shifted his hand to the hilt of his sword. And Coronata smiled wider.

The shopkeeper squirmed. "Please do not touch those," he said, his voice less squeaky this time. "What do you need from me, travelers? I have only parchment and ink to sell. And even those are quite sparse this time of year."

"This time of year?" Merewen asked, her curiosity turned from the books to the bookkeeper.

"It's about time for the Night of the Souls," the shopkeeper said, the words spilling out of him now. "It's a Shadowvar thing. They make notes and trinkets to throw into the noktum. A colossal waste, if you ask me, but I don't have horns, so it's not for me to understand. Now are you here to purchase something or may I direct you to the nearest *shkazat* tent?"

"I'm comfortable right here," Coronata said and the shopkeeper stopped breathing for a moment. Coronata laughed and Ksara gave her a look. The pirate queen shrugged, feeling no shame at the power she wielded over the man by just standing near him.

The shadows began leaning in toward Ksara, so she resumed her pacing of the store. And, eventually, the shopkeeper resumed control of his lungs and mouth and he blubbered out more words, "I must insist you buy something right away or leave my shop. I have no interest in housing travelers."

That was new. They'd walked into dozens and dozens of shops in the past several hours and none of the shopkeepers had been so anxious to have them leave. Something wasn't right here.

She could feel it as surely as if her arm bracer had hummed—which it hadn't.

The shopkeeper looked like a hare cornered by a Kyolar. His back pressed against the wall. His eyes wide. And the parchment still clutched to his chest as though the paper would serve as armor should weapons be drawn.

Beneath the awkwardness of the man was a wealth of terror. But why? Atlas hadn't even threatened him. Yet.

"When is this festival?" Ksara asked, stopping for a moment between Merewen and Coronata.

"Tomorrow night," the man said.

Coronata and Ksara exchanged a look. Tomorrow night was the end of their allotted time to find the kid. That was more than a coincidence.

"And you sacrifice what is most dear to you to the noktum?" Ksara asked.

"Yeah. It's one of the oldest Shadowvar traditions."

That was it. The Dorumai had taken what Ariston valued most—his only son. And they were keen to sacrifice him at the Night of the Souls. It was the perfect way to send a shiver of terror not just through Ariston, but the whole of Nokte Murosa. This was why they only had a day and a half to find the kid. And why Ariston was desperate enough to ask Ksara and the *Falco* crew for help.

The shopkeeper furrowed his brow. "You aren't with the Dorumai at all, are you?"

Silence reigned in the small shop as all eyes turned to the shopkeeper. He squirmed a little, rallying the threads of his dignity. "If you have no purchases to make, I think you should leave. You should leave. Now."

Atlas drew his sword and the sound of the blade pulling free might as well have been a Kyolar's roar in the small room. The shopkeeper yelped and cowered.

Before Ksara could give Atlas the go-ahead, the Imprevari closed the distance to the shopkeeper in four quick strides, hurdling over the desk and catching the academic by the stained collar. "What do you know of the Dorumai?" Atlas breathed.

"Nothing! I-I-I know nothing."

"That's not entirely true," Merewen said.

Atlas kept the shopkeeper pinned to the wall and sighed. "Explain."

Merewen moved three stacks of books to show a full, blank parchment on the shopkeeper's desk. "All of these parchments are made of thin, treated animal hides," she replied as though giving a lecture at the academy. "These have a distinctive scrape pattern. Same as the Dorumai propaganda scrolls I studied at *The Saunter.*"

Atlas brought his sword up just inches from the shopkeeper's neck. "So you're one of the Dorumai?"

"I-I'm not! I s-swear."

"He isn't Dorumai," Ksara said.

"And how do you know that exactly, Demaijos?" Atlas growled. "You now have power to hear thoughts?"

"You're afraid, scribe," Ksara said, ignoring Atlas altogether. "Why?"

The shopkeeper's lips trembled and spittle flew from his mouth as he spoke, "They're supposed to come. The Dorumai. They'll be here any moment."

Atlas leaned into his sword, bringing the edge to prick the other man's neck. He yelped.

"We'll just wait right here until your friends arrive. Kill you all at one time." Atlas breathed.

"I'm not one of them! They come for a bundle of parchment. I tried to refuse. They killed my birds. Best carrier pigeons I've ever had."

Coronata sat atop the desk, legs crossed. "And they just let you keep breathing?"

"They need the parchment for their messages. I'm the only place they can get it. But I'm not one of them. I never took up the mask."

Atlas bared has teeth. His restraint wearing thinner and thinner. He really needed to kill someone soon. "And if I don't believe you?"

The shopkeeper gasped. "I swear! I-I-I swear it!"

"How can we believe the word of a man ready to betray his city to madmen?" Atlas said, drawing another droplet of blood from the edge of his sword.

Ksara moved around the desk to join the men, standing at Atlas's side. In an instant the shadows began to pull from the wall behind the shopkeeper and toward Ksara. The man noted the unnatural phenomena. His eyes widened. His mouth chewed on empty words. Then he began to weep.

Ksara stepped back and away from the man, taking the shadows with her. "He's telling the truth."

"Doesn't really matter whether he's Dorumai or just a regular coward," Atlas said. "We wait here long enough and we get more of them."

"Not necessarily," Merewen said, picking up a folded letter from the ground just beside the shop door.

Coronata slipped off the desk. "What is that?"

Merewen looked up at Ksara, her stormy blue eyes even more somber than before. "It's addressed to Ksara."

"To Ksara?" Coronata said, her smile faltering.

"And it's marked with the Dorumai's sigil," Merewen said. "Same as the street."

Ksara whipped the door open and dashed onto the street. She stared at the chaos that met her, searching for eyes that were directed her way or someone slipping quickly away in the crowd. Carts passed by. Merchants shouted. Kids ran along wagons and prodded the horse's legs with sticks until the driver tried to whip them. None of the heaving chaos paid any attention to Ksara standing in the open doorway of the shop.

Whoever had delivered this Dorumai note was already gone.

She reentered the shop to find Atlas with a bloodied nose and his sword pointed at Merewen, who now stood between Atlas and the shopkeeper.

"We do not get to judge his innocence or guilt," Merewen said in the same even tone she'd used to talk about how parchment was made. She stood like a mountain between Atlas and the shopkeeper, no axe in her hand to defend against Atlas's sword. Ksara wondered in that moment if the towering warrior woman would need a weapon at all to beat any one of them, should she choose to.

"Enough!" Ksara said.

Atlas kept his sword aimed at Merewen, but he cocked his head toward Ksara. His eyes bright with the challenge.

Ksara walked around the bristling, violent Atlas as if he were a piece of furniture in her way, sat down at the scribe's desk, and reached a hand out to Merewen. She placed the Dorumai letter in Ksara's palm and she examined the thing for a moment. Her name, Ksara Sajra, was scrawled on the front of the folded parchment with a red wax seal closing the back. The seal pressed with the same symbol that had been scrawled in blood outside their door this morning.

A message from the Dorumai right to her. As if the blood on the street weren't message enough. She opened the letter and found two lines written in a neat, upright script. She read the words aloud: "One willing sacrifice or precious blood taken. We will be paid."

"They could have at least made it rhyme," Coronata chimed in.

"Grina's skirts! It's a threat. Do threats need to rhyme?"

Merewen leaned closer. "What does it mean, Captain?"

Ksara turned and looked into the shopkeeper's eyes. He wasn't looking at Atlas or the sword at his neck. Nor at Ksara or any of the crew. But the door. Even with a sword at his throat, the man feared what might walk in the door more.

The Dorumai didn't just kill people, they tormented them. Killing this man's courier pigeons. Which probably stood in for his closest friends. Maybe even family—

"Ulric." She said and the whole room quieted. "They're coming for Ulric."

CHAPTER TWELVE

CLEM

lem Lyshan spent the morning tending to the unconscious Demaijos lying on his worktable and taking inventory of the elixirs on his shelves.

He'd need to brew a few more bottles of the new recipe for Quick Beat. The mandeville root took nicely to his magic and the combination had restarted the Demaijos heart more than once last night.

Of course, Deidre would scold him for spending his time and magical stamina on stocking up on an unproven elixir. She loved to tell him that one patient doesn't prove an elixir, they merely test it.

He smiled, imagining Deidre speaking the rebuke with her auburn curls bobbing about her face. The more stern she tried to look, the cuter she was. Sometimes she'd start into an argument, catch his warm gaze, and just sigh and leave the room. And sometimes she'd start an argument just to start something else entirely.

She hadn't come by much since Eshe had been taken. They'd both been doing their part to find the Shadowvar—Clem at the

Guildmaster's side and Deidre fletching arrows for the city guard as all prepared for a war with vague enemies.

He sighed and swirled the green liquid in the vial. Deidre was probably right—each person reacted to an elixir differently. He'd had the same elixir save a life one day and jeopardize it the next. The body was not a simple science. And his magic lay in enhancing the qualities of medicinal herbs, not healing the body itself. If he guessed the wrong herb or enhanced it too much or too little, the patient could die. And all Clem could do was try more elixirs and hope the patient's body would react well to them.

That the Demaijos man on the table had pulled through spoke to both Clem's creative problem solving and the man's own will to survive.

The door opened and Clem turned toward it, a practiced smile appearing on his face. He rather hoped it would be Diedre and not the Imprevari soldier. That man had the reek of violence on him. Among other things.

Neither stood in the doorway, but a man with oarsman's arms and a black traveler's cloak clasped about his thick neck.

Clem bowed. "Welcome. I am the mage Clem Lyshan. What ails you?"

The man studied the room with a blunt, forceful gaze. Weighing a choice without words.

"If the ailment is unseemly, good sir, you shall have my honor! I will be discreet."

Still the man didn't speak. He carried something in his hand. Clem hadn't noticed it at first; the man carried it loosely at his side like a sailor might a flask of Triadan whisky.

But this wasn't a bottle of any kind. It was flat, circular, and white.

Curious.

It was possible the traveler had brought in some magical trinket from his voyage and had come to Clem, the resident mage of Nokte Murosa, to divine its magical properties.

Clem sighed. Oh, that he could educate every citizen of Noksonon on the rudimentary differences in the five streams of magic! His own life magic could connect with anything that grew, whether flesh or plant. Land magic manipulated the non-growing elements. Lore magic was the ability to discern the future. Love Magic twisted thoughts and feelings. And line magic could do any of the four other streams using runes or symbols, but to lesser effect.

Did anyone else in Nokte Murosa grasp this knowledge firmly?

No.

Clem had had scholars who studied magic come to him with a coin, gem, or amulet and beg him to give more information on its nature. And unless it was the elixirs he'd made with his own hands, he had no idea what magic might lie within the treasure. He could sense the magic, but could no better discern it than a blind man could the subject of a painting.

After years of explaining this very thing, Clem had taken to just lying. No one else knew the difference and the lie got the person out of the shop in moments.

Clem nodded at the thing in the man's hand. "Have you something you'd like me to see?"

The traveler nodded. Then he slid the object over his face and Clem's breath caught in his chest.

It wasn't a magical artifact—it was a Dorumai mask. Long and white with angled slits for the eyes.

The Dorumai unsheathed a dagger from his belt and held it before him. "You will see and you will tell all. The Dorumai will not be stopped. One willing sacrifice or precious blood taken. We will be paid."

Clem garbled sounds instead of words, his mind lethargic with shock and his body quickened by fear.

The Dorumai stepped to the Demaijos, the dagger tight in his thick fist and suddenly the haze cleared.

The Dorumai had come to kill the Demaijos. To deal another blow to Ariston. And to make Clem, Ariston's own mage, watch helpless as he did.

Clem's hand tightened around the Quick Beat elixir. He

sensed his own heart, felt the magic in his own blood, and infused more and more of it into the vial in his hands.

The Dorumai raised the knife, just above the patient's own heart, aiming sure and true for a single, lethal strike—

And Clem unstopped the elixir and sloshed it into the man's ear.

Mouth or eyes would have been better, but both were covered by the mask. And the ear would get the elixir into his blood faster than just skin.

At first the Dorumai just tilted his head toward Clem, growling a curse. Then his body stiffened, and his free hand groped at his chest as he gasped for air. He collapsed to the ground, kicking and sputtering sounds.

Clem sagged against his cabinet, doing his own bit of panting as adrenaline raced through him. He'd call for Ariston and his guards as soon as the Dorumai's heart stopped completely.

Then he'd let the *Falco* crew sleep in his shop all they wanted—Clem would be in the Guildmaster's own home, protected by his own guard, as soon as possible.

The Dorumai quieted and silence filled the room once more.

Clem put the stopper back on the empty Quick Beat bottle and replaced it on the shelf.

Something slapped the table, and Clem spun around to find the Dorumai pulling himself to his feet, the dagger still clutched in his hand.

"Tested, not proven," Clem said in that strange moment between seeing the Dorumai get to his feet and seeing the dagger plunge into his own heart.

A dozen thoughts and sensations warred for Clem's final attention. The heat of the wound. The cold shock of seeing the hilt of the blade pressed against his skin, the point hidden within his flesh. The anger at being another victim. Even the contempt at being a mage and yet still helpless to the crudest of deaths.

But the thought that won out in Clem's mind as blood gurgled from his mouth and black overtook his vision was Diedre's face. Angry and lovely. And weeping over him.

CHAPTER THIRTEEN

ULRIC

Ulric stood before a gnarled tree the size of a city and he knew this was a nightmare. He'd lived this moment over and over and over again. But there wasn't anything else to see, nowhere else to move toward except the tree-shaped nuraghi. This was the last place he remembered being awake.

Or alive.

There was a chance he'd died here with Ksara and the crew. On a mission he devised to get a treasure that seemed entirely insignificant now.

And ever since he'd been trapped here with only one path to the nuraghi, he'd died countless times. And, after every grisly death, he'd blink and be back exactly at this spot, wondering these very same questions.

It certainly seemed more like an eternal torment than a nightmare. But Ulric smiled and drew the long sword at his back. If he was here for eternity, at least there were things to kill.

Resting the blade flat against his shoulder, he strode into the trunk of the enormous, blackened tree. As soon as he crossed the threshold two things happened. First, all light extinguished around him. That was a trick of the magic still soaked into the nuraghi's very walls. A twist of light to confuse explorers just long enough for—

Ulric whipped the sword in a high arc and pivoted to the left, cleaving the head off a human-sized bat lunging toward him.

Now he ran, counting his steps in the dark. Twelve strides and he ducked, just missing the swooping claws of another bat. That one had killed him and reset the nightmare four times in a row.

He hurried on. Seven more steps and he ducked right, into a hallway indiscernible from the black around him. He'd spent several lives clapping his hands and illuminating the nuraghi with his magic to chart his course, dying the most terrible deaths of them all. These creatures hated the light. But maybe, just maybe, if he killed the monster that guarded the nuraghi at its center, he could leave it. Whether to wake or to fade into a different existence. He'd find out one way or another.

He held to the right wall and jogged another twenty-three steps, avoiding the spears of wood coming down from the ceiling that had impaled him twice.

Now he ducked left and flew up a narrow, winding staircase. The stairs were huge and he bashed his knee on the first one and then his muscle memory took over, vaulting him over too-tall steps he couldn't see.

Injuries in this place were strange. He felt his knee collide with the stair, but the pain was muted. A tickling sensation, no matter if he stubbed his toe or had his torso ripped in two, the sensation was the same. A small tickling and he could keep on fighting. A prolonged tickling and he'd be blinking awake just outside the nuraghi once more.

Ulric counted ten steps and then paused on the landing where the real challenge began. Six bats waited for him there and they ambushed just the same way every time. He'd only made it beyond them all once. And just past this room waited the real guardian of this place—its thousand eyes already upon him. Waiting to deal out his final test once again.

Ulric allowed himself four counts to breathe. It steadied his nerves and put the next bat into the perfect position to kill. Two lunging steps and a sideways slash and his sword sliced an unseen bat clean through. It screamed as it died.

Ulric ducked backward two steps and swung again, meeting another bat he couldn't see and sending it to a shrieking death. A low lunge forward and he impaled another unseen bat, crawling toward him on the ground. He jumped over the howling body, raised the sword over his head and brought it down on another bat as it swooped at him, rending its wing from its body and sending it careening into a wall with a crash.

Four steps forward and a mighty slash felled two bats with a single stroke and before he could finish the blow, he contorted sideways, throwing himself to the right, but the claws still raked across his shoulder. That tickling sensation marking the wound.

This is where things got messy.

Either way he swung his sword now, he was about to lose it. He took his best guess at where the last bat's head would be, struck there, but only the middle of the blade caught the creature's skull and the tip sunk into wood.

The bat howled but didn't die.

Ulric released the sword and leapt at the creature. He collided with its warm body, the thing's foul, hot blood tickling his skin. He guessed the stuff was acid and would have left some sizeable burns if any of this were real.

The bat thrashed, pummeling him in the head with a wing. More prickling sensations on his head.

Ulric lashed out with his thick arms and cinched them around the bat's neck. The bat lashed out this way and that and its head wound oozed more of that acidic blood across his arms, his skin tingling longer and longer.

But Ulric held on, constricting the creature's throat tighter, until it couldn't howl or shriek, only gurgle and flop down to the ground. When it released its final sigh, he held on for another count then released the creature and got to his feet.

He'd made it through the gauntlet, but his skin still tingled with the bat's acid blood and his head and back ached with their own muted injuries. One more hit, even a small one, and he'd be back at the start.

And the monster beyond made these man-sized bats look like flies.

Ulric retraced his steps until he found his sword and pulled it out from the wall. It hadn't helped him much with the big monster last time, but he felt even more foolish facing it with his bare hands.

He knew three things about the guardian awaiting him. First, it was made from the blackened, gnarled tree that composed the nuraghi itself. The branches wove into arms and claws and even the most insignificant scratch from one of those claws would leave him blinking back at the beginning.

Second, even stooped over like an ape, the thing was the height of two houses with an easy reach of forty feet.

And, finally, the thing had milky white eyes all up and down it's back and legs and arms. The eyes glowed in the darkness, like a cluster of stars turned toward him.

The first time he'd stood at this threshold, he'd been there with Ksara. The crew were finishing up the bats in the room behind and he and his sister swapped a few quick ideas on how to distract the monster long enough to get the treasure on the far wall. Ksara had insisted on being the decoy, but she wore the bracer on her arm that could sense the magical object, even in the pitch black. She was the best person to retrieve it. So she'd reluctantly agreed to let Ulric play the hero.

He'd made it only a step into the chamber before the monster had struck him, a grazing wound on his arm he'd tried to rally through. But in a moment he'd lost sensation in his body. Ksara had screamed and he'd blinked awake here, in the shadowy replica of his final moments.

Had Ksara died here, too? Had he urged them all to their deaths because he'd wanted to test his strength against monsters instead of men?

The uncertainty tore through him deeper than any blade could reach. He didn't mind the idea of being dead so much as the thought that he'd killed Ksara.

All of this doubt and speculation flashed through Ulric's mind in the space of a few breaths. Just enough time for more of the monster's milky white eyes to blink open and the twisted branches of its body to creak and groan as it leaned in toward him.

Ulric adjusted his grip on the long sword and charged toward the nearest splattering of white eyes. Branches snapped and cracked as the monster pivoted to counter his attack, but it moved slowly, uprooting its legs from the ground so it could turn its hulking shoulders toward Ulric.

He barreled forward and sunk his blade into the first eyeball within reach. His sword caught in the wood as the thing growled, branches twisting closer around him.

Ulric released the hilt of the sword, and beckoned magic to his fingertips. Heat raced from his chest down his arms and into his fingers in an instant and he clapped his hands together.

Light flashed from Ulric's hands, illuminating the monster.

Ulric's sword was stuck in the creature's ankle and its thorny arms were all around him, moments from sinking sharp wooden claws into him from a dozen directions. The eyes on the thing's legs and arms blinked closed in the light and the leech-like mouth at the center of the monster's chest stretched open wide as it leaned its torso toward him.

Just as the light from his magic faded, he pulled a dagger from his belt and jammed the blade up and into the monster's mouth. The next moment tingling sensations speared through his torso in six different places. He cried out. Then blinked.

And he stood outside the nuraghi again. The long sword on his back. The knife at his belt. And nowhere to go but back into the haunted place to face another death.

Pain erupted in Ulric's shoulder. Not the tingling sensations of a wound here, but searing hot pain that robbed his breath. He turned about to look for his enemy, shock working through him.

He found only air.

Tearing the sword from his back, he slashed it about the blurry space. Whatever enemy had come for him now, he wasn't about to die flat-footed.

He blinked again and the world blurred more. Light burned his eyes. Blood and something even more bitter tinged the air.

He blinked and slashed the blade again and his vision cleared.

But he wasn't standing at the nuraghi. He wasn't standing at all.

He lay on a table. Sunlight in his eyes. And a man leaned over him, wearing a white mask.

Holding a dagger wet with blood.

Ulric swung a fist at the man. At least, that's what he'd told his body to do. All that actually happened was a spasm in his shoulder where blood spilled out of a hole there.

The attacker clutched at his own chest and sagged against the table, wheezing. Then he met Ulric's eyes and rallied, steadying himself and raising the blade to strike again.

Ulric watched the blade descend on him and he kicked at the man. This time his body almost complied and he kneed the attacker in the chest, knocking him sideways into a cabinet. Glass vials tumbled from the shelf, raining down on the masked man. He gasped, clawing at his own heart, and staggered back toward Ulric, and fell.

Ulric willed his body to stand and he rolled off of the table instead, landing atop the writhing man. His bulk helped him now and, while he didn't have full use of his fingers yet, he put his hands down on the other man's arms and pinned him to the ground.

The attacker convulsed, more in distress from Ulric's weight atop him than anything else. And he gasped. Choked. And went limp beneath Ulric.

He held the man down another moment or two and then leaned back against the wall, panting out his own exertion. His whole body trembled. Sweat beaded his brow and his stomach churned bile up his throat. Each sensation was a thousand times more acute than dying had been in the shadow nuraghi and now his body seemed intent on cycling through one poignant complaint after another.

The door slammed open and Ulric flinched, trying to get to his feet, but only managing to lurch to his knees and sag back against the table.

"Ulric!"

Ulric smiled and his whole body relaxed. A moment later his sister had her arms wrapped around his torso, squeezing him tight enough to make the dagger wound bleed on them both.

He held her anyways. The comfort of being near her again, of knowing she was alive, far outweighed the ache of the wound.

"I told you he was hard to kill," Coronata said with a laugh.

Ksara laughed or wept into his shoulder. He couldn't quite tell which.

CHAPTER FOURTEEN

KSARA

sara clung to Ulric until she felt the blood then she pulled back and Ulric laughed, his voice raspy and weak.

"I'm fine," he said.

Ksara pulled back the tunic to examine the wound. It was two inches long, but shallow. "Atlas!"

Ksara didn't have to call the Imprevari twice—he was kneeling beside Ulric in a moment, prodding the wound with firm precision.

"Just a scratch," Atlas said, leaning back. "I'll stitch it."

Ulric gave Ksara a grin. "See? Just a scratch."

She wanted to clap him upside the head and laugh with him all at the same time.

Atlas returned with his satchel and Ksara reluctantly stepped back to allow the Imprevari room to tend to the wound.

"How many lives do Demaijos have?" Coronata asked with a grin of her own.

Ulric wheezed a laugh. "More than you have lovers."

Coronata chuckled and leaned her slight shoulders against the wall. "You're going to like the new barmaid. Just your type."

"Really?"

"Oh yes."

"Tall. Auburn hair. Blue tattoos. A Usaran accent—"

Ulric winked. "Just my type."

In the corner of the room, Merewen choked a little, and flushed a deep red.

Ulric smiled wider.

Merewen composed her expression and crossed the room to kneel beside the dead Dorumai. "This is Dockmaster Gid's man. We fought him at the tavern."

Ksara cut between her brother and the Usaran to look down at the dead Dorumai. Merewen had removed the man's mask and, sure enough, the dead man was one of Gid's goons.

"Did you kill him, Ulric?"

"No. Just held him down until he died."

"The mage—Lyshan—he threw an elixir," Merewen said. "He killed the Dorumai."

Ksara looked at the dead mage. His body had been the first thing she'd seen as she'd stormed into the room. His glassy eyes staring at her had brought all the despair crashing in. Ulric had to be dead. She was too late and Ulric was dead.

Then she'd seen Ulric, heard his voice, and hope had returned. Impossible, painful, battle-weary hope.

She hadn't thought about the mage after that. All her focus had been on Ulric and keeping him breathing and laughing and smiling. She looked at the mage now, an elixir stopper in his fist and a dagger wound through the chest.

"The Dorumai came after Ulric first," Atlas said. "This wound started as a puncture and then slashed downward. The attack was interrupted."

"And the Dorumai smells of herbs. A root elixir, I'd guess," Merewen added.

Glass crashed on the ground and a flash of black and white bounded about the room. "Khyven. No. Khyven. Khyven! Don't eat that. Don't eat that!"

Coronata snatched Khyven off the ground and removed a full elixir bottle out of its mouth moments before its sharp teeth broke the seal. "That's not for you," she chided the creature and then examined the vial. "So the Dorumai busts into the shop, the mage splashes him with an herbal perfume, gets stabbed anyways, and then the perfume does its thing before the Dorumai can use up another of Ulric's lives?"

"The Dorumai was here for Ulric," Ksara said. She still had the letter bunched in her fist. "The mage saved his life. Again."

All eyes turned to the Life Mage slumped against a cabinet. His tunic stained red and his eyes vacant. One last worry frozen on his brow.

Even in death this man looked entirely ordinary. A face in a crowd you'd see and forget the next moment. He'd fumbled and bowed to the Guildmaster in the Assembly Hall. But here, in his own shop, he'd moved with certainty. And he'd saved Ulric from the nuraghi's curse.

Then gave his life to save Ulric again.

Silence hung in the room and Ksara felt more like an intruder in this space than ever before. This man should be surrounded by people who knew him. Loved him. Instead he was just one more dead body in a place none of them wanted to be.

The shadows pulled into Ksara, as if beckoned closer by her ill ease. They swelled high and twisted about her waist with their inescapable chill cutting into her. Her chest tightened. Her pulse thundered so hard in her skull it almost sounded like a voice. Like a murmur of words.

"Ksara."

Ulric's voice startled her. He smiled at her, but for the first time since he woke, the gesture looked sad. He wriggled off the worktable, waving away Atlas's protests, and reached through the dark to grab Ksara by the shoulder. The shadow bit into him, but he didn't flinch, pulling her out of the darkness.

She looked up into his Demaijos eyes. Every Demaijos had one dark eye and one Lux eye. His Lux eye was a vivid green. Ksara's own was a pale blue. It was the only bit of home Ksara still found comfort in.

"You haven't slept."

It wasn't a question. Part of her wished she could hide her fatigue and hurt from his gaze. And part of her was grateful she didn't have to find words for them. He just saw her. Understood her.

"It's my sister's turn to rest," Ulric said to the crew as much as Ksara.

"We have to—"

"No," Ulric said, cocking a brow at her. Willing her to argue. She wasn't going to win. Not now.

"One hour," she said, letting him guide her to the other side of the room and up the stairs.

When Ulric shut the door to the dead mage's room, Ksara mounted her last defense. "We have to find the Guildmaster's son. He's been taken by a cult. It was the only way to save you. And we only have until tomorrow night—"

Ulric guided Ksara to the small bed tucked beneath the house's rafters. Tables full of jars and plants filled the room. The bed was almost an afterthought to everything else.

"Or we could leave," she said. "The *Falco* is almost repaired. We could get out of the bay before the Guildmaster finds us."

"And abandon a kid to a cult?"

"It's not our problem," Ksara said. "You're awake, so we can leave. If the *Falco* isn't ready, we can take another ship. I'll row out of this port if I have to."

Ulric cocked a brow at her. "You gave your word you'd help, Ksara."

"And you almost died!" The words burst from her, then she reined her voice back to a whisper. "Twice."

Ulric's expression softened, but Ksara didn't let him speak. "There's no saving this kid. This cult—the Dorumai? They've been hiding for centuries. It could take weeks ... months! To root them out. And we have hours. Hours until Ariston pins all the failure on us and we finally meet the gallows. And you want to stick around for that?"

"They're going to kill a kid."

"And I can't stop them!" That time Ksara did yell. Loud enough for the crew downstairs to hear her. And loud enough to bring tears to her own eyes, but she did not let them fall.

"It's not your fault, 'Sar."

Ksara shook her head, not trusting her voice.

"I walked into that nuraghi. I thought it was a good plan. I wouldn't have blamed you if I—"

Neither of them wanted him to finish that sentence, so he didn't.

"Ulric, I led us to a place we didn't understand and you almost paid for it with your life," Ksara said. "I'm not doing that again."

He caught hold of her elbow and pulled her into a slow, gentle hug. He held her there, not saying a word, until her breathing relaxed and her heart steadied. When he let her go, the fight was out of her.

"This cult is dangerous, Ulric."

"I know."

"The shadows are wild here."

"I know."

Ksara sat down on the bed. "I still think we should leave Nokte Murosa. Now."

Ulric smiled. "No, you don't."

"If we stay," she said, laying her head down on the pillow. "I can't protect us."

"Rest, 'Sar. We'll figure the rest out when you wake."

She closed her eyes, sleep already anchored into her and dragging her downward. "The shadows—"

"I'm here, 'Sar. You're not alone. Rest."

Ksara smiled. Actually smiled. Then she slept.

◆　◆　◆

Ulric stayed at Ksara's side until the shadows chased him away.

As soon as Ksara fell asleep it started. The shadows detached from behind the desks and tables and spilled out from beneath the bed and began inching toward her.

The strange march had a ridiculousness to it. The shadows weren't alive; Ksara's power drew them to her. They couldn't rally an ambush without her call.

Land magic didn't work that way.

The light in Ulric's own chest felt wild, like a tempest of fire, before he'd learned how to control it. After those hours of training the power felt like a roaring hearth. Constant. Contained. Comforting, even.

But, for all of Ksara's trying, she'd never reached that level of control over the shadows. And now, as she slept, her subconscious must be directing the dark close to her.

Or that's the explanation that made sense at first when the shadows pulled to Ksara, hemming her in on all sides.

But when Ksara's brow furrowed, the shadows changed. They seemed to take notice of Ulric. And they shifted toward him, mounting high into a wave that brushed the rafters.

He tried to call his own power to his fingertips, but the heat moved sluggishly down his chest and arms. His own injury and fatigue inhibiting the magic.

And still the shadows swelled, curling over top him like a wave about to crash.

Ulric staggered backward, bumping into a desk and knocking a plant to the floor. The pot shattered. Ksara stirred.

And the dark attacked.

In an instant, Ulric knew he wouldn't be able to access his power before the black engulfed him, so he leapt for the door, threw it open, and slammed it closed behind.

Just outside the door he waited for Ksara's voice. Or for the shadow to gush beneath the door.

"It's time for the truth," a voice said from behind Ulric. He flinched and found Atlas at the top of the stairs. His expression dark and his voice commanding. "The truth before she kills us all."

CHAPTER FIFTEEN

ARISTON

Guildmaster Ariston sat in his son's room, staring at the bloodied sheets. He'd calculated the size of the blood stains. Eshe had been cut by a blade at least twice as they took him away. One wound high, near the pillow. Maybe his shoulder. Possibly his neck or face. And the second wound left stains nearer the foot of the bed. A leg wound. Maybe even a quick cut to the back tendon to keep Eshe from running off.

Either way, they'd wrapped him up in his blanket and hauled him away. All with Ariston sleeping in the room beside. All with two of Ariston's guards in the house and the rest in the two guard houses on either side of his.

Ariston imagined the fear on Eshe's face. The boy wasn't quite a boy anymore—nineteen and just returned from a trip to Nokte Shaddark and Taur-El. It had been a celebration trip under the guise of securing more trade partners and meeting the growers on Taur-El. Eshe had returned more experienced in the world. Bright-eyed, but seasoned. Tempered.

But Ariston had still seen his young child standing there at the docks. One crooked horn and that mischief on his face. No matter how many trips he went on, Eshe would always look like a child to his father.

And now Ariston imagined both versions of his son fighting off the Dorumai in the night. His nineteen-year-old son had clearly put up a good fight. Though he hadn't woken Ariston or the guards, he'd struggled enough to warrant two injuries to subdue him.

But what about the young Eshe that was still living inside that fierce, stubborn boy? Had he tried to call for Ariston? Plead for his dad to hear him? To come and stop this nightmare from stealing him away?

A knock sounded at the door and Ariston stared listlessly at Eshe's bed, ignoring the sound.

"Guildmaster," the voice familiar voice said. Omri. Captain of the Guard and one of Ariston's oldest friends. "Something happened to the Assembly Hall."

Ariston kept his gaze trained on the blood stains. "The Assembly Hall?"

"More vandalism from the Dorumai," Omri said.

"And?"

"It's drawing a crowd. Gid's asking for you to deal with it."

He looked about Eshe's room one more time. The faded brown traveling pack that hung around the bedpost. The map of Noksonon pinned to the wall, old trade routes to and from Nokte Murosa marked in meticulous lines. New scholar's robes slung over the chair Ariston sat on. And a wood carving of a round goddess he didn't recognize lying on the desk.

It felt like Eshe could walk back into this room any moment and all would be right again.

Only the bloody sheets broke the illusion.

"Ariston?"

Ariston startled. He'd forgotten about Omri waiting on the other side of the door. He eased himself upright, studied the room one more time, and then left.

Omri joined Ariston in step as soon as he exited the room.

"We will not bow to these monsters," Ariston growled. "We cannot."

"As you say, so it will be done, Guildmaster."

All twelve of his guards escorted Ariston the quarter of a mile between his home and the Assembly Hall—a route he'd known by heart since he was four years old. It should have been utterly ridiculous to have his personal guards encircling him as he strode past houses as familiar as family.

But this was Nokte Murosa. And in Nokte Murosa, your only friend was a dagger clutched in your fist.

Somewhere in his fourteen years as Guildmaster, he'd forgotten that. He'd thought he could rule villainy with civility. That changed now.

As he swept up the stairs to the Assembly Hall, miscreants and urchins scurried off the steps and out of his way. As they cleared, he caught sight of their handiwork and fresh rage filled him.

There, on the door to the Assembly Hall—a door that had been crafted by a renowned Land Mage in Triada centuries ago—were crude smears of mud.

No. Not mud. Darker than mud. This was ash.

And the smears weren't random at all, but a rough depiction of a man in a mask with slits for eyes and a black cloak.

Someone had vandalized the Assembly Hall with a depiction of the Dorumai.

"Arrest them all," Ariston growled.

His guard responded without question, darting forward and laying hold of any nearby vagrants. They wriggled and howled, many of them taller than the Shadowvar guards that held them. One of the vandals threw a single punch toward his captor and had his face slammed into the cobblestone the next moment.

"What shall we do with them, Guildmaster?" Omri asked.

The prison was already full of suspected Dorumai. There

wasn't even standing room for these seven. And, if he released them, they'd scurry away from this place like cockroaches in torchlight and he wouldn't find them here again.

"We'll question them ourselves," Ariston said. "Bring them into the hall."

Omri hesitated and then nodded. The pause lasted only a second, but it spoke volumes. The Assembly Hall had been built by Rastavan, a demigod among Nokte Murosan Shadowvar. And the Hall had been made for the explicit purpose of dealing justice and good will to the citizens of the city.

And Ariston had just causally ordered the place be used as a prison and interrogation room for a handful of beggars and addicts that likely had no real information on who vandalized the door or the Dorumai at large.

If the image of Eshe's bloodied, empty bed wasn't burned into Ariston's mind, he would have faltered. Instead he reached out and grabbed the Assembly Hall's door to swing it open.

A stab of warmth entered his fingertips. He gasped and withdrew his hand as the sensation worked through it and up his arm, spreading across his chest to his shoulders and down his spine, ending in a buzzing at the base of his neck that itched.

"Guildmaster?"

His heart thundered in his chest. He gasped for breath. He swung his head about him, searching for an enemy his body could feel, but his eyes didn't see.

Had he been hit with a dart? Poisoned somehow while the vandalism distracted him?

He pivoted again and again and again. Every time he felt like an enemy was coming up behind him. Every time he was more certain than the last that if he turned fast, he could catch sight of the spineless coward who had incapacitated him in an instant.

Then something moved on the Assembly Hall door and all of Ariston's focus turned upon it.

The black lines smeared on the wood began to shift. The Dorumai's cape flowed around him. Eyes blinked behind the slits of the mask.

Ariston fell backward, scrambling on his hands and knees away from the impossible sight and not daring to look away from it, either.

"Guildmaster? Guildmaster! What's wrong?"

He tried to reply. But even if he could force enough air into his frantic lungs to form words, he had none. Instead, he scrambled to his feet and ran.

There was no comfort in the houses he knew so well. No steadiness in the familiarity of the path. Only a wild panic thumping around his chest and an unquenchable need to be back in his home.

Omri stopped asking questions after two blocks and just kept stride with him, eyes roving over every citizen of Nokte Murosa with his naked sword in his fist and the rest of the guards sprinting to keep up.

When he spotted his house, Ariston rushed to the door and almost missed the human man standing just beside it. He stopped abruptly, only a few feet from the man, while his mind fought through the fog of panic. He knew this man. Not in this dust-covered state with hands stained in charcoal—

"Genove." Ariston spoke the word and his thoughts sputtered forward. All the ink and parchment they'd found. Lyshan had been certain Genove used these implements with his power, but couldn't say how.

Now, with the man smiling down at him with charcoal on his fingers—the same substance used to defile the doors. The same substance that moved as though it were alive—

Omri took a half a step forward, still gripping his sword. "Stand aside, Genove LeGrande."

Ariston put a hand on Omri's shoulder, pushing him aside so he could point directly at Genove. "You! You did this to me!"

Genove's smile grew. "You should have kept me as a friend."

Ariston opened his mouth, the command to send Genove to the gallows ready on his tongue—but he stopped.

Genove began to change.

His clothes transformed from dust-caked tunic and trousers

to long, black flowing robes with a hood that draped over Genove's head. His face shifted, features simplifying. Smoothing. And growing paler until his face was just a white mask with slits for eyes.

Ariston dug his fingers into Omri's shoulder, but words eluded him. His whole body convulsed with waves of fear and rage.

"Guildmaster?"

All he could see was that Dorumai mask. Those black robes. Genove's laugh rang out in the silence.

"Guildmaster?"

How had Genove done this? Was he the Orator? Had he taken Eshe and plotted to take all of Nokte Murosa, too?

"Ariston!"

Ariston turned his gaze toward Omri's voice, but he didn't find his oldest friend at all.

Ariston didn't have his hand on the shoulder of the captain of the guard, but another Dorumai, robed in black. White mask bright under the cowl.

Ariston startled backward.

"Ariston!" The Dorumai said with Omri's voice. How did they have Omri's voice?

No. Not Omri. Omri couldn't be a Dorumai. He couldn't!

But the panic thumping through Ariston's body offered no other explanation. There he was dressed in Dorumai robes in the middle of the day. Reaching a hand toward Ariston to grab him.

Ariston ducked around the hand and darted for the door to his house, throwing it open and slamming it shut behind him. He secured the bolts and leaned his back against it just as hands pounded on the thing to burst it open. Pleading in voices Ariston had trusted just moments before.

CHAPTER SIXTEEN

GENOVE

When Genove locked eyes with Ariston, when he saw the sheer terror barely held at bay in the Guildmaster's eyes, pure joy filled him. An elation that made losing all of his prestige and possessions mere irritations.

For a moment, at least.

Then Ariston had lost control over the panic and had turned on his own guard and had locked himself in his house without them. The captain of the guard, a Shadowvar by the name Omri, sheathed his sword and banged on the door with his fellow guards joining in, hollering for Ariston, and openly vexed at the man's strange shift in behavior.

Then Omri stopped and turned to Genove. The Shadowvar had been with Ariston when they'd raided Genove's lab. He'd been the one to haul Genove out of his home and torch his belongings.

Omri stalked toward Genove and in an instant Genove realized he'd lingered in his victory too long. He'd relished the panicked cries of Ariston inside his house too completely and now he didn't have time to flee.

Genove turned all the same, trying to duck down the nearest alleyway. Omri caught hold of his tunic in a flash. Genove tried to bat the Shadowvar away. He had three inches on the captain of the guard. Omri's grip tightened, and he pushed Genove off balance and swung him head-first into the corner of the house.

Light exploded across Genove's eyes and the fight seeped out of him as he sunk to the ground.

"What did you do to him, mage?"

Genove tried to focus in on the black blur in front of his face. The blur grew bright white horns. Then angry eyes formed. Then a nose and teeth drawn back in a snarl. Omri.

"What did you do?"

Genove remembered Ariston's face. The apathetic dictator of Nokte Murosa devolving into a babbling idiot. Genove smiled and blood spilled out of his mouth.

Omri struck Genove so swiftly he couldn't even be sure if it was a punch or a kick. All he knew was another wave of pain and that growing sense of contentment. He'd struck at Ariston in a way no beating could undo.

"What did you do?"

Genove laughed again. And Omri stopped asking Genove questions. He just punched and kicked and stomped on Genove until even the mage couldn't laugh any more.

When the beating stopped, Genove wiped the blood and dirt from his eyes to blink up at the Shadowvar. And he hated how weak he must look, curled up in the dirt and bleeding. "You will regret me for an enemy, Captain," Genove mumbled with swollen, cracked lips.

The Shadowvar wiped his bloodied hands on his tunic. "I am not a politician," he said, reaching for his sword, pulling the blade out of the scabbard in a long, slow motion. "I do not leave my enemies breathing."

"Captain!" A voice called from near the house. "We've made it in!"

The captain gave Genove a long, calculating look.

Genove smiled up at the Shadowvar. "Vengeance or duty, Captain? Fateful choices."

"You won't get far," Omri said. Then he jammed his sword back into its scabbard and sprinted toward the house.

Genove urged his body to flee. If he was still on the street or anywhere close when Omri returned, the captain would get to fulfill duty and vengeance after all.

He tried to stand only to find his ankle wouldn't hold his weight—probably sprained or worse from the captain's boot heel. His arms trembled and buckled beneath him and his rib cage burned with every breath. Broken ribs. And his shoulder where the Kyolar had bitten him a decade ago throbbed as if this defeat awakened the first.

Thoughts of being an apex predator flitted through Genove's mind as he dragged his bleeding, aching body through the dust and into an alleyway, stopping every foot or two to spit blood and wheeze air into his burning lungs. He'd just been taken to the dust by a single Shadowvar. Not a group. Not an ambush of any sort. Just a single, albeit well-trained, Shadowvar and Genove hadn't stood a chance.

He realized then, bleeding in the dark of an alley soiled by piss and rats, that his power was as fleeting and intangible as the hallucinations he inflicted on others.

Yes, Ariston now suffered from the manic fear and images of the Dorumai closing in all around him—his shouts so loud Genove could still hear them muffled through the walls—but come tomorrow the hallucinations and terror would be gone. And so would Genove's power over him.

None of the phantom Dorumai following Ariston's every step right now could draw a single drop of blood with their daggers. Only Ariston's mind would bear the wound.

He glanced down at his bloodied body through his swollen eyelids. Bodies healed, but they kept record of the deepest injuries with scars and aches that never quite went away.

But the mind?

The mind was a hive of Zekroaches. Should you rally a strong enough attack, you might scatter the swarm. With repeated, concentrated effort, you may even kill the hive queen. But you will never control the hive with violence. You will only rally them against a common enemy.

He sidled up to a wall and leaned against it, choking out a few more agonizing breaths.

Genove would feel this pain for days and weeks and months. But what of Ariston? Would he feel the edge of this agony tomorrow? Or will he pretend it away in a matter of days, burying it in the deep recesses of his mind?

The air shifted about Genove and he turned back to see if Omri had come upon him after all, silent and full of rage, sword bare.

But the alley was empty. He strained to find horns in the shadows around him—those damn Shadowvar could slip in and out of the dark effortlessly.

Blood dripped into his eyes and the sting blurred his vision. He blinked and rubbed at them. He should get moving. Even if Omri wasn't here now, he would return soon and he would waste no time killing him.

With a few more haggard breaths, Genove pushed back against the wall and inched himself up a little higher, testing his ankle again.

"You were not meant to kneel, Genove LeGrande."

Genove startled, his leg gave out, and he fell back to the piss-stained dirt. Swearing, he turned toward the sound. But it wasn't Omri's voice. This voice boomed like thunder, even in a whisper. Genove caught sight of the white mask and the black robes that seemed to pull out of the shadow itself.

A Dorumai.

Possibly even the Dorumai: the Orator himself.

"I'm not meant to follow blindly, either," Genove said, wiping his hands on the front of his pants, but only smearing the urine smell around rather than ridding his palms of it.

"We encourage sight," the Orator said. "Sight into the past, into our creation and our purpose. Into the present, where our purpose has been tangled by greed and hubris. And into the future, where our potential can only be realized when our masters return."

"Your masters?" Genove wished he had use of his legs now. He'd learned a move or two from Omri that he could certainly try out on the Dorumai.

"The Lords of the Dark," the Orator continued. His voice brimming with pompous enthusiasm. "The Giants of legend. They were our creators and we spurned them. Now they are returning and we have a chance at penance. At assisting them in retaking creation and restoring it to balance."

Genove's irritation faltered. "Balance?"

"Surely you—scholar of the noktums—have noticed the imbalance in this world. We weren't meant to live distinct from the dark. We were meant to embrace it. To be one with it. The noktums suffer for our insolence. We suffer away from the place of our creation. Torn from our purpose."

"And what is our purpose?" Genove asked, some of his irritation returning.

"For many, it is to die."

Genove smiled as best he could with his swollen, bruised face. "I am not going to die. Not by the captain's hand. And not by yours."

"You are not one of the hapless livestock that will feed the Kyolars and Sleeths," the Orator said, stepping farther away from the wall, his black robes shifting around him. "Your destiny is linked with the monsters of this land. But you crave more than apparitions. More than the monsters of the mind."

"And?"

"What do you know of the isle of Hayvonlar?"

Genove studied the Orator, but there were no features evident behind the bright white mask. No body language beneath the shifting, floor-length robes. Just that understated, powerful voice and words that cut right to Genove's center.

"Few know that name."

The Orator crouched down to look Genove in the eye, the white mask just inches from his face. "Fewer still have been its master."

Genove forgot his pain. His humiliation. He imagined a monster with three heads bursting out of the Nokte Murosan streets. He imagined the look on Ariston's face as he tried to reason away the sudden horror.

But it would be no apparition this time.

"Show me, Orator. Make me believe."

CHAPTER SEVENTEEN

KSARA

K sara."

Ksara startled awake and blinked but the black didn't leave. She blinked again and rubbed her eyes. Her eyes were open, and still the black remained.

"Grina's skirts!" Ulric muttered and a burst of light filled the room. The shadows retreated to the ceiling and Ksara covered her eyes with her arm.

"What's that for?"

Ulric pulled Ksara to her feet and propelled her to the door. "It wouldn't let me near you."

"What wouldn't let you near me?"

"The shadows." Ulric hesitated at the door, eyeing the shadows writhing on the ceiling before looking Ksara in the eye. "They know. They know you can't control it."

Ksara's breath caught in her throat. "How?"

"The shadows chased me from your room. Atlas saw."

"By the gods," Ksara whispered. Her mouth suddenly as dry as the Eternal Desert.

"I didn't have the strength to use my power. I couldn't chase them back. I'm so sorry, 'Sar."

A hurricane of thoughts ran through her and her body stiffened, stilled, a husk for the torrent inside her.

The crew knew her lie. They knew her weakness. What would they do now?

What would she do if she were them? Would she follow a leader who'd lied so completely about their ability? Who was, at best, not a magical strength to the team and, at worst, a danger to them all—

"Ksara!"

Her gaze focused on Ulric and only then did she notice the swaths of shadow peeling off the ceiling to whip around her.

Ulric winced as some shadow brushed across his skin and he snapped his fingers, igniting a flash of light and pushing the shadows away again.

"They're gone," Ksara said. It wasn't a question. There was no question. It's what she would do if she were them.

"For now," Ulric said, opening the door and pulling Ksara through it. He shut the door fast behind them as if the shadow couldn't follow. As if the shadow weren't in every crack and crevice of the house and every house in the whole of Nokte Murosa. "They'll be back. Some of them will be back."

"Coronata?"

"Paying Junli a visit. It's how she works through things. She'll be back when she's ready."

They moved down the stairs, the wood creaking loud in the empty house.

"Merewen?"

"At the academy doing research."

"Research?"

"She doesn't like things she doesn't understand."

Ksara sighed. "If she's researching me. My power. We won't see her for a long while."

Ulric shrugged. "Maybe she's better at researching than you are."

Ksara almost laughed but it came out as another sigh. "And Atlas? Is he miles away from Nokte Murosa or finding someone to kill?"

"The second one," Ulric said as they arrived at the shop where the two dead bodies still lay. "He's going after the Dorumai on his own."

"He's going to get himself killed!"

"I think that's one of his goals, yes."

Ksara moved to where her staff leaned against a wall and fastened it to her back. "When did he leave?"

"An hour ago."

"An hour! He could be dead already!"

"I couldn't get to you before now. I didn't have the stamina to use the light."

That gave Ksara pause. What exactly had the shadows done while she was sleeping?

Ulric stepped in front of her. He moved slower, each motion a deliberate expenditure of energy rather than his usual barely contain exuberance. Using his magic to penetrate the shadow to wake her had taken a steep toll on him. "We lied to him, 'Sar. We lied to an Imprevari who was banished from his home for speaking the truth to the wrong people."

"He'll die if he faces the Dorumai alone."

"Dying is always a part of Atlas's strategy. It's what makes him terrifying in a fight."

"I should have told him," Ksara said, her voice tightening. "I should have told them all the truth."

"We met them in a Triadan prison. All of us in chains and hoping to build something more together. Not really the place for confessions."

"I brought them here," Ksara said. "And I will get them all out alive. I owe them that, at least."

Ulric smiled a quiet, knowing smile. "If we go after him, we could die, too, you know."

"Then you should—"

Ulric clapped Ksara on the shoulder and laughed. "Not a

chance."

❦ ❦ ❦

Ksara scrawled a note for the others while Ulric stripped the Dorumai man of weapons and gulped down two elixirs that looked vaguely familiar.

"Where would he go?" Ksara asked as she tucked the note between two elixirs on the shelf.

"The Western Noktum," Ulric said, fastening the sword and dagger to his waist and tucking another knife in his boot. "Merewen suggested it was the most likely place for the Dorumai to be waiting now. It's where some ceremony is being held. I didn't catch it all."

Ksara rolled her eyes. "You have to stop staring at her like that."

"It's not my fault! She gets this look on her face when she's explaining something...."

"We've talked about this."

"We're a professional crew, I know. I know. But Merewen should be the exception to the rule. There's always at least one exception to a rule. That body ..."

The only body on Ksara's mind was Atlas's. She kept seeing him dead in an alley somewhere, beaten and stabbed nearly beyond recognition. She crossed to the shop door and opened it.

The street had throngs of people rushing back and forth under the high noon sun. The shadows pushed back into the alleyways. She took a moment to scan for any Dorumai watching them. She felt their eyes upon her. Felt the shadows lean into her, too.

Ksara turned her gaze to her brother standing at her side. His mismatched eyes bright with hope. Excitement. Certainty.

She borrowed these from Ulric now. Borrowed them against the chasm of dread opening up wider and wider inside her soul.

"Let's go rescue our suicidal Imprevari," he said.

CHAPTER EIGHTEEN

EZELL

zell Lamar straightened a stack of parchment on her desk, took a half a step away from it, then returned to straighten it again.

She absolutely loathed late deliveries. One of the perks of being the chief librarian of the Nokte Murosan Academy Library—the only proper library east of Nokte Shaddark—was prompt and reliable deliveries.

She fussed with the stack of parchment once more. Not even the news of Genove LeGrande's fall from the Guildmaster's grace had been a proper distraction. Nor the rumors of Jocosa Daw— the beloved prodigy of history department—bedding the lecherous LeGrande then fleeing the city on the first boat out.

So much for a pedigreed mind.

Ezell didn't seek out such gossips, but her desk was outside the library's only entrance and while she stood sentinel over previous knowledge, student and professor alike would spot Ezell across the rotunda and scurry over to offer bits of common dribble no ink or parchment should bear record of.

Footsteps clapped loud on the stone floor and Ezell heart leapt. Forty-five minutes late is a travesty, but at least it is done—

She frowned and made her way to sit on the single stool behind her desk, glaring over the rim of her spectacles at the approaching stranger who very much was not an Academy courier.

The stranger loomed over the desk like a noktum over a chicken coop. She had thick, red hair tied into a strange braid and blue tattoos curling about her jawline like waves. What's more, the strange woman wore furs that covered her bosom, but not her full torso and carried two axes at her belt. Axes! Not only did she bring weapons inside the academy, but the most rudimentary and primitive of ones.

"I wish to access your library," the strange woman said in a stiff Usaran accent.

Ezell stared at the woman, blinking long and slow. "Are you a student of the academy?"

It was a foolish question, but one foolish question begat another.

"I am not," the stranger said.

"A professor, then?"

"No."

Ezell smiled a poison smile and pushed her glasses up higher on her nose. "Then I cannot allow you access to the library, but there are plenty of taverns and *shkazat* tents to meet your needs, be they what they may."

More footsteps sounded in the rotunda and Ezell leaned sideways on her stool to look around the stranger, nearly toppling off her perch. When she caught sight of a young, frantic student with a fistful of letters, Ezell's mood improved dramatically. "You'll find the exit the same way you arrived," Ezell said. "Good afternoon."

The dense, mountain of a woman, didn't move. Perhaps she hadn't quite heard Ezell's polite dismissal from her altitude. Perhaps she was too barbaric to know a dismissal should Ezell track down a ladder and scream it in the woman's ear.

The student gave the strange woman a wide berth then mumbled apologies and something about the last courier not showing up for her shift. Ezell took the letters, dished out her disapproval in a sharp glare, and the courier hurried away.

The stranger hadn't moved an inch.

Ezell craved privacy for the next bit of her routine, but the late delivery and obstinate stranger had her miffed. So she flipped through the envelopes, pretending she was alone and sinking into the routine to calm herself.

Two letters came from students, one who was a zealous reader and the other one who no amount of extra reading would save from mediocrity. Both, no doubt, requesting additional texts for their studies. The third envelope came from the mage, Clem Lyshan. The mage often wrote Ezell when he'd discovered new properties to an herb or elixir and just as often wrote to argue with established texts on the same subject. The former was an intellectual delight and the latter was a prickling thorn that clung to her thoughts.

The final envelope in Ezell's hands had no writing on it at all. Her pulse quickened and she glanced up at the stranger. The woman still stared down with stormy-blue eyes. Content in the silence.

Ezell frowned and hid her hands behind a pile of parchment before flipping the blank envelope around.

Her heart leapt again at the sight of a black wax seal with an upside down pentagon symbol pressed into it.

The Orator had called her. Her!

She'd barely caught a glimpse of the Dorumai leader at the gatherings. He'd stepped out of the noktum, the dark curling away from him as if by command. He'd spoken to them, his voice clear and strong.

History was coming for Noksonon. The Giants were returning. And the citizens could see the truth or die in ignorance.

Nokte Murosa was a glutton for ignorance. From the Guildmaster pretending at peace while criminals ran the streets to the academy feigning a quest for knowledge while adopting every wandering merchant with blue robes as a scholar and master teacher.

There were texts in her very own library that depicted how these follies would end. She'd tried to share them, but no one wanted to hear her. No one wanted knowledge when it challenged power.

No one except the Orator. He quoted from these texts more fluently than even Ezell. He would lead Nokte Murosa away from decay and into the future.

And now he called on her to act. This envelope contained his handwriting. His instruction just to her.

She memorized the texture of the parchment, the perfect portion of wax for the seal, the crisp folds to create the envelope—

"Are you well?"

Ezell startled off her chair, pitching her precious envelope to the ground and crying out more at that tragedy than her head cracking into her desk. She caught herself on her knees and scrambled to the where the Orator's call to her lie on the ground like refuse. In an instant it was back in her hands and she cradled it to her bosom for a moment, breathing hard and noting the blood trickling down from her brow.

"You're injured."

Ezell cursed beneath her breath. The Usaran beast of a woman was still there, like a talking, red-headed statue of Senji herself sent to curse her in this moment of elation.

"Do you need help?"

"No!" Ezell bit back, then took some of the edges off her words. "I'll be but a moment." She turned her attention back to the letter, broke the seal, unfolded each precise crease, and drank in the words:

Ezell Lamar, guardian of history and curator of truth, we call upon you now.

For even a mountain can be changed by a single stone tumbling down its face, carving a path for the rest to follow.

History is seen in sieges and sweeping wars, but history is made in the quietest moments no scribe records.

There are strangers to Nokte Murosa who strive to undo destiny. Two Demaijos mages, a Sandrunner pirate, an Imprevari captain, and a Usaran warrior. The warrior comes to you now. Detain her. Be certain she will not escape. And then join me at the noktum and I will receive you.

Ezell, you are the stone. This is the moment.

-The Orator

Ezell read the note three more times and then cradled it in her hands.

Her heart pattered with excitement. She'd always known she was meant for something more. Fate hadn't passed her by, it had found her here. Right now.

"I can tend the wound," the Usaran woman said. She'd moved around the desk with a silence most impressive for her size and stared down at Ezell like a stony peak beholding a stone.

A stone.

A smile spread across Ezell's face and she tucked the letter inside her wide belt. "I am fine. Help me to my feet and I will let you in the library."

The Usaran grabbed hold of Ezell by the arm and tipped her onto her feet. "Thank you. My research is quite urgent."

"Curiosity doesn't abide library hours," Ezell replied. "Exceptions must be made."

Ezell retrieved her keys from a drawer and did her best to walk calmly to the library's thick, wooden door. The library had once been a keep, a stronghold against raiding pirates before the rest of the academy and Nokte Murosa grew up around it.

Ezell hefted the heavy door open, inch-by-inch. Cool, stale air exhaled from the room. Followed by the sweet taste of lamp oil. Even in the afternoon light, the library maintained its grim shadows.

"Lanterns are at the back," Ezell said. "And I will shut the door to keep errant students from disturbing your study."

The Usaran considered Ezell for a moment and Ezell fixed her askew glasses and beckoned the stranger into the library with a single hand.

The Usaran bowed her head and entered in.

Ezell listened for the woman's quiet boots to cross to the center of the library before she heaved the door closed—and locked it.

She checked the clock across the empty rotunda. With the Night of the Soul tonight, there wouldn't be more than a handful of teachers moving about the academy for the next sixteen hours.

Ezell pulled the spare library keys from a hidden drawer, extinguished the oil lamp on her desk, and hurried across the rotunda.

She was the stone. This was her moment.

CHAPTER NINETEEN

JUNLI

Junli lie in his bed, staring at the ceiling. Coronata slept on his bare shoulder.

She'd found him at the shipyard, sauntered up to him, whispered in his ear, and in all possible haste, he'd led her right back here.

He hadn't had time to feel guilty then. Coronata wielded lust and temptation more masterfully than a Ringer swung his sword. And only now, when they'd had their fill of love and her favorite Triadan whiskey—when Coronata slept with her naked body against his, did Junli have time to feel the sting of his betrayal.

The note had come just after Coronata's first visit. And it had come stamped with the Dorumai sigil and tucked inside a carton of Triadan whiskey. Coronata's favorite.

Death is a Kyolar, the note had read. *It waits for the unwary. The ill-prepared.*

You couldn't save Malene. You loved her, but you let her choose. She boarded that boat, and the sea took her.

Coronata's arm lie draped over him. He brushed his fingertips across her smooth warm skin. Trying not to imagine that spark in Malene's eyes after she'd kissed him goodbye. The spring to her step as she boarded the ship. He'd done everything he could to make sure the vessel was up to task. He'd even tried to suggest a different navigator than Malene to the captain. But Malene was the best in the city and Malene wanted it.

So he let her go.

But he'd been right. It had been recklessness renamed as adventure to try to chart the waters east of Taur. The Taur-El had found pieces of the ship washed up on their shores.

Junli traced his fingertips across Coronata's brow.

Death is a Kyolar and you hear it's screams, the note had read. *Coming for those you love.*

They thunder through the ground now—Behemoths awaken. Civilizations will crumble. Only those who hear can be saved.

You know the Bloody Queen cannot hear the death coming for her.

The drink will not kill her, it will save her. Take away the choice and you take away her death.

Junli wrapped his free arm tighter around Coronata and watched her sleep.

Chapter Twenty

BREY

Brey, the beggar watched the Imprevari stomp into the tavern, seething with violence.

When the man exited a half an hour later, the Imprevari had a busted lip and a slur to his words as he shouted back at the tavern patrons.

"The Imprevari is his own enemy," Brey recited, clutching the poisoned dagger tight to his chest. "You only have to deal the final blow."

The masked man had said those words. He haunted the alleys at night. Moving about like the ghost and speaking mesmerizing words.

Brey asked coin of the masked man every night. And every night he ignored the request, moving about on the business of death.

But last night the masked man had paused, staring down at Brey's empty, grimy palms. He'd reached into the billow of his own cloak and offered Brey a white, wooden mask instead of coin.

At first Brey chuckled at the offering. He couldn't eat the

thing. Nor could he sell it without losing his own head. That painted bit of wood was the most dangerous bit of garbage in all of Nokte Murosa!

But then the masked man had started speaking. He spoke of history and destiny. Of purpose for all. Of loss and redemption.

And, before Brey fully understood why, he took the mask from the masked man's hand and clutched it tightly within his own.

But the masked man hadn't stopped there. He told Brey of those who would thwart progress. Those who despised change because they could not comprehend it. Because they could not see past the crust of gold on the refuse of their lives.

But Brey could. Brey saw them all as they were—scared children rushing about. Too terrified at the fragility of their own fortune to look misfortune in the eye.

"The Imprevari is his own enemy. You only have to deal the final blow." Those words and the dagger had been the masked man's final gifts and he'd faded into the alley as though spawned from the night itself.

The Imprevari made quick progress to the next tavern. He shouted about the Dorumai. He blasphemed the masked man. He wanted a public fight. To kill an enemy before he died.

Brey saw the feeble fear behind the bravado. The ache for belonging. The self-hatred so immense it swallowed everyone around him.

The masked man had been right about this, too. The Imprevari would destroy himself. It was his truest desire.

The armored foreigner entered the next tavern two streets down and Brey kept pace in the alleys. The Imprevari made a ruckus and never looked behind him. He was easy to follow.

At the door to the next tavern, a throng of sailors met him. A few had knives in their hands.

The Imprevari's voice fell too low for Brey to catch every word, but the sailors heard every breath of it. In a moment, the group attacked.

The Imprevari drew his short sword in a flash and narrowed

in on the three strongest of the group, dealing them slashes to their legs and then letting the force of the ambush press him backward into an alley. He'd have the advantage there.

At least against the enemies he knew about.

Brey hurried down the alley, climbed two stone walls, dropped into the back of a *shkazat* tent, wove about the lounging, dead-eyed patrons, and then dashed across the street and into the alley with the wild abandon of a rodent about to feast.

This alley smelled of chamber pots and cloying *shkazat* smoke. He followed it and the sound of the battle grew louder. By the time he traced the alley around the building he found Atlas standing alone, leaning against a wall, blood dripping from his sword.

The sailors groaned and muttered curses up at the Imprevari. One of them started crawling out of the alleyway, holding a stomach wound.

Brey crept forward, the bandages passing for shoes stifling each footstep. His palms sweating, making the dagger harder and harder to hold.

He'd killed a man before—a blue-breath addict who'd leapt upon him while he was sleeping. Brey had wrestled the man to his back and squeezed the air from his throat. And the addict had just let him. Like death was the release he'd been searching for and Brey had been a tool to get there.

The Imprevari yearned for the same. So Brey would give it to him. For the Dorumai and the destiny of Noksonon. But also for the man who was imprisoned in a life he no longer wanted.

The Imprevari bent down and cleaned his sword on the tunic of one of the sailors. The sailor flinched but couldn't flee with his thigh sliced open and weeping blood.

Just as the Imprevari was about to stand, Brey leapt forward and stabbed him between the plates of armor.

Or, tried to stab him.

The blade barely scratched skin before the Imprevari twisted around and slashed his sword right across Brey, cutting him open from shoulder to hip.

The dagger, barely wet with the Imprevari' s blood, slipped from Brey's fingers and clattered to the ground. He stared down at his horrific wound as his tattered rags changed from dusty brown to wet crimson.

Brey lost sensation in his legs and he sank to the ground. He didn't fight to keep his blood inside him. Death was not as terrible as he'd imagined. It was warm, lying in a pool of his blood. And his stomach didn't ache for food nor his heart for greater purpose.

With one final gargled breath, he drifted away from it all.

CHAPTER TWENTY-ONE

KSARA

I count two in front," Ulric said.

Ksara leaned into the foot traffic around them, letting an oncoming Shadowvar knock her shoulder. She used the hit as an excuse to pivot and glance behind them.

"Four trailing," she said low enough only Ulric could hear. "Six people are following us."

"At least Atlas will be happy."

Ksara raised a brow at her brother.

He shrugged. "More people to fight."

"We're trying to keep Atlas alive."

"Tell him it's an 'I'm sorry' gift."

"More people who want to kill him? That's how I should apologize?"

"Have you *met* Atlas?"

Ksara shook her head and smiled. They could have a mountain toppling over on them and Ulric would make a joke about the quality of the shade.

She led them across the street to a tavern door. It was the seventh one they'd checked and so far the only thing they'd found were sour glares and more people who wanted to track them across town.

As soon as Ksara paused at the door to open it, the shadows swarmed closer to her. These were the stalkers she didn't need to count. The ones she never truly broke free from. And they invaded her mind like a pack of Kyolar rushing at her. They pressed against her skin as cold and fierce as a blast of Usaran winter air. Her whole body wanted to flee. Every ounce of her begged to get farther away from the noktum. To climb aboard the *Falco*, seaworthy or not, and sail far away from this cursed city tucked between two nightmares.

Her heart raced and her body tightened, but she kept the fear from her face and she stayed right where she was. There would be a time to flee, but not now. Now her crew needed her.

Ksara sucked in a short breath between clenched teeth and she entered the tavern.

The room smelled sour sweat and sweet mead. Half-empty bowls of stew littered the tables and a woman exited the back room carrying a tray. She had thin arms, a sharp jaw, and a bright smile that didn't quite reach her eyes. "Meade or soup? What will please you?"

Ksara walked the perimeter of the room, making a show of examining the tattered tapestry and the fake Kyolar head, stuffed and mounted on the wall, but all the while staying a pace or two ahead of the rabid shadows.

Ulric smiled wide and moved to one of the tables, grabbing a bowl and giving the stew a sniff. "Sansarillian spice?"

The woman nodded.

"All the way from Usara?"

The woman's cheeks warmed a little. "My uncle runs caravans north."

Ulric gave the uneaten stew a long look and shook his head. "Shame to see such quality eating go to waste."

The woman began collecting the bowls and placing them on the tray. "Got fresh stew for you and your woman. What will you have?"

"I'm his sister," Ksara said, shooting a warning look at Ulric. Her brother was a few lines from pulling the inn keeper into the back room for some private hospitality. And this wasn't the time for that. "Your patrons rushed out in the middle of supper. Was it to chase after an Imprevari soldier?"

The woman scooped the bowls onto the tray faster, the flush of emotion fading from her face.

Ulric moved a little closer to her, lowering his voice to the gentlest of tones. "He's our friend. We just want to see him home."

"They fought. Took it to the alley," she said, putting the last bowl on the tray.

Ulric dropped a coin on the table. It was one of their last. "What's uneaten should not go unpaid."

The woman met Ulric's eyes and her smile returned. Stronger than ever.

Ulric beamed back at her.

Ksara strode toward the door, but it burst open before she could arrive. Six men filed into the room. Each with faces she recognized as the Dorumai who'd tracked them through Nokte Murosa.

Ksara stopped, planting herself between the men and the rest of the room. The shadows writhed and danced around her, swelling as high as her waist.

The inn keeper gasped and Ulric beckoned her into the back room before returning to Ksara's side.

The men stared at Ksara and the shadows playing around her. Then they each reached inside their tunics and robes and retrieved white masks and slid them over their faces.

"Leave Nokte Murosa now and your crew leaves with you," the man at the center of the group said. He wore a blacksmith's frock with pincers and a hammer still tucked in his belt.

Ulric chuckled. "Aren't you a polite cultist!"

"We have no qualms with a mage of the dark."

"Mage of the dark?" Ulric said. "That's not a bad title, 'Sar."

Ksara reached over her shoulder and pulled the metal staff

free. She twisted it in her palms, clicking it three times to the left and two to the right. Two spikes extended out the top and bottom of the staff, each four inches long.

Ulric spread his hands wide. "That's a no from her. Better luck next time."

He clapped his hands together. Blinding light exploded in the room. And Ksara attacked.

CHAPTER TWENTY-TWO

KSARA

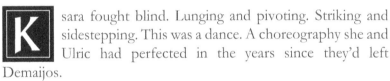

sara fought blind. Lunging and pivoting. Striking and sidestepping. This was a dance. A choreography she and Ulric had perfected in the years since they'd left Demaijos.

She dropped three men before the light began to fade. She loved fighting in the light of Ulric's power. She loved living in that moment, free for an instant from the lurking weight of the shadows on her mind. She fought with a joyful ferocity that no one saw, but many unfortunate foes experienced.

As the light returned to normal in the room, Ulric drew his own blade and tested it in the air before him. He had a way with new weapons. He loved the challenge each one brought. The worse the balance or the stranger the craftsmanship the better. Ulric loved elevating his skill to any deficiency the weapon at hand brought.

To the Dorumai's credit, they did not flee when their sight returned and they caught the glinting metal of Ulric's swinging sword in their face, nor when they beheld three of their company writhing on the ground at their feet nursing welts and puncture wounds.

Ulric smiled and the three Dorumai attacked.

Two of them had long knives and the other his blacksmith hammer. Ksara incapacitated the blacksmith first, dealing a quick slash to the back of the man's leg and then reversing it to slash at the Dorumai behind her. Ulric finished the man off with strike to his thigh and then clocked the final standing enemy with the butt of the sword. He crumpled to the ground with a groan.

"So much for Atlas's gift," Ulric said.

Ksara stepped over the bleeding men and opened the tavern door. "Keeping him alive will be gift enough."

"You really don't know Atlas well at all."

Out on the street, Ksara ducked around the western edge of the tavern and into an alleyway. There she found mounds of bodies, some of them still breathing. And, at the center of the chaos, Atlas.

She hurried to the Imprevari and the shadows hurried with her, sweeping around her and cloaking the carnage about them in black. She knelt beside Atlas and touched his arm. His eyes fluttering open.

"Atlas!"

Sweat covered his face and his whole body quivered. "Ambush."

"We'll get you back to the mage's shop ..."

"No."

Ksara's throat tightened. Surely the man wouldn't choose death over trusting Ksara just one more time. "Ulric can take you. You need help."

"Get out," Atlas said. "Ambush."

Ksara tugged at Atlas's arm, but fully clad in armor and nearly unconscious, he was too heavy for her to lift alone. "Ulric!"

She tried to haul Atlas to his feet again and failed. "Ulric!"

Glancing up, she found Ulric a half a step behind her, his eyes searching the alley around them.

Ksara stilled and she slowly rose to stand beside her brother.

"There's someone out there," he said.

Deliberate footsteps echoed from farther down the alley. Boots against dirt and stone, but something else, too. A gargled breathing and claws scraping.

"Asper's ass," Atlas wheezed. "Get out of here!"

The shadows churned around Ksara. "Get him up!"

Before Ulric could obey, a creak and crash shook the alley. Ulric cried out. Ksara spun to find a wagon tipped over and blocking the exit. Its cargo of crates spilled into the alley and atop Ulric, who'd stepped to meet the new attacker and met the trap instead. He wrestled to get free, blood trickling from a new cut on his head when a low, loud, growl trembled through the air, the sound humming in Ksara's very bones.

Centimeter-by-centimeter, Ksara turned her head and found yellow eyes staring back at her. Whatever the thing was, it stood four feet from the ground and had a vaguely feline shape, though its coat blended almost perfectly with the dark of the alley.

"What … in … all … the … gods … is … that?" Ulric said, his voice strained as he struggled under the pile of crates.

The shadows pulled tighter into Ksara, the cold piquing her terror. She clicked the staff three times and spikes emerged from every inch of the metal rod, leaving only the grip at the center free of the short blades.

The creature stalked closer. Only a dozen feet away now.

Atlas groaned and pushed himself up on his elbow.

"Stay. I've got this."

"Shall I take your word on that, Demaijos?" Atlas said and the words stung.

The cat hissed and its long, white teeth shone bright.

"Hold."

The voice rang from somewhere behind the creature. The thing peeled its black lips back and growled louder, the sound so low Ksara felt it as much as heard it.

The creature's sides heaved and its tail flicked, but it obeyed the voice.

A white mask appeared behind. The body of the Dorumai just

as fluid with the dark as the creature was.

"The Dark delights in you, Ksara Sajra."

"You are the Orator."

The masked man nodded his head, showing the nubs of his sawed off Shadowvar horns, if only for a moment. "I am."

"Grina's ass," Atlas said. "Just kill each other. Or kill me. I can't stand any more talking."

"You're only my enemy by circumstance," the Orator continued. Atlas groaned. "You sought healing for your brother and the Guildmaster leveraged your need to match his. But you know how Nokte Murosa festers under his rule."

"You came after Ulric," Ksara said.

"A misstep. I have not killed the Usaran."

Ksara gripped her staff tighter. "Where is Merewen?"

"She is locked in the academy library," the Orator said. "Nor have I killed the Sandrunner pirate. She lies drugged in a lover's arms." The Orator inclined his head to Atlas. "Even this Imprevari I would spare. There is an antidote for the poison infecting his wound. But there is always a choice and a cost."

"Just kill him," Atlas said, his voice much weaker than it was before.

The shadows circled Ksara, looping and curling around her. "You're the leader of the Dorumai? They follow you?"

"Yes."

"Good," Ksara said and set her jaw in a firm line. "Then I'll only have to say this once. We take care of our own and we make our own way. And right now, you're standing in it."

The cat let out deep growl, but the Orator laughed, genuine mirth in the sound. "You cannot deter destiny. And I am your destiny."

Atlas groaned. "Stab your destiny or die already."

Ksara stepped over Atlas's prone body and stood between him and the Orator and creature.

"Look about you, mage. The Dark is your destiny. And I am the voice of the Dark. We are bound. You can no more be rid of me than you can be rid of the shadows now. But you do have a choice."

The Orator raised his hand and a gold ring with a ruby gem glinted there. The bracer on Ksara's arm hummed. That was the Ring of Salgimore. The ring that was supposed to be on the Shadowvar kid's finger so she could find him before these very Dorumai ended him. Now, seeing it in the Dorumai's hand, Ksara felt that familiar stab of despair. Even if she could get out of here alive, even if she could get her crew back together in one piece, she had no way to succeed in saving the kid. No hope of finding him when the ring sat in the Dorumai's hand.

"You know what this ring is, mage. And you've been scouting the city in search of it. Treasure hunters using this artifact to find the boy, Eshe." The Orator tilted his head. "But Ariston was given his choice. And the boy must pay for it."

Ksara narrowed her mismatched eyes. "You gave Ariston a choice?"

"Ariston could have forfeited his own life and his boy would be safe in his room right now. But he showed himself a coward, unfit to rule in the new world. And now his son will die. And he will still kneel before us as the Dorumai take Nokte Murosa. But that was his choice. Your choice is just as simple. Go back to the Mage Lyshan's shop and stay there. Let the Night of the Soul be as it will be. Then, in the morning, you and your crew will be free to leave Nokte Murosa."

"You're going to kill more than the kid," Ksara said.

"Nokte Murosa must shed its skin like a serpent in order to grow. But what do you care of these?" The Orator motioned to the city at large. "Miscreants and vandals. Sycophants and small minds. They are tools for you. You came here only out of dire necessity and nothing more. You owe them nothing."

Ksara considered for a moment, the darkness lapping against her and sending chills across her skin. The Orator knew so much about them. Likely he and his spies had been watching them from the moment they came barreling into port as someone who could disrupt their plans. And now she had a way out. A way to turn from Ariston and Nokte Murosa and go their own way, mostly whole and with the sea beneath them.

Her gaze fell to that golden ruby ring in the Orator's black hand.

They were that kid's only hope at living through the night. Ariston couldn't stop the Dorumai. Nor could any of the criminal factions within Nokte Murosa who might have wanted Ariston's favor over the Dorumai's.

"Where is the kid?" Ksara asked, the words spilling out before she could stop them.

"Far from your reach."

"He's in the noktum," Ksara said. "That's why I'm a threat. Because I can follow you there."

"Can you now?" The Orator said, a smile in his voice. Then he dropped the Ring of Salgimore and it landed near Atlas. The Imprevari groaned and rolled closer to it before growing still once more. She could no more follow the Orator into the noktum than Atlas could leap up and grab hold of the ring. And the Dorumai knew it.

"Then why give me a choice at all? You could kill us now."

"He could try," Ulric said, stepping up to Ksara's side. She glanced at him in surprise. He must have wriggled free of the crates in the time Ksara had been talking. The effort had drained him and if the verbose leader of a violent cult wasn't standing in front of them with his pet monster, Ulric would have surely been leaning against a wall to keep upright.

"You carry the power of a Lord of the Dark," the Orator said. "You are a type of what is to come. A signal that the Giants' return is imminent. A reminder of their ultimate power."

Ksara opened her mouth, but her tongue dried and the words didn't come.

The Orator turned from them and strode back down the alley way and the creature rumbled a growl and stalked closer toward them.

"Come," the Orator called back over his shoulder and the monster breathed a high whine and turned its hungry gaze from them, and ran on heavy, quiet paws to its master's side.

"We didn't even leave the baby monster for Atlas to kill," Ulric said. "Atlas is going to be so mad when he wakes up."

CHAPTER TWENTY-THREE

KSARA

K sara held the Ring of Salgimore tight in her fist as she and Ulric hefted an unconscious Atlas back through the crowded streets of Nokte Murosa. The black ring on her arm hummed at the proximity of the magical artifact while Ksara's mind buzzed with the Orator's words.

He'd offered her everything she'd wanted since she'd stepped foot into Nokte Murosa three days ago—a way to leave.

But he'd done it while holding her crew hostage.

Measure a man by what he bleeds, not what he breathes. That's what their father had said. The fact that he'd been willing to send Ksara off into exile to preserve the reputation of his gem business only ratified the words.

A person was measured by what they were willing to sacrifice, not the words they spoke.

By that measure, the Orator was willing to lose a Shadowvar kid, all of Ksara's crew, including Ulric, and most of Nokte Murosa.

And for what?

This was more sinister than a bid for power. It was a righteous entitlement to political power sent down by a prophecy the Orator dictated and enforced in fear.

The thought made the skin between Ksara's shoulder blades itch.

The Orator and his Dorumai were more than just a violent cult steeped in history. They had a hold over the people. A strength in numbers not even Ksara had guessed. They'd watched Ksara's every move since she'd come here. Catalogued it and reported all to the Orator. And, when called upon, they'd incapacitated Ksara's crew in an hour without any apparent strain.

Ariston was right to worry. Ksara glanced about the busy street. The orange dusk cast the faces around them in sinister hues. How many of these citizens were actually Dorumai? How many would be willing to stick a knife between her ribs, just to gain the favor of the Orator and some mythical Giants?

"You're too quiet," Ulric said as they arrived at the dead healer's shop.

"Merewen and Coronata are being held hostage by a gilded-tongued maniac and I have to figure out a way to keep someone from dying of poison. Again. In three days."

Ulric chuckled, his voice hoarse. "At least the shop is probably safe."

"Probably?"

"Well, the Dorumai want us to stay here. So they *probably* won't try to kill us while we sleep."

Ksara kicked open the shop door and sidestepped through.

The shop was pristine with all of the vials upright and labels facing forward. The bodies were gone. The mage's blood wiped clean from the cabinet.

And a single, unmarked vial sat on the table.

Ksara and Ulric paused just inside the door. Listening for a whisper of breath. But the only thing that filled the room was shadows twisting from their regular forms to draw closer and closer to Ksara.

"Get him on the table," Ksara said and they heaved the

armored man up and onto the workspace, moving the unmarked vial to the edge, and turning him over onto his side. The actual wound was small, barely an inch long. She prodded the skin around the scratch. It was an angry, bright red with veins of black spreading across Atlas's back.

"What are the chances that this is the actual antidote?" Ulric asked, picking up the unmarked vial and shaking its contents. "And what did they do with the dead bodies?"

"High," Ksara said, taking the vial from Ulric and tipping some of the contents into the wound and the rest into Atlas's mouth. "If he kills Atlas, the deal's off."

"You're taking his deal, then?"

Ksara leaned close to Atlas's mouth to listen for his breathing. It had steadied. This wasn't nearly as deadly a poison as Ulric had survived.

"He's going to murder innocents, 'Sar. A lot of them."

"And Merewen and Coronata will be among them if we leave this house."

"We could go in disguise."

"You have a cowl and a mask I don't know about?"

He motioned at the swath of black air swooshing around her with every movement. "You have your own perfect disguise right there. Move through the city Shadowvar-style. Quite fitting for Nokte Murosa, I think."

"I can't control this, Ulric," she said. "You know I can't control this."

He shrugged. "We try a different meditation technique. There has to be a way—"

"No!" she shouted with enough force to rattle the elixirs on their shelves. "No," she said again, calmer than before. "That's not a plan. That's hope in harlot skirts."

"We can give them hope, 'Sar. The kid. The whole city. Isn't that worth the risk?"

"I don't have any hope to give," Ksara said.

Ulric's smile faded and the room felt colder without it there.

She parted her lips to say more, but he turned and climbed the stairs to the mage's room, shutting the door behind him.

She stayed in the silence of the room, guilt joining the shadows haunting her at every turn.

● ● ●

Ksara watched the orange light beaming through the window as it burned red and began to fade. The streets outside the shop were quiet. The Night of the Soul had nearly begun.

Ulric hadn't left the mage's room. And Atlas lie on the worktable in full armor. It looked about as uncomfortable a position as she could imagine and she couldn't tell if the deeper-than-normal scowl on his face was from the discomfort of the table or the poison receding from his veins. Either way, his eyes were closed and Ksara had nothing to do but watch the night roll in on Nokte Murosa and pace the room.

She circled the table in quiet, careful steps, pausing at the door. The shadows caught up with her, pressing their chill against the backs of her legs before swelling around to engulf them.

Shouts sounded up and down the street. Feet clapped against the cobblestone. Ksara moved to the window and watched a dozen robed and masked Dorumai patrolling the streets. Most of the citizens had already gone to the Noktum Plaza—an entrance into the western noktum where there was an altar specifically built for the Night of the Soul.

But the stragglers walking through the streets had just encountered these silent, marching Dorumai and the panic had begun.

Ksara began pacing again, faster than before. Screams sounded several houses over. A door slammed. Voices murmured. Pleaded.

A quiet knock sounded at the back door.

Ksara froze mid step, and the shadow washed its icy embrace across her skin. She shivered, but crept silently to the wall, lifting her staff into her hands, and moving to the back door to ease the door open without a sound.

The parchment merchant stood in the orange light of dusk, wearing Dorumai robes and holding a mask in his hands. He met Ksara's eyes, then stared at the ground.

"They killed Lyshan?" The man whispered. The words hollow.

Ksara nodded.

"Nokte Murosa is a lot of things." He turned the mask about in his hands. "But this? This isn't it."

"It is now."

"Lyshan was the first person to be kind to me here," he said. "Closest thing I had to family. Someone has to stop them."

"I have family here, too," Ksara said. "They're dead if I leave."

"They're dead if they see you," the merchant said, and he offered the mask to her. "Take it. Stop them."

More screams poured out of a nearby house. A child cried. A woman wailed.

She should shut the door and ignore the merchant. Ignore the terror pulsing through the air as though the whole of Nokte Murosa had a heartbeat and she could feel it thundering faster and faster.

This wasn't her problem. Her allegiance was to her crew. And she had to get them safely out of this city.

But she couldn't get herself to close the door.

All she could see was Ulric's face when she'd told him she had no hope. The way the light dimmed in his eyes as his smile faded. Hope led them out of Demaijos to traipse across Noksonon with a handful of coin and each other. Hope had brought her here to Nokte Murosa and it had saved Ulric's life.

Hope was terrifying, but Ulric didn't want to live in a world without it. And neither did she.

"Come in."

The merchant's face brightened. "You're going to stop them?"

"I'm going to try," Ksara said. "Don't make a sound when you're inside. And only tell my brother all of this when he finds you."

The merchant nodded and she beckoned the man inside.

CHAPTER TWENTY-FOUR

GID

ockmaster Gid waited for the Demaijos Devil to skulk past him wearing Dorumai robes.

And he didn't have to wait long at all.

The arrogant woman strode right across the street without a single visible hesitation. As though a Dorumai could defect without the Orator knowing. As though the Orator hadn't planned for this possibility from the very beginning.

When he'd found the Orator standing in his home, Gid had considered clocking the Shadowvar over the head and turning him in to Guildmaster Ariston. The move would have given him copious amounts of goodwill, maybe even enough to position himself as the next Guildmaster of Nokte Murosa. The first human in their history to do so.

But he had just lost a tavern brawl to the Demaijos and her crew. Limping and bleeding and his mind pulsing with a lustful rage. He'd taken his best men to the tavern. He should have been able to overcome the Demaijos woman and her crew at the tavern. Hold her down until fear entered those defiant, eerie eyes.

That's when the Orator had offered him this—a chance to catch the Demaijos woman in her most desperate moment and exact revenge on her when she least expected it.

All it took was a robe, a white mask, and a little trust.

But that trust was already paying off.

Pulling from the doorway of a shop, Gid hobbled the path that the Orator had told him to go—a shortcut right to a lesser-used entrance of the Western Noktum. There, the Orator had promised Gid his prize.

Gid caught a flash of the Demaijos running to the noktum and he staggered faster on his bruised and swollen leg. When he arrived at the noktum entrance, the Demaijos woman was still standing just outside the noktum's reach. Or what should have been outside the noktum's reach, but the shadowy tentacles stretched farther than they ever had before, coiling around her. Brushing about her shoulders and pulling her closer step-by-reluctant-step.

He stared at her neck, that pretty little neck, as he heaved his bulk soundlessly toward her. She would bend to him. Beg him. Serve his every pleasure or die squirming as he squeezed the life from her.

He half-expected her to turn on him. Notice him in a flurry of movement and lash out like a cornered viper. But the black air had her seemingly mesmerized, maybe even paralyzed.

Until he wrapped his fingers around her throat from behind and began to squeeze.

She pivoted then, or tried to, but he threw her to the ground, headfirst. The shock of the blow kept her down for a moment. And he used his good foot to stomp her head then. Again and again.

Blood trickled out of her nose and mouth and he halted the assault. Let her look up at him with those strange, wild eyes.

He would tame this woman. He would—

Something hit him from behind. At first he thought it was a wagon. Then, as the thing pinned him to the ground and a wet ripping filled his ears, he knew it was something else. Something big.

And the ripping, shredding sound was his own flesh being peeled from him.

He screamed and thrashed but even his best efforts, fueled by pain and panic, did not unsettle the creature atop him.

That's when he saw the Orator step from the noktum, flanked by two more Dorumai. Hope gurgled up in his throat. But the Orator motioned, not toward Gid, but at the Demaijos woman who was trying to get to her feet. One of the Dorumai struck her in the head and she crumbled unconscious to the ground. Then they each grabbed her by the arms and pulled her into the noktum.

The Orator watched Gid for an impossibly long moment. Gid couldn't form words. He could barely draw breath and any air that fluttered into his lungs only served to fuel the fiery agony raging through every inch of his flesh.

"Come," the Orator said, and the creature paused.

"Thank ... you," Gid tried to say, but the words were just a sound. A moan.

"Finish your meal inside the noktum."

"No ..." Gid flailed. He tried to crawl away, but his arm wouldn't move. His legs barely twitched. He had to escape. He had to get away.

But the creature bit into his shoulder, its teeth grinding against bone, and dragged him into the black.

Gid screamed and it was his final sound.

CHAPTER TWENTY-FIVE

KSARA

The black all around Ksara might have been the nothingness of death, had it not been so cold and noisy.

The icy touch of the shadows engulfed her. Seeping into her bones and numbing a thudding pain in her skull. She shivered so hard, her back spasmed. She tried to move her arms, but her wrists and ankles were bound behind her back.

Dozens of voices murmured all around her, but the loudest was a voice she recognized. "The time has come," the Orator said in his clear, lilting voice. All other voices quieted. The only sound still permeating the dark was a wet, tearing, crunching somewhere behind them.

Someone whimpered near Ksara. She guessed the sound belonged to the Shadowvar kid. And that she'd just joined him as another offering in the Orator's flamboyant display of power.

Beneath these sounds was a drumming in Ksara's head. At first she thought it was from the hits she'd taken before being dragged into the noktum, but the rhythm wasn't steady. And the tone rose and fell. Like words. A voice.

This was the same voice she'd heard when the shadows drew very near her. It pulsed from the noktums. And now, it permeated her every thought, beating its rage against her. The murmur almost forming commands.

Feet shuffled toward Ksara and rough hands wrenched her upright, holding her by her arms and letting her bound feet drag behind. Another whimper and she felt more than heard the Shadowvar kid get the same treatment.

"Citizens of Nokte Murosa!" Ariston called out from the other side of the Noktum. They must be close to the Western Plaza now. "The Night of the Soul is more than a tradition among the Shadowvar people—it is a reminder to all the races of Noksonon that freedom must be guarded. The depravities of the past can so easily return, should we forget our oppressors. Or, worse, bend to those cowardly few who mimic them. The Dorumai. They would have us hide in our homes. To comply with ransoms and threats. But we, like the Shadowvar of old, will not be ruled by fear nor tyrant." A cheer rose up around Ariston. When the crowd quieted again, he continued. "Toss your sacrifices into the Dark and remember we are a people free of fear."

Something small clattered against stone very near Ksara. The first offering thrown into the noktum.

The Orator's voice boomed through the black air: "Watch your leader now, Nokte Murosa. And see if he is void of fear."

A knife pulled free of a sheath and the Shadowvar kid cried out in pain. Before Ksara could make a sound in protest, she was pitched forward out of the all-consuming black and into the bright oranges and violet hues of twilight, crashing head-first into the flagstones.

The crowd screamed. Ariston shouted. They swarmed around Ksara and the Shadowvar kid, pulling the rope off their hands and feet. Faces and feet and voices.

"Eshe! Get Lyshan! Now!"

"He's been stabbed!"

"Stop the bleeding!"

"Ksara!"

She heard Ulric's voice, just as her wrists and ankles were cut free. Staggering to her feet she tried to see her brother in the crowd. "Ulric?"

"Ksara!"

He'd climbed the plaza's stone wall and was pushing through the throng of people now standing between Ksara and the noktum.

When the Dorumai rushed from the wall of black and began hacking people down, it was something out of a nightmare. Each strike seemed to slow and the blood splatters fell in lazy droplets.

Then the Kyolar joined the fight, leaping from shadow onto the back of a Shadowvar woman, tearing into her neck before she could even cry out.

Six citizens fell. All in the span of a single breath. The crowd hadn't even had time to fully turn toward the threat. Many more would fall before the first scream escaped a throat.

And Ulric was there. His back turned to the Kyolar. Only five feet away from tooth and claw and certain death.

She imagined him lying on the stones beside her with only her hands to staunch the blood and keep him alive. Watching him smile for the last time as he slipped away.

The voice from the shadows thumped louder and louder in her skull. Angry. Powerful. This time, instead of pushing the voice away and hiding it at the edges of her thoughts, she leaned into it. Let it course through her mind like a river released from a dam.

Cold shivered through her and the shadows rushed toward her, faster than ever before. In an instant she had a vortex of black air whipping around her with tentacles reaching out from the black halo like miniature noktum.

The first thing the tentacles grabbed was the Kyolar. The creature hissed, then growled, then yelped as the tentacle of black air picked it up and then cracked it against the wall. It slid motionless to the ground.

The voice grew louder and the beat of that wordless murmur overtook Ksara's thoughts. Instead of being in the center of the battle, somehow Ksara was now just a witness to it. She saw the tentacles go wild, snapping out at citizens and Dorumai alike, wrapping about waists and heads and necks. Flinging anything that moved as easily as the wind scattered dry leaves.

Ulric dodged the first onslaught, clambering out of the way. Now he stood twenty feet away from Ksara, his arms stretched out wide as he beckoned his own power to rival Ksara's.

The tentacles shifted their attention toward him.

No.

Ksara tried to speak the word. Tried to scream it. But she couldn't move. She stood at the epicenter of the wild shadows, that thundering voice booming through her mind, and she couldn't speak. Couldn't shout a warning to Ulric.

The shadow struck, faster than a viper and Ulric clapped his hands the same instant. Light burst around them. That voice in her skull bellowed its rage. And something struck Ksara in the head.

A new black emerged around her, this one quiet and warm. Her legs gave way beneath her, her body met the flagstones, and the new black embraced her.

CHAPTER TWENTY-SIX

ULRIC

Ulric watched as they hauled a limp and bleeding Ksara off in chains. They should have been hauling away Dorumai. But no Dorumai who'd stepped from that noktum had survived their encounter with Ksara.

Then again, very few of the citizens had made it through the experience unscathed either.

At a glance, there were several dead innocents among the bodies of Dorumai. Some had surely been victims of the Dorumai's ambush. But many more had clearly been crushed or bludgeoned by the shadow.

Even Ulric had wondered if Ksara were controlling the malevolent shadow for the briefest of moments. She'd been standing in their center. Her face stoic. Her arms raised out at her sides.

And the power had been astounding. In moments she'd ended a force large enough to take a city by force. She'd batted away a Kyolar like it was a mouse. The immensity of the power had shaken him.

Would she have been able to stop?

He'd used his burst of light and Atlas had leapt from a nearby wall to strike Ksara in the head and, as soon as she'd lost consciousness, the shadows had disappeared. A tide of black receding back into the noktum.

Atlas directed volunteers now, helping the most direly wounded himself and getting those with minor injuries away from the plaza. Ulric cut through the commotion and angled toward Guildmaster Ariston. He found the Shadowvar leader kneeling beside the body of his son, cradling his head.

A pool of blood wreathed the boy and stained the Guildmaster's clothes. This much blood and no Atlas meant that the kid was dead. But the Guildmaster cradled the broken, lifeless body of his only son still, whispering words the boy would never hear.

"Guildmaster—" Ulric began, but the Shadowvar looked up at Ulric with such intense hatred that Ulric choked on his own words.

"She will die for this," he breathed.

"The Dorumai did this, not Ksara."

The Guildmaster's whole frame quivered with emotion.

"The Orator did this," Ulric tried again. "He stabbed—"

"Where is the Orator?" The Guildmaster hissed. "He is not among the dead."

Ulric's lips parted, but he found no words. Finding the maniacal cult leader had been Atlas's first priority among the fallen. He hadn't found the Shadowvar with sawed off horns. The leader must have slipped back into the noktum during the chaos. Injured or no, he was not here to shoulder the blame.

Only Ksara could do that.

"May I see her?"

The Guildmaster lifted his dead child into his arms, grunting to carry the weight. The Guildmaster's eyes were cold. Empty hearths where ambition and charisma had burned only hours ago. "You may see her when we all see her. At dawn. With a rope about her neck and her feet without the ground."

"Ariston!"

The Guildmaster turned from the devastation and trudged back into Nokte Murosa, carrying the body of his dead son.

Ulric stood rooted in place. There would be no recourse for Ksara. No argument would assuage the Guildmaster, nor the voice of the people. He glanced up at the sky and his stomach sank. Night had come upon the city, the moon cresting over the noktum and the stars splattered across the sky.

This would be Ksara's last night.

Unless they stole her away first.

Atlas moved to Ulric's side, refastening a satchel to his waist. "You're planning something foolish," he said.

"We can't let her die for this."

"I told you she was dangerous."

Ulric's throat tightened. "She was trying to help."

"They're still dead, Ulric."

"It's never been this bad," Ulric said. "It's always worse around a noktum, but it's never been this bad."

"What kind of mage loses control of their power?"

"Her power has always been—unique." Ulric wiped a palm across his face and his shoulders sagged. "She hated Nokte Murosa the first time. Maybe it's this place. Maybe that's why...."

"She killed a dozen people."

Ulric glared at the Imprevari. "She's not a murderer, Atlas."

"These people are dead."

"And how many would be dead if the Dorumai had succeeded? Did she not stop them?"

"She delayed them," Atlas said. "The Orator lives."

"Grina's corset! Atlas! She's my sister! She wouldn't be here at all if it wasn't to save me."

"She's a danger. To the city. To us. Even you could not stop her."

"She's my sister," Ulric said, his voice breaking. "I will not watch her die."

Atlas sighed. "Then I guess it's time we find the bawdy pirate and a know-it-all Usaran."

"You'll help her, then?"

Atlas glared back at Ulric, anger bordering on hatred in his gaze. "You saved my life from poison. This squares us."

Ulric flashed a fleeting smile. "This squares us."

They found Coronata first, lying naked and alone in her lover's bed. Atlas searched for the lover, a shipyarder by the name of Junli, while Ulric went about trying to rouse the retired pirate queen without getting too close.

Waking Coronata was a dangerous game even when she hadn't been drugged and betrayed. Now? Well, Ulric would rather be wrangling a nest of two-headed Lux vipers than waking Coronata.

He threw a sheet over Coronata's exposed backside and turned his gaze away. If she woke to him leering at her, he'd hurt for months and months. "'Nata?"

The pirate didn't stir.

Ulric glanced about the room for options. He didn't want to get nearer than two steps. He certainly didn't want to touch her. But they didn't have time to just yell at her and hope she'd wake up soon.

Then his gaze settled on a half empty bottle of Triadan Whiskey.

Atlas reentered the house. "Even I know that's a bad idea."

"When all you have is a bad idea …" Ulric said, moving to the bottle of whiskey.

"It's still a really bad idea."

Ulric pushed the whiskey into Atlas's hands. "You should do it. She already hates you."

Atlas backed away from the offering, hands raised. "If this is how you want me to repay the life debt, then so be it. I splash her, take my beating, and I'm gone."

Ulric sighed and kept the bottle. Then he turned and sloshed the liquid right at Coronata's face.

The woman woke and leapt to her feet in the same motion, whipping the sheet off the bed and twisting it into a rope between her hands. Naked and seething. Her black hair falling down her shoulders in waves.

Ulric raised his arms in the air. "'Nata! It's me! It's me!"

She panted and glanced about the room. Her eyes wide. Her shoulders heaving. She looked entirely too practiced at the notion of strangling an attacker with a bedsheet.

"Junli drugged you," Ulric said. "He was with the Dorumai. No, we haven't found him. Yes, you can skin him alive when we do."

Coronata slowed her breathing. "Khyven?"

Atlas motioned at a cage draped in a blanket near the door. "We didn't do it. But we're not undoing it either. I like my face just the way it is."

Coronata crossed the room, unabashed at her nakedness, and freed the kapicat from its cage. The thing screeched and chittered in a constant stream and Coronata nodded along, as if receiving a report from a crewmate. She gathered her clothes strewn about the room and dressed without a word. Ulric held his tongue, waiting until the kapicat had quieted and Coronata sat on the bed, lacing her boots.

"There's a storm in your eyes," Coronata said.

"Ksara's in trouble."

"What kind of trouble?"

"The hanging kind," Atlas interjected.

Ulric winced at the words. Somehow saying them aloud made them more real. Made the image of Ksara trudging to the gallows spring to his mind.

"We have until dawn to free her," Ulric said, his voice tight.

Coronata finished with her boots and sat still as a statue on the bed. Somehow the motionless, stone-faced pirate was even more formidable than when she had been actively ready to strangle them. "We'll need Merewen," she said. "Where is she?"

* * *

The Academy had two guards and both of them looked more like homeless academics with swords than anything resembling a fighter.

"Halt there!" The fattest of the two called out, putting a hand on the hilt of his sword with all the confidence of a pig farmer with a paintbrush.

Ulric led the crew closer.

The second guard hurried out of a *shkazat* tent several yards away, strapping on his sword coughing a trail of blue smoke. "Come no closer!"

Ulric didn't slow. "We're here for the Usaran woman."

"The academy is closed until morning," the fat guard said. "Return then for your woman."

Ulric rushed at the fat guard, catching him by the grimy collar and pinning him against the academy wall before the man could so much as yelp. Coronata's rapier rang and the *shkazat*-addled guard now needed both hands to keep his trousers on his waist.

"We can't let you in. Not now with the Dorumai and all," the fat guard wheezed.

The *shkazat*-addled guard lost his grip on his belt, fumbled his pants, and his trousers fell to his knees. His face flushed a deep red as he gathered his pants back up to his waist, holding them there with both hands while Coronata wagged her rapier in the air between them. "Th-th-they don't look like Dorumai."

"Let us in," Ulric said without so much as a hint of a smile on his face. "Or we let ourselves in."

The fat guard bobbed his head up and down. "We'll let you in. We'll let you in."

Ulric released the fat guard's collar. "And you'll show us to our friend."

The guard hesitated and Atlas drew his short sword. The man threw his hands into the air, "Okay, okay! I'll take you right to her!"

"Now," Ulric said. The fat guard flinched, ripped the key ring off his belt and stuck it into a hidden keyhole in the wall. In a moment, a section of the wall swung backward.

The guard holding his pants in his arms waddled through the door first. Coronata and Atlas followed, then the fat guard. Ulric moved at the back of the group, shutting the door behind them.

Inside the wall, the academy was a collection of the oldest, and most pristine, buildings Ulric had seen in Nokte Murosa. Only the Assembly Hall rivaled them in size and grandeur.

If the Academy held anything more than books and those who cherished them, that wall and two poorly-trained guards would never be enough to keep the criminals of Nokte Murosa from looting the place. As it were, the stained-glass windows would have been in jeopardy of random vandals if they had been clearly visible outside the walls.

The guard with two hands on his trousers led them to the biggest of the structures, a wide gray building with a single black, twisted tower. The frames of the wooden doors had faces carved into them. Some grim and wild and others kind and happy. All of them staring down at the intruders with unblinking eyes.

Once inside the building, oil lamps lit a vast rotunda of red and gray stone. One scholar in floor-length robes crossed the rotunda, but she didn't even look up at Ulric and the crew, her eyes distant and her mouth chewing on words only she could hear.

They crossed the rotunda, stopping at a long wooden desk with a darkened lamp. The desk stood sentry to a single, wooden door that had all the affectation of a siege barricade.

"This is the library," the guard said. He moved around the empty desk and to the door beyond, trying the door. "But it's locked."

"That's what those shiny keys are for," Ulric said.

"Only the librarian has that key," the fat guard said, sweat dribbling down his face.

Coronata exchanged a look with Ulric. He saw the edge to her gaze. Each moment they wasted here was time they didn't spend getting Ksara to safety. And they had no plan. No allies. Only the resources they carried with them now. And the Guildmaster would use every ounce of his power to keep them from succeeding.

Those were poor odds, even with days of planning.

A knock sounded from the other side of the door. A measured, calm rap of knuckles against wood.

"That's our friend," Ulric said and he motioned to the clock on the opposite side of the rotunda. "You have four minutes to get her out."

The fat man raised a brow at Ulric.

"Atlas?"

Atlas stomped on one guard's ankle and punched the other in the nose. They howled in unison, surprise and pain unifying them. When they recovered, they eyed Atlas.

"Now three minutes," Ulric said, and he didn't need to say more.

They had the door removed from its hinges in two minutes and spent the last minute wrestling the heavy block of wood up and out of the way.

Merewen stepped through the opening with three seconds to spare. The guards panting and sweating as they leaned against the wall.

"There's a whole section of scrolls missing from that library," Merewen said. "We should alert the librarian."

"By the gods," Atlas growled. "You've been locked in the library for hours and that's what you're worried about? Some missing paper?"

"Missing scrolls." She looked from Atlas to Coronata and finally Ulric and her own mouth settled into a grim line. "Where's Ksara?"

CHAPTER TWENTY-SEVEN

KSARA

Unconsciousness might have been a refuge if the screams hadn't followed her there.

Ksara's mind replayed the sounds of the dying. Shouts of surprise that turned to terror. The cries of pain that stopped short. The slap of flesh against stone.

Even as she fluttered back toward consciousness, she couldn't escape the sounds. And she didn't want to.

She had finally fulfilled all of her father's darkest predictions. She was a curse upon the land. A scourge. A mark of death and destruction. Nothing good could come from the shadows.

As she lie on a cold, stone floor, chains cutting into her wrists and her head still trickling blood, she regretted running away from her father's edict at all. She should have stayed. They'd planned on sending her away to a Brightling colony in the east to live in seclusion and light for the rest of her days.

If she had, eleven citizens would still be alive right now.

Ksara coughed out a bitter laugh that dissolved into a sob. Oh how her father would delight in being proven right, even with so grisly a price for it.

A door opened and torchlight burned Ksara's eyes until she pressed them closed. Two people walked through the hall, their boots clapping harshly against the silence. They grunted and struggled through the door and down the stairs.

They were carrying something.

In a pang of realization, Ksara didn't want to open her eyes at all. Even if they'd adjusted to the sudden light. But she forced her eyes open anyways. She made herself see Ariston's guards bring in another dead body and put it on the dais. Twelve dead now. She'd killed twelve people.

The guards left the body, wrapped in bloody cloth, and made their way to the exit. She showed no emotion when they veered their course toward the pillar where Ksara lie chained. She knew what was coming next, but she made no attempt to stop them.

The kicks and stomps landed on her unprotected face and ribs. Her head gushed blood again and she gasped for breath, each movement of her rib cage bringing a fresh wave of pain.

The guards tired of the beating and left. Ksara drank in the pain, clinging to it. No amount of physical pain could compare to the agony tearing through her soul. She'd killed those people! She'd tried so hard to save them. To be the hero. To protect those who couldn't protect themselves.

And she'd killed them.

She remembered the thundering voice inside her. The way it had pounded louder and louder. The cold coursing through her. The desperation. And even the glimmer of hope as the shadow dispensed of the Kyolar poised to attack Ulric.

Then seeing the tentacle pick up the first person and smash them against the ground. The horror of knowing somehow she'd beckoned the violence. That she had no idea how to banish it. And even her body would not obey her pleas to turn and run from the plaza, to take her curse far, far away from this place and these people.

When the door to the Assembly Hall opened again, Ksara leaned her back against the pillar and closed her eyes. She hoped the next beating was longer and more effective. Ariston must have ordered that Ksara be kept alive for whatever formality of a trial he had planned and a prompt public execution after.

But maybe if she taunted the guards, they'd go too far. End her now where she didn't have to look into Ulric's face as she died and see the way her final disappointment destroyed him.

The boots stopped just beside Ksara, but they didn't move closer. Whoever had come walked with a limp. Gid come to get his final violence?

When no meaty hands grabbed at her or pummeled her in the face, finally, reluctantly, looked up and found a man in tattered scholar robes standing before her.

He held a lantern in one hand and the light danced in his green eyes. There was something similar to the violence she'd seen in the guards' eyes in this man. A hunger. A craving. But not for Ksara's death. Something more.

"I am Genove LeGrande," the man said, his words slightly slurred. He had a swollen lip and a map of bruises and cuts on his face. And as atrocious as his face looked, she imagined hers looked worse.

"I'm not exactly in the market to make new friends."

He smiled and it felt more like a predator showing its teeth than anything warm.

Maybe this man would kill her after all.

"I have come to give you a choice," he said.

"Choice?" Ksara croaked out the word. It tasted like poison. "Choose what?"

Genove smiled wider. "Freedom or death, of course."

"Let me check," Ksara said. Then she watched blood drip from her head onto the front of her black, deep cut tunic. "Death. I choose death."

"That's only because you think death is the only way to control your power. To end it," Genove said. "It's not."

Ksara eyed the man, fighting the compulsion to laugh. After a few more painful breaths, she leaned back against the pillar. If annoying conversation was all this man was going to inflict on her, then so be it. She deserved much, much worse and all she had to do was wait long enough and she'd get it.

"Do you know of the isle of Hayvonlar?"

Ksara stared up at the ceiling and watched the shadows dance and dodge the lantern light. How did this man get in here at all? He looked like he'd lost many more fights than he'd won. And she doubted that lame ankle let him climb to the second tier of the Assembly Hall and pry open a window.

Then again, how he'd gotten here wasn't even the best question, but why. Why was he here? And why was he teaching a dead woman about islands?

"Few scholars even know its name. It's a fortress of rock. Nearly impossible to navigate. And full of monsters."

More blood dribbled from Ksara's head, this time trickling down the bare skin from her collar bone to belt. The Demaijos-cut tunic had been a curiosity in Laria. A fashion statement in Triada. A shameful display in Imprevar. And downright cold in Usara.

Now she wished she'd left all the Demaijos clothes in Demaijos. She wished she'd taken on the fashions of the places they'd visited, just as Ulric had. Although, Ulric had only bought a piece of clothing in a new land when he'd also found a lover there, so the mismatched tunics, vests, trousers, belts, and boots, all spoke a quiet story of the love he'd found.

Thinking about Ulric made her want to close her eyes and never open them again.

"Few see the merit in studying monsters, but you, a mage of the dark, should take special notice of them."

"I die in the morning. I've run out of time to care about anything. Least of all monsters."

"That's where you're wrong, Ksara Sajra. So very wrong. You see the monsters of Noksonon are more than monsters. They are weapons crafted by the Giants millennia ago to use against each other."

"Giants?" Ksara eyed the man, fighting the compulsion to laugh. After a few more painful breaths, she leaned back against the pillar and shook her head. It was entirely possible this man had come to pontificate to a truly captive audience.

"We can learn *everything* from monsters," the man said. "Including how to remove shadow."

"Remove shadow?"

"The monster was called the Allarune and it was designed to suck the noktum air away from the monsters that needed it to survive."

"And?"

The man's green eyes lit up. "We can use it to remove your power."

Ksara turned her mismatched eyes on the man then, studying his face for evidence of his lies. The most dangerous thing to enter this room wasn't man or weapon. It was hope. And she felt it stirring, unbidden and unwanted, in her chest. "A monster can take away my power?"

"The remains of one, yes."

"And you know this how?"

The man patted his tattered clothes. "I may not look it, but I am Master at the Nokte Murosa Academy, specializing in noktum wildlife both ancient and modern."

She blinked, willing her mind to focus through the pain. To hear the words he'd just said. It was impossible. Mages didn't just divest themselves of power. It was linked to their very life force. To bleed that out would be certain death for any mage—

But she hadn't been any average mage. Her power had defied the understanding of Land, Life, Love, Lore, and Line Mage. None had been able to help her control the power.

"I'm going to die at dawn. That will solve the problem nicely."

"One problem, yes. But the Orator lives. He will return. And who will stop him?"

"Someone else."

The scholar shook his head. "The others tried. They were either in league with the Orator, or too weak to stop him. Nokte Murosa will fall without your help."

"My help?" Ksara almost choked on the words. "I killed

twelve people!"

"The families of those dead," Genove said. "They will join them soon. Blood will stain every street of Nokte Murosa before the Orator is sated. If you want to deal them justice, then offer mercy to the living. Live long enough to do that. Then you can die for your conscience."

Ksara narrowed her eyes at the scholar. "And what is the price of your help? There is no unselfish deed done in this city."

Genove smiled wider. "I would go to Hayvonlar."

"Then go."

His smile faltered. "It is near impossible to gain entry to the land. And I would require escort while I was there."

"Then hire my crew," she said. "They'll need another job real soon."

"They need their captain. Or there will be no crew."

Ksara closed her eyes. She could barely form a thought through the pain. But the cold chill of shadow returned to her skin, haunting her even now.

If she could be rid of it—if she could bring the Dorumai to justice—would that be enough? Would she be able to live with herself then?

Ksara opened her eyes and watched the shadows twist and curl across her skin. Helpless to send them away. Unable to turn them from their dark design. "I never wanted this power."

Genove's eyes glittered bright. "What would you do with your freedom, Ksara Sajra?"

She imagined a life without shadow and fear. A life where she could finally rest....

"Tell me more about the isle of Hayvonlar."

Chapter Twenty-eight

ULRIC

Ulric strode toward the Assembly Hall alone. His pace quick and sure and his whole body seething with anger.

He immediately drew the attention of the three sailors working on the gallows. And the eyes of Ariston's guard followed after.

"Oi!" A sailor called out at him. "We can build it for two, ya know. A family affair, as it were."

Ulric pivoted on the workers, closing the distance between them in seconds. Ariston's personal guards ran at him from the steps of the Assembly Hall. But they wouldn't reach him before he got a little justice of his own in.

He grabbed the mouthy sailor by the leg and ripped him off the platform they were making, flinging him aside like the refuse he was. Then Ulric went right for the structure's support beam, pulling out his stolen sword and giving the beam three swift hacks.

The workers shouted. The gallows swayed. And Ariston's guards encircled Ulric, their crossbows leveled at his heart. He dropped his sword to the ground and raised his hands to the gray morning sky.

"You've been warned, Demaijos," the center guard said. There were six of them. Not the whole of the force, but enough that even Atlas would be satisfied with the unlikely odds of victory.

Ulric looked between the guards and back at the gallows. "Would you let your sister die?"

"If my sister were a murdering Dorumai mage," the guard replied, "then yes."

"Could you say that louder?" Ulric said.

The guard blinked at him.

"If my sister were what?" Ulric coaxed him. "If my sister were …"

"If my sister were a murdering Dorumai mage then I would let her die," the guard said, loud enough that the words echoed about the courtyard.

Ulric threw the guards a half smile. "Thank you. Makes my life easier when she's right and truly angry."

A barrel flew through the air and hit the brazen guard in the back of the head. As soon as the crossbows turned from Ulric to the new threat, he used the toe of his boot to flip the sword from the ground back to his hand and attacked.

Merewen joined him a fraction of a second later, wielding a length of wood intended for the gallows. She turned the wood as a shield, absorbing the crossbow bolts with ease and then cracking the plank against more skulls until guards and sailors fell.

Ulric made them bleed. None of the wounds were fatal, but they wouldn't be chasing after the crew. They wouldn't be walking at all for a good long while. The sailors tried to flee and Merewen dealt each a blow to the head; they crumbled to the cobblestone. Ulric turned his vitriol to the gallows itself, landing two more blows on that center support beam and then backing away as the whole structure crashed to the ground.

The sound was loud enough to wake every criminal, addict, and merchant for a mile.

Merewen cocked a red brow at Ulric. He shrugged. "Coronata

asked for a distraction."

She nodded and scanned the three streets that emptied into the courtyard. Already there were figures running toward them from two of them. "I miss Ksara's plans."

"Yeah, well," Ulric said, rolling a sore shoulder. "Me, too."

"Which mob would you like? Left, right, or center?"

He picked up a few pieces of the broken gallows and smiled at Merewen. "Do you remember the Pass of Selvo?"

"This is a street. Not a canyon."

"Oh, I remember the canyon. It was warm. Too warm to wear your furs.... That's hard to forget."

Merewen blushed a little then hid a smile by turning back to the pile of debris and filling her arms with timber. "A barricade could work."

"A barricade or two."

Merewen sighed. "Two?"

He nodded at the narrow streets. "This is a street not a canyon! And they were so kind to give us all this lumber...."

"Very kind of them," Merewen said and this time she couldn't hide her smile. Her whole face lit up and her blue eyes sparkled like a sunrise over an ocean horizon. And, for a moment, the light there filled him with hope. With calm. And he drank it into his anxious, aching soul with desperate greed.

She believed in him. She thought they would succeed at this haphazard plan to save Ksara. She didn't doubt him—as far as he could tell, she'd never doubted him.

And, for a moment, he dared to trust in her glowing adoration of him.

A half-smile curled up on his face and he grabbed more timber. "Last one finished buys rounds."

Merewen laughed. The sound so pure and happy it made his heart leap about in his chest. "Deal."

♠ ♠ ♠

Atlas stood atop a cart, bracing his arms against the outer wall of the Assembly Hall, while the pirate climbed up his back and onto his shoulders like a human-sized kapicat. He winced as she clambered over the dagger wound there, but he kept his footing and let the woman settle her feet upon his shoulders so she could reach the ledge above.

They'd stolen a few supplies on their way from the Academy to the Assembly Hall: the wagon he now stood on, a change of clothes for all save Atlas, two unlit lanterns, a barrel of whiskey, and the retired destrier that Atlas had rigged to the cart with a few ropes. It stomped its hooves, rocking the wagon back and forth. If Atlas didn't return to the horse's side, no amount of rope was going to keep it attached to the cart.

Coronata stepped from his shoulders, dangled from the ledge by her fingertips, and pulled herself easily up and onto it. Once on the ledge, she tied the last bit of spare clothesline around a Shadowvar statue on the ledge. Then she went to work on the window, cutting a wide piece of stained glass from its mount, removing it, and slipping inside.

The destrier fidgeted forward and Atlas eased himself out of the wagon, careful not to make too many sounds as he made his way back to the war horse's shoulder. He held to the makeshift rope bridle and stroked the horse's shoulder. The animal steadied, lowering its head and blowing out a contented sigh.

It was rare to find a war horse in any stable, least of all Nokte Murosa. But this war horse had the look of Imprevar to it. A red roan coat with a thick red mane and tail, but an agility to its physique. This wasn't just a plow horse ridden by a knight—this horse could carry a warrior and still move swiftly about the battlefield.

But how had it gotten here?

Atlas traced a scar from the horse's chest to its withers. Four more paralleled the first.

Claw marks. Very large claw marks. Probably only a Kyolar or another noktum monster could make them that wide apart.

He imagined the horse with a knight atop it riding near the noktum. The rider urges the horse closer to the noktum to test his nettle and the noktum surprises them, reaching farther than they'd guessed and pulling horse and rider inside the nightmare.

The horse has instincts no rider has. It has a sense for where food and water and home might be. It runs blind through the noktum and ends up in Nokte Murosa where the only use for a horse is as a cart animal and none of them know the merit of the animal that just appeared on their streets.

Atlas gave the horse another long pat, then he used the wagon to mount up on its back, taking his makeshift reins in hand. The horse danced a little underneath him, then blew a contented sigh and settled.

He was right. This was a horse accustomed to rider, not cart.

He sat deep and calm, guiding the horse and cart back to where Coronata had left them and settling the animal again. They'd need the horse, and all of Atlas's skill, when Coronata returned.

And a lot of luck.

❧ ❧ ❧

Coronata paused for a breath on the ledge just inside the Assembly Hall, the stained-glass window at her back. Waiting for her eyes to adjust to the dark.

As soon as she could be sure there wasn't a guard directly below her, she grabbed hold of the rope, held it taught against the statue outside the broken window, and rappelled down the curved wall with barely a whisper of her boot scuffing against the stone.

She landed in a crouch, waiting for an ambush. When it didn't come, she released the knots holding the rope around her waist and legs and stalked farther into the room.

Black outlines marked the room's pillars, the amphitheater seats, and the dais at the center of it all. At noon, with the sun beaming down through the stained-glass windows above, the space would have been resplendent in color. But now it clung to the dark like a jealous lover and only a single lantern at the far side of the room cast any light at all.

Coronata stole toward the light, keeping her body low and her boots silent against the stone. A murmur of voices echoed across the hall. And they were talking. Not yelling. Just talking.

This gave her pause, if only for half a second. By all appearances, Ulric and Merewen's spectacle outside had drawn all the guards away from Ksara. But if she encountered a guard within the hall, she'd expected them to be belligerent. Violent.

What she heard now had none of that edge. The words were soft. Entreating.

She recognized Ksara's voice in reply in the same, calm tones.

Ksara had every making of a great leader. She was decisive and level-headed. She moved three steps ahead of those around her and, what was rarer still, she cared deeply about her crew. Once she'd decided upon her crew, there wasn't a force on Noksonon that could dissuade her from protecting them.

She'd have made a terrible pirate.

And that was precisely why Coronata had been fascinated by the Demaijos mage. And, as they'd crossed the Selvo Sea and on through the Selvo Pass, that curiosity had evolved into respect. Then loyalty. And now a kinship Coronata couldn't quite explain. The captains of her armada would have gawked at this display of weak affection. And the old Coronata would have gawked right alongside them.

But there was something compelling about Ksara's single-mindedness. It was both naive and wise. Innocent and as tried and true as ruts in an ancient road.

Then again, the woman was full of dichotomies. Light and dark. Love and self-hatred. Trust and secrets.

Maybe it was the pride of the Demaijos, with their two different colored eyes, to house these contradictions in one whole. And maybe Ksara was the best example of them all, being the selfless hero of her crew and now about to hang for the death of a dozen innocents.

"Hayvonlar," Ksara said, her words finally clear as Coronata came within twenty feet of her.

"It's due east," the man said. He wore a tattered blue robe, the face of a man recently beaten, and not a single weapon, hidden or otherwise. "Five or six hours of rough sailing away. Is that about right, Bloody Queen?"

Coronata's hand flashed to her side and a dagger appeared in her palm. The man turned deliberately toward her, the lantern casting its light across her.

"Coronata," Ksara said between swollen lips and wheezing breaths.

Coronata's heart raced just looking at her friend. The Demaijos had taken at least a dozen beatings. Her face was a patchwork of bruises, trickles of fresh blood, and swollen features.

If Ulric had been standing here, the scholar would be dead. Whether he'd laid a hand on Ksara or not. Beating a woman chained to a pillar so that every breath she took before going to the gallows was agony?

Even pirates had more honor than that.

Well, most pirates had more honor than that.

Coronata had once stripped a crewman naked, tied him to the mast of her flagship, and sailed the armada all the way from Triada to Laria—all because he'd spoken her name in a tavern. The legend of the Bloody Pirate Queen was built on tales of the survivors, not her crew.

And it wasn't a stunt she had to pull twice.

Coronata turned the dagger lazily in her palm, catching the lantern light with the edge of the blade. "It's time for you to leave."

The scholar sized Coronata up, his gaze lingering on her curves. "I am here to help."

Her free hand slid a ring of keys from her belt and held them in the center of the lantern light. "How helpful can you be?" Coronata asked as she sauntered around the stranger and began unlocking Ksara's chains.

"He can take away my power," Ksara said in that haggard voice.

"He can't even stave off a beating."

"I can't live with the shadows anymore, Coronata. I won't."

Coronata released Ksara's other hand and then stared deep into her eyes. There was so much hurt in those pale blue and brown eyes. So much hurt. And now, a little stirring of hope.

"Is that even possible, Ksara?"

"What's the worst that can happen? I die?" Ksara coughed out a weak laugh. "The Orator won't stop. He'll come back for Nokte Murosa. We have to stop him." Her gaze drifted to the dais at the center of the room. "I have to try."

Coronata unlocked Ksara's ankle shackles and helped her to her feet. She teetered and fell against Coronata, but stayed upright.

The scholar watched it all, his eyes bright with a craving more complicated than a lust for bodies. "What exit have you devised, pirate?"

"An exit for two," Coronata answered, giving Ksara a long side-eye.

"He's coming," she said. "I need him. Adapt."

Damn that scholar. If he'd just promised her more than he could deliver, she'd fillet him alive with a dull blade.

Coronata nodded and said no more, guiding Ksara toward the rope and window.

Atlas was going to hate all of this.

♠ ♠ ♠

Merewen placed the final timber of her barricade as the first of the citizens charged her. Or, rather, charged at the barricade and began dismantling it.

That was strange.

When Ulric had suggested that they build barricades, it had been a fun challenge. A good way to ultimately slow the mob and be able to incapacitate the angry citizens in a more orderly way.

But something else was happening entirely.

It was as if this barricade were a threat to the city unto itself. An anomaly. One more disruption that they couldn't abide.

A perfect distraction.

The first citizen at the barricade ripped at the timber and flung it behind him. And Merewen clocked the man on top of the head with a scrap of wood and he fell to the ground. Three more men rushed at the barricade, two sailors and a Shadowvar. "Get back!" Merewen bellowed. They didn't listen. Nor did they make it through the beams of wood to reach her before she smacked them each with the wood and they fell.

More citizens came and soon the best barricade Merewen made was of the unconscious bodies piling up on the other side of the woodpile. Sweat dripped from her now and she played with the idea of pulling her axes from her belt to fight.

But she'd seen the blood in the noktum courtyard. Heard Atlas's retelling of the event that had landed Ksara in custody and on her way to the gallows.

Too many innocents had died this night. These citizens were angry. Hurt. Scared. As would any who'd witnessed a cult ambush, a Kyolar mauling, and a mage apparently commanding the dark itself to murder.

They didn't know Ksara. Didn't know she had been trying to help them. But that small ignorance shouldn't be a death sentence. So she took the care, and time, to knock out her attackers rather than dealing fatal blows.

The mob swelled. Merewen backed away and assessed the new threats. Four men. One had a torch that he put to the barricade, trying to light it on fire. The other three rushed at her, knives slashing, as a fifth clambered over the pile with an axe to join them.

She threw the timber at the three closest attackers, taking them out at the knees and then pivoting to catch the axe man by the shoulder and throw him up and over her to crash against the cobblestones on the other side. The barricade caught fire and the man with the torch stood with his implement, suddenly alone on this side of the barricade and very, very uncertain.

"Here they come!" Ulric shouted just before wagon wheels and horse hooves cracked against stone. Merewen turned to see Atlas riding atop a thick, frothing steed pulling a cart that bumped and careened across the courtyard toward her. Coronata sat in the driver's seat, her wild black hair billowing behind her and a grin on her face.

Merewen and Ulric ran at the wagon. Merewen caught hold of the edge of the cart and vaulted into the back of it. Ulric pumped his legs to catch him, the strain on his face. Merewen reached out and caught hold of his hand in hers and hefted him into the wagon.

Ulric had barely hit the wagon bed before he pivoted and found his sister. He was at her side in an instant.

Merewen took in her beaten friend and then caught sight of another person pressed into the corner of the wagon. Bright green eyes on the scene.

"Who is that?"

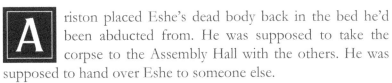

CHAPTER TWENTY-NINE

ARISTON

Ariston placed Eshe's dead body back in the bed he'd been abducted from. He was supposed to take the corpse to the Assembly Hall with the others. He was supposed to hand over Eshe to someone else.

But he couldn't stand the idea of letting Eshe out his arms until he trudged up the stairs and dropped the boy where he was supposed to be—sleeping in this bed. Dreaming. A whole life left to live.

He sat beside Eshe's bed, staring at the body and seeing his boy. A babe wrapped in a red wool blanket. A quiet toddler hiding beneath the bed with a stolen sweet roll in his hands. A teen robed in academy garb and bringing home armfuls of scrolls.

Now he was shrouded in bloody sheets. Glassy-eyed. The pain and despair of his final moments chiseled onto his face.

An ache lanced through Ariston. A grief so potent it made his chest heavy and breathing a chore.

A crash echoed through Nokte Murosa, and it was loud enough, surprising enough, to turn Ariston's gaze toward the door where Omri stood.

"Eight guards watch her," Omri said. "And the whole of the city wants her to face her dues. She will not escape. Eshe will have his justice."

Ariston flinched at the name spoke aloud and his eyes drifted back to the body.

A young guard opened the door and pressed his horned head through the door. "The gallows have been destroyed. Two streets have been barricaded. One's on fire."

"And the eight?" Omri asked.

"No sign of them, but—"

"Take me to the docks," Ariston said.

Omri frowned. "We can stop them at the courtyard. If her crew has somehow managed to get her out of the Assembly Hall at all …"

"They have succeeded," Ariston said. "Take me to the docks or I walk there alone."

Omri nodded and opened the door. Ariston strode through, working his way through his empty, quiet house and feeling more and more like the whole place was dead. That the part of Ariston who'd lived here, thrived here, had died, too.

What was left inside him, the jagged pieces of him that still animated his body and thoughts, wanted to see the Demaijos woman bleeding and broken and begging for her life at his boot. He wanted to stab her and watch the pain enter her eyes. Hear her scream. Feel her wish for death, but deny her that relief as long as he could draw out the pain....

He burst out the front door to the waiting horses. Omri had ordered horses to be at the ready. Probably as a way to get Ariston away from trouble, should the Dorumai return. Now Ariston mounted up on the first horse, gathered the reins, and kicked it into a gallop.

Omri shouted, but Ariston didn't slow.

All he could see was that Demaijos woman writhing in agony. And his mind and body focused on that one design. He didn't dodge around the people in the streets.

When he arrived, he found a horse and wagon without any passengers and the Demaijos ships still bobbing at the docks. He guided the horse around the wagon and onto the swaying docks and toward the Demaijos' ship. The horse complied fitfully, shaking its head and stumbling about as the waves pitched the dock to and fro. If the horse fell from the dock, it would break its legs on the rocks and die. And the horse knew the danger intuitively.

Ariston beat the horse on, funneling his rage into the thing until all it knew was to move forward or face his wrath.

In moments he made it to the Demaijos ship and he leapt from the horse's back, catching the railing of the ship and hoisting himself aboard.

The commotion aboard the ship paused. The pirate at the helm. The Usaran holding the sails rigging. The Imprevari pulling up the anchor. The brother standing over the Murderer lying on the deck.

Ariston produced a dagger from his robes and charged at the woman on the ground. All he wanted was to sink the blade into her chest. Feel her blood flow past her fingers. To know her body would soon become the same, empty husk as Eshe's now was.

Someone caught Ariston two steps before he reached the woman. Yet, none of the crew had moved at all. They'd been surprised by the Guildmaster's appearance. And his Shadowvar skin had given him an advantage. He'd already been lunging forward by the time they saw him at all.

The hands that held him now, spun him around away from his design, and Ariston sputtered a curse. "Genove! Bastard! I-I should have killed you!"

The pale scholar smiled. "You will yet regret making an enemy of me, Ariston."

The brother Demaijos laid his thick hands on Ariston next and picked him up with ease, and pitched him overboard without so much as a grunt of effort.

Ariston hit the waves and lost the dagger to the sea. He spat saltwater from his mouth and struggled to keep his head above water. The anchor lifted from the *Falco*, the sails shifted to catch the wind, and the ship slipped away from the docks and into the bay.

Ariston watched them go; his view blocked every few seconds by another wave crashing atop him.

When Omri fished him out of the water, Ariston didn't speak a word. He didn't answer a single question. He just sat at the edge of the docks where the *Falco* had been anchored and watched the ship speed away.

There would be no justice for Eshe. No person to step into the gallows and die. Ariston hadn't even had the power to do that for his son.

CHAPTER THIRTY

KSARA

K sara lay on the deck of her ship, each wave jostling her broken ribs. She bit her lip and kept quiet, focusing on the taste of the ocean spray in the air and the sound of her crew working seamlessly together to get the ship out and away from port.

"Your injuries are more serious than you let on," Genove said as he sat himself down beside her, those hungry eyes fastened upon her. Always fastened upon her. Even when she wasn't looking at him, she felt the man's gaze.

"Did the Guildmaster drown?"

Genove just watched her with those eager green eyes for a long moment. "He survived the ocean. Ariston is difficult to kill."

Ksara let out a relieved sigh and closed her eyes. At least she hadn't been the reason one more person was dead tonight. Twelve was enough for a lifetime—

"You're happy he's still alive?"

Ksara opened her eyes. "I killed his son."

Curiosity clouded the scholar's face. "You were a captive of the Dorumai. Thrown into a courtyard to be the public sacrifice to the Orator's pet Kyolar. And the Guildmaster's son was stabbed by the Dorumai while you were bound and waiting for death. And yet you still blame yourself?"

The *Falco* cut through a steep wave, rolling Ksara into the ship's railing and igniting her chest in red-hot agony. She breathed in tight, short gulps. Her stomach churned. When the pain subsided, she found Genove still staring at her. Still waiting for an answer to satiate him.

"I was conscripted to find the kid," Ksara said between slow breaths. Her ribcage throbbed and the sea promised more turbulent waters before they broke free of the bay. "I didn't find him in time. And when I did, I couldn't control my power enough to save him. Instead I killed eleven more people."

Just saying the words aloud made Ksara want to vomit. It made her wish for the pain. She deserved to die. She should have a noose about her neck right now, but she'd run away.

"You are curious," Genove said and Ksara couldn't be sure if it was her relief in Ariston's survival or her enduring guilt at hurting innocents that baffled the man more.

"Ariston knew you," Ksara said, squeezing her eyes shut and breathing through another bout of pain.

"Indeed," Genove said.

When the *Falco* steadied and Ksara opened her eyes, the scholar was still staring at her. Or through her. A distant look twisting his features and his body tense. Like a viper waiting to strike.

"He's the one who gave you that beating," she said. "You wanted him to die."

He didn't answer, but his hungry green eyes found her again and she wanted to wince away from his gaze, but every movement brought new pain. Her thoughts spun back to the Allarune. He'd said he'd wanted to go to Hayvonlar because of some professional curiosity. But now that she lay beside the man, she knew there had to be more.

"You'll be bedding in the stern," Ulric's said, arriving at

Ksara's feet and crossing his arms over his green, Luminent silk vest.

"Of course," Genove said. "I'll go now. It is wise to rest before we arrive on Hayvonlar."

Genove nodded to Ksara and then he rose up from the deck and strode to the stern of the ship where Atlas waited with a rolled up blanket and a glare.

Ulric knelt beside Ksara, placing gentle fingertips to the wounds on her face. Concern and anger warring for control of his expression.

"I'm okay," she said.

He laughed a little then he caught a glimpse of the sun just peeking up over the horizon and his laugh died. He looked back to Ksara. "You would have been in the gallows right now. You would have—"

"I killed those people," Ksara said, her voice cracking. "I should die for that. If I cannot repay my debt to justice, I will die for that."

"No."

"Ulric! I killed them!"

"It wasn't your fault."

She shook her head, pain radiating down her neck. "I've spent my whole life pretending. I have to own the dark now, Ulric. I cannot run from my curse or I share it."

Ulric looked away. He couldn't meet his sister's eyes.

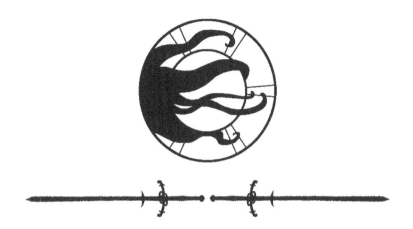

CHAPTER THIRTY-ONE

KSARA

Ksara might have been a perfect patient to Atlas's ministrations, if the shadows hadn't joined in. Atlas had to dodge tendrils of black air while bandaging Ksara's ribs. Twice the air cut through him as he applied an herb salve to her broken, bruised face and he spat obscenities. By the time he finished, more shadows had come to loop and curl around Ksara and he just threw an elixir at her. She caught it.

"Drink," he said. Then he spun on his heel and stalked away from her, muttering more curses.

Ksara unstopped the elixir, swirled the pale orange liquid a moment or two, and then chugged the whole of the vial down. It tickled her throat, and, as it churned in her stomach, her whole body began to tingle. Her eyes drooped heavy. Her vision swayed steeper than even the ship in the steep waves. Dark circled her vision and this time it was unconsciousness, not shadows, that plagued her.

Sleep came not as a request or even a dire need, but as an overwhelming urge she could not deny. It commanded her body.

This was the elixir's effect.

And the small part of her that still had strength fought against it. She wrenched her eyes open. Caught a glimpse of Genove watching her from across the ship. His green eyes never leaving her.

"What's wrong?"

Ulric's voice.

"It's safer for us all if she's asleep."

"Atlas!"

Still Genove stared at her. Oblivious to all but Ksara.

A chill ran through her and she couldn't be sure if it was a tendril of dark moving too close to her skin or those cold, green eyes piercing through her.

"You asked me to tend to her wounds, so I tended to her wounds!"

"I didn't ask you to drug her!"

"She just killed twelve people in Nokte Murosa, Ulric. Not even you can ignore the danger now."

The words stung. She fought the sleep harder than ever. Parting her mouth to add words. To tell Ulric that Atlas was right. That she was dangerous. That she could hurt people, even when she didn't mean to—

But the sleep took Ksara, pulling her from one nightmare and dropping her into another—

She stood in a forest of purple trees.

Purple trees!

The vibrant leaves whispered in the wind. She froze, looking to the warrior at her side.

The man was a living weapon. Tall and alive with power, with imposing muscles and a scarred face. Lightly armored, he moved with a Kyolar's grace. And when he drew the largest sword she'd ever seen from his back, it somehow looked balanced, natural even, in his hands.

He scanned the trees ahead, sensing a danger she couldn't detect. Ksara's heartbeat stuttered inside her chest and she glanced from tree to tree, shadow to shadow. And still she saw nothing.

But the warrior smiled, playful mirth and violence blending in the simple curve of his lips and he stepped between Ksara and the threat.

Twang! The sound disturbed the serene forest. The warrior rushed forward, moving so fast he was almost a blur.

Then something collided with Ksara's chest and she hit the ground. A sword clanged and whirred through the air. Footsteps crunched through the grass. A roar split the sky. A dragon hovered above them, encompassing the horizon with its shiny, black body.

Someone new hobbled in front of her on one real leg and the other metal. The dragon breathed an inferno at them, melting those purple trees. There was a burst of orange light and the fire bent around them, incinerating the grass just feet from her face.

While she watched the grass smolder, the pain began to deepen. To slow her breathing. And she glanced over to see the fletch of an arrow protruding from her chest.

She reached for the arrow and her skin was an inky black with long, thick nails and indigo hair on her knuckles.

Ksara startled. She wanted to jerk the arrow free of her chest. She wanted to push free of the strange body altogether. But she didn't have control. The body moved of its own volition, curling a little into the wound and waiting. If she made a sound now, the warrior and mage would notice. And they were still in danger. She couldn't distract them now.

When the forest quieted, the mage found her first, calling the warrior to his side. The warrior's scarred face grappled with anger. Then guilt. Then rage. And the mage knelt beside her, pulling at a pouch at his waist and thumbing through a stack of clay discs there until he found the right one.

Both warrior and mage spoke, but Ksara didn't hear their words. She only saw their mouths move and felt the pull of pain sinking her into something darker than unconsciousness.

The mage cracked a clay disk and orange light exploded in front of her eyes.

When she blinked, the nightmare had changed. She drifted up

and over the scene, seeing her body as she left it. A Shadowvar body. Male and young, but not Ariston's boy. This Shadowvar wore a Usaran tunic with a high collar, breaches, and a black vest.

As she drifted up and away, the voices came. One she recognized as the thunderous voice inside the noktum. But two more joined the first, a higher, calmer voice. And a mumbling murmur.

The voices surrounded her and she couldn't escape them. They absorbed her, swallowed her, exploding through her mind and rending her soul with their collective screams.

Ksara screamed, but the sound didn't leave her mouth.

"Ksara!"

It was Ulric's voice, but she couldn't open her eyes. She barely felt her body on the deck of the *Falco*. She sucked in another breath and screamed.

This time she felt the cold sea air reenter her mouth and throat and fill her lungs. And the sensation anchored her to her body again. The pain returned, but it came from her ribs and face, not her shoulder. She'd been beaten by Gid and Ariston's guard. She was on the *Falco*. Not in a forest. Not near those voices.

A new taste splashed into her mouth and her eyelids grew lighter and lighter. She blinked and found Ulric crouched near Ksara, an empty elixir vial in his hands. He was pushing back and away from her as a torrent of black air whipped between them. Ksara struggled to her feet, her ribs aching, and she staggered through the shadows, dispelling them.

As soon as the dark was gone, Ulric pulled Ksara into a slow, firm hug. She leaned on his strength, her body weak from fatigue and her insides buzzing from the nightmare.

"What the hell did you give her?" Coronata asked.

"Sibson extract," Atlas said.

"And?" Coronata pressed.

"Just Sibson extract. That's what the label said."

"Likely Sibson paired with Kaciter leaves," Merewen interjected. "A common pairing for sleep, but sometimes results in hallucinations."

"Let's stop trusting the labels created by the dead mage, yeah?" Coronata said.

Ksara held Ulric until pain bit into her ribs and she had to let him go.

"I'm here, 'Sar," he said, his mismatched green and brown eyes somber even as his mouth cracked into a smile. "Genove told us about the Allarune."

Ksara nodded once and her skull started throbbing.

"You think he's telling the truth?"

Ksara glanced past Ulric to Genove only to find the scholar staring at her. She'd yet to find his gaze anywhere else. "I think the Allarune is real. And he wants to take us there."

"But what does he gain?" Ulric asked, his voice low.

"As long as I am done with this curse, I don't care."

Ulric frowned, but he only let it linger for a moment. Then he returned a smile to his face and examined the wounds on her face with gentle hands.

"There's a ship behind us," Merewen said. Her voice had no alarm to it, though Atlas immediately cursed and the kapicat chittered its own obscenities.

Ulric left Ksara with a squeeze to her shoulder and strode to Merewen's side. "A merchant on their way to Taur-El?"

"No," Coronata said. "I recognize that ship from the Nokte Murosan harbor."

"Then who is it?" Atlas growled. "The Guildmaster come for Ksara?"

"The Dorumai."

All eyes turned to Genove, but his never left Ksara.

Ulric shook his head. "The Dorumai are dead."

"Some are dead. The Orator is not," Genove said.

"Why would the Dorumai follow us here?" Coronata asked.

"They worship the Lords of the Dark," Genove said, a small smile curling the edges of his lips. "And Ksara shares that power. She's the human link between Dorumai and Giant."

Nobody spoke. The waves crashed against the *Falco*. Coronata cranked the helm back and forth, the creaking loud in the tense quiet.

Ksara felt the weight of her crew's gaze. She was beaten. Her power wild. Now they faced an unknown island filled with monsters and a murderous cult. They needed a leader. A good leader. And all they had was her.

Her pulse thundered in her head and the shadows pulled toward her, but she fought for control over her face. "We will annihilate the Dorumai on Hayvonlar. Bring the Orator back to Nokte Murosa for trial. Justice will be met."

Ksara turned, crossed the deck, and gingerly climbed the ladder up to Coronata at the helm. She stood beside the pirate, willing her strength to her legs to keep them from buckling. She kept the effort from her face and held this position until the crew stopped staring at her. Until they stopped expecting her to fall.

CHAPTER THIRTY-TWO

KSARA

K sara didn't sleep again on the ship. She couldn't get a straight answer from Atlas about the sedative he'd given her and she couldn't quite shake the dream she'd had when she'd been under its influence. The strange sensation of living in someone else's body. And the three voices coming alive inside her and then rending her apart with screams.

Besides, the crew needed her awake. Ulric needed to see her alive. Atlas needed to see her not murdering people with shadow. Merewen needed her ear as she explained all she'd learned in the library about the dangers of dampening or altering magical powers. And Coronata needed Ksara's gaze at the stern of the ship as the Dorumai closed the distance between them.

All this Ksara did with a four-foot-wide pool of shadows sliding around her boots. It was more than she'd ever seen follow her about this far from a noktum. A fact she tried hard not to think about.

The ship pitched to the left and only Ksara's years on the sea kept her on her feet.

"Hayvonlar ahead!" Coronata called into the morning wind.

She circled back around to face the stern of the ship in time for Coronata to spin the wheel hard one more time and jump the ship farther to the starboard.

To Ksara's eye, the pirate was just zigzagging about in the wake as they drew within two hundred feet of the sheer rock cliffs of the Isle of Hayvonlar. But Coronata had had more experience on a ship by the age of ten than Ksara had now and whatever the pirate was avoiding, was the best course.

The sea grew angrier the closer they came to those mammoth gray cliffs. Hayvonlar looked as if it were forged from nuraghi stone with the barest of evergreen trees jutting out the top of the jagged cliffs like a barricade bristling with spears.

Coronata had the *Falco* aimed right at one of these cliffs.

If it had been any other person holding the helm, Ksara would have been at their side in an instant to take away the controls. But Ksara returned to her pacing, keeping one step ahead of the shadows and her gaze on the implacable wall of stone beating back the sea.

As they drew closer to the cliffs, Ksara spotted a break in the stone. A notch barely wider than the *Falco*'s berth. Coronata aimed the ship right at the notch, deviating from her course only to catch a crosswind and slow the *Falco*.

The crew quieted. Merewen stored her scrolls below deck. Khyven the kapicat clung to Coronata's shoulders. Even Genove retreated from the bow to skulk by the mast.

In an instant, the *Falco* was riding a five-foot-high crest and tipping into a deep trough. Ksara grabbed hold of the railing as the ship slapped against the water. Before she could blink, another swell carried the *Falco* up and through the notch between the cliffs, the roar of waves all around them.

The *Falco* fit inside the notch with only inches to spare on either side and the passage continued through the cliffs, a shadowy corridor where the angry sea could not reach them, but the stone on either side certainly could.

"And they say *I'm* the one with a love affair with death," Atlas breathed. "Asper's ass! That was close."

Coronata laughed and Ulric's booming chuckle joined along.

Ksara peeled her grip off the railing. Her boots were wet with the waves that should have carried the *Falco* right into the cliffs to crack the vessel like an egg. Should that have happened, there would have been no survivors.

But they'd survived. By Grina's smile, they'd made it!

Ksara turned on her heel, opened her mouth to voice her praise to the pirate queen, when a sound tore through the air—a screeching sort of scream, neither human nor entirely animal. The sound stole the breath from Ksara's lungs and made her, for just a moment, forget the dark swirling around her. She glanced about to find the source of the noise, but found nothing but the stone cliffs on either side and the unnatural canal leading them deeper into the island.

Water lapped quietly between the stone wall and the hull of the ship. Coronata turned the helm instinctively and the accompanying creak disturbed the tense silence.

The canal that had been their safe harbor just moments before now felt like a killing corridor. They couldn't turn back. Not until they reached wherever this canal took them and hoped it had enough space for the *Falco* to do an about-face. They would be at the mercy of whatever came at them now.

The animal scream split the air again.

"What sort of hell did we just wriggle ourselves into?" Atlas breathed in barely a whisper.

CHAPTER THIRTY-THREE

KSARA

o one aboard the *Falco* made a sound while the ship floated through the canal and into a perfectly circular bay just big enough for three ships to anchor. The stone cliffs on three sides of the bay were smooth. Pristine. Almost polished. And the beach on the eastern side of the bay—the one part of Hayvonlar that wasn't sheer cliffs—held ominous black sand and a forest crowded with trees as tall and thick as giants.

And that's when Khyven the kapicat lost his nerve.

The creature yelped as if struck by something, clawed up to the top of Coronata's head and leapt to the mast. There it scurried up to the tip top and chittered a warning down at them all.

"For once we agree," Atlas murmured. "There's something wrong with this place."

"You mean the screaming?" Coronata said with an almost carefree smile. "That happens on loads of nearly impenetrable islands."

Merewen frowned. "Really?"

Coronata's smile grew. "No. There's definitely something

wrong with this place."

Genove hobbled to the ship's rails and stared out at the island. "We're the first to look on this island in centuries. Millenia, even."

"I'll count my good fortune when we leave," Ulric said, placing himself conspicuously between the scholar and Ksara and staring down at the wisp of a man.

"Drop anchor," Ksara called from behind her brother. "Prepare supplies and board the dingy. We disembark now."

"Should we really drop Atlas in the sea?" Coronata asked as she glided about the deck tying down the masts.

Atlas grumbled something beneath his breath and stomped away to tend to the actual anchor.

Genove boarded the dingy immediately. Merewen entered close behind. Ulric waited with one foot on the railing.

Coronata pulled a piece of dried fruit from her pocket and offered it up the mast toward Khyven. The kapicat wagged its butt back at them and chittered its unequivocal response.

"Coward!" Coronata yelled back.

Another scream tore through the air, echoing throughout the bay.

Ksara flinched. Atlas swore. And Khyven the kapicat bared his teeth at them.

"He'll be safer here anyways," Ksara said, shifting her feet away from the groping shadows.

"You're right." Coronata made a dramatic gesture of putting the treat back in her pocket. "And there's no treats for cowards!"

The kapicat wagged its banded black and white tail back at them.

Ksara strode to the dingy and Coronata and Ulric followed. In moments Merewen lowered them all down into the water and began rowing them to shore. Ksara slid out of the boat first, helping to drag it onto the black beach. Her ribs ached with the exertion, but soon Merewen, Ulric, Ksara, and Atlas were in the surf helping her along and they moored the boat in the black sand.

"That's not ominous at all," Ulric said pointing at deep animal prints pressed into the wet sand all around the dingy. The prints were the bigger than Ksara's head with impressions for the claws and a wide vertical mark that smudged them all where a tail dragged behind.

Merewen knelt at the print and prodded it with her fingertips.

"Master of the Noktum and shit," Atlas said, turning to Genove. "What made that?"

Genove shrugged his shoulders. "A reptile of some sort."

"You studied where?"

"I trained at the Nokte Shaddark Academy."

"And all you can do is point at that and say lizard?"

Genove just smiled. "Would you prefer I tell you that it is likely a flightless version of the Elder Dragons? Or that, judging by its size, it could easily consume a man of your size?"

Atlas's face pinched in a snarl. "Which monster had its way with your arm, Master of the Noktum?"

"Probably a Kyolar," Merewen said. "By the depth of the scar—"

"We don't have time for this," Ksara interrupted and marched forward, following the creature's tracks right into the forest. The reptile, whatever it was, carved a nice path through the underbrush, making the trek all the easier.

"'Sar," Ulric said, hurrying to catch up with her. "Did I miss the part where you tell us all the plan?"

"We don't argue on the beach while on a strange screaming island. With a murderous cult trying to follow," Ksara said, stomping on the bent underbrush. "We don't get eaten by whatever left those tracks. And we get this curse off of me as soon as possible. That's the plan."

Ulric walked beside her and kept his silence for fifty feet. The rest of the crew filed in behind them.

Ksara dodged around a boulder and continued on in the monster's wake as best she could in the shadow of the canopy. This was exactly the kind of half-considered plan that Ulric usually made. The kind of plan she would have turned down before Ulric had finished saying it. The kind that had almost gotten him killed.

But the shadows clawed at her. The thundering voice from

the dark that had overwhelmed her in Nokte Murosa beat inside her still. An undercurrent to her every thought.

She needed to be rid of this power. Then she could deal with the Dorumai.

"You still want to die," Ulric said.

Ksara faltered, but only for half a stride. "I killed twelve citizens of Nokte Murosa."

"Your power did that," Ulric said. "You were trying to save them."

"They had families. Friends." Ksara's voice cracked and she pressed her lips closed. She didn't need to explain this to Ulric. He knew her heart better than anyone. He knew the toll this was taking on her, the toll this would always take on her.

"We'll follow you, 'Sar."

She gritted her teeth to keep from screaming. She should have left them in Nokte Murosa. Should have sailed to Hayvonlar, just her and Genove.

But she'd never have been able to get out of Nokte Murosa without their help. Never mind navigate the notch in the cliffs to arrive in the bay. There was a reason the pirate fleets hadn't used Hayvonlar to cache their loot and hide their ships and that treacherous entrance was it.

That, and whatever monsters awaited them here.

"I can't keep you safe—I can't keep anyone safe," Ksara said. "Not until this curse is gone."

"We'll look after ourselves," Ulric said with a smile. "Just slow down and ask that quill-for-brains scholar which direction this Allarune might be."

Ksara slowed, stopped, then sighed. She'd stomped into this forest like a petulant child. And now she had to own that.

She turned to look at her crew. Atlas strode beside Genove, just behind her and Ulric. Coronata and Merewen were at the rear. All of them stopped when Ksara did. Atlas looked irritated. Genove alive with excitement. Coronata content and Merewen concerned.

"We need to get our bearings. Genove—" A new sound

entered the forest and Ksara held her tongue to listen. These were not the screams of monsters, but the murmuring of men.

"It's coming from the bay," Coronata said.

"Some of Genove's monsters?" Ulric asked.

Genove shrugged. "Possibly."

"Or the Dorumai," Atlas said. "They watched Coronata enter. They could have followed."

Ksara exchanged a look with Coronata. "It's possible," the pirate said. "I showed them the way."

"Genove," Ksara said, turning on the scholar. The only one among them who looked entirely unperturbed by the voices. "Get us to the Allarune. Now."

Genove's eyes glowed all the brighter. "Yes, Captain."

CHAPTER THIRTY-FOUR

GENOVE

enove knew the course to the Allarune. He'd studied all the Orator's maps before abandoning the Dorumai camp.

The isle housed a nuraghi called Serkir. The nuraghi were monuments built by Giants, either to house them or their endeavors.

The Serkir Nuraghi housed monsters. And it would be at the center of this island—a land mass likely created specifically to house this nuraghi.

Even as Genove mentally calculated the correct course to Serkir, he feigned strain on his face and paused to check the trees on either side of him. Ksara stood near him, studying his face. The darkness swelling about her. Her crew on their heels. She trusted him. Not implicitly. Not even willingly. But out of necessity. And that's all he needed to get what he wanted.

He didn't need the rest of the Demaijos crew with them now. It was best they met their end earlier rather than later. Eliminate the distraction so Ksara could focus on getting to the Allarune and forfeiting her power to him.

Genove ducked left this time, leading the group two hundred feet in that direction before he found a distinctive, entirely irrelevant tree and paused again, only to angle them forward and to the right again.

The Imprevari glared at him, the man's dark eyes could be forges for the heat they scorched him with. But even if the Imprevari guessed Genove's ill intent, he didn't speak. The voices were close enough now that even a whispered conversation would give the group away.

Genove halted again, this time for a half second as he checked the blue sky peeking in between the canopy and directed them yet farther to the right. Ksara kept stride with him, moving silently through the forest. Even injured, she exuded a quiet strength that had nothing to do with the shadows flowing around her. It was the way she carried her shoulders. The way her eyes moved about the landscape. The way she stepped through the underbrush with calm intention. She was more than the girl prodigy from the academy in every way. A prey Genove could have only dreamed of.

And soon he would have her. He already knew her weakness. She was already playing by his rules. Soon he'd tear down that strength and she'd be an even more pathetic, blubbering pool of a psyche than the academy girl.

His pulse quickened and he fought the grin off his face.

They walked in the prints of the creature from the beach for a few strides, then he wound them away from the prints, back into the thick of the forest where their progress would slow. But even away from the prints, he kept them in view, more as a fascination than an actual guide.

The monster that made those prints had to be bigger than a Kyolar. Closer to the size of a Sleeth. He guessed the creature was twenty feet long, including its thick tail. And, most incredible of all, it lived outside the noktums.

Had it adapted to the light? Or had it been designed to operate in the light by the Giants that created it?

So many questions and they'd only just entered this paradise of lost monsters! Hayvonlar was the pinnacle of his old academic career—and the beginning of so, so much more.

He spotted an incline with loose stone and couldn't fight the smile off his face. Instead he hid his expression by hurrying forward, pretending at urgency, but stealing himself for the injury he was about to endure. On purpose.

He clambered up the slope, set his sore foot on the loose stone, and let his ankle buckle and twist and his body follow. In an instant he was crashing down the embankment, colliding with the crew's legs and taking down Atlas with him.

The Imprevari's armor jabbed at Genove as they fell and the man growled a curse when they landed in a heap, tangled with each other, and a thorny bush.

Ksara and Coronata hurried down the slope to help the two of them to their feet, as silently as they could. But it was too late. The crash had drawn all the attention of their pursuers.

Genove held his ankle, tried to put weight on it and didn't have to fake the pain that radiated up his foot and leg.

"They're coming," Merewen said, looking to Ksara.

The whole group looked to her and she considered a moment. "If it's the Dorumai, they're here for me. Merewen and Atlas, get behind the group and wait for the signal. Ulric and Coronata, you do the same from the sides."

The group divided to their tasks without a word until only Ksara and Genove remained.

"What of me, Captain?" Genove said with a small smile.

"Whether Dorumai or monster, you face it with me."

CHAPTER THIRTY-FIVE

KSARA

Here!" The voice called and a robed, masked figure charged at them. Sword raised.

Ksara's heart raced, but she stepped to meet the attacker. Her hands itched to pull her staff from her back. The metal could parry the blade. And with a turn of the grip, she could add edges to the weapon.

But she left the staff on her back. The Orator had wanted her alive in that alley in Nokte Murosa. Now that he'd seen her violent display at the Western Plaza, his eagerness had brought him across the sea to find her. He wouldn't kill her now.

So she strode slowly, letting the dark air billow around her. Feeling that low voice beat faster, louder, in her mind. And the shadows moved and twisted about her, forming tentacles about her.

Flashes of her attack at Nokte Murosa invaded her mind. Screams. Bodies flying in every direction.

The Dorumai remembered, too. The robed man faltered, lowering his sword and slowing to a stop. Twenty more Dorumai joined the first, swarming around Ksara and Genove.

Hands snatched Genove. He thrashed and struggled, but they wrestled him to the ground, punched him in the face, then dragged him to his feet, nose bleeding.

Ksara watched the spectacle from the corner of her vision. "He's with me."

"He is with no one," the Dorumai answered. "He only serves himself."

Ksara stopped before the first Dorumai. "Today, he serves me."

"And tomorrow you will have that dagger in your back," the Dorumai replied.

"Where is the Orator?" Ksara said, loud enough for the Dorumai all around her to hear.

"You speak to me, yet you know me not?" The Dorumai said.

Ksara spent only a moment on hesitation. She knew the Orator's voice, it lived in her mind where the nightmare replayed over and over again. She turned from the fake Orator and scanned the crowd. This was some sort of test. Part of the spectacle the Orator loved so much. And now, while her crew moved through the forest, Ksara appreciated the Orator's penchant for the dramatic. It bought them precious time.

"You are not the Orator," she said. She strode in a small circle, taking her time to examine each Dorumai in attendance. Thirty-two Dorumai sprawled around her. Twenty-seven humans and five Shadowvar, including the Dorumai who first rushed at them. Each was armed with at least a dagger. Most also carried a sword. Two a halberd. Four crossbows.

As she held each Dorumai's gaze, Ksara's unease grew. They didn't reach for their weapons. There was a reverence in the silence. An awe. For her!

She had the adoration of murderers.

A scream bubbled up through her chest and caught in her throat. She wanted to push through this crowd and run headlong to wherever the Allarune lay. To rip her power from herself with her fingernails if she had to.

Wrestling some calm back into her body, Ksara continued her perusal of the crowd. She was supposed to be identifying the Orator and if she prolonged the moment too long, even the Orator would see through the ruse and start asking about her other crew members.

"Why should the Orator seek me out, only to hide?" Ksara said, her voice steadier than it had any right to be.

"You have much to prove, Prophetess of Shadow," the first Dorumai said.

A chill ran up Ksara's spine and this time it had nothing to do with the frigid shadows all around her.

"Choose the Orator," the Dorumai said. "Choose and prove yourself."

She considered signaling the crew just then. Three of the Dorumai held Genove upright, one for each of his arms, and another with a blade pressed against his neck. That made for twenty-nine other Dorumai in the group. Almost six-to-one odds.

But if she had the Orator? This fight ended faster and without pulling her crew into danger.

She searched the crowd again, looking at the five Shadowvar for any sign of disfigured horns beneath their hoods. None showed the Orator's sawed-off horns clearly.

Ksara stopped in front of one of the Shadowvar. He didn't have anything about his appearance that separated him from the other Shadowvar men. He had the same height and build. Even the same boots.

But there was something about the eyes behind this Dorumai mask that kept her where she stood. Something about the way this Dorumai felt at ease and eager at the same time. Calm and violent. In control and wildly volatile.

"You are the Orator," Ksara said, drawing out the words.

The Shadowvar Dorumai removed his hood to show his sawed-off horns and then removed his mask as well. He smiled and turned, raising his hands to his fellows, "She knew me."

The gathered Dorumai bowed their heads. Genove struggled against his captors, but even with their reverence, they held the scholar fast.

"We made this mage a sacrifice to the Lords of the Dark and she was remade," the Orator said, stepping into the center of the circle beside Ksara. "This is the conduit—she is our connection to the Lords of the Dark! Our Prophetess foretold by Sandretti and then Laynra—"

Ksara turned with a quick punch, hitting the Dorumai holding the knife to Genove in his own throat. Before he could cough, she wrenched the dagger from his grip, kicked out at the back of the Orator's legs, and caught the Orator's fall with a dagger at his neck.

The Dorumai flinched toward her and she pulled the dagger against the Orator's neck, drawing a trickle of blood and careful to keep the Dorumai with the crossbows in front of her.

"Weapons on the ground," Ksara said, her voice loud and clear and the shadows looping eagerly about her. "You're going to leave this island and forsake Nokte Murosa. Or you die with your Orator now."

Not a single Dorumai lowered their weapons.

"You are our Prophetess," the Orator wheezed from behind the dagger's edge. "You have confirmed their faith. This you cannot run from."

"I am no prophetess," Ksara said. "Soon, I won't even be a mage."

The Orator laughed and that shrieking, rending scream filled the air. Even the Orator quieted at the sound. It trembled through the earth and trees and straight through Ksara's ribcage, humming in her skull.

Heavy footsteps thudded through the forest moving faster and faster and faster. Crunching bushes and stone. Rumbling closer and closer and closer.

"And here we meet the first monster of Hayvonlar," Genove said with a bloody-mouthed smile.

A thirty-foot lizard darted into the clearing, caught a Dorumai in its wide mouth and swallowed him before he could do more than yelp. A massive man sat astride the lizard. He studied the shocked group with yellow, reptilian eyes. Strange gashes marred his pale, bare chest. The wounds on his body twitched and opened, exposing teeth and tongues within each.

The wounds weren't wounds at all, but dozens and dozens of mouths.

Mouths that opened, sucked in breath, and screamed.

CHAPTER THIRTY-SIX

ULRIC

Ulric beheld the monster and the lizard it sat upon and beckoned light to his fingertips. The warmth had barely left his chest to travel down his arms and to his fingers when the monster opened its mouth—mouths. It had mouths all over its chest and arms and neck and back! And they twitched and clacked their teeth and licked their lips. Then they all opened in unison, sucking in air.

The scream that followed sent Ulric flying twenty feet backward, colliding with bodies and a tree and, finally, the ground.

The next several moments were robbed of sound. He heard only the dull thump of his own pulse in his head and a relentless ringing.

Pushing free of the bodies around him, Ulric staggered to his feet. His head spun and he collided back with the ground again, getting his arm and face wet. He glanced at his arm. The wet was blood. But he couldn't tell if it was his own or another's. Pain hadn't pushed through the shock yet.

He'd lived this nightmare before. Monsters and dead around

him. But he wasn't alone here. He had to find Ksara. He had to keep her alive.

Stumbling to his feet again, Ulric stepped on a few bodies that didn't move and clung to a tree that was wetter than even his arms and face.

The lizard stood just where it had been when it had entered the clearing, licking its forked tongue into the air while the monster atop it watched the scene with unblinking, yellow eyes.

There was no sign of Ksara.

The monster's scream had thrown everyone back. Ulric had been flung across the clearing. A dozen feet to his right, Coronata also wobbled to her feet among several Dorumai, their masks knocked off their faces.

Merewen stood next, her height giving her away even when she was twenty feet away from him. Several more Dorumai joined her, dazed. One of them tight-fisting a sword as if it were a talisman of prayer rather than a tool of death.

Ulric stretched his arms out wide and beckoned the magic to his fingertips again. The warmth complied, tingling down his arms and heating his fingers.

The rider turned to him and it looked less and less human the more Ulric looked on it. It had no mouth between its nose and chin. Just slitted eyes that matched the reptile it rode and skin that had a sheen to it, like a cream-colored python's skin stretched over a human body and then slashed open at random to allow for the thirty mouths at every angle on its surface.

Coronata joined Ulric at his side, a stolen crossbow in her hands. She spoke, but he only heard gargled sounds. She frowned and tried again. More sounds.

"Ksara," he said, his own voice ringing distant in his ears. Whatever Coronata's question, Ksara was the answer.

Coronata didn't speak again. She cocked the crossbow, aimed it at the monster, and shot.

With a twang even Ulric could make out, the bolt released, soared across the clearing, and buried itself in the monster's shoulder, right between two mouths.

The monster didn't even twitch nor glance at the bolt protruding from his skin. A black ichor leaked out of the wound and the mouths on either side of it lapped up the dark blood.

The monster's lizard, on the other hand, swiped its tail back and forth and lumbered two steps closer, crushing any bones and flesh beneath it as if they were bits of fallen, rotten fruit.

Ulric stepped to the right, keeping his hands wide and the magic alive there. The lizard and rider followed, its tail swiping bodies aside as it listed heavily from left to right, stalking closer and closer to Ulric.

Another twang and a second bolt shivered into one of the monster's mouths. It gargled and gasped, more ichor oozing from the wound and the other mouths beneath it licking up the black ooze. The lizard hissed and Ulric ducked behind a tree. Its mouth snapping down around air that Ulric had just occupied. He danced around the tree, pulled a Dorumai sword from his back, and struck at the lizard's neck. The sword made contact, but bounced against the plated scales, jarring Ulric's grip free of the weapon as it flew through the air and landed a dozen feet away.

Ulric dove behind another tree and the lizard's mouth almost caught him then. He felt the warmth of the lizard's as he landed in the scrub and rolled across his back and shoulder to his feet and clapped his hands together.

A flash of blinding light burst from his hands and the monster screamed.

This second flight through the air was more terrifying than the first. He couldn't even see the trees and ground whir by him. He didn't know if he was about to collide face-first with a trunk or crunch down on a boulder or even how far he was from the ground at all.

When he did land, the impact stole his breath. He wheezed and pain found him. All of the pain found him, a tidal wave that overwhelmed his mind and body. He willed his legs under him, but they didn't comply. He flopped to his stomach and clawed at the dirt. Pulling his stunned and heavy legs along. Had they broken in the fall? All he knew was he had to get away. And that he could never get away fast enough. Not like this.

The lizard's footsteps thundered around him, the tremors knocking Ulric face-first into the dirt. That hot breath would be upon him any moment. He dragged himself forward again and again and again.

A cold wind gust past him. The shadows fled from the trees. And Ulric stilled.

"Ksara!"

He craned his neck up and found Ksara standing in the epicenter of the fallen Dorumai.

No, she didn't stand, she levitated. The black air propelled her upward, suspended her five feet from the ground. Her body was still limp. Her eyes still closed.

The reptile hissed, its whole attention on Ksara now. And the monster's golden eyes stared down this new anomaly with something close to interest.

A small noktum pivoted around Ksara. A Dorumai groaned and stood, taking in the mounted monster and then the pillar of black air with wide eyes. Then one of the black tentacles lashed out, grabbed the woman around the waist and cracked her back into the ground with a grisly crunch.

Ksara twitched but didn't wake.

"Shit," Ulric said.

The lizard hissed again, snapping its jaws around a tentacle of shadow but finding only air.

The mouths on the monster's body twitched, lips smacking. Tongues tickling the edges of skin. They opened wide, sucking in a deep breath.

"Ksara!" Ulric bellowed, but the tentacles were faster. They lashed out at the monster, choking a dozen mouths with shadow and whipping both beast and rider with several more. The lizard recoiled, turning to swipe its tail at Ksara and the miniature noktum only for it to pass through air as the shadow lifted Ksara far above the scene and out of reach of the creature. She hung limply in the grips of the darkness, head lolled back.

The mouths wheezed in another breath and the tendrils of

shadow rushed to attack, but they could not choke every opening. The monster screamed. Ulric slid backward across the forest floor, blood dripping from his ears. He blinked away the daze to find the small noktum of black air that had been holding his sister was gone.

The shadow had been expelled. Pushed back just like everything else by the monster's scream.

And Ksara plummeted through the air, reeling head over foot toward the ground.

CHAPTER THIRTY-SEVEN

KSARA

The Shadowvar was there again. The one in the tidy, black vest with a silver chain in the breast pocket. He wore such worry on his face, it looked to be a permanent expression.

At least he didn't have an arrow in his chest anymore. That should have made him at least a little happy.

"What are you doing?"

Ksara shrugged. She glanced about the dream, but found only a hazy gray. A hazy gray and this Shadowvar glaring at her. "Dreaming."

"No," the Shadowvar said. "You're letting him have control."

Ksara blinked at the Shadowvar. She remembered the horrors of Nokte Murosa. Their plight to Hayvonlar. Genove and the Allarune. And she suddenly found the Shadowvar a little less charming. "This is the only way."

"You can't give him control!" The Shadowvar's body began to shimmer and then fade into the gray. His arms disappearing first. Then his legs and torso. Finally his face, eyes, and horns. But still his voice remained, chiding her through the gray haze. "Do you know who he is? What he is?"

"Ksara!"

Ksara blinked her eyes open to find the ground rushing up at her. Warm air pressed at her face and arms and legs. She couldn't even yell. All she managed was a choking gasp just before she hit the—

The deep voice in her mind boomed like thunder and the cold air cut into her, ripping her upward. Her neck jerked backward and pain coursed through her body, but her lungs filled with air and she rose slowly, reorienting upward. The shadows held her. Raised her into the air and turned her to face the monster and its lizard mount.

And a low, beating voice of the shadows thumped through her mind. Loud and commanding, its words still a jumbled slur, but their presence heavy.

Then there was a second voice. Much softer than the first. *What are you doing?*

Someone stood, armor creaking and a sword scraping free of its sheath. Ksara turned to see Atlas on his feet, blood spilling from his head, but he held his short sword steady. Then he smiled and charged the lizard and rider.

"No!" Ksara yelled. She willed the shadow to reach out and stop Atlas. To keep him from rushing right at death this time. The dark didn't comply. It just held her above the ground, keeping her from leaping between.

But the monster did not hesitate.

The lizard spun about, but instead of the thing swallowing Atlas down, the rider caught hold of Atlas by the neck. He lifted the Imprevari by the throat with one hand. Atlas slashed the sword at the monstrous man, dealing long gashes down the thing's arm. More black ichor dripped from its body and more of the mouths about the wound opened and licked it up.

Then the monster cracked Atlas's head into the lizard's plated shoulder and he went limp.

"No!"

Ksara put all her will into the shadow. She wished it to attack the lizard now. To stop the monster.

But the voice just beat its own, unintelligible words into her head, and the air whipped and curled around her.

The lizard spun away from the carnage and lumbered back into the forest. The rider still holding Atlas by the neck with a single hand.

"No!" Ksara screamed the word this time. Then she gritted her teeth and screamed inside her head at the voices there. *Stop it! Stop that monster!*

Her heart flailed against her ribcage. Sweat gathered on her brow. She kicked her legs, but still the shadow held her tight and away from the ground.

Ulric limped from the trees and as close to Ksara as the protective shadows would allow. Coronata joined Ulric, steadying him under one arm and Merewen shuffled near, her shoulders and arms slashed and bloodied.

Ksara met Ulric's eyes and he nodded, snapping his fingers and splashing the clearing with a small flare of light. The shadow fled and Ksara fell. This time only from a few feet. She landed on a cold Dorumai corpse and shot upright in an instant. Swaying a little.

Ulric pulled Ksara into a tight hug. He smelled like blood and dirt, but he was alive. And that simple truth steadied Ksara some.

"I couldn't stop it," she said into Ulric's shoulder. "I couldn't keep him safe."

"We'll get him back. Besides, it's Atlas. Getting throttled by the neck by a new monster? Dream come true."

Ksara coughed a little laugh into Ulric's shoulder. The man's truest magic was making her laugh when she wanted to cry.

He released Ksara from the hug, but kept an arm around her shoulder.

"The Horror Knight went that way," Merewen said.

"Horror Knight?" Coronata asked, a bloodied hand resting on her hip. "Is that what we're calling them?"

"Are we really going to argue over naming a monster?" Ksara

asked.

Coronata shrugged. "Atlas is hard to kill. And how often do we get to name a new monster?"

Ulric smiled. "What about Screamy Mouths Monster and its Oversized Angry Lizard?"

Ksara gave her brother a sharp look.

He pointed at Merewen. "She started it."

Merewen shrugged. "Genove should probably be the one to name it anyways."

"Genove!" Ksara pulled away from Ulric and surveyed the bodies around them. Two dozen Dorumai lie in the clearing with more spread out into the tree line. A few had fled into the woods during the fight.

"Can't we leave him?" Ulric said. "Atlas isn't *that* hard to kill. Not for the Screamy Mouth Monster and its Oversized Angry Lizard."

"We need him," Ksara said, stepping around another dead body.

"We?" Ulric pressed.

True anger flashed on her face now.

Ulric softened. "'Sar—"

"No," Ksara turned back to her brother, her shoulders square. Her back straight. She looked clearly and deeply into her brother's eyes. "I cannot save anyone with this curse on me. Not Atlas. Not you. Not me. We find the scholar and the Allarune."

Ulric sighed. He had an argument brewing in his eyes, but he limped about the clearing instead, moving bodies off of each other and searching for the scholar.

Ksara continued doing the same. She hadn't seen the scholar since the monster—the Horror Knight's—first scream. He'd been right behind her then. What if he were dead? What if she could never find the Allarune remains?

Her throat tightened. The shadows drew nearer to her. And she hurried to the next body. The man lay at an unnatural angle, his head and feet nearly touching. Had the Horror Knight or her own power killed the man?

They rifled through twenty bodies before Ksara caught a glimpse of blue cloth. Moving two more bodies, they uncovered Genove. For half a moment, Ksara waited for Atlas to push between her and the wounded and take over. But Atlas was gone. Injured gravely himself. And being marched toward a fate they could only guess at.

Ksara felt for a pulse on Genove's neck and found it. Listened for breathing and heard a steady wheeze. He had no obvious injuries; the blood staining his tunic was from the Dorumai above him. As best as she could tell, he'd been knocked unconscious and then protected from the rest of the onslaught by the dead above him.

She tried to wake the man, shaking his shoulders and tapping his face. But he didn't stir. She glanced about the clearing. How long could they wait here until he woke? What would happen to Atlas while they did? And would the Horror Knight return for more of them?

Then again, they had no idea where the Allarune remains were. And Hayvonlar was a large island. They could wander for days, not find the Allarune without the scholar's help.

"I think there's a nuraghi here," Merewen said.

And it was such a random exclamation that even Ksara turned to stare at the giant Usaran.

"Nuraghi are ancient places of power," she continued. "They house artifacts and monsters. Hayvonlar is rumored to have both."

"If the Allarune is in a nuraghi, we don't need the scholar after all," Ulric said with a smile. "Just go to the scary, black building and find the Allarune yourself."

"We don't know what it looks like. We bring Genove." She shook Genove again. He still didn't wake. With a sigh, she looked up at Ulric. "Can you carry him?"

Ulric limped closer. He'd injured his right leg during the fight. She didn't see blood or bone, but he couldn't put his full weight on it. And he hid the pain from her. Or tried.

"I will carry the scholar," Merewen said, but she waited, eyeing

Ksara.

Only then did Ksara see the shadows that had skulked in between her and the rest of the crew. She stood and stepped back, taking the black air with her.

Merewen strode forward, lifting Genove from the ground and hefting him over her shoulder like a child.

Senji's boots! The woman was strong.

Ksara glanced at her crew, or what was left of them. "Any chance the rest of you will go back to the ship and wait for me there?"

Coronata laughed. "And miss saving Atlas's ass again? Not a chance."

Ulric clasped an arm around Ksara's shoulder. Merewen motioned ahead and said, "After you, Captain."

"You're all crazy," she said with a sad, proud kind of smile. "Not a lick of sense in you at all."

CHAPTER THIRTY-EIGHT

THE ORATOR

The Orator clung to a tree and watched the Prophetess. His Shadowvar skin blended in with the shadows. Usually that was enough. Usually he could stay still inside the shadows and, with his horns sawed off, all of him remained hidden, even from other Shadowvars' eyes.

But here, so near the Prophetess, the dark was alive. It was the tide and she the moon. So he swayed with it, following its fluid movements silently around the trunk while he watched and listened.

She walked about the blessed dead—these Dorumai had died in service of the Truth. Their debts were paid and now they could peacefully await the return of the Lords of the Dark.

And she spoke of finding Genove LeGrande—the faithless scholar.

He'd known she'd arrived on Hayvonlar with him. The scholar had deserted the enlightened cause. Spies had seen him enter the Assembly Hall where the Prophetess had been taken. And caught sight of him again, leaving with the Prophetess and her crew as they fled Nokte Murosa.

It was one of the few times he'd orchestrated events and regretted their outcomes.

When he'd first given the scholar the idea of taking the mage's power and using it for himself, he hadn't known the extent of the woman's magic. He hadn't seen the magnificence of it.

The Night of the Soul had changed him. Purified his purpose.

This was a woman, not to be used as a tool, but to be a guiding light for the Dorumai.

So, he'd rallied his most loyal and followed Genove here. Usually he was as adept at unraveling unwanted plans as he was at crafting destinies.

But this time a monster had disturbed it all. Leveling his forces and making the Prophetess all the more determined to strip herself of her divinity.

Rage quivered through his body so intensely he almost growled and gave away his disguise.

How could someone so elevated by destiny be such a fool? How could she be so very, very blind?

When they pulled the scholar from among the dead, the Orator reached for the dagger at his belt and gripped the hilt until his fingers ached. All he needed to do is end the scholar and the knowledge of the Allarune stayed in the Orator's own head.

But even with powerful purpose guiding his hand, the Orator could not ambush and kill the scholar now. Not with the Prophetess and her crew gathered about him. They didn't hesitate to fight and kill. He wouldn't make it within three feet of the scholar before he met his end.

And then who would guide the Prophetess? Who would prepare Nokte Murosa—and the world—for the return of the Lords of the Dark?

He pried his fingers from the hilt of the dagger, sheathed it, and clung to the tree beside him. No, he would strike from the shadows. That was the way of the Dorumai.

The Usaran lifted the scholar over her shoulder and the Prophetess led her crew where the monster had gone. After one of their own.

And the Orator followed.

CHAPTER THIRTY-NINE

ULRIC

They were moving too slowly and Ulric knew it.

He pushed his throbbing leg faster, hobbling around stones, over fallen trees, and through swatches of brambles, but after nearly an hour the agony could not be ignored any longer. He took shorter and shorter steps, breathing heavier and heavier between each. The pain lanced up from his leg and forked across his torso and nothing seemed to tame the injury's fire.

Ksara stopped, turning to scrutinize Ulric.

He gave his sister a winning smile that turned into a wince.

Worry deepened on her brow. "We rest here."

They'd lost sight of the Horror Knight in the distance. Couldn't even feel the tremors of the thing's lizard stomping through the forest. It left a wide trail for them to follow, but if they arrived too late, it didn't matter much at all. "'Sar ..."

"We rest here," she said again, and the shadows flared around her when she spoke.

Ulric opened his mouth to argue and Coronata elbowed him

in the side as she passed. He groaned, rubbed his ribs, and gave the pirate a sidelong glance.

She grinned at him. She had her own gash just under her hairline with blood caked into her black hair and across the left side of her face. And somehow, even with the blood and dirt, she could have turned all the heads in the tavern with that smile. With that saunter.

He smiled back at her. Wondered what it would be like to wrap his arms around her and—

"Sit down," Ksara said. "Rest."

Ulric's imagined euphoria dissipated and the pain returned, louder than ever before. He found himself the tallest boulder in sight and eased himself down to sit upon it.

Merewen slipped Genove off her shoulder and onto the ground. She checked the man for a pulse and breath then left him where he lay. Coronata lounged against a tree trunk near Ksara, speaking in a low voice.

Merewen joined Ulric where he sat. She knelt and almost touched his injured leg before her hands froze and her eyes, the color of the Demaijos Sea, found his. "May I?"

Ulric grinned. "I never say no to a pretty woman."

Merewen blushed and hid her gaze. She prodded his injured leg and he gritted his teeth to keep from cursing. She was the only one among them that didn't appreciate a good bout of blasphemy once in a while. But the way she kept prodding at his injured leg, she was more and more likely to get a dose of it.

"It's not broken," she said. "But it needs a splint. I can make one now."

"You can fix me up any way you like," Ulric said. "After we get Atlas back."

"Gather the supplies; I'll splint it now," Ksara said.

Ulric flinched. He hadn't noticed his sister's approach. But, with the swath of shadows constantly crowding her feet, her footsteps rarely made a sound.

Merewen stood, pulled one of the hatchets from her belt and began hacking off small branches from the trees about them.

"Atlas can't wait," he said. "My leg can."

"Coronata and Merewen are going on without us," Ksara said, raising her hand to stop the argument she knew was coming. "We'll be right behind them when Genove wakes. And they'll get to Atlas first. And we'll use the time to come up with a proper plan."

"And if the Horror Knight comes here?" Ulric said. "We barely survived the first attack when we were all together *and* we had the Dorumai as target practice."

"You just said Atlas can't wait."

"And we can't get separated," he said. "The Horror Knights might just be the beginning."

She nodded. "It's the best of the worst plans."

Merewen returned with several long, sturdy branches and Genove's belt. She handed the supplies to Ksara, careful to avoid the black air around her.

"Be well, my friend," Ksara said.

Merewen nodded. She glanced at Ulric, opened her mouth to speak, and then closed it suddenly, turning from them and striding to catch up to Coronata who'd already started down the trail toward Atlas. The pirate turned and gave a flamboyant wave back to them before returning to her task at a brisk jog.

In seconds Coronata and Merewen were both out of view.

Ksara splinted Ulric's leg in silence. Every time Ulric parted his lips to argue with her, she tightened this or that and the discomfort kept his argument quiet.

When she'd finished, Ulric pushed to stand and she clamped a hand down on his shoulder. "We rest," she said.

"We can at least hobble after them, 'Sar!"

"And who's going to carry Genove?"

"We leave him behind. Should have done that a while ago."

Ksara stiffened and the shadows swelled around her. Coming alive with his sister's aggravation.

As much as Ulric would never admit it to Ksara, that was a new and concerning development to her power. The shadows had always responded to her fear. That had been a constant since they were children. But now the dark air came alive with any of her strong emotions. And he'd seen exactly how little control she had over them, conscious or otherwise.

But there had to be another way around this. Ksara was taking a snake's offer for a ride across the river and not expecting to get bitten.

"I need you to trust me," Ksara said, her voice strained.

"I need you to stop wanting to die," he bit back. The pain laying bare his truth.

The shadows grew taller, dancing around her waist. "You saw what I did in Nokte Murosa! Grina's ass, Ulric! It just happened again an hour ago. None of you will admit it, but I see it in your eyes. You're afraid of me! My own friends!"

"That was different. You weren't awake that time."

"And that makes it *better*?"

"It makes it different."

Ksara shook her head. "I could kill you. All of you. And not even know I was doing it. That's no way to live, Ulric. If I hurt you ..."

He motioned at his bound knee. "Me? I'm invincible."

She didn't smile. Instead, her gaze grew distant. "No. You're not."

Ulric had hoped to lighten the mood. To shake Ksara from her white-knuckled-grip on despair. But the change in her eyes. The hollowness to her voice. She'd seen him walk the path to death and only just avoid the destination.

And now he had to do the same for her. He had to walk the path *with* her.

"We've tried everything else," she said. She had none of the fire in her voice anymore. "We've met with every mage. Searched for every artifact. This is the only lead we have. And I have no more time to wander."

He held his throbbing leg between his hands and thought for a long moment. She wasn't asking for permission; she'd decided on this course before she'd left the Assembly Hall. And Ksara was incredibly hard to dissuade once she'd set her mind to something.

No, she wasn't asking for permission. She wanted him to understand her. She wanted him to forgive her for being foolish. For risking so much. For hurting so many.

He smiled a sad smile at his sister. She had all of those things, but he told her anyways. "I'm with you, 'Sar. No matter where we go or what we do, I'm with you."

Genove cried out then, his cry so near the Horror Knights that both Ksara and Ulric leapt into action—Ulric launching up to his uncertain legs and Ksara whipping her staff from off her back.

CHAPTER FORTY

GENOVE

Genove woke as soon as the Usaran put him on the ground, but he kept his eyes closed and his body limp as she checked his neck for a pulse and then moved away. He listened as the crew decided their course and his own.

When the Usaran and the Pirate left, the Demaijos siblings began a quiet argument a dozen feet away from him. That's when Genove opened his eyes to slits—and saw the Orator crouched in the shadows.

He could have alerted the Demaijos right away, called out to them and let them chase down the Shadowvar. But the Orator was stalking closer to Genove, not the Demaijos. The glint of a dagger in the Shadowvar's hand.

Certainly Genove had earned the Orator's ire for joining the Dorumai and then abandoning them. But if that had been true cause to kill him, he would have done so as soon as he had Ksara and Genove in their grasp.

But he hadn't. He'd tried to leverage Genove to gain power over Ksara.

Now the Orator apparently wanted Genove dead. Which meant that the Orator had discovered Genove's purpose with Ksara and he disapproved of his supposed prophetess being stripped of her power.

Genove shifted a hand inside his tunic and found the pouch he'd sewn there. Opening it with two fingers, he found three small bits of parchment with the top edges dipped in wax. He'd made it from the last bits of supplies he could beg from the Nokte Murosan parchment merchant. Now, careful to only touch the wax edge, Genove removed one and held it tight between two fingers. Waiting.

The Orator stalked through the underbrush, darting between trees, and then blending with shadow. His small frame lending itself to stealth. He stood over Genove for scarcely a moment before he crouched and plunged the dagger toward Genove's heart.

Genove rolled out of the way and slapped the parchment against the Shadowvar's face.

He felt a snapping, sizzling kind of sensation in his stomach and the magic activated.

The Orator's eyes went wild, staring all about him and backing away from Genove.

Then he screamed.

The Demaijos ran to them then, stuttering to a halt when they found the Orator there, screaming and turning about in circles, evaluating enemies only he could see and slashing his dagger at empty air.

Genove crawled a distance away from the madman and then got to his feet. Ksara and her brother joined him, never turning their back to the Orator.

"What happened?" Ksara asked.

"Shouldn't he be dead?" Ulric said. "What's wrong with him?"

"He hit his head. Hard." Genove watched the Orator scream again and swing the blade back and forth. "But if he doesn't quiet down, we'll all be in trouble."

Both of the Demaijos quieted then, exchanging looks.

"He will stand trial in Nokte Murosa," Ksara said.

Ulric shrugged. "We can't leave now."

"We can't leave him, either," she said. Then she nodded at Genove. "Give me your robe."

"What?"

Ksara's glare hardened. "Give it to me."

He slipped out of the filthy cloth. He had no belt now. Just trousers and boots. He handed the robe over.

The Demaijos immediately began cutting it into strips.

"Knock him down," she said. "We're keeping him right where we can find him again."

Ulric pulled his sword from its scabbard and eased in closer to the Orator. The Shadowvar whipped about with his dagger, the white of his eyes bright. No pattern to his attack. No rhythm to predict.

But the Orator didn't seem to see Ulric either. So he batted away the man's weapon, then shoulder-checked him into a tree trunk. Ksara was there the next instant, tying the man's hands together with strips of cloth and then securing him around the trunk of the tree.

The Orator kicked and spat and screamed, but the Demaijos made quick work of the Shadowvar.

Ulric stepped back, panting hard. "Now can we leave him? Nokte Murosa might have heard all that shouting."

"We can leave him, for now." Ksara turned to Genove. "Take us to the Allarune."

CHAPTER FORTY-ONE

CORONATA

oronata jogged swiftly up the hillside and down another, dodging the loudest bits of broken debris and using boulders as stepping stones through brambles.

And Merewen kept stride.

The Usaran was at least a foot taller than Coronata. Thick and muscled. Although her footsteps landed louder against the earth than did Coronata's, the woman was lighter on her feet than many half her height.

And she had a warrior's stamina. She'd taken quite a blow from the Horror Knight. The blood from the other Dorumai had hidden most of her wounds from the others, but now as they were running, the gash down her head, neck, and shoulder spilled new blood. Each wound as thick as Coronata's finger and longer than her hand.

The ground shuddered just as Coronata was about to leap from a boulder. She stood poised there for a moment, balancing her body and listening for the sound again.

The thud came again.

"Horror Knights?"

They hadn't felt the first Horror Knight's footsteps in some time. But this wasn't a place she wanted to just sit and wait to find out what new and exciting death was coming for them.

Coronata pivoted toward the nearest tree trunk and leapt to the lowest branch. She caught hold of it, hoisted herself up, and climbed the fifty-foot tree as easily as if it were the *Falco*'s own mast. Standing at the top, her head breaking through the shadow and into the waning afternoon light, she saw Hayvonlar's treasure.

The Serkir Nuraghi.

It rose from the landscape like a crown with twisted spikes, each reaching a hundred feet into the air. The outside was adorned with pillars and gates, all made from dull, black stone and metal, the same material she'd seen at other nuraghi.

And just like with the other nuraghi, Coronata felt an urge to flee. Every instinct that brought her from the sands of the Eternal Desert to rule the seas told her to turn away from that place and leave. Death awaited her there.

She knew this was part of the magic of the place. It wasn't a place for humans and so it pushed them away. But the impulse buzzing inside her felt every bit as real as any she'd felt, so she stayed in the tree, steadying her nerves.

And that's when she saw six Horror Knights dispensing out of the gates of the nuraghi at a run. And coming right toward them.

"Get up the tree!"

"What?"

Coronata lowered herself beneath the canopy so she could look down at Merewen. "Get up a tree. Now!"

The Usaran frowned and hurried to a tree.

The ground bucked and the tree swayed. There were so many of the lizards, it didn't even sound like footsteps, but a roar of thunder in a cloudless sky.

Merewen reached for a low branch but couldn't grab it. She jumped, but the jump was pathetic. Perhaps, being as tall as she was, Merewen had very little experience needing to jump at all.

She moved to a different tree and tried again.

Coronata glanced up through the canopy just as the first cracking began. The troop of Horror Knights were barreling through the forest, trampling the underbrush, the lizards' tails whacking trees as they rushed by. "Hurry!"

Merewen reached a branch on her tip toes and hauled herself up, blood dripping from the wounds on her neck and shoulder. Then she began to climb. Slowly. Deliberately.

The thundering was almost upon them now. "Faster!"

She got up one more level, just fifteen feet from the forest floor, before the first Horror Knight crashed through the forest below. Merewen was barely higher than the Horror Knight's line of sight, but she had the good sense to stay completely still as it barreled past her.

More footsteps. Another Horror Knight. Then another. They each had that pearlescent white skin and reptilian golden eyes. Bodies larger than any human she'd seen. Exaggerated and large. Hulking chests and arms and necks with bloodless gashes all over their bodies. Gashes that looked rather harmless when they weren't licking or clacking their teeth.

Coronata kept her eyes on her friend clinging to the tree as another Horror Knight passed. The trees swayed with the lizard's heavy footsteps. Coronata kept one arm wrapped around the trunk and the other near her rapier. Merewen did the same, her free hand on one of her axes.

But what good would a rapier or a hatchet do against one of those monsters? Not even Ksara's magic had been enough to dissuade it. It had born the magic and weapons with a suffering sort of calm and then plucked Atlas up like a child and left.

Another Horror Knight rode past and the lizard was larger than the rest, its plated scales scraping against Coronata's tree. The tall pine shivered and bucked. Coronata snaked her free arm around another branch and hung on tight. The top of the tree tipped five feet back and five feet forward, brushing against the neighboring trees, their branches clawing at her. Her hands, calloused by years at sea, held true and she kept atop the tree until it settled and stilled.

Glancing down, she found another Horror Knight and its lizard. But this one didn't speed past them. The lizard plodded through the forest, its tongue licking the air. Then it stopped abruptly. The Horror Knight atop the lizard turned its golden eyes about, scanning the clearing.

Merewen crouched on a branch of a tree a mere ten feet away from the creature.

The Usaran didn't flinch. She kept still as stone in the tree.

The lizard's forked tongue tasted the air again and again. Then it lumbered closer to Merewen's tree. To where a trickle of Merewen's blood splattered the ground.

Then it raised its head and licked the air, finding the source of the blood.

The Horror Knight locked its golden eyes on Merewen and the slashes on its milky skin opened, clacking their teeth and wetting their lips.

Merewen pulled the axe from her belt and threw it at the Horror Knight. The blade sank into one of the strange mouths and black blood spilled out of it. The Horror Knight didn't even flinch. And the other mouths lapped up the blood like Merewen's attack had just done them all a great favor.

"Senji's braid!" Coronata swore and flew down the trunk as fast as she could. "Senji's damn braid!"

CHAPTER FORTY-TWO

MEREWEN

Merewen aimed true. She threw with force. And the axe hit its mark.

The hatchet sank deep into the Horror Knight's only soft skin—one of its many mouths.

But the Horror Knight didn't seem perturbed by the blow in the slightest. It just beheld her with those unblinking reptilian, golden eyes. The lizard, however, flicked its tail side to side, and hissed. Exposing the wet, soft pink of its wide mouth as it did.

Merewen threw her second axe.

This strike was noticed.

The lizard hissed louder than ever before, swinging its head back and forth to dislodge the weapon from its mouth. Copious amounts of blood pouring down its lips and chin. All the while, the Horror Knight never looked away from Merewen.

She reached for the next branch and climbed.

Her shoulder burned with each reach and then pulsed with agony when she pulled herself upward. Six more handholds and the waves of pain were so intense, they blurred her vision and she had to pause for a few seconds to distinguish the next branch to reach for.

The lizard stopped hissing. Stopped thrashing. And there was quiet on the forest floor.

Merewen hauled herself up a little higher, held tight to the trunk as her vision swayed, then glanced down to find the lizard lying still at the base of the tree. And the Horror Knight standing on his own two feet, staring up at her, the mouths all about its body opening, smacking, and twitching—gathering breath.

Suddenly she knew that no matter how high she climbed, that monster's scream would still reach her. Would propel her out of the tree to meet the ground with a force she wouldn't wake up from.

She had no more weapons. Not even a stone to throw down at the thing—as much good as it would do.

She tightened her grip on the tree and sent gratitude to the gods. She'd outlived all of her kin by a decade. She'd traveled Noksonon and learned all she could about its people and history. She'd found new kin, though most of the time they fought like street dogs, but she defended them. She protected them—doing for her new family what she'd failed to do for her first.

That was enough for Merewen. And if it was enough for Senji, Asper, Libur, Grina, and Lotura, then she'd be rewarded with another chance to defend her kin in the next life.

"Jump!"

Merewen turned her head, the movement bringing another wave of pain.

Coronata crouched in the adjacent tree, one level higher than Merewen. How the pirate had gotten there, and so quickly ...

Was that a belt cinched around the woman's upper arm?

Merewen blinked at the woman.

She hissed a curse. "Just jump! I'll catch you!"

Maybe it was Merewen's last gift from the gods that she didn't think too hard about how ridiculous Coronata's proposal was. Maybe it was the pain dominating her body. Or the final wheeze of the Horror Knight below gathering the last gulp of air, but

Merewen pushed away from the trunk, ran down the branch—barely the size of her arm—and leapt toward Coronata.

As Merewen reeled through the air, feet pedaling for purchase, the Horror Knight screamed. The blast struck her in the back, tearing at her wound and propelling her up and away from the tree. She closed her eyes and cried out; the sound swallowed up in the Horror Knight's long shriek.

She tumbled through the air, arms wheeling. Her stomach flipped inside her and pressed up into her ribcage as she transitioned from flying to falling.

Something grabbed hold of her hand and her body jerked, arresting her fall and tearing her wound open wider. She cried out as pain cascaded over her body.

Her eyes snapped open and she saw Coronata clinging to her wrist with her right hand and dangling from the tree by the belt fastened to her left arm.

Coronata strained. Her lean muscles taut and her face flushing a deep red.

Merewen clenched her jaw against the pain and caught hold of Coronata's hand with her free hand, clinging to the pirate.

"I won't let go," Coronata said in a rough whisper. "Swing toward the tree."

Merewen glanced at the tree Coronata was tethered to. It was four feet and another reach to the closest branch. She kicked her feet and began swinging them back and forth. Coronata's grip was as sure as any Merewen had known, but she couldn't hold her for long.

Her boots scraped against the trunk and she kicked off of it a final time. One more swing and she could take one hand off of Coronata's and grab for the branch.

The ground trembled. The trees groaned. And Merewen swung back at the tree, released one of her hands from Coronata, and caught the branch. The stretch opened up her wound yet wider and blood rushed down her back now. She pulled herself closer to the branch, rallying the rest of her strength to wrap her legs around it, relieving her arms of her own weight.

Coronata panted and smiled. "Don't let me go, now. Just pull me a little closer and we'll cut the belt. Ideally, before my arm loses all blood flow. Then again, a hook for an arm would only improve my reputation."

Merewen wriggled her body atop the branch, keeping hold of Coronata, when the tree shuddered again, almost pitching her off.

Coronata glanced down and her good humor faded. "Don't worry about that now. Just get me closer."

Merewen leveraged her legs and pulled the pirate closer to the trunk. Coronata twisted her body with the ease of a Triadan street performer and wrapped one leg around the branch and then let go of Merewen's hand to grasp the tree instead.

Merewen let out a breath she hadn't realized she'd been holding and Coronata pulled a knife from her boot and got to work on the belt attached to the branch above them.

The ground shivered again and Merewen looked down.

There was yet another Horror Knight and lizard waiting beside the first. This lizard was a deep red and larger than any she'd seen. The Horror Knights didn't look at each other. They didn't speak from any of their mouths. But the red lizard reared up on its back legs, its thirty-foot length teetering in the air while the Horror Knight kept astride it without exertion.

Then the lizard fell against the tree, its front claws crashing against the trunk. A crack split the air. The tree groaned. The branch pitched underneath Merewen. And for the second time in minutes, Merewen was in a free fall from one of the enormous trees.

This time the hand that caught her did so by the throat. A lightning-fast grab that stole her breath and clamped down hard on her wound. She couldn't gasp. She could barely wheeze in a whisper of air as she stared into the face of a Horror Knight, dangling from his grip like a rabbit in a snare.

CHAPTER FORTY-THREE

CORONATA

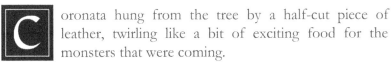

oronata hung from the tree by a half-cut piece of leather, twirling like a bit of exciting food for the monsters that were coming.

She'd lost her dagger in the fall. Although, all things considered, she was lucky that the branch hadn't landed between the trunk and the ground. Then she'd be a dead bit of twirling food for the monsters. And that would be less exciting for both of them, really.

Merewen cried out and then the sound stopped short.

Coronata arched her back and kicked her legs, willing her body to turn faster. It didn't work. She spun as slowly as she had before, inch-by-inch to the left until she caught a glimpse of the Horror Knights. The one seated upon the red lizard had Merewen by the throat.

"Hey!" Coronata growled. "Leave her be!"

Merewen ripped at the Horror Knight's hands, gasped, and went limp.

"No!" Coronata yelled. Anger getting the better of her good

sense. "You bastards! You mouthy, creepy bast—"

The golden eyes turned on her. Two pairs of eyes that held no emotion. Not hunger nor anger nor triumph. This wasn't a predator, just a body animated by cold purpose.

And the lizard-less Horror Knight stomped in a straight line right to her, batting away branches and sending them flying a dozen feet out of his way.

Coronata had laughed in the face of death dozens of times. But she hadn't felt this panic, this cold, consuming fear since she'd faced down an army in the Eternal Desert. Her mother at her side. She'd been eight years old. Barely strong enough to wield a dagger. And an Imprevari army rushed at them, their armor glinting in the sun. Hooves beating down the sand dune toward them.

They'd been doom incarnate. Destiny come to destroy. That moment she knew that everyone she loved might die that day. That life could be snuffed out like gnats pinched between fingers, no matter how much you adored them.

She was that girl again, hanging from the belt, watching the Horror Knight march toward her. Hope left her like a breath she couldn't draw back in. Instinctively her fingernails clawed at the leather holding her to the tree, but she knew her fate.

She'd danced around death enough times to know when it outmaneuvered her.

The Horror Knight stopped a foot from Coronata's face and looked at her eye-to-eye.

She spat at him. The thing's eyes didn't blink. It didn't flinch. The spittle dripped down its mouthless face and one of the mouths on its neck opened and licked the saliva off its skin.

Then she kept twirling, her back to the Horror Knight now. She writhed and turned, but the momentum continued.

Her skin crawled. She could feel the monster's nearness. His gaze was a cold mist pressed against her skin.

She'd almost made a full circuit around when the hand clamped down on her throat and jerked her downward. The belt snapped. Her lungs burned.

And she fought. She kicked and wheezed a scream through

her throat and she whipped the broken belt at the thing's face. She used every ounce of her strength beating and thrashing at the thing.

All it did was wait. Wait until her strength failed. Until the lack of air blurred her vision and made her hands and feet heavier. More sluggish. Until sleeping felt like the best way to fight. Until closing her eyes was the only option she could think of.

The last thing she saw were those yellow eyes like dunes in the Eternal Dessert. Peppered with an army about to destroy everything she loved.

CHAPTER FORTY-FOUR

KSARA

The shadows swelled around Ksara, rising like a wave before her.

Not a wave. A shield.

A moment later the ground shuddered.

"Here's hoping that means rain," Ulric said, hurrying a little faster and hiding the pain on his face with a smile.

"They're coming," Genove said.

Ksara glanced about the forest. She saw no sign of the lizard and rider. But another tremor worked through the forest floor. "What do you know of these monsters?"

The scholar wore a gaunt frown. "The texts speak of the Witnesses. Guardians of the Serkir Nuraghi that serve it without a word."

"These ones are rather loud," Ulric said.

The ground pulsed now with a succession of rumbling steps. Ksara paused, listening. Panic pumping through her. There was no way that sound was a good thing. And, as best as she could tell, the sound was getting louder and louder with each passing second.

"They're coming for more," Genove said.

"More?" Ulric whispered back. "They took out thirty Dorumai."

Genove glanced about the forest with something near wonder and glee in his eyes. "They serve the nuraghi still."

"What does that mean?" Ksara said, louder than before.

Genove turned his irritatingly calm eyes on Ksara. "It means we should run. Or hide. Or prepare to enter the Serkir Nuraghi on the Witness's terms."

Ulric chuckled hoarsely. "Have any ideas of where to hide an invalid, a mage, and a scholar with a scroll stashed up his arse on an island full of monsters?"

"We could always give them the invalid," Genove said. "Lean into the inevitable."

"Stop," Ksara barked and the shadows grew taller. She glanced about the forest and found two boulders stacked nearly on top of each other with a three-foot crawl space beneath. By themselves they wouldn't offer much cover at all, but perhaps the shadows haunting her could help. Once.

"You two, get in there."

The ground shivered. Genove and Ulric looked about ready to argue at the same time, with her instead of each other, for once, but her expression hardened. "Do it."

They complied, crouching into the cramped space. Ulric's shoulders took most of the room and Genove hunched below them like a chick beneath a hen's wing.

Ksara stood in front of both of them, the top of her back pressed against the boulder, and the swell of black air between her and the rest of the forest.

But the air was only as tall as her shoulders and it curled and looped in front of her. Would it draw more attention to them? Or would they be able to hide in the patch of unnatural shadow?

The ground shuddered longer and louder than ever before. Ksara's heart thundered right alongside it and she ducked as best she could beneath the rim of black air.

Massive footsteps crashed through the forest a dozen feet

away from them. Ksara winced behind the cold shadows, but the footsteps didn't slow.

And more and more of them came.

She counted the Horror Knights as they passed and by the time an uneasy silence resumed in the forest, six of the monsters and their steeds had rushed by.

Ksara kept Ulric and Genove in the alcove another few minutes, just to be sure the danger had passed. Then she stepped forward, the icy breath of the shadow cutting through her until she got ahead of the shadow enough to draw it away from the boulders and the men.

Neither of them left the alcove. Ulric's eyes were wide, his gaze darting wildly about the empty air. Genove had a hand on Ulric's shoulder, some version of concern on his face.

Ksara was at Ulric's side in an instant. "What's wrong?"

"They're here," he said. "They found me!"

Ksara frowned. "Quiet."

"They're here!" Ulric bellowed. "Can't you see them? They're here!"

Ulric brushed off Genove and pushed past Ksara.

"Ulric!"

Drawing his sword from the sheath at his back, Ulric pivoted in a circle, holding the weapon at the ready before him. His mismatched brown and green eyes darting back and forth and his breathing getting faster and faster.

"You won't get my sister," he growled. "You won't get my sister!"

"Ulric!" She hissed. "Quiet!"

Ulric began swinging the broadsword left and right, pivoting and lunging, only to skewer empty air. *"Run!"*

"Ulric!" She lunged toward him, dodging a swing and catching hold of his forearm. As soon as she touched him, he turned on her, slamming the pommel of the sword into her face. She reeled backward, blood springing from the wound on her cheek and dripping down to her jaw.

Genove caught her before she fell, pulling her away. Ulric

reversed the blade and began attacking the empty air behind him.

"What's going on? What's wrong with him?"

Genove kept dragging Ksara away. She wriggled free of his grasp and held her ground, now a dozen feet away from her brother's imagined war. "What's wrong?"

"The Witnesses. They have more power than I guessed."

Ulric slashed and growled at an imagined enemy, sweat dripping from him now as he wielded the heavy sword with unrelenting ferocity. Yelling as he swung.

"It happened to the Orator, too."

"But why not us?"

"Some are more susceptible to Love Magic than others," Genove said, his voice low and calm. "You know better than most that sometimes magic defies explanation."

Ksara looked at Genove, measured him again in a moment. He seemed genuine. Concerned. Thoughtful. But carefully so.

But his words made a certain kind of sense. And she certainly couldn't explain it any other way.

"I will kill you all!" Ulric bellowed louder than ever before.

The ground shuddered beneath them. The trees swayed.

Ksara flinched and moved toward him again. "Ulric! Quiet!"

Genove grabbed her by the arm. "It's not safe. He's not himself."

"He'll bring the Horror Knights down on us all." She pulled her metal staff from her back and the black air whipped faster around her legs. "We have to quiet him."

"That will just cause more noise. It will bring them here faster."

Ksara leveled her gaze at Genove. "I will not leave my brother behind."

Something flashed across the scholar's face then. Irritation? Anger? But it was hidden behind crafted calm the next instant. "We go your way, then, Demaijos."

Ksara stepped to meet Ulric, parrying one of his strikes with the center of the staff. His eyes turned on her, but no recognition flashed there. He gritted his teeth and struck at her again. She sidestepped this blow, aiming her own strike at his shoulder, knocking him back a step.

"Ulric. It's me."

"You will not take her," he sputtered, his voice unsteady but the next several blows as sure as any he'd swung.

Ksara did not parry the long sword directly—Ulric's strength behind that kind of blade could send her to her knees, blinking in surprise as he followed it with a killing blow.

Instead, she moved with the momentum of the attacks, ducking, pivoting, twisting, and keeping the metal staff between her and the sword's edge.

The ground shivered again and again, each vibration growing in strength.

"Ulric! Snap out of it!" Ksara said, dodging a strike aimed at her neck and then dealing a bone-bruising blow to Ulric's good leg.

"You will not take my sister, demon," Ulric spat.

"It's me," Ksara said, the dark air swirling about her. When she moved, and fought, the air retreated a foot or two away. Now as they stared each other down again, the shadow returned. It caught Ulric's eye and the hatred on his face hardened. "I will kill you."

The words shouldn't have hurt. She knew he wasn't seeing her. It was some twisted, magic-altered version of her. But the hatred in his voice. The revulsion on his face. Somehow they still stung.

But not as much as the thwack of her metal spear against the side of his head.

His legs buckled and he fell to his knees. Blood flowed from a gash on his head. "I will end you!" His voice cracked, softened. "I will save my sister ..."

"Ulric?"

He looked up at her, and his eyes softened. The confusion dissolved. He was her brother again. "'Sar?"

Trees and underbrush cracked and crunched. A lizard hissed, the sound like a hot wind behind them.

Ksara grabbed Ulric by the arm and ran.

CHAPTER FORTY-FIVE

GENOVE

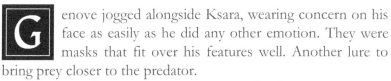

G enove jogged alongside Ksara, wearing concern on his face as easily as he did any other emotion. They were masks that fit over his features well. Another lure to bring prey closer to the predator.

He'd hoped Ksara would have seen the futility of dragging Ulric along with them. That she'd have been willing to leave him behind as she had the Orator.

But he'd underestimated her attachments. A thing Genove couldn't wear as easily as expressions.

They were going to get taken by the Witnesses. They'd had only slim chances of evading them before. Now it was a surety.

The *Falco* crew had called these creatures Horror Knights, but they were so much more. Even upon first glance at them, moments before he was blasted into the crowd and knocked unconscious, Genove had known their maker.

These were the sentries created by the Noksonoi Giants. Not quite human and not quite Giant. If even a fraction of the legends were true, each of the monster's mouths had once belonged to a slave who'd promised undying devotion to the Noksonoi. And this was their wish granted.

These were not simple Kyolars, serving only their instincts and their survival. They had a purpose. And collecting live humans and taking them back to the nuraghi was seemingly part of that purpose.

A single Witness had incapacitated thirty Dorumai, two mages, and three rather competent fighters in an instant. Now, several hunted them.

They were going to get taken by the Witnesses. What remained now, was whether Ksara and Genove could survive what happened after they arrived at the nuraghi, or not.

It would be easiest if Genove and Ksara were the only survivors. All else were a distraction. A nuisance. Particularly Ulric. He was the one person who might still be able to dissuade Ksara from using the Allarune at all.

And he'd certainly object to Genove walking away with the power while Ksara died on the floor.

But Genove did not yet have the power to dispense of Ulric himself. So he used Ulric to draw the Witnesses back to them. And he hid his smile as the first Witness broke through the trees behind them, closing the distance in seconds. They might as well have been rabbits fleeing Kyolars.

Ulric was the slowest, staggering with his injured leg and slower still from the fatigue of fighting monsters only he could see. Ksara tugged him along, but it wasn't enough. The first Witness rode up beside them and grabbed Ulric by the throat, effortlessly lifting him from his flight.

Ulric thrashed and kicked. Ksara screamed and the shadow billowed around her. The whole sky seemed to darken with the amount of shadow rushing to Ksara's aid now. The Witness paused, its prize in its fist and its golden eyes on Ksara.

Tentacles of black lashed out all around Ksara, thicker than the tree trunks about them, faster even than the Witnesses' Drakanoi steed. "Let my brother go."

CHAPTER FORTY-SIX

KSARA

sara ran at the Horror Knight, beckoning the shadows to her as she did. The voice thumped faster with her footsteps. Tentacles flew around her.

When she neared the Horror Knight, she let the shadow move before her, slapping the lizard's head to the ground. She leapt, landed one foot on the flat of the lizard's head and vaulted to Ulric. In a breathless instant she collided with her brother, and wrapped one arm around him and the other on the Horror Knight's hand. She'd tear Ulric from the Horror Knight's grip, then hold him in the center of the shadow's vortex and let the wild dark take care of the rest.

The lizard hissed and screamed. Ksara ripped at the Horror Knight's hand, prying at the finger. But they might as well have been iron. Even as dark air lashed out all around her and Ulric, the lizard bucking and swaying, the Horror Knight's grip showed no signs of waning.

But Ksara's did. She could only hold onto Ulric and the Horror Knight so long.

She let go of the Horror Knight, drew a dagger from her belt and started sawing at the hand. Black blood wept from the wound. Ksara's grip slipped and turned. Ulric choked and gagged and gasped.

And the shadows whipped about her in the deafening roar of a tropical storm. The voice boomed in the violent vortex. Triumphant and murderous.

The Horror Knight screamed and the sound tore through the low roar, cut through the shadow, and sent Ksara flying.

Her back cracked against a tree trunk and the impact sent lights dancing in front of her eyes and pain stabbing through her. She slid to the forest floor.

There she fought back a different kind of black as unconsciousness threatened her, clawed at her. It weighed on her limbs and rimmed her vision, but she bit her lip until she tasted blood and kept her eyes open. Ulric needed her. She would not let them take him.

Staggering upright and then swaying on her feet, Ksara only caught a blur of black scales before a hand clamped down on her throat and lifted her from the ground. She blinked and gasped. Her throat burned. Her lungs flailed inside her ribcage.

And the Horror Knight stared back at her with those impassive yellow eyes.

The ground shuddered and another lizard lumbered near. Genove cried out, the sound cut short and replaced with a gasping, wheezing. The same sound she made now.

The lizard pivoted with remarkable dexterity given its size and the density of the forest. Then it followed another lizard, that Horror Knight holding a limp and bleeding Ulric. A third following behind.

She pulled at the Horror Knight's fingers, tears welling in her eyes and the shadows dancing about her dangling feet.

She'd failed. Again. Now it wasn't just her that would die for it. But Ulric, too.

CHAPTER FORTY-SEVEN

ULRIC

lric couldn't yell when Ksara turned back with that fire in her eyes, ready to take on the monster that had him by the throat.

He couldn't beg her to leave him when she clung to the monster's arm and sawed at it with her knife.

He couldn't cry out when the monster screamed and sent her flying.

He couldn't even weep when another monster plucked her up from the ground by her neck.

Every sound, every emotion, every thought came out in a hoarse mouthful of air. Just enough to keep his lungs inflating, but no more. So the same chuffing gasp accompanied all the agony tearing through him. The guilt at having been the first to fall—the one who'd needed saving. Again. And Ksara had run right at this nightmare of a monster to do just that.

The lizards moved through the forest at a brisk, deliberate pace, in single file. Ulric's Horror Knight took the lead, then Genove's, and finally Ksara's. Ulric could barely see Ksara and her captor behind Genove's. Trying to catch a glimpse of her was the only thing that kept him fighting to stay conscious. If he succumbed to the sleep pulling at him, he could lose Ksara forever.

Ulric's arms and legs swung left and right with the lizard's sidling gait like the ticking of a clock as they traveled. He lost sensation in his hands and feet, then his legs and arms. And, by the time they exited the forest, the only thing Ulric still had control of were his eyes and eyelids, which he kept open wide and darting left to check for Ksara.

They crossed into shadow and Ulric's heart raced. He flicked his gaze back toward Ksara, expecting to see that swath of black air around her. Her power had flared when she'd been knocked completely unconscious, but now it gathered around her legs and arms in a cocoon of black, but it didn't attack. And it certainly wasn't the thing blotting out the sun now.

Chains groaned and metal scraped. Ulric blinked at the new sound. The shadow about them intensified and suddenly the forest was replaced by black pillars and black walls. The scent of earth and pines and water replaced by decay and dust.

More metal scraped and, at the end of the sound, the Horror Knight finally moved his pale arm, flinging Ulric.

He flew through the dark air, his lungs greedily sucking in a deep breath. The air tore through his raw throat like daggers and Ulric collided with a ground he couldn't see. It was softer than he'd guessed, some kind of sand, and it absorbed the impact of his limp, lifeless limbs.

The lizard lumbered on and another took its place. A thunk and groan marked where Genove had hit the ground. That lizard moved on and the third lizard stepped forward, its footsteps sending shivers through the sand.

Ulric waited for the lizard to pause like the rest. For that thud and moan to mark Ksara's spot in the dark, so that he could crawl to her. Find her.

But the lizard didn't stop. The metal scraped and a gate slammed closed.

"Ksara," Ulric wheezed and the words hurt worse than the deep breath had. He willed his arms and legs to push him up, to chase after her, to keep the monsters from having her, but he barely got one hand beneath his chest before his whole arm quivered and he fell face-first back into the sand.

Footsteps shuffled through the sand and a hand grabbed hold of Ulric's shoulder "'Sar?" He wheezed. Maybe he'd been mistaken. Maybe it had been Genove, not his sister, that the monsters had kept.

"Ulric?"

That was a voice he knew, but his thoughts came slow. It wasn't Ksara. It wasn't Genove.

"I found the sniveling scholar," a voice growled.

"Where's Ksara?"

A hand pushed Ulric over onto his back, the grip firm, but gentle. Strong and calm as the voice that followed, "Ulric."

"Merewen," he wheezed, the words bringing on a coughing fit that tore at his throat and finished with him spitting blood onto a floor he couldn't see.

"I'm here," she said, her own voice hoarser than usual. "Where is Ksara?"

Now that he had his voice, the emotions held his words back, choking them in his throat. He swallowed it all down. There would be time for self-loathing and regrets, but it wasn't now. Ksara needed them now more than ever. "They have her," he said. "The Horror Knights still have her."

CHAPTER FORTY-EIGHT

KSARA

K sara drifted between worlds.

There was a world of pain—a throbbing, desperate ache in her throat and a chill pressed against her skin that didn't numb the hurt, but added to it.

And then there was a world of fear. Fear that wasn't quite her own. Two figures ran through a cavern brimming with treasure. The kind of treasure that Coronata would trade her favorite lovers for. Both of the figures were some kind of Luminent and they bounded across the stone floor as swift and agile as deer.

A claw the size of a wagon smashed down between the two Luminents and they tumbled to the ground with the force of the blow.

Lorelle! The softer voice pleaded in her mind. *Get up! Run!*

The dragon lowered its face down to the woman Luminent. Its scales were as black as any noktum and its curved claws scratched lazy scars into the cavern ground. Its voice rumbled low and Ksara's fear peaked. Her whole body willed to be there. To stand between that woman and the dragon. To whisk her far away.

But she'd never seen that woman before in her life.

Then back to the pain. That throbbing that started in her throat and rattled through her teeth and skull. She blinked her eyes open but saw only black. She still smelled the musk of the lizard. Heard its heavy footsteps shuffle against the sand. If she listened close, between the pulsing beat in her own skull and the thump of voices that weren't her own, she could even hear the Horror Knights many, many mouths twitch and smack their lips or click their teeth.

Back to the fear, but this time the quiet voice was gone. And that pulsing, angry voice hammered through her skull with words she couldn't quite understand. It commanded her. Challenged her. She saw a hulking silhouette standing on the parapet of a dark castle, looking out on bursts of light in the distance. Greens. Blues. Reds. And smoke accumulating on the horizon. An invasion. An army.

And a new plan.

The figure dissolved into shadow. A darkness. A wave of black that engulfed the castle, the forest—everything. Then the thoughts fractured. The voice screamed louder but the words became a chorus of sounds.

Ksara's body fell, her eyes opened, and the pain took her away from the vision. Pulling her back into the torment of every wheezing, burning breath. A hand grabbed her by the hair and new pain burned across her skull as it dragged her across smooth stone littered with sand. The sand rubbed her skin raw as she tried to kick and struggle, but mostly just flailed weakly under the Horror Knight's iron grip.

This time when the pain stopped, Ksara hadn't drifted into another dream, another world. She'd merely stopped moving and the hand released her.

What's more, she could make out the outlines of the Horror Knight as he strode away from her then stopped a few paces from her, turning back. As she stared at him, she realized he was not alone.

She was not alone.

Four more Horror Knights encircled Ksara where she lay, each the same distance from her in a circle. And each watching her from those bright yellow eyes.

A beam of light came from an entryway beyond where the air smelled less like the stanch of lizard. If she could get to her feet—and somehow get through the barrier of Horror Knights—she could escape. Find Ulric and the crew. Get the Allarune and leave the island behind.

"Who do you serve?" A voice whispered and Ksara startled. That was not a voice from her head. But it was quiet. Furtive. She glanced about the room to find its owner, but found only the five Horror Knights and their impassive stares.

"Who is your master?" The squeaky voice repeated. "Speak or die."

Ksara pivoted on the ground. "I—" she croaked the word. The sound burned and slid about in her throat. "I—don't know what you're asking."

"You bear the master's mark," a different voice said, this one a grumble of thunder.

Something moved to her left and she swung around, but as soon as she'd turned the movement was gone. "Who are you?"

A hoarse voice replied and this time she saw the mouth move on the Horror Knight just in front of her. The mouth was on the thing's shoulder and its lips formed the words, "We are the Rha'jaheem."

"The Witnesses," another voice rumbled from another Horror Knight. The one sounded old and weathered.

"The Waiting," a high, young voice added.

"What do you want from me?" Ksara asked.

"Which of the Masters do you serve?" A new voice asked, this one smooth and calm.

"Masters?"

"Eldroi."

"Giants."

"Masters of all things living."

The chorus of voices quieted and Ksara rallied her strength

and got to her feet. It took more effort and focus still to keep her legs from buckling beneath her and crumbling back to the ground. She swayed. She gritted her teeth. But she stayed upright. Then she said, "I have no master."

"Lies!"

"I feel him near!"

"She's a worm who only sees the soil not the garden."

"Insolent mortal!"

"Xos ..."

The quiet shadows gathered about Ksara's feet agitated at the name, swirling and whipping and curling.

The Horror Knights and their many mouths quieted then, but the voice inside Ksara's skull grew to a fevered frenzy. She held her head between her hands and breathed. The voice shouted louder and louder. She clenched her jaw. Her head was going to tear in two like an overripe melon on a vine, but she couldn't let that voice free. She couldn't let it overtake her thoughts as she had in Nokte Murosa. She screamed and fell to her knees.

As soon as her knees touched the stone floor, the voice quieted to a whisper.

"Insolent mortal," a mouth on a Horror Knight's chest said, its voice booming and deep. "You will learn reverence to your Master."

"Master?" Ksara breathed the word and her whole body went numb.

And the voice inside her mind answered, clear and booming: *I am Xos!*

The shadows rose around her then. They passed through her skin and entered her veins and muscles and bones and the cold owned her body. Moving her legs without her consent and bringing her to stand with strength that wasn't her own. The shadow lifted her then, propelling her high above the Horror Knights' heads.

The Horror Knights lowered themselves to one knee and bowed their heads.

"I have returned," Ksara said in a booming voice she recognized. But it wasn't her own.

CHAPTER FORTY-NINE

ULRIC

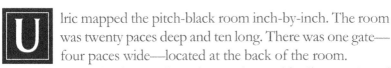

Ulric mapped the pitch-black room inch-by-inch. The room was twenty paces deep and ten long. There was one gate— four paces wide—located at the back of the room.

In between the four walls, as best as he could tell, was a lot of sand and the captainless *Falco* crew.

He examined the gate for the fourth time. Testing its weight. Feeling for its hinges. Trying to jostle it back and forth.

"Ksara hid you from the Horror Knights that passed us," Coronata said from the corner of the cell where she'd no doubt done the impossible and found a spot against the wall where she could lean and look comfortable.

"Yes," Genove replied. Coronata and Merewen had wanted the story from Ulric, of course. But he'd been sullen and pacing the room, so they'd settled on the scholar for information. "Ulric and I tucked into a crevice between two boulders, as Ksara instructed, and then she stood in front of us and the shadow hid us all from view as the—well, what you call Horror Knights— passed."

"How did they find you, then?" Merewen asked. She was closer to Ulric than the rest. She hadn't been more than three paces from him since he'd landed in a wheezing, gasping pile of numb limbs on the cell floor.

Genove sighed and the emotion sounded rehearsed. Mimicked. And Ulric realized that he hadn't seen the man react in genuine feeling since he'd been challenged by the Orator in the forest. And the only raw emotion he'd shown then was a cold, contemptuous rage.

"We could have been safe," Genove continued, "But as soon as they'd passed, Ulric had an … episode."

Coronata scoffed. "Episode? What do you mean, *episode?*"

Ulric's shoulders bunched up near his ears and his fingers clenched into fists. He wanted to find the flimsy scholar in the dark and rip him in two.

But mostly because Genove was right.

"He means I lost my mind," Ulric said. "Thought I saw monsters all around me. And I ran out to meet them. To give Ksara a chance to escape." He laughed a dry, hopeless laugh.

"You saw monsters? That weren't the Horror Knights?" Coronata asked.

He couldn't explain what had happened to him. It had been as if he'd blinked and he'd stepped back into the nightmare he'd had during his wrestle with death. Except this time Ksara was near. She was just behind him and the monsters' eyes were looking for her, not him.

He'd rather die over and over for an eternity than watch his sister get ripped apart in front of him.

"They weren't the Horror Knights," Ulric said after a long pause. "They were in the trees."

"Scholar, you're an expert of monsters and nightmares," Atlas said.

Ulric startled a little at the voice.

"Praise Grina, Senji, and all the rest," Coronata said with a smile in her voice. "Atlas is awake."

"I don't make a habit of sleeping with an enemy in the camp," he said.

"You were snoring a minute ago," Coronata said.

"And you were about to ask me a question," he said. "Then you didn't. It's a specific kind of skill."

Coronata laughed. "If I start actually liking Atlas, someone please get me to a healer!"

"And if the pirate starts to tolerate me, please just gut me with my own sword," Atlas said. "But I'm rather curious what the esteemed scholar, master of the Nokte Murosan Academy thinks of the monsters Ulric saw."

"There were no monsters save the Horror Knights," Genove said. "I suspect whatever he saw was an effect of his injuries or the Horror Knights themselves."

"The Horror Knights themselves?" Atlas asked.

"The Orator had a similar episode."

The cell quieted for a long moment.

"I was hoping to skewer the lunatic with my own sword anyway," Coronata said with a forced laugh.

"If the Horror Knights cause hallucinations," Atlas said, "then why haven't we had any?"

"Weaker minds."

Rage flashed through Ulric and he stepped toward Genove's voice. Merewen's hand clamped down on his shoulder, keeping him where he stood. He hadn't even realized the Usaran woman was so near him until that moment.

"How about we kill you now, scholar," Ulric growled.

"And doom your sister?" Genove replied, a smile in his voice. "I am her salvation."

"Her salvation?" Coronata scoffed. "Ksara doesn't need anyone's salvation. Least of all yours."

"She was about to be hanged for killing twelve citizens of Nokte Murosa," Genove said.

"We were going to free her," Merewen interjected.

"But would she have gone with you?" Genove asked. "Ask her own brother—Ulric! Would Ksara have left that hall without a plan to redeem herself?"

Ulric swallowed down the tightness in his throat and the motion made it ache anew. "And you would not have entered the Hall if you didn't think you could benefit from her power."

"I never claimed to be doing this for charity."

"Then what have you to gain from my sister?"

"Knowledge," Genove said, but the word rang hollow. It was a half-truth, at best.

Ulric wrapped his hands around the gate and squeezed tighter and tighter until the sharp edges bit through his skin and his blood wet the metal. Then he threw his shoulder into the barrier again and again and again. The pain came and he welcomed it. He needed to get Ksara out of here. And he'd rip free of this cell with is bare hands to do it.

Sweat joined blood and dirt and sand to coat Ulric's skin. His bad leg screamed with each impact and pivot, but he toiled still.

Then the gate shuddered and Ulric stopped. Listened.

"It worked!" Coronata called out with a laugh.

"And he's still mostly alive," Atlas said. "That's something."

The gate rattled again and Ulric's leg throbbed anew. He frowned.

"That's not the gate," Merewen said.

A moment later, sand rushed around them, emptying like a cracked fountain. Ulric beckoned the light to his fingertips and the heat moved slowly from his chest and down his shoulders and arms to his fingertips. Fatigue had the better of him, but he called the magic anyways.

When he snapped and filled the cell with light, he saw the black sand on the floor tumbling to the edges of the room and pouring down a crack there.

And the floor inched upward.

He glanced up, but there was no ceiling above them. And the floor propelled them higher and higher, ripping his hands free of the gate and thrusting them into the darkness above.

CHAPTER FIFTY

KSARA

 s soon as the voice in Ksara's mind resolve into words—as soon as it declared itself as Xos—Ksara lost control of her own body.

She wanted to scream. To run from the room. To flee the Horror Knights bent before her. All her will thrashed about her mind, but she couldn't even get her small finger to obey.

That thrumming, deep voice of the shadow had control of her now and as soon as the shadow brought her back down to the stone floor, she strode past the kneeling Horror Knights, coming within inches of them. She exited the room at a determined clip, passing through an opening Ksara hadn't even seen in the black wall and then mounting steps triple the height and depth of any stairs she'd climbed. And while she wheezed her exertion through her raw throat, her body would not relent the pace.

Footsteps followed her up the stairs, heavy and steady.

At the top of the staircase, orange and red light spilled across the black stone and she walked toward it, blinking away the temporary blindness while her feet stepped quick and sure.

When she stopped, it was at the edge of an audience box at the top of an open-air stadium. It was big enough to seat all of Notke Murosa's citizens. Three spires jutted out of the walls hundreds of feet into the sky and every inch of the building, the seats, the walls, the spires, were made with the same dull, black stone.

And below, at the center of the spectacle, was a pit with a black sand floor and dozens and dozens of gates embedded into the walls. Even at this distance, she could see movement behind those gates.

Not gates—cages. Those were cages.

This was the Serkir Nuraghi.

Ksara's insides churned and her heart raged so hard against her chest that it should have knocked her off center. But her body didn't even tremble. It stood steady, her face forward, watching.

The five Horror Knights arrived and moved to either side of her. She winced at their nearness, or tried to. Again, her exterior remained implacable.

"We have cared well for your creations, Master Xos," the Horror Knight to Ksara's left spoke, the words leaving the mouth on his neck. "We shall show you its strength."

Xos.

Even the name filled her with terror. Who was this voice in her mind? And how could it now control her body like a puppet on a string?

The Horror Knights had said the word Eldroi. Had called Xos a Giant. She'd heard of Giants in stories told in the Demaijos court, most often on the lips of her own mother. She'd delighted in the legends and had flourished them differently depending on the guests they entertained. Nobility from Triada? Then Senji and Grina were forbidden lovers who die in each other's arms on the battlefield. Ambassadors from Imprevar? Grina created a winged horse and outwitted a sword that speaks to her mind. When the visitor knew all of her mother's stories, she'd tell the one about the Giants—enormous magical beings who created land and noktum and even the races, only to turn on all of them.

The legends were stories. Trifling little entertainments her mother used to prove she was more than the queen's personal guard, but her sister. Her equal in education and polish, despite her duty.

But Ksara was living one of those legends now as she stood beside the monsters who'd plucked her up by the throat like a wayward chicken and hauled her to this very nuraghi and now stood at her side. Her very own court of monsters and she their unwilling master.

One of the Horror Knights spoke, this time from a mouth near his navel, "The exhibition is ready, Master."

Ksara stepped forward, the movement unbidden and that low, pulsing voice inside her head now exited her mouth, "Release the Worldbreaker."

The Horror Knight sidestepped to the right and triggered a stone on the floor, indistinguishable from the rest. The stone shifted down with a thunk and a rumble echoed throughout the arena.

For a moment, all Ksara could feel was the tremor beneath legs that wouldn't flee. She was more a captor now than she ever had been and that terror would have chilled her, if there'd been anything inside her that wasn't numb already from the shadow.

A split appeared in the arena floor, dividing it into two jagged halves with a deep crevice between. The rumbling stilled and the sound of metal grating on metal overcame the air as all of the cages inside the arena opened at once and monsters slithered, stalked, and flapped out of their enclosures.

The first to exit was a spider on thirty-foot-tall legs. It launched out of the small cage and scuttled about the arena, the pincers at its mouth snapping.

Three giant otters flew into the air, each the size of a horse and wagon. They bared their teeth at the spider and the spider froze, coiling its legs beneath it, readying for the attack.

A Manticore staggered out of one of the cages, flapping its wings and shaking out its mane.

Opposite the Manticore stalked six Kyolars. Each black cat

was smaller than the Manticore. They grouped together and avoided the larger cat-like monster, opting instead to circle toward dark, scuttling monsters Ksara had never seen before.

They looked like cockroaches. Ridiculously large cockroaches, but on their antenna were round orbs. Flesh colored orbs. Faces! They had human faces on their antenna.

The last creatures to tumble out of their cage were five humans who might as well have been Delvers for the way the other monsters dwarfed them.

No!

Ksara tried to scream the word. She tried to wrestle any sound out of her mouth at all.

No! Not them. No!

But none of the words escaped.

You gave him your power, that quiet, agitated voice replied in her head. And somehow she knew it belonged to the Usaran Shadowvar. *You gave Xos back his mind and now he'll use your body.*

Help me! That's my brother ... my family. Help them! Please!

I cannot fight for you. But I might be able to show you the way.

CHAPTER FIFTY-ONE

ULRIC

The cell jerked to a stop and Ulric's leg finally gave out. Pain exploded through him like a blacksmith's billow, hot and unrelenting. He gasped and writhed in the sand. His hands tightened around his left knee, but the pain would not abate. He breathed through each wave of it through gritted teeth and a hand found his shoulder.

"Be still, Ulric," Merewen said as she knelt beside him. Her touch settled the panic rising in him. And he breathed a little deeper.

"What happened?" Coronata asked, her voice closer in the absolute dark.

"Ulric is down," Merewen said. "The splint could only hold for so long. Should we make another, Atlas?"

"Sure," he said. "In the pitch dark. With only sand. Let's make a splint!"

"We have to do something," Merewen said.

"Grina's smelly boots," Atlas swore and his armor clanked as he stomped his way over to Ulric. Soon his hands joined Ulric's, prodding and feeling the aggravated injury.

Finally, Atlas sat back and sighed. "What do we have other than sand?"

"I have arm bracers," Merewen said. "And laces from my boots."

"Atlas has—I don't know—a lot of armor," Coronata said. "If it's okay this bracer smells like a chamber pot and horse shit."

Atlas growled.

Coronata laughed. "Right. Sacred armor. Can't help out."

"We each hold something sacred," Merewen said.

"Must it also smell bad?" Coronata asked with a chuckle. "To be sacred I mean."

Ulric wrestled his jaw open between waves of hot radiating pain to chide the group, but he only succeeded in groaning louder. Which worked in its own way. For now.

"Give me the bracer and the laces," Atlas said.

Merewen shuffled about in the dark to comply and in a moment Atlas repositioned Ulric's leg, wrapping the bracer around the back of his knee and cinching the cording around it. The air left Ulric's lungs as the Imprevari worked. Heat overwhelming his body and sweat gathering on his brow.

Merewen's hand found his shoulder again, light and gentle.

He wrapped his hands around hers and clamped his jaw shut tight. No need to moan and wiggle while Atlas worked.

Ulric wanted to look up into Merewen's face and see the soft concern in her blue eyes. See her cheeks flush pink under his gaze. And smile to tease out more of the color. The complete black hid all of her from him, but just imagining it kept him breathing deep and long.

"Done," Atlas declared.

The pain waned some. The new splint kept whatever had gone wrong in Ulric's leg in the right area, but his leg throbbed against the restraint so hard it felt like his leg might burst through it at any moment.

"Can he walk?" Coronata asked.

"Any other person and I'd say no. Not for weeks," Atlas said.

"But this Demaijos? He'll hobble around. I mean, a seventy-year-old beggar with half a leg and a reed for a walking stick will be faster, but he'll walk."

"Now's the time for him to try," Genove said.

"Really?" Coronata asked. "What insight do you have now, scholar? Is it another monster that can miraculously heal Ulric's leg and whisk us off this island in a blanket of clouds and rainbows? No? How about—"

The grating of metal against metal cut off Coronata's words. The sound grew louder and higher, the screech almost deafening and then bright light spilled into the cell.

"Grina's corset …"

Their cell had opened out into a vast arena floor covered in the same black sand as the cell. More cages, just like theirs, rimmed the fifty-foot-tall arena walls, their gates grinding open in unison and then quieting at the same moment.

Empty stadium seats extended out from behind the walls culminating in wicked spires stabbing into the blood-red sky. New sounds spilled out into the arena. Clicking, scuffing, groaning, and finally a roar that reverberated in Ulric's ribcage.

Atlas stepped toward the opening. "What in the gods was that?"

"Monsters," Genove said, the word joyous in his mouth.

Ulric stared at the arena with new apprehension. This wasn't just an island where monsters still lived. This is where they fought. "Then we don't enter," Ulric said. "We let them kill each other and find a way out."

"It won't work," Genove said, that stupid smug tone to his voice.

"And you know that how?"

The ground lurched again, raising them upward inch-by-inch. Genove pointed up at the ceiling where dozens of black pikes jutted from the stone, each crusted with dried gore and corpses too old and mangled to identify.

"Shall I say more?" Genove said with a curve of a smile.

Atlas marched out into the arena. Coronata followed with a

smile, unsheathing her rapier from her belt. Genove followed behind the soldier and pirate. But Merewen hesitated within the cage, staring at the pikes in the ceiling mere moments from impaling her head.

Ulric heaved himself up from the ground with a groan and shuffled his leg as fast as he could, but Atlas had been right—an ancient beggar could have beat him in a foot race just now. The opening was barely two feet and he bent over double to avoid being skewered.

Merewen stood her ground, reaching up and ripping one of the pikes out of the ceiling with her bare hands, brandishing the rusted, grimy weapon as if it were a gift from a king. Then repeating the maneuver.

Ulric still had two normal steps to the opening, but at his rate, he wasn't going to make it. Not even if Merewen ripped out a dozen more of them.

"Merewen," Ulric said. "Get out!"

Merewen didn't reply. But she grabbed Ulric by the collar of his shirt and threw him toward the opening. He let out a surprised shout, tumbled out the opening and down a ten-foot drop to the arena floor.

The impact knocked the breath out of him and clapped his legs together. He wheezed and coughed into the sand, blinking back white spots on his vision.

Merewen landed on her feet beside him, pulling him back upright. "Sorry."

"I owe you one."

"More than one," she said with a smile, handing him one of the four pikes in her hands. Then her gaze moved passed Ulric and the humor left her face. Her jaw set in a hard line. "Not here, Atlas. Not here."

Ulric pivoted on his good leg and swore. This time Merewen didn't even chide him for the blasphemy. They both just started forward, Merewen at a sprint and Ulric at a hobble.

"Atlas!" Ulric hollered, but the sound was lost in the roar of a pack of Kyolars. All of which were sprinting toward them.

And the Imprevari was racing to meet them with Coronata's rapier in his hand.

Coronata knelt beside a collapsed Genove, then, when she spotted Merewen, she dashed after her, grabbing a spare pike from her and rushing toward Atlas and the Kyolars. Both of them still thirty feet from catching the Imprevari. Atlas bellowed his own roar at the charging Kyolars and slashed the blade at the first monster, slicing it with the tip of the blade. The monster roared again and its fellows converged on him, engulfing him in black as surely as any noktum.

Ulric limped past Genove, who groaned on the sand, blood oozing from a wound on his arm. "What happened?"

Blood spilled past his fingers and he laughed. Loud and clear.

Ulric almost paused to stare down at the maniacal scholar.

"Predators and prey," he said. "You're all going to die."

CHAPTER FIFTY-TWO

MEREWEN

When the Kyolars folded in around Atlas, Merewen slowed her steps, leaned backward, and vaulted a pike through the air with all her might. It landed in the throng of black bodies and something cried out.

Four Kyolars turned from the pack and loped toward her. One of them with her pike lodged in its shoulder. She widened her stance, clasped her last pike between her two hands, and readied herself for battle.

Bursts of profanity came from the other pile of Kyolar and that gave Merewen a measure of hope. Atlas was alive. For now. And she intended to keep him that way. No matter how hard he tried to the contrary.

The Kyolars came at her from three sides, the fourth lingering a step back. Their attacks came all at once. Claws slashing from the front. Jaws the length of her arm snapping at her sides. In a split second, she calculated her odds. She could take a few slashes from the claws and keep fighting, but if she ended up in one of their mouths, that was the end.

So, she jammed the point of the pike into the mouth on the right, aiming up and holding tight to the shaft of the pike and jamming it into the cat's throat. It gargled and its momentum knocked her back five feet, pushing her farther away from the other Kyolar. She still caught a single claw down her shoulder. The wound burned hot. She thwacked the ground flat on her back, skidded across the sand, and then rolled to her side just as another Kyolar was on top of her, slashing its claws at her stomach. She twisted, rolling to her side to dodge the first strike, but catching the second down her back. She cried out, turned, and kicked her boot into the Kyolar's eye socket. It took a turn to scream and she staggered back to her feet.

Only to find Coronata leaping at one of the Kyolars, grabbing hold of the embedded pike and ripping it from the monster's shoulder. Blood sprayed them both and the creature collapsed to the sand, hissing and spewing blood. The two standing Kyolars hesitated now, sizing up the women. Coronata stood panting and smiling. Staring down the monsters with a bloody pike in her hands while Merewen's back wound dripped blood to the black sand.

Obscenities still flew from the other group of Kyolar and one of them fell dead, its anguished cry sending a shiver through its fellows. All of the monsters retreated, regrouping a dozen feet away from the humans and leaving the dead and dying alone on the black sand. Atlas leaned against the dead Kyolar, covered in so much gore none of his armor was visible beneath it.

Ulric hobbled up beside them. He breathed heavily and the pain of his leg showed on his face. But he smiled at the dying monster. "Three monsters down and only their angry kin to go. And whatever that is." Ulric pointed at the center of the arena where a thirty-foot-tall spider paced back and forth, interested but unwilling to cross some kind of threshold.

"And those," he said again. This time pointing back and to the right of the spider where hundreds of insect-like creatures scuttled back and forth. They were hard to make out at this distance, but they were big, even at the feet of the impossibly large spider.

"And that," he said again, but this time he didn't need to point. The Kyolars had turned their attention on the thing, too, their heads low and their tails twitching quickly back and forth. They growled; the sound so low it seemed to rumble through the ground itself.

It was a black cat, double the size of any one Kyolar with a thick black mane and leathery, dark wings. It loped closer and the Kyolar backed away, snarling and baring their teeth.

"A Manticore," Merewen said. She should be terrified of the creature, but instead she felt an awe overcome her. These creatures occupied whole legends in the north. Beloved and feared. Thought to be lost souls of heroes, bound to the noktum to bring order to the chaos.

And it did have an almost human expression of abject determination as it charged at Atlas and the dead Kyolar.

"Atlas!" Merewen sprinted toward the soldier.

"Let him be!" Coronata called after her. "Merewen!"

The pirate didn't speak with conviction. Though she bickered with the Imprevari, though Merewen sensed the woman had been genuinely hurt by the Imprevari people, the pirate queen didn't actually want Atlas to die. She shuffled after Merewen, letting Ulric lean against her as they moved after her.

Atlas leaned against the dead monster, panting hard and looking about the arena. He stiffened when he saw the Manticore approach, but he did not run. He just pulled the stolen, gore-crusted rapier from the Kyolars neck and turned toward death. And Merewen wondered if the man were blessed with luck in battle or cursed to never die and end his misery.

Merewen reached the Imprevari just as the Manticore leapt forward, unfurling its wings and covering twenty-five feet in a single bound.

She tackled the man to the ground and pitched him sideways and away from the carcass. Sand rubbed into the wounds on her back and she bit back a groan as she held Atlas fast. He tried to cry out and she crammed her hand against his mouth.

The Manticore landed atop the dead Kyolar and ripped into

the flesh the next instant, feeding in wet rips just feet away from where Merewen and Atlas lay. All the thing would need to do was turn its head a few degrees to the left and it would see them. Weak, very killable additions to its feast that they were.

But it tore zealously into the meal, bits of flesh and flecks of blood splattering across Merewen and Atlas. For a moment, she thought Atlas would lean into his better sense. That he wouldn't taunt death when it drooled carnage from its jaws.

She was wrong.

Atlas's expression darkened and an instant later he whipped the rapier in a wide arc and sliced the Manticore's front leg with the blade.

Blood sprang from the wound, but the Manticore didn't make a sound. It just lifted its head out of the carcass and stared down at the two humans, prone on their backs with only two pieces of metal to fend off tooth and claw.

A shadow crossed over top of them, large enough to eclipse the dying light of the sun.

Two more shadows, just as large, crossed over the light again. The Manticore finally moved its attention upward and the hair on its spine raised. It roared a deep, ear-splitting roar and a blur of brown dove down at the Manticore, screeching high and loud.

The Manticore flexed its claws into its meal and roared up at the sky just as two more of the flying attackers came after it. One of them slashed at the Manticore's back and it turned to deal with the strike while the other grabbed hold of the dead Kyolar's head and began lifting it into the air.

The new attacking monsters looked like otters, but exaggerated to the size of a wagon, with sharp fangs and small eyes. They dipped and twirled through the air as freely as their kin did water.

These were Sleeths.

The Manticore bellowed its rage again, raking the second Sleeth across the head and shoulders. The Sleeth cried out, but didn't release its prize and the second Sleeth attacked the Manticore from behind, lodging its own teeth on the Manticore's neck. The Manticore shook its head, tossing the Sleeth aside, but the second Sleeth already had the dead Kyolar several feet in the air.

The Manticore coiled and leapt into flight after its meal.

Merewen pushed from the ground in an instant, dragging Atlas to his feet as well.

"You are a fool," she said to his face. Or the bits of his face still visible beneath the blood and black sand. "We'll all die trying to keep you breathing."

"Then let me die," Atlas growled back.

Merewen grabbed hold of Atlas by the collar of his breastplate and hauled him away from the battle happening just above their heads. He tried to resist, but whether it was wounds she couldn't see or just battle weariness, he didn't have enough fight in him to stop her.

She spotted Coronata and Ulric and stopped short for a moment.

Her friends had the other two dying Kyolar at their back, the pack of its fellows all around them, and a Sleeth swooping down just over their heads.

Atlas jerked Merewen's hand free of his armor. "Now who's running at death?"

"I'm running to my friends," she said. "Maybe you'll live long enough to know the difference."

Merewen took off at a jog. She had no weapons. But she wasn't about to watch any of the crew get dismantled by a monster while she could do something. Surely she could do something.

Something.

Just six feet from the closest Kyolar, Merewen prepared to leap on its back. Surprise seemed to work well on these Kyolars, surrounded as they were by even fiercer predators than themselves.

As she planted her foot to jump, a tremor rumbled through the ground and pitched Merewen to the sand. Kyolar feet were all around her, stepping on her legs and side. The claws puncturing her skin. She kicked and punched at the limbs, waiting for the teeth to sink into her.

In an instant the limbs were gone. The Kyolar were gone. Merewen pushed herself up to her elbow and she saw Ulric and Coronata running around the dying Kyolar toward her. Atlas was coming, too.

Coronata reached her first, prodding the bleeding wounds and then pulling her up to her feet.

"Where did they go?"

"Away," Coronata said. "They ran away."

"Away from what?"

"That," Atlas said.

A dark mist rose up and out of the center of the arena, curling over the sand and spreading out in every direction.

"What is that?" Merewen asked.

"Let's let one of the monsters find out first, eh?" Ulric said and he began limping toward the nearest wall of the arena, at least a hundred feet away.

Merewen moved to Ulric's side, put her bleeding shoulders beneath his arm and helped him along. He didn't protest. Neither had the energy for that game. Coronata took his other side and Atlas strode to the lead, holding his stolen rapier in front of him and perpetually scanning the arena around them for more and new hazards.

They made it twenty feet before the sounds began.

Merewen had heard animals in distress. A bear cub beside its dead mother. An injured calf. An angry wolf. But she'd never heard sounds like these.

They shook her to her center. Roars of utter rage. Sounds that could only be interpreted as an outright challenge. Each voiced in different tones and pitches.

Atlas glanced behind them and his face grew even more solemn.

"What's happening?" Merewen asked. She couldn't see around Ulric and couldn't stop pulling the man forward to look.

"Nothing good," he said and he took up a jog.

Screams of pain joined the rage-sounds. Punctuating them like beats to a drum.

They made it to the wall, wheezing and bleeding, but Atlas didn't stop. He turned to the right and took them along the edge of the wall even faster than before.

As they turned, Merewen caught sight of the full arena again. The Kyolars had turned on each other, ripping into their own kin until it died and then moving onto the next. The Sleeths did the same and when only one victor flew through the air, it dove at the spider and tackled the thing to the ground, ripping out flesh as the spider kicked and twisted, plunging its pincers into the Sleeth.

Every monster in sight was doing the same. She hadn't realized the restraint displayed in the monsters before until beholding this savagery.

And the dark mist rolled on, covering all but the edges of the arena. Only five feet from them now. The had nowhere to run. The cages were gone. The wall beside them stretched fifty feet into the air. And they couldn't outrun or outthink this sinister air.

It hit Atlas first. He reeled backward to try to avoid it, but paused, his body going stiff and then he inhaled a long, deep gulp of the air.

And turned toward his friends.

The whites of his eyes were gone. All of it was black. The color of the sand, the mist, the nuraghi stone behind him.

Then he adjusted his grip on the rapier and lunged right at Ulric's heart.

CHAPTER FIFTY-THREE

KSARA

Don't watch, the Shadowvar's voice insisted.

Don't watch the Kyolars ripping into her friends. Don't watch their desperate, futile defense. Don't watch Ulric hobble about, wounded and nearly left behind. He wouldn't be able to keep up with them. He wouldn't be able to survive long at all....

Her stomach twisted tighter and bile burned her throat. Coated her tongue. She wondered if she could vomit or if that action, too, had been taken from her by this curse. By this being living inside her body.

Not a curse, the spirit of a Giant. Xos. Now focus. Senji's boots! You have to focus or they're all dead!

Ksara wanted to scream. She wanted to race down the steps and rip the Kyolar off of Atlas and away from Merewen. She wanted to put her shoulder beneath Ulric and let him lean on her. She wanted—

Stop! There was power to this other voice. It usually held a quiet sort of certainty, but now it raged inside her. A coal stoked into a crackling flame. *You're running from him. Hiding from him. You have to face him if you want to save your friends!*

She ground her teeth and pulled her focus away from the horror playing out before her eyes. How could she be running or hiding from this thing, this so-called Giant when she couldn't move?

Your power connects you to the Dark. He is a part of the Dark. One of many. He's used that connection to take control of your body. But you can use the same bridge to disrupt it.

How?

Close your eyes and see. See what he is seeing.

Ksara wanted to argue. To fight against this other voice—whoever he was! What did he know of this torment? How could he possibly be able to guide her through this nightmare?

And did she have a choice?

Forcing out a shallow breath, Ksara wrestled her eyelids closed. The commanding voice—Xos—growled inside her head and her eyes shot open again, her grip on the smallest part of her own body slipping away in an instant.

Let him have it for a moment. Wait until he's not thinking of you anymore. Try again.

Try again! Ksara glanced toward the arena and caught a glimpse of a maned cat with dragon wings feeding on a dead Kyolar. But where was Ulric? Had Atlas fallen? Merewen? Coronata?

Senji's boots! Quiet your mind! It's a wonder the whole arena can't hear your thoughts!

She frowned, or tried to, but only succeeded in lowering her brows a fraction of a centimeter.

Your panicked thoughts might as well be whales flopping about on a marble floor. They draw attention to you! You must be silent or you will never cross over into Xos's mind. And you will never have a chance to help your friends.

She would have nodded then, but her head held perfectly still. Instead she settled the fear raging inside her and let it sink to the bottom of her gut. She'd feel that sensation later. Deal with that terror when safety came. Right now she was in a battlefield. One she didn't quite understand, but she knew how to treat a battlefield. Calm, decisiveness filled her.

Better. Now close your eyes.

Ksara didn't fight to close her eyes—she just let them slip closed. Centimeter-by-centimeter. Keeping her mind quiet. Her fear subdued.

She didn't feel Xos stir. And her eyes slipped closed and stayed there.

About time. Now find that place inside you where Xos is. Enter like a thief. Like a shadow. See what he is seeing.

She gritted her teeth, suppressed the wave of fear swelling inside her. Ulric described the seat of his power as a Lux inside his ribcages. But she'd always imagined her own power as a noktum. And not just a noktum overtaking the wild lands of Noksonon, but a mass of angry air invading the palace in the Demaijos city of Merneith.

A bitter chill throbbed through Ksara as she realized that Xos had invaded her as completely as the noktum had the palace in her mind.

But she conjured up the image anyway. The solemn stone steps. The seven pillars carved in the likenesses of the Seven Sisters—the seven women who had forged Demaijos out of war, plague, and obscurity. That her mind conjured this place as the host of the abomination of the noktum was blasphemous to her very core.

She imagined herself walking up those familiar white steps. Imagined herself, not in her typical Demaijos tunic, but in black leathers and cloth bound sandals that made not even a whisper of sound against the stone. Stalking like a thief in her own mind, she mounted the final stair.

The noktum waited for her there. Hungry tentacles and foreboding black.

Enter in. Don't wait for him to see you.

Gathering her wits, her will, Ksara took one step toward the noktum, passing that threshold on the stone floor where she knew the tentacles could reach her. The tentacles didn't grab her, though. They quested about the space mindlessly. Distracted.

She guessed that was a good sign, held her breath, and entered into the noktum proper.

Black overwhelmed her sight for a moment and she wanted to scream at the voice in her head—what was she supposed to see here when she couldn't see at all?

Don't.

His voice was quieter than ever. Not a distant sort of quiet, but a tense whisper just in her ear.

They won't last long.

Ksara spent a fraction of a second imagining Ulric, Coronata, Merewen, and Atlas battling monsters with scarcely more than their hands. Her concentration faltered, the noktum wavered, and her eyes almost opened.

You help them here. Now hurry. By Senji! Hurry!

Steadying herself, she strode deeper into the black. Even a few steps in, she couldn't be sure which direction she'd entered the noktum from. All she could do was take another step into the darkness and try not to think of Ulric. She had to focus. She had to try.

She didn't know how long she wandered in the black. Soon it became a sort of rhythm. Feel the suffocating panic of the place, breathe, take a step. Repeat. Again and again and again until the black began to lighten to gray and the gray began to form into images.

The first thing she saw was a woman. Tall in a long, black gown. A thick braid of black hair cascading down her shoulder. Her indigo eyes bright as they looked right at Ksara and right through her at the same time.

"I will join the project," she said.

Ksara hesitated. There was something in the woman's face. She wasn't quite human. And her words held no affection, but an iron-clad certainty.

What is this? Ksara whispered to the voice in her head.

Xos's mind. His memories, the voice muttered back. *Disrupt them and you disrupt his control.*

Ksara strode closer to the woman crafted in shadows only to find she stood twice Ksara's height. She stared up at the apparition like a child.

And, like a child, Ksara swung a hand toward her leg, petulantly trying to get her attention. If she could distract the vision, maybe she could distract Xos.

Ksara's hand moved through the shadow, but the woman didn't turn her gaze downward. She just stared forward with those chiseled features and eyes alive with purple shadow.

She tried again, punching the shadow this time. Still her hand moved through the air without effect.

It's not working.

Try something different.

Like what?

You're the one sharing a link with a myth, the voice retorted. *Stir up some ideas. And fast.*

"Like what?" Ksara let the words burst out of her mouth.

The Giant woman's gaze dipped down to find her. The noktum whipped into a fury around her, tentacles striking her, passing through her. Filling her with that bitter, numbing cold.

He heard you. Run!

Ksara dodged a tentacle and sprinted into the dark. When her legs tired, she walked again. As soon as she did, the black began to lighten around her. This time the lighter air swirled and formed a pit of wretched creatures. Humans, Delvers, Taur-El, Luminents, and races she'd never even heard of in Merewen's most obscure legends. All of them starved and beaten. Ribs showing. Eyes hollow. Blood and dirt crusted on their tight skin. They shuffled about in the hole, restless and reeking of despair.

Three more of those towering statues of beings stood at the entrance to the pit. One looked repulsed. The other aloof. And the third one smiled down on the scene with a pinched face and pinpricks for eyes. Delighting in it.

Ksara's anger boiled up in her and she turned back to the pit, wishing that there was something in that pit that they cared about.

Something that might, at the very least, startle them.

She imagined the woman Giant standing in the pit, as ragged and hopeless as the rest.

As she imagined it, the shadow changed. The woman stood in a ragged version of her long, black gown and she stared up at the three Giant men.

"You cannot escape me," she said.

The gleeful Giant straightened and his expression soured.

It's working. Run! Try it again!

CHAPTER FIFTY-FOUR

ATLAS

When Atlas breathed in the dark mist, his tension dissolved in a soft exhale. He didn't have to worry about monsters. He didn't have to worry about dying with the last shreds of his honor intact or proving to his own heart that he was no coward.

Worry fell away. So did the loneliness of forever wandering in a land that wasn't his own. The grief at never seeing his parents again. Never holding his sister's children and teaching them how to ride. Never galloping across the plains of Thelca in the glow of sunset where the sunlight painted the fields in streaks of burgundy and orange.

All of it left Atlas in an instant and it was blissful.

The only emotion, the only thought, that remained was rage. Simple, pure rage. It sped up his heartbeat. It added strength to his frame. Steadiness to his mind.

He adjusted his grip on the rapier in his hand and turned around to find something to stick it in. The impulse itched at his mind like biting ants scurrying about on his brain. He had to attack. To fight. To kill.

Behind him he found three candidates for his violence. A woman with a thick braid of red hair and blue tattoos curling about her jawline. Another lithe as the rapier. And a man with two different colored eyes and a wounded knee.

And he stabbed the rapier into the man's gut.

Or tried to.

The tip of the blade pierced the man's vest and tunic and kissed his skin, but went no further. Blood blossomed from the pinprick of a wound and it slithered down the thin blade, dripping to the ground.

Both Atlas and the man watched it fall.

The rage built up in Atlas then, at the sight of the blood. A promise unfulfilled. He gritted his teeth, screamed his rage into a sound more animal than human, and tried to punch the tip of the blade through the man's heart.

But his arm didn't move. The sword didn't move.

Atlas screamed and leaned into the blow. His arm quivered. He clenched his jaw so tight the bones ached. Sweat dribbled from his brow down to his beard.

Still the blade did not end the man.

The man spoke, but he didn't hear the words. The women, too.

But there was nothing in his mind and heart but hatred and this single purpose: violence.

And even here he had been thwarted.

He screamed again, pivoted his body, and punched the man with his free hand. That blow did land.

CHAPTER FIFTY-FIVE

KSARA

The shadows reformed into a forest and she stared at the trees until they transformed into copies of the Giant woman. Soon every tree wore the woman's face, the space between her humming with her intensity. Her quiet rebellion.

The shadows changed again into a hilltop bare of vegetation. Slabs of stone rimming the top of the hill where the tortured lie suffering there on slabs of stone, held with chains, but pulled apart with glowing silver threads so that their innards were on display.

Ksara ran to each face and touched them with her fingers, changing the humans and Taur-El into her face.

It's working.

And the image changed again. Ksara didn't even have to run. She stood right where she was and the shadows reformed around her now. This time to a castle wreathed in night and besieged by dragons. Fire exploded all around Ksara, boiling stone.

She stood among the pillars of flame. There were no trees to transform. No faces but her own.

So she did. She reformed her own face, her own height, her own figure, to that very Giant woman and the noktum shifted. Fled from the image.

And there, standing with the visage of another, Ksara saw the noktum itself change. Rather, it shifted into focus, the utter black actually a deep indigo with speckled lights swirling within it. Each light bobbed and danced about the ink-blue landscape forming long threads that laced back and forth, encompassing every inch of ground and air. It was like stepping into the night sky and breathing in the life of the stars.

Now you see.

And she did see. What it was, she had no idea. But she saw.

The noktum is more than shadow. It is a spell. It is magic alive with the sentience of Giants.

As she watched, the purples and indigos braided together and pulled apart, twisting and pulling and probing through the air and all the while the flecks of light inside them bobbed about.

Open your eyes.

Ksara opened her eyes and the vision of stars merged with the arena below her. The indigo air swirled around the ground of the arena, the lights bobbing about in a patchwork of lights that oozed out of the crack in the center of the arena and danced toward the outer edges. These lights acted strangely. They moved more erratically and blinked red when they neared another living creature. When the creature breathed them in, the red light beamed from inside the monster and then went dark.

And the monster attacked anything near it. Kin or foe, it did not matter. It was all claws and teeth and terror.

The lights flowed toward Ulric and the crew. They blinked red and Atlas breathed them in. His outline flashed crimson and he struck out toward Ulric—

And Ksara's hand shot out in front of her, her fingers gripping the air. Not the air in front of her, but the air inside of Atlas. The tainted lights bobbing about inside him. She grabbed hold of those, just as she had the shadow inside herself.

Atlas wrenched his other hand free and pummeled Ulric in the face.

Ksara gritted her teeth and twisted her grip tighter on the lights inside Atlas. She could barely see them now, but she knew they were there. And she threw them backward. Away from Ulric.

Atlas stumbled backward, knocking against the arena wall. He breathed out some of the lights and she wrenched the rest of them out of him. He crumbled to the ground just as more lights, more mist, inched closer to Ulric.

The thundering beat began in her head. Her hand trembled and the cold of Xos's control seeped down from her shoulder toward her fingers. She knew once the cold reached her fingertips she'd lose control of the lights. Already her vision of them began to fade.

"No," she gritted out the word between her tight jaw and she closed her hand tight and jerked it toward herself, beckoning the lights up toward herself.

Shadow shot toward her and, just before she lost sensation in her hand, she steered the dark at the Horror Knight beside her. A flash of red lit up his eyes and her hands went numb.

The Horror Knight turned to Ksara, hands outstretched and its dozens and dozens of mouths twitching and clacking their teeth. Before the Horror Knight could touch her, Xos's voice swelled inside her and her hand punched up into the air. Shadow speared up from the ground and impaled the Horror Knight. It gasped from its many mouths and went limp, black ichor splashing against the stone below.

Ksara's hand fell down to her side, her jaw tight, and the thump of Xos's voice louder than ever in her skull.

I am your master, mortal, Xos said, and her left arm rose again, hovering right in front of her face. Pain seared through the arm and she watched in horror as the flesh split in two, skin and muscled dividing to show the bone beneath. The burning agony overwhelmed her. Her legs trembled, but she couldn't fall. She gasped, but she couldn't cry out. The tear began to extend, stretching from her elbow down to her wrist. Her vision swayed. Sweat burned her eyes. She closed them—at least then she only had to experience the horror, not watch it.

Help me! Please!

She tried to go to the noktum in her head. She strained to hear the other voice inside her. But all she could hear was the panicked hammering of her own heart. All she could see in her mind was the image of her own flesh splitting in two before her very eyes.

Xos pried her eyes open again and blood rushed from the wound. As if Xos had just released the dam and now the river of red could weep down her arm, delaying the spectacle just for her.

Tears tumbled down her face. More and more blood rushed from her. Her whole body and mind swallowed in the agony pulsing from the supernatural wound.

Then, the blood stopped flowing. The muscle and flesh knitted back together and it felt as though hundreds of hot needles were doing the work. She gasped and panted, staring at her arm covered in blood, but without even a scar to mark the horror of what just happened.

I am your master. It is a lesson I do not teach twice.

Chapter Fifty-six

ULRIC

Ulric held his face. Lights flecked his vision and he blinked back the shock of the blow. His vision returned in time to see Atlas fly through the air and smack, back-first, into the arena wall. He twitched as he slid to the ground, jerking and spasming, until he finally crumpled to the black sand. When he did, he exhaled some of the dark mist from his lips.

The mist advanced on them faster than ever before. Ulric had to leap toward the wall to keep it from him, landing heavily on his injured leg with a moan. Coronata and Merewen rushed to the wall as well, Coronata in a graceful jump and Merewen in a hearty sprint.

In an instant, they'd run out of places to run. The arena was full of the supernatural mist and few of the monsters had survived its effect—Ulric spotted two Sleeths fighting in the air, the Manticore issuing a final bite to the spider, and a few of the huge roaches still swarming each other on the far side.

Thirty feet from them was another cage door, but this one had jammed before the floor had completely risen up into the ceiling, leaving a three-foot gap at the top of the opening. It would be a strain to get up in it, but it would keep them from the mist and probably the monsters.

But even that bit of hope died as the mist rushed at them.

Ulric reached to his magic, the warm core inside him that fueled his light, and found only wisps of warmth left. He'd been battered and fatigued for days on end now and the reservoir of power was all but extinguished. If he emptied that reservoir entirely—well, monsters and a supernatural mist would suddenly be the easiest of his problems.

He called the magic down to his fingertips anyways. Their prospects were slim and maybe if he used the last of his magic to create a burst of light, he could keep the mist away from them a moment or two longer.

The warmth left his chest and crept down his veins toward his hand and the black air rushed toward them, billowing into a wall that would overtake them in moments.

Ulric readied his hands in front of him. His magic might not get to his fingers in time, but he'd be ready. He'd banish the dark one more time before he died.

Merewen hooked her hand around his, lacing her fingers between his. He stiffened, surprise taking him, and then shot her a smile. She didn't even look afraid. Senji be blessed, this woman had a glimmer of hope in her bright blue eyes as she faced the doom.

He grinned wider. There were worse ways to die.

Squeezing her hand, he let the black air overwhelm them. The cold air slinked into his nose and throat. It choked him and all of his muscles tightened.

Then the air rushed away from him, thrown back by an invisible force.

He coughed as regular air reentered his mouth and his muscles released. Merewen gasped beside him, but she didn't release his hand. And he clung to hers.

Coronata recovered first, wheezing for a few breaths and then snagging Ulric by the other arm and pulling him toward the half-open cage. The black air had retreated for thirty feet in all directions and a cloud of it flew up and into the stadium.

Coronata dragged Ulric to the opening. He couldn't maneuver his injured leg fast enough so she just hauled him. Merewen picked up Atlas and carried him on her shoulder. They'd just faced down death a few times over and the gods had smiled on them somehow—none of them were willing to go another round.

At the broken cage, Ulric reached up and grabbed hold of the opening. He had to stretch to his toes to get a purchase, but he managed it. He hauled himself up and Merewen and Coronata pushed his legs up behind, careful of the bandaged one. As soon as he'd leveraged himself up into the hole, he leaned an arm down to help the others. Coronata took his hand and alighted quickly. Merewen, who stood taller than Ulric, lifted Atlas upward and Ulric and Coronata pulled him up. Then the Usaran grabbed the lip and pulled herself up with barely a grunt.

When they were all huddled inside the hole, Ulric turned to examine it properly. There were pikes in the ceiling above them and they scarcely had enough room to crawl without scraping their backs on the ancient spears. Merewen went to work right away to pull a pike down. The pike creaked and the ground rumbled.

"Don't do that," a voice said from the deeper recesses of the hole.

Ulric spun on the sound. Merewen tugged a little more on the pike and it groaned louder.

"You pull that out and we all die," the voice said again and only this time did Ulric recognize it.

"Genove?"

As soon as he said the name, he made out those bright green eyes nearly aglow in the dark a dozen feet deeper into the recess.

"You survived," Coronata said with the closest thing to respect she'd had in her voice when talking to the scholar.

"If you remove that pike, the cage will reset and this tunnel will be for naught," Genove said.

"Tunnel?" Ulric and Coronata said at once.

The scholar's eyes twinkled with that bright yearning. "I have found a way to the Allarune."

Coronata laughed. Merewen let out a captive breath. But Ulric didn't move. He'd barely trusted this man when they'd fled Nokte Murosa. Now they'd followed him through a forest, been thrashed by Horror Knights, and nearly extinguished in an arena of monsters. All with the scholar calmly and happily in the lead.

"We can't stay here," Merewen said. "The cage could reset any moment."

"And that Manticore was just crazy enough to come looking for us."

Still Ulric didn't move.

"You didn't see Ksara at the top of the stadium," Genove said, that gleeful tone to his voice. "You didn't see the Horror Knights with her. She commands them now."

Ulric's mouth dried. "You lie."

Genove's bright green eyes never wavered. "Your sister needs the Allarune more than ever before, Demaijos."

It couldn't be true. Ksara couldn't be in league with the Horror Knights now. That was a fabrication. Another way for the scholar to manipulate and move people.

But he'd seen her be overcome by the dark. He'd seen it control her while she was unconscious. What if it did the same now? Except, instead of just controlling the shadow with her unconscious mind, she was also controlling monsters?

"After you, scholar," Ulric said. "I'll be right behind you."

Genove flashed a smile in the dark, then turned and led them on.

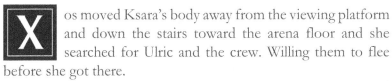

CHAPTER FIFTY-SEVEN

KSARA

Xos moved Ksara's body away from the viewing platform and down the stairs toward the arena floor and she searched for Ulric and the crew. Willing them to flee before she got there.

They couldn't guess what had taken hold of her. She imagined walking up to them, screaming in her mind for them to flee, only to have Ulric rush to her and wrap his arms around her and pull her close. She would stand stiffly there, unable to return the embrace or answer his questions. Ulric's excitement would sour to concern and all she would be able to do is stand there and wait until Xos decided what to do with them.

And the Giant had pulled apart her skin and muscles just to make her watch. Just so she'd know just how insignificant her strength was.

But she was useful to Xos. Maybe even necessary. It was the only reason she could think of that he'd be occupying her body at all.

What would he do to Ulric and the crew? He had no need for

them. And he might just tear them apart, bit by bit to prove he could. To make Ksara watch. To quell the last bit of rebellion inside this body he'd overtaken.

That thought galvanized something inside Ksara's soul. This wasn't a war she could lose. She'd didn't know how she'd win, but she was going to. She didn't have a choice. Her power had hurt enough people in the past days, but this being? This Xos?

She would die before she let him use her to hurt anyone else.

Xos's mind thumped harder and faster in her, like a pulse that wasn't her own coursing through her. She wondered if he could feel her new resolve.

She listened beneath the drum of Xos's thoughts for the quieter voice of the Shadowvar. But if he was there, she couldn't hear him.

The ground began to tremble beneath her boots. Then quake. Then pitch left and right as the crack at the center of the arena expanded into a deep chasm. If Xos hadn't had full control of Ksara's body, the movement would have thrown her to the ground. As it was, she walked a little slower, but kept her feet all the way down to the fifty-foot wall that separated spectators and their horrific sport.

She caught sight of the crew for the briefest of moments and then lost them again. They'd been running along the wall's edge and then two Sleeths killed each other in the air near them and the battle obscured her friends. When both Sleeths fell and the Manticore below keened a haggard victory over the field of monster corpses, her friends were nowhere to be found.

At the wall, Ksara climbed up and over the lip. Her pulse quickened as her gaze darted to the arena sand below the wall—a fifty-foot drop at least. That was a fall that would kill her no matter who had dominion over her mind.

Her toes teetered over the edge of the wall, but she could not steady them. Felt the warm wind tickle across her skin, but she could not withdraw.

She closed her eyes and imagined the noktum there again. She recreated the stone steps. The seven sister pillars each baring a carved, solemn face. All was the same as ever before, but the noktum wasn't there.

Just an empty stone floor between seven pillars.

Wandering the space, Ksara stared at the faces in those pillars. She still felt Xos inside her mind. A pulse. A drumbeat. An iron hand at her neck.

But why wasn't he here?

And if she couldn't find him here, then could she find him at all?

Ksara's stomach wretched and sloshed up into her ribs. Her eyes flew open. She was falling from the arena wall. Her arms outstretched, ready to meet the black sand. The wind ripping at her.

Her throat ached with the scream she couldn't release. The terror remained captive in her ribcage, burning and writhing and feeling as though she might burst from the inside out before she ever even met the ground.

Shadow rushed up to meet her, billowing from the ground to catch her around the waist and arrest her fall.

Her insides sloshed again, this time to the front of her stomach and chest, but the only sound that escaped her was a breath cut short. Then the black air pulled her upright and cradled her feet, and lowered her gently until her boots met sand.

As soon as she stood upon the arena floor the ground gave one final rending. The chasm at the center of the arena now stretched thirty feet wide. Sand from the edges trickled into the black abyss.

The injured Manticore tried to flee, hobbling away from the chasm with slashes torn into both shoulders and a mangled leg. It whimpered as it struggled and it kept turning to look back at the chasm, hurrying faster and faster until—

Out of the chasm, a dragon-like head on a long, sleek neck rose from the depths. The head was six feet long, black and skeletal. It had a hole between its eyes and an eerie orange light pulsing from within its skull, the light leaking out where the things eyeballs should have been. And tendrils of tainted smoke drifting out of its jagged-toothed jaw.

The Manticore moaned and limped away faster.

Another head rose from the chasm, identical to the first.

The Manticore froze, the hair raising up on its spine and its body coiled defensively beneath it.

A third head joined the first two. None of the heads made a sound, but the Manticore hissed at the new menace like a kitchen mouse cornered by the lord's hunting hound.

Each of the new monster's heads turned to apprise the annoyance. Then with a blur of black and a wet crunch, the Manticore was gone. Blood dribbling from one of the monsters' mouths was the only sign of the kill.

"All these millennia," Ksara spoke words that weren't her own. "And you are still my champion, Worldbreaker."

The three-headed beast turned six eyes on Ksara and a primal terror overtook her. Never before had she looked upon a predator and felt so small. So weak. So entirely insignificant. Every muscle in her body wanted to run and climb and flee. Every other thought in her mind quieted. Escape occupied her now. How could she escape those eyes and the death they promised?

Then she saw something flash across her mind. A thought that wasn't her own.

It was this creature—the Worldbreaker—perched at the edge of a noktum. Its heads peeked through the edge of the noktum and even the tentacles ever-reaching for new victims stilled for a moment. Then the head breathed out that tainted mist and it rolled before it, slipping down the streets of a quiet city. In moments the screams began. Glass crashed. The first scream cut short, but more soon joined the grisly song.

And still the Worldbreaker breathed and breathed and breathed the black air. Soon the haze had grown into a faint noktum of its own and the Worldbreaker itself entered the city and the true terror began.

"I created you for more than tournaments and corpses, my champion," Ksara said, her tongue moving of its own volition. Her own words sending a chill down her spine.

The monster held Ksara's gaze and she wondered if Xos, for all his power, could keep the creature from eating them anyways.

The center head snapped forward and caught a Kyolar corpse mere feet away from Ksara's boots. It held the Kyolar in its jaws and leveled those yellow glowing eyes at her. More tainted smoke trickled out of its open mouth and black skull.

Ksara barely dared to draw a breath. The monster's skin was something between hide and scales and it glistened in the low light of dusk.

Somehow a laugh bubbled up from Ksara's breathless throat.

"I will not deprive you of your feast," she said. "Eat. Then we shall return and you will be the champion of all of Noksonon."

The Worldbreaker swallowed the Kyolar whole with a juicy gulp.

CHAPTER FIFTY-EIGHT

ULRIC

Walking had been difficult for Ulric. Crawling was nigh impossible. Crouching was worse.

They oscillated between crawling and crouching, descending and ascending in the maddening dark of the tunnel. The sheer exertion of it had him swaying, his wide shoulders bumping into the tunnel walls on either side. Bruises developed on both shoulders so that every time the strength in his legs faltered and his shoulders knocked into the tunnel, his irritation flared with the discomfort.

But the true source of pain was his leg. The injury in the forest had been bad enough. Traveling on it and then having the ground jerked about beneath it had been the final blow. It now existed in a constant state of agony that amplified with each movement. He breathed hard between clenched teeth so that Coronata and Merewen wouldn't hear his pain. They were dragging Atlas along, after all. And all Ulric had to do was keep himself between the slimy scholar and his friends. And not lose track of that same slimy scholar in the utter dark.

He'd been pretty tolerant of night and shadows and darkness before coming to Hayvonlar. It had been a constant hazard of being Ksara's brother. The shadows had always loved her and that had given him plenty of opportunities to ignite bursts of light into the world to dazzle and comfort her.

But he'd had just about enough of black and black and more black. What he wouldn't do to be transported in a blink of an eye to Laria. To see the veins of light in every building, and fountain, and stone. The way the place pulsed with the brightness. Alive with life and hope.

And to see all of the beautiful Luminent maidens. That certainly added to the place's charm.

One woman came to his mind now, as he hobbled after the scholar in the dark. She'd worn the brightest blue gown Ulric had ever seen. Simple and ornate in the same turn, draping from her bare shoulders in a long trail and adorned with glowing embroidery that would have taken a human artisan their whole life to achieve.

She'd glided so solemnly through that celebration. Black hair tied in a long braid down her bare back. Her slender grace was alluring, but it was her sadness that drew him in.

He'd followed her to the gardens outside the hall and to a bench beside a quiet pool where Golian turtles crowded the bank and basked in the light of the moon, adding happy, melodic chirps to the night.

He'd asked if he could sit beside the Luminent maiden and she'd ignored him, so he'd sat down beside her anyways. For an hour they didn't speak a word, just listening to the turtles' song.

"I'm dying."

Those had been the first words she'd spoken to him.

Ulric had smiled. "We're all dying."

She'd looked at him then, really looked at him. Then she'd told him about how her soulmate had died. How half her soul had gone with him. And now there was nothing left for her in this life but to fade into a shadow of what she was before and then just cease to be.

Ulric took her hand and she'd let him. By Grina! Her skin was soft as the silken dress she wore. He didn't say a word. There were no words for grief that deep. So he just held her hand, anchoring her here. Seeing her.

She smiled at him and the light in that solemn face made his heart skip and his hands tremble. Then she spoke of her life before. Her childhood running among trees and mapping them like stars. How she'd apprenticed with a seamstress and made the dress she now wore. She spoke of lovers and friends. Fears and dreams.

The moon waned and dawn blushed above them and still she talked, and he listened to the lilt of her voice, relishing the spark in her eyes.

She'd stopped talking abruptly and he'd flinched. The air so much colder without the sound of her voice. Even the turtles stopped chirping. Waiting for her to continue so that they could compete with her voice.

She'd kissed him then, a burst of light into his soul that started at his lips and radiated through him.

He'd smiled at her and tried to draw her close. She'd rested her hands on his chest, and for a moment, he'd thought she might actually take him. A Luminent and human!

Then she'd pulled from his grip, slipping out of his hands as easily as a moonbeam and drifting back toward the hall, now empty of party-goers. That afternoon a parcel had been delivered to the *Falco* containing a silken, green vest embroidered and vibrant.

Centrin. In this relentless dark tunnel where his body was wracked with agony and his mind uncertainty, he thought of Centrin. He imagined returning to Laria and finding her and wrapping his arms about her. Winning a smile from her lips before he kissed them again.

Ulric ran into the scholar and his face collided with the other man's backside. All thoughts of Centrin left as he untangled himself from the scholar's rear end and regained his unsteady footing. "Warn me next ti—"

"Shh!" Genove hissed.

Ulric's smile faded. He strained to see something in the black—anything. He had no idea how the scholar could navigate them through the dark. Maybe it was a special skill given only to the academics twitchy and unhinged enough to actually study noktums.

The only sounds were the scuff of boots behind them where Coronata and Merewen drew nearer, and the scrape of Atlas's armor as they pulled him along behind.

"What's wrong?" Ulric whispered back at Genove, as much to be sure he was there than anything else.

"It's getting lighter," he said.

"Isn't that a good thing?" Ulric asked.

"No," he said with finality.

Ulric shook his head. "Not all of us love crawling around in the dark."

"The noktum is moving."

Ulric humor faded. "Move. Move how?"

"Move away from here," Genove said. "Upward to the surface, would be my guess."

"Hold on—we've been walking through a noktum?"

"Yes."

"And now it's leaving?"

"I don't enjoy repeating myself," Genove said.

"Then speak some sense!" Ulric said, his voice louder than ever.

"Quiet," Genove whispered back. "We may not be the only ones disoriented by the change."

Ulric took a beat to listen for sounds of an attack. When he didn't hear any, he continued in a whisper, "Have you ever seen a noktum move like this?"

"No."

"Well, at least we have that in common. Why is it moving? Where is it going?"

"Up," Genove said. "Your sister is calling it up."

"Ksara? She's up there?" The words burst from him and

echoed about the tunnel walls.

A hiss like steam from a teapot answered from somewhere in the dark. The sound swelling, starting at a distance but filling the tunnel around them in a moment.

"Is that the noktum?" Ulric said, his voice much quieter than before.

"No," Genove said. "Those are the creatures that built these tunnels."

Ulric sighed. "I don't suppose they're friendly?"

"No."

He looked over his shoulder to where he'd just heard Coronata and Merewen settle in behind him. They were breathing hard, but he hadn't heard a word of complaint from either of them in the seemingly infinite journey through black. "Time to wake up Atlas," he said. "We found more monsters.'"

"More monsters found us," Genove said and pride resonated in his voice.

CHAPTER FIFTY-NINE

KSARA

The Worldbreaker consumed all of the monster carcasses strewn across the arena floor in mere moments. The heads swallowed Kyolars two at a time. They crunched down thirty-foot long spider legs. And they scooped dozens of man-sized cockroaches into their mouths. The three heads did not quarrel for food, each taking the portion of the arena nearest them and, when they'd finished, only patches of black sand wetted with blood spoke of the mighty melee.

Ksara strode toward the apex of monsters, in calm, even steps she could not control. Her insides hummed in rebellion. She called out to the Shadowvar. She searched for the noktum inside herself. But neither came, so she walked toward the impossible beast.

When she finally stopped she was only twenty feet from the Worldbreaker, its hulk blotted out the last red bursts of the sunset. She could see the lizard's muscles flex and slacken beneath its shiny black hide. Hear the rasp of three throats drawing breath. Feel the tremble of the earth every time the monster moved; its body still hidden beneath the ground.

Ksara's hands raised in front of her. They were trembling. Apparently the proximity of the Worldbreaker filled her with enough terror that not even Xos could completely quell the reflex.

Her hands flexed and a low-pitched rumble began. A tremor of cold worked through her—the touch of shadow inside her veins—but she couldn't avoid it. She couldn't divert it. It just rushed right from her head to her toes and raced through every vein in her body.

Xos was using magic. A lot of magic.

The idea of him conducting power through her made her want to vomit. Somehow that was worse than him overtaking her body and forcing her to be a wordless observer.

She didn't want this power. It was wild. It hurt people. And now Xos could use it, too.

But, if the Shadowvar was to be believed, it had been Xos's power all along. The noktums were built by spells imbued by the sentience of Giants. Her magic connected her to more than shadow, but also the minds within them.

That's why the shadows had been drawn to her. The reason they had gathered to her and not obeyed her. Her presence was an echo of their masters.

Ksara stayed in the sensation of magic drawing into her body. She couldn't run from it. She had to endure it.

And, on the other side of the stinging numb that needled at her organs, was a calm. She breathed a little deeper and felt more than darkness in her body—there were also those lights! The ones she'd seen in the arena mist while looking through Xos's eyes. Pinpricks of stars in a galaxy that swelled and expanded and grew. The lights accompanying the dark, no matter how small they were in comparison to it. There was always light.

That idea resonated with Ksara. Maybe there was more than destruction destined with this curse.

Xos turned her hands and noktum air gushed up through the crack in the arena floor.

She was moving a noktum.

Any inkling of peace shattered in that moment. She wasn't just cursed by shadow, but she was a slave to its master.

He beckoned more and more of the dark moving her arms so that it would spin around the Worldbreaker. The monster hummed in delight, the sound deafening at this distance. She wanted her hands to cover her ringing ears, but they thrust into the air and beckoned more shadow, then twisted it around the Worldbreaker again and again until the thing was swathed in it. Until its whole attention was on the black air.

Then, Ksara threw her left arm outward and the noktum moved where she pointed, right at one of the arena walls. With a grunt and a thunderous crash, the Worldbreaker destroyed the wall. Fragments rained down on the sand.

Ksara would have flinched, ducked, reeled backwards. Instead she stood firm, whipping a hand above her to bring a wisp of dark above her head to swipe the dust and debris from around her and then walking toward where the Worldbreaker waited just outside of the wall.

When she got near the ruined nuraghi wall, the shadow lifted her again and the sensation made her nauseous. When her feet touched the ground bile burned her throat and for the second time in minutes, she wondered if she could vomit at all or if the Giant in control of her body now would keep her choking on it.

More of the Worldbreaker peeked out of the ground, revealing where the necks merge into a single, serpentine body.

Ksara's arm shot out again, pointing toward the ocean. The dark obeyed, hurrying onward. And so, too, did the Worldbreaker, splitting the ground as it went. Trees crashed. Stones cracked. And Ksara caused it all as she unwillingly marched the monster out of its centuries-long cage and toward its freedom.

CHAPTER SIXTY

ULRIC

 o Atlas's credit, he woke ready to fight.

To Atlas's detriment, he woke ready to fight Ulric, Coronata, and Merewen.

Ulric limped back toward the women to add his weight to the scuffle and earned a kick in his mangled leg for his trouble. He collapsed to the ground and wheezed, listening to the fight between bouts of excruciating pain.

"Get his hands!"

"Where are his hands?"

"Bastard Imprevari! We're trying to hel—shit!"

"He can't see us! He's disorien—ow!"

Ulric wrestled through the pain and summoned heat to his fingers. In his current state of exhaustion and depletion, he had only whispers of his magic, but he used one now and, with the snap of his finger, lit up the tunnel in a momentary brilliant flash of light.

Atlas crouched with his back against a wall, a chunk of stone in his bloody fingers and his eyes wild. Merewen had fresh blood trickling down her temple and Coronata was getting to her feet.

The light only lasted an instant, but it was enough. Atlas's eyes focused, the feral rage lowered to a simmer, and by the time the all-consuming black returned, the fight was done.

Or at least the fight with Atlas.

Genove ran past them, leaping over Ulric on the ground, dodging around Merewen and shouldering past Atlas and Coronata to flee back up the tunnel. The clicking sounds thundered ever closer and the black resumed around them.

"Follow the scholar!" Ulric bellowed, rolling to his shoulder and using his thick arms to prop himself up again. His legs screamed in pain, but he did his best to ignore the annoyance. Dying would be far worse.

Atlas hurried off first, his armor clanking as he closed the distance with the wily scholar. Coronata jogged after, her steps light and sure. Ulric waited a second for Merewen to go next, but fought back a smile when he felt a hand on his shoulder.

"You first."

"No," Ulric said. He knew very well he was the slowest. He'd rather grapple with the monsters than jeopardize whoever was behind him.

"Then we wait here for them," Merewen said, picking up a stone from the ground.

"You're difficult," Ulric said, a smile touching his lips.

Merewen threw a rock and it cracked into something behind them. The thing hissed and scurried closer.

Ulric picked up a rock of his own and tossed it backward. Another hiss and the rustling legs drew closer. Ulric reached out for Merewen, caught hold of her arm, and propelled her in front of him. She resisted for a moment, but only a moment—their time for arguing was spent, and then some.

Merewen ran and Ulric dragged his injured leg in a hunched, sidling gait that would have made even the street beggars of Triada take pity on him.

Merewen tried to stay near him. He heard her footsteps slow in front of him, but he decelerated much faster. He'd thought he could run for at least a little while, but he just couldn't push his body anymore. Not even through sheer will. His legs slowed. His breathing ripped in and out of him through his raw throat in wet, haggard gasps.

And the sound of the approaching monsters overwhelmed him. He knew they were feet from him now. He turned to meet them, picking up a rock from the ground as he did and launching it at the dark.

Another crunch and hiss. And still the sounds came. The monsters came.

A pincer caught Ulric by the shoulder and pulled him in. He couldn't even see the thing that had him, but it didn't matter. Not now. Now all he had was blind punches into the abyss anyways.

He flailed and punched, catching the thing in a soft spot, but not before getting a gash down his shoulder and forearm. This pain settled him somehow. He stopped fighting to survive and started to fight to inflict his rage on something, anything, else.

He thought of Centrin sitting alone on that bench in Laria. The whole world looking right through her, discarding her while she had so much more life to live.

Three more punches and he won another cut down his arm. A pincer caught his forearm and this time Ulric twisted and jerked his arm, ripping the mouth free of the head. The monster's hot blood adding to his own.

He thought of Ksara attacking the Horror Knight that had him by the throat. Prying at its fingers. Hacking at the hand with her dagger. The black wild around her. Fear and determination sharp in her eyes. Then a hand grabbed her by the neck and he watched her dangle and kick there. Heard her gasp and wheeze.

Gritting his teeth, he threw himself into the blind fight with the monsters. A pincer touched his neck, but he grabbed both sides of it and ripped outward, splitting the monster's head in two before another took its place, biting at his good leg. Ulric stomped on it with his bad one and used the consequential pain as a boon. Fuel to fight. To kill before he died.

Three pincers had him now, one on his thigh, another his

shoulder, and the third had his arms pinned together. And those were just the three beasts that could fit simultaneously in the tunnel. The rest of its fellows clicked and hissed behind the attacker, eager to add their own pincers to the death blows.

The ground shuddered. Dirt rained down on Ulric's shoulders. A deep, muffled roar came from somewhere above and the monsters in the tunnel quieted in an instant. The silence came on so suddenly that Ulric might have thought the cockroaches had just disappeared had three of them not had his flesh caught in their mandibles.

The ground shuddered again and the mass of monsters pressed forward. Two of the pincers let go of him, but the one that held his arms did not. The thing lifted him off his feet and rushed forward. He cried out, but the clicking sound subsumed his own.

They raced through the tunnels with wild abandon, turning and scuttling faster than Ulric had thought possible in the space and wheeling him about like some kind of accidental trophy still caught in the lead insect's jaws.

A muffled roar shook the earth. The monster tightened its grip on Ulric's arms and scuttled all the faster, ducking right and left, down and up in a synchronized course with its fellows.

Ulric's feet dragged on the tunnel floor, but he could not get purchase and his arms, wet with blood, turned and twisted in the monster's pincers, the sharp edges getting closer to the bone.

Whether he traveled in the panicked monster's jaw for seconds, minutes, or hours, Ulric could not say. Facing backward, held in the pincers of the creature in the utter black of the tunnel, he couldn't delineate time. He knew that he should have run into the crew by now, but wrestled between relief and disappointment that he hadn't. They might have been able to free him, but they probably would have just been trampled over and killed by the strange stampede.

He even called down his magic toward his fingertips three times, but the power never made it past his shoulder. His reserves were too low, his body too weak. Pain owned him and it stabbed from his arms and occasionally from his leg when it collided with wall or stone or the monster's own cold, hard exterior.

The sound of the monsters' scurrying feet changed, it echoed louder. The air was colder. And he could feel more than see the swarm of creatures fan out around the one that held him, expanding and filling the new space.

The ground rent again, this time a crack of blinding light accompanied it. The monster hissed at the change and dropped Ulric to the floor. He barely had time to groan before thousands of legs were stepping on him. He curled up into a ball as best as his swollen, mangled leg would allow, and took the stiff scurrying legs up and down his body, the impacts feeling like dozens of strikes with the blunt end of a staff.

When the blows stopped, Ulric stayed on the ground. The air was quiet and his skin warm and not just near the open wounds where his blood trickled out of him.

No, this was a pleasant sort of warmth that made him think of Demaijos courtyards and sunrises.

Inch-by-agonizing-inch, Ulric straightened his body and opened his eyes. The light made his vision speckle and he laughed: a weak, coughing sort of laugh.

There was sky above him, peeking through a crack in a high ceiling. And it wasn't the sun that offered up its light, but a full, bright moon winking down at him.

He lay on his back staring up at the moon and Centrin entered his mind once more. He remembered the way the moonlight illuminated her skin. The way her dark hair lit up, strand-by-strand when she spoke of her deceased mate, like stars winking to life in the night sky.

He'd wanted to tell her there was more to live for. More than pain and sorrow in this life. Now he lay on cold stone, his body a beaten pulp of bruises and cuts, and he wondered at the words. Had they been hollow all along?

And could he believe them now? Lying mangled, broken, and lost in a nuraghi where he was supposed to be rescuing his sister, but now didn't even know if he had the strength left to roll over and crawl?

No inspiring messages came into his mind. No relief from his pain. But he did see Centrin's face transform the moon. Saw her sad eyes. The sharp angle of her jaw. The night sky her dark hair spilling out around her as she lay facing him.

She didn't speak a word in his imagination or hallucination. Not a word. But he knew he couldn't give up on living while she was watching. He had to die fighting, just as he wished with all of his soul that she would, too.

There was more to life than the pain wracking him now. There was beauty and love. Serene, unexpected moments in a Luminent garden.

Ulric rolled to his shoulder and his flesh and bones ached and throbbed, but he ignored their complaints and slapped his palms down on the stone floor, heaving himself upward only for his arm to give out and his body to clap back down against the stone. He didn't wallow in the defeat. Not with her watching. And the next time he tried, he made it to his good knee before his arms gave out and landed face-first on the ground again. The third time his body didn't just complain at the movement, black rimmed his vision and that cold calm of unconsciousness pulled at him. If he collapsed again, he could succumb to it. He could sleep and escape the agony and perhaps never wake back up to it. He would die under Centrin's gaze.

But he pressed his palms against the stone and raised his body up, first to his good knee and then, readjusting one hand to push against the knee, up to his feet, dragging his lame leg upright with him. He swayed, unconsciousness coming for him again, but he fought it off, blinking his eyes and shuffling forward.

Walking brought another level of exquisite pain, but he would not surrender to it. And, as he hobbled forward inches at a time, he began to see the room around him. Stone floors and stone walls, each slab placed so perfectly it made every other room he'd been in seem entirely flawed. Not even the debris of dirt from the ceiling nor the dust of time diminished the craftsmanship.

And the floor and its accompanying twenty-foot-tall ceiling

led on in a magnificent corridor forward. As best as he could tell there was only the single tunnel he'd come from—a place where a single stone slab had been pushed to the ground and the creatures had burrowed there—and the path forward.

He glanced up at the moon, gave Centrin the best smile he could with his swollen face, and followed the path before him.

Two hundred feet from where he'd fallen he saw a new monster lying very still on a stone pedestal. Ulric froze, his heart pounding quick and sharp in his bruised ribcage. He listened for a sound that indicated the thing sensed him. It looked like a horse, but four times bigger than any plough horse he'd ever seen with a head like a bear, and a tan, shaggy coat.

Ulric stood still for several long minutes waiting for this new threat to manifest. He could not run. He didn't have the strength to fight. And with his injured leg, he wasn't exactly moving stealthily through this corridor.

But the monster didn't move at all. Not a twitch of its ear or tail. Not a blink of its eye.

That's when Ulric focused on the thing's ribcage. It didn't move either. Not even a fraction of an inch.

Perhaps the thing was in a deep sleep, so deep its breathing was almost non-existent. Deep enough, perhaps, for Ulric to move past undetected.

He shuffled forward, keeping his gaze riveted on the thing's head. If it flicked even an ear in his direction, he'd have to try to run. As futile as that might be.

When Ulric was side-by-side with the stone slab and the creature atop it, he saw the gash across its neck and down its chest to its abdomen. The wound bloody and the fur wet. It looked as fresh as if it had been done minutes ago, though the blood didn't spill from it.

Ulric paused again, this time his eyes catching the writing around the base of the stone. "Voru. Defeated champion."

He dared to breathe a little freer. This was a fallen champion to whatever the nuraghi stadium was designed to do. Some sort of conquest of monsters, he guessed. And the dead champion of a game centuries past, was preserved here on this pedestal by some sort of magic. A testament to the creature's legacy.

Ulric stared a moment at the thing and then hobbled on.

In a hundred feet or so, he found another monster, this one primarily tentacles and teeth. He slowed only to read its name, Dhensun, and continued on.

The third monster was the strangest yet. It's head and body looked like something the fishermen of Demaijos pulled up from the depths of the sea and brought before his parents to shock and amaze them. It had fin-like spines going down its back and a mouth that gaped open with four teeth, each the length of Ulric's leg and coming to an arrow-head's point. Jutting out of the body were six dog-like legs with wide paws and curled claws.

This one had a deep gash at the back of its neck, the insides of the thing still somehow pink and juicy.

As he was about to shuffle past the monster, he read the name and froze: Allarune.

CHAPTER SIXTY-ONE

KSARA

K sara strode through a nightmare of her own creation.

The Worldbreaker split the earth in two as it went, creating a deep ravine for its body to wriggle through while its three heads whipped about in the air, snapping up fleeing flocks of birds in lazy bites. The thing's heads glowed with a pulsing yellow-orange and tainted smoke leaked out of its eyes and nose.

It turned one of its heads toward her now and those yellow-orange eyes tore through her as easily as it cleaved the ground. Sweat beaded on her skin and her hands trembled, even under Xos's command.

But Xos held her still. Kept her standing firm before the monster's unnatural gaze. Four Horror Knights flanked Ksara on either side, so that even if she could break Xos's grip on her, she'd have to evade them as well to escape the doom glancing down at her.

Cold stabbed into the base of her neck and Ksara braced for the magic to course through her. She'd gotten accustomed to the sensation, as unpleasant as the chilling needles might be. Once the stinging exploded out across her lower back and infiltrated her gut, she knew her hands would move and focus the power, beckoning the shadow forward and ushering the monster on.

Her hands moved. The shadow complied. And the Worldbreaker continued its devastation.

As the chill faded, the fatigue took hold.

When Xos had first used her as a puppet for his power, the exhaustion had only lasted only a few moments. But now nausea settled into her stomach, sloshing bitter bile up her throat where she couldn't even swallow as it burned. Her strength seeped out of her and her knees buckled, but held. Xos wouldn't let her fall. He'd use the shadows themselves to keep her standing if he had to.

But for how long? How long would he use her as a puppet, trapped in this torment she couldn't escape? Hours? Days? Weeks?

Not weeks.

At the rate he was using her magic, she'd get Mage's Sickness by this time tomorrow and be face-down in the grass, cold and lifeless.

The mages her parents had hired as tutors had taught long and hard about Mage's Sickness. It was an ever-present threat and the most likely way to die once the mage knew how to draw on the power intentionally.

Ksara had laughed at the tutors. Not only did she not know how to draw on her power on purpose, but if she'd died doing it, her parents would have been relieved. Surely they would have grieved some. But they had grieved the loss of the daughter they'd wanted every day of their lives.

Now Mage's Sickness and the death it caused might be her only salvation. In the hour or two it had taken to travel from the arena to here, Xos had called on Ksara's power seventeen times. For an immortal Giant, that was likely nothing. But for a mortal? Each long draw of magic could be the one that pushed her into an unconsciousness very few woke from.

And that was if she was lucky.

Some mages, Love Mages particularly, lost their minds before then. Detaching from reality and drifting between worlds only they could perceive.

A tutor had taken Ksara and Ulric to visit one of these invalid mages once. A woman with a young face, but a body with skin hanging off here bones. Her eyes had darted about the room, tracking movement that wasn't there.

She hadn't been able to answer a single question. When she started yelling at an empty corner, the tutor had ushered them out of the room and the woman's mother had tried to calm the girl.

Ksara still heard the girl screaming and hitting the walls of her home. Trapped in a prison her own magic had created.

If that was her fate, would Xos still be able to use her? Would he command her body still if her mind fractured?

She preferred the idea of dying. Of ending Xos's reign alongside her own. Then Ulric wouldn't have to see her changed. He wouldn't have to see her becoming the exact monster he'd always insisted she could never be.

Her boots sank into sand and she stirred from her thoughts, staring out of eyes that were mere windows into a reality she couldn't control.

They'd arrived at the bay where the *Falco* and the Dorumai's ships were anchored. Both ships bobbed in the water, ripples from the Worldbreaker's movement through the earth causing bigger and bigger waves.

The Worldbreaker hesitated at the water's shore, all three of the thing's heads turning back to stare down at Ksara. Or, rather, to stare at Xos.

"It is a necessary pain," Xos said with Ksara's tongue. "We must get you to the great Noktum now. In the cover of night. And this mortal does not have the strength to lift you there with shadow."

Two of the Worldbreaker's heads turned back to behold the water and the third kept its gaze trained on Ksara.

Cold needles pricked into her neck and the power moved

through her again. It cascaded down her spine and then out. This time the nausea brought a mouthful of vomit and she couldn't swallow it down. It sloshed about her tongue and teeth, nearly blocking her airways.

Then her hands shot out, but this time the shadows caught her up by the legs and carried her weak, trembling body two hundred feet across sand and waves to alight on the deck of the *Falco*. Dark air wreathed in a cloud of black that lapped and curled against the hull of the *Falco* just above the water. "Come," she commanded in a voice that wasn't entirely her own.

The Worldbreaker hesitated for a fraction of a second and then plunged into the bay. The ship pitched and yawed, ocean water wet the deck, but the *Falco* stayed afloat.

When the ship steadied, something pulled from the shadows. Xos and Ksara alerted to the movement at the same time, though the Giant was the one that turned her to face the newcomer.

It was a Shadowvar with sawed off horns and tattered, bloodied black robes, kneeling at Ksara's feet.

The Orator.

Surprise bubbled through her mind and Xos seemed to flip through her memories a moment before summoning the shadow with that stinging cold in her bones. The Giant wanted to kill this mortal, a distraction from his purpose, and be on his way.

"Lord of the Dark," The Orator said. His voice was simultaneously clear and reverent. "I have prepared an offering for your return. A city. A place where you may show your power and fulfill prophecy."

Ksara felt Xos's mirth before it bubbled up her throat and into the night air. "I have no need for prophecy. Nor offerings. This world belongs to the Noksonoi. And I will take it."

"Notke Murosa is the closest city, Lord," the Orator persisted. "And it is rimmed by two noktums. Plenty of Dark to fuel your desires, whatever they may be."

Ksara remembered that flash of thoughts that hadn't been her own—where the Worldbreaker had been demolishing a town on its way to the noktum. She imagined Nokte Murosa and the thought gave her a chill. She saw the twelve bodies covered in sheets lined up in the courtyard. And then more bodies joined them. Small forms of children lying beneath bloodied sheets beside their parents. Rubble where the houses had been.

Ksara's stomach dropped like cold iron. She imagined returning to Nokte Murosa—not free from her power and with the Dorumai under her boot, but with a monster in tow and the Orator at her side. She stiffened, even within Xos's control. *No,* she thought. *No.*

A laugh bubbled out of Ksara's own chest. "Show the way, servant."

The Orator rose from the deck and pointed to the west. "That way, Lord."

That familiar, terrible chill cascaded down her back, then she raised her hand to mimic the Orator's, shooting shadow that direction.

Each of the Worldbreaker's heads screamed into the night air, a terrible delight in the sound. Then one of the heads grabbed the *Falco* by its anchor like a Kyolar with a child's toy on a string, and it pulled the ship through the water as the monster cut through the surf.

CHAPTER SIXTY-TWO

ULRIC

lric stared at the Allarune until his aching body could not abide the stillness any longer and he hobbled closer to the thing.

The incisors of whatever killed the Allarune left deep puncture wounds all the way to its spine. The wound looked fresh, wet. But drained of blood. Like the wound that killed the Allarune was just as much part of the display as was the creature who'd sustained it.

It was grotesque and fascinating. At any other time, he'd be tempted to prod the wet atrocity with his finger. Maybe even smell the wound to see how foul a century-old corpse sustained by magic would be.

But right now curiosity was the least of the turmoil inside him.

This was the creature, the corpse, that had given Ksara a glimmer of hope. It's what Genove had promised would rid Ksara of her powers and give her the normalcy she'd always craved. She had never wanted to be a mage, but she'd always been a natural leader. Fair and honest. Compassionate and decisive in their proper turns. She'd always seen the power as an impediment to that. A weakness.

But he didn't see her that way at all.

The power was unique. It ebbed and flowed depending on where she was. It had a playful nature. A wildness to it. It was something to be explored and cherished.

But their family had never seen it that way. And no matter how much Ulric had tried to protect Ksara from their skewed judgments and shame, she'd absorbed it all the same. She'd let them discard her. Ignore her. And ultimately, almost let them exile her to a Brightling settlement for good.

And while they'd left Demaijos that night, stealing away on a ship, Ksara had never left behind that judgement. That curse had followed her because she'd accepted it.

And this Allarune, this relic, was the pinnacle of that thinking. She treated her magic, this part of herself, as a sickness. And this was the cure.

He could hobble away from this place and pretend he'd never found it. It would be hard enough to find an exit and meet up with Coronata, Merewen, and Ksara without the detour. No one would suspect he'd found the Allarune and ignored it.

But could he look into Ksara's eyes again, if he did? Could he see that haunted expression when the shadows closed in on her at every turn, when she had not a moment of relief day or night, and be able to look back into her eyes without remorse?

As much as he believed that this power was a boon, not a bane, he'd also seen the courtyard incident at Nokte Murosa. He'd seen the power overwhelm her and the line of dead that had come from that moment.

Far fewer bodies than if the Dorumai had pursued their plan uninterrupted. Yes, she'd done the magical equivalent of starting a village on fire, but she'd also thwarted an invading force bent on murder and mayhem. She was a hero. Only the Guildmaster with a mind twisted by grief and his own guilt would make Ksara into the face of evil.

But that wasn't the logic Ksara followed. Just like with the curse, she'd absorbed this story about herself, too. She was a murderer that must be redeemed. And in order to exact justice on the Dorumai, she must first cure herself of the illness that had caused her to kill so many.

It was a new way for her to hide. For her to diminish herself and he hated every bit of it.

But could he make this choice for her? Could he turn down the help the Allarune tooth might give, just because he was so certain of his own rightness?

His body throbbed and he tried to shift his weight to give his legs relief, but there was no position he could maintain that didn't radiate a different series of pain throughout his body. He'd survived two encounters with the Horror Knights. And another with a pack of Kyolars. Then a fight with the deranged version of Atlas. And again a scuffle with the human-sized cockroaches in the pitch-black tunnels.

And all of it so that Ksara could have this relic and the choice it represented. He couldn't rob her of that, no matter how much he didn't want her to choose to rid herself of her power. It was her choice to make.

That was the truth of it. He could impose his will and stack the deck against most people. But not Ksara.

He urged his aching body closer to the Allarune. Genove had said the monster's bite was what dispelled the dark. Wrapping a bloodied hand around one of the four massive teeth, Ulric pulled on it and it didn't budge.

"Grina's skirts," he breathed and readjusted his grip. When he yanked again, the tooth wiggled a fraction of an inch. Just enough to encourage Ulric on as he twisted and leveraged the tooth out of the Allarune' s skull. When the tooth finally came free, the gaping hole where it had once been became one more grisly, perfectly preserved wound on the strange corpse.

He glanced at the creature one more time, wondering how it used this power to best so many monsters and become a champion.

Wondering if the piece of it that he now held would kill his sister.

And if he could live with himself if it did.

Using the tooth as a staff, Ulric shuffled away from the Allarune. His footsteps echoed through the tunnel. He stopped every dozen steps. Sometimes to wheeze his exhaustion into the dark. And sometimes to stare at the relic clutched in his hand. But each time he rallied and continued on, following the crack in the ceiling and the meager light from the moon above until the crack spidered down from the ceiling to the wall in front of him. He paused there, but when he caught a whiff of pines and grass from the crack, he started the process of wriggling his tender and swollen body through the hole and out the other side.

It was an arduous process. Halfway through as he was crammed between the stone slabs and running dangerously low on energy, he wondered what it would be like to be crushed between the two pieces of rock. For better or for worse, he was still a Demaijos. And a Demaijos didn't give death an easy time of them.

He fell out of the crack on the other side, tumbling onto upturned earth and grass. He lay there for a moment, clutching the Allarune tooth in one hand, breathing shallow, painful breaths, and staring up at the moon.

That's when he heard hushed voices. He stilled. He didn't have speed on his side, nor strength. All of his advantage might be in silence and surprise.

"We're not leaving without him."

"And what of Ksara? You saw her walk by here!"

"We're not leaving without him."

"There's more to discover within the nuraghi—"

"Shut up!" Three people said in unison.

Ulric smiled. "I'm here," he said hoarsely. "I'm right here."

Merewen found him first. The moonlight played in her auburn braid and illuminated her marble-white face. He reached a bloodied, dirty hand up toward her and traced the blue tattoos sweeping about her jaw.

"You okay?" She asked; not waiting for an answer she prodded his bones and examined him for critical wounds.

"Ow."

"What hurts?"

"When I'm away from you? My heart," he said, smiling up at her. She gave him a look.

Ulric smiled back. "See. It's getting better all the time."

Atlas arrived with a rustling clang of armor. Merewen stepped backward and her calm, gentle presence was replaced by the smell of horse sweat and firm, unsympathetic hands digging into the deepest wounds. Ulric squawked and writhed, but Atlas didn't even give the reaction a second glance.

When he'd finished the wounds ached anew, but there was confidence in Atlas's voice. "He'll make it to the ship. Let's go."

Coronata stood a step behind Atlas. She flashed Ulric a grin. "Race you there."

"Deal."

"What is ..."

Someone tried to grab the Allarune tooth out of Ulric's hands and he ripped it out of their clutches, holding it tight to his chest.

Genove peered down at him now, his fingers twitching and his bright eyes on the tooth. "You found the Allarune."

"And you found Ksara?" Ulric said, pushing up to an elbow and breathing out the pain for a moment.

"Yes and no," Coronata said.

"Yes and no?"

"She—she wasn't herself."

"What do you mean?"

"Well, she was commanding a three-headed monster like it was an alley dog," Coronata said.

"She was what?"

"Telling the monster where to go," Atlas said, rising to his feet. "Right to the ships, by the look of it, too."

Ulric got to his feet and Merewen was there in an instant to steady him. Genove lingered close to the side that clutched the Allarune's tooth. Ulric waved both of them away and used the tooth itself as a staff again, hobbling along in the grass toward the bay.

"The Allarune relic is two millennia old," Genove said. "And you use it as a staff."

Ulric shrugged. "A multipurpose relic."

"And if you dull the tip of the tooth and the siphon goes from a narrow tip to a gaping hole, how will your sister survive the process?"

Ulric's shoulders stiffened. "If she doesn't, neither do you."

"It is safe ... in the proper hands, of course." Genove moved closer to Ulric, his palms extended toward the Allarune tooth. "It will be even more delicate now. With her transformation."

Ulric's mood darkened. "Transformation?"

Genove smiled and Ulric had the urge to signal Atlas and start in on a good pummeling on the scholar. But Ulric held his temper. They needed information and Genove had it. That's why he'd come along in the first place.

"What do you mean transformation?"

Genove's eyes glittered in the darkness and he held his smile tight on his face for a long moment. "She wasn't in control of herself when she entered the arena," he said.

"More than the usual?" Atlas asked.

Coronata glared at him.

Atlas crossed his arms over his chest. "She lied. She said she could control her power and she can't."

"And you went black-eyed savage and tried to kill Ulric," Coronata retorted. "Let's take your opinion on control *very* seriously."

"I did what?" Atlas said, his voice faltering some.

"You attacked Ulric," Merewen said, her voice as calm and even as ever. "I suspect it was an effect of the Worldbreaker's breath. It caused the Kyolars to turn on their own pack. And the Sleeths killed each other, too."

"And how did I—you know," Atlas said.

"Ksara," Genove said. "I think it was her last effort to control the magic before it overtook her."

"What overtook her?" Ulric asked. "The shadow?"

"Yes and no," Genove said, that sparkle in his eyes. "I knew her power was special. That it was linked to the noktums. But she's even more."

Ulric tried to suck in a deep breath, but pain stabbed through his shoulder. He choked on the half breath, glanced up at the wide, full moon, and then settled his gaze back on Genove.

"Now is when you tell me what happened to Ksara," he said. "Or I find a monster who would like to eat a pompous, bony academic."

Genove glanced over Ulric's wounds and smiled. He was in no danger of being the easiest prey for a predator. Ulric might have more substance and strength to him, but now that muscle mass was torn up and bleeding. An easy meal for any number of predators and that truth lay bare on Genove's face.

"Ksara's power isn't what we thought it was," Merewen said, squinting at Genove as if she could hear his thoughts. She had a way of penetrating through facades and catching hold of the person beneath. She did it now with Genove, her azure blue eyes as bright as Genove's. "She's not a Land Mage at all, is she?"

Genove beamed at them. "No. She's not."

"She's a Land Mage," Ulric said. "We both are. I of light and she of shadow."

"Is your light alive, Demaijos?" Genove asked. "Does it yearn for you? Protect you? Animate you when you're unconscious?"

Ulric's cracked lips parted, but his words died there.

"The shadow isn't just shadow," Merewen said. "It's the Dark."

"Now we're just saying words," Atlas growled. "Of course the shadow is dark."

"The Dark," Merewen said. "It's what makes the noktums."

"And that makes it alive somehow?" Coronata asked, placing a hand on a cocked hip.

"The noktums reach out," Merewen said. "They sense people near them and try to drag them in. That's not normal shadow."

"We already knew she was connected to the noktums," Ulric said.

"Did you know she was a Life Mage?" Genove said with that

tight smile on his lips. "Did you know that her true power wasn't commanding the dark, but connecting to the creators of it?"

Ulric shook his head. Ksara was his twin. She had land magic because he had land magic.

But the more he thought about it, the more it felt true.

His parents had hired every Land Mage they could find within four hundred miles to train Ksara and none of them had been even remotely successful. Their parents had blamed Ksara—telling her she didn't want to learn badly enough.

But Ulric had seen Ksara trying. He'd seen her sitting on her bed in the middle of the night, bathed in a pool of moonlight, and trying to pull and push the shadows in and out of the circle of light.

She'd tried then. She'd tried in Nokte Murosa. She'd never stopped trying to keep the shadows at bay, but she'd failed despite her tremendous effort.

That she was approaching her magic from an entirely wrong way made a certain kind of sense.

"Who created the noktums?" Ulric asked, his words slow. Unsure if he wanted to hear the answer.

"If he says one more made-up word," Atlas growled, "I get to beat him."

"The Noksonoi," Genove said.

"There it is!" Atlas drew his short sword and had two steps on the scholar before Ulric could shout at him to stop.

Atlas twirled the hilt of the sword in his hand, eyeing the scholar, but not cutting him down. Yet.

"Merewen?" Ulric asked.

"They're the Giants of legend," she said. "Creators of the world. An evil force long since dead."

Ulric shook his head, the motion sending another ache through his body. "It doesn't make sense."

"It makes perfect sense," Genove replied. "It just seems impossible."

"What does it matter?" Coronata asked. "If she's a Land Mage or a Life Mage, she's still a mage."

"Because it's not the shadows that have been playing with her," Genove said. "It's a Giant. A being of immense power. And now its awake. It's alive in her." He pointed at the Allarune relic. "And that's her only chance at stopping it."

CHAPTER SIXTY-THREE

KSARA

Ksara's hands clasped the *Falco*'s helm, but she'd never felt so helpless. She didn't direct the ship. She didn't even have control of more than the tips of her fingers, and even if she could mount a rebellion on that barest bit of her body and manage to grab hold of the helm with her own power, she still could not stop the ship.

The Worldbreaker pulled the *Falco* through the sea with one of its heads while the other two reached far ahead, their long, serpentine necks cresting against the waves.

All the while she felt Xos relishing his victory. Reveling in this body he'd found to focus his mind and power once more.

In the hours at the helm, her mannerisms began to change. She stood taller. Whenever she left the helm, her steps were heavier. Marching about the wooden planks. Her brows crowded her eyes in a perpetual squint and anytime her hands left the helm, she clasped her hands at the small of her back like some kind of commodore.

And her own thoughts grew smaller and smaller. As if the

space inside her mind was dwindling and she could only focus on one idea at a time. If she thought about rebellion, she couldn't worry about Nokte Murosa. If she worried about Nokte Murosa, she couldn't think about how to stop Xos.

If she worried about Xos, her thoughts grew smaller still. He seemed to find her then and, like a python, constricted around her, suffocating her mind.

She turned her thoughts, instead, to the Shadowvar. She hadn't heard him in her mind since she'd succumbed to the dark. The moment when she'd thought she was going to save herself and her friends but lost herself instead.

His had been the voice of caution. The voice telling her not to trust the dark. Not to give into it.

And the other sounds in her mind? That thumping, urgent beat she'd felt when the noktum was near?

She recognized that, too. That had been Xos's voice, although his words had been slurred. Incoherent. Now she knew their tone and cadence.

And she'd become a slave to them.

The image of the Worldbreaker tearing through Nokte Murosa took hold of her mind again and all other thoughts slipped away. She imagined the faces of the people fleeing. The way they'd feel terror for a moment at the sight of the monster and the crack dividing their town. And then the Worldbreaker's breath would seep up and out of that crack.

Then they would become their own enemies. And the Worldbreaker need not spend any energy at all on its meal. They would kill each other and, when the streets were still and stained with blood, the Worldbreaker would feed.

And when it was done feeding, where would it go?

Ksara thought of the line of twelve bodies hidden beneath blankets. The innocents she'd killed in the courtyard of Nokte Murosa.

Now she imagined those bodies multiplying again and again and again and again until she couldn't see the end of bodies. Couldn't escape the knowledge that she'd brought this death to these people. She could have stopped it—somehow—but she'd failed.

No.

If she failed, it would be after she did everything she could do.

So she eased her eyes closed and sent a pleading thought out toward the Shadowvar. Then she conjured the Merneith palace in her mind.

She passed through the gardens first where blue, red, and gold birds flittered back and forth between the boughs of wide-leafed trees. Up the white, stone steps and into an open-air courtyard. The breeze brought the scent of blooming flowers, rich earth, and a distant sea to Ksara's nose and the scent calmed her.

The courtyard held the Seven Sisters and they looked grimmer now than ever before. There was still no noktum here. No easy access to that connection between Ksara and Xos.

But she felt Xos close. She knew him by that chilling presence. So she followed that sensation forward, crossing the courtyard, weaving around the circle of lavishly polished chairs, and through the narrowest of three corridors.

Pools of water lined either side of the path with ornate white walls framing them in. Paintings leafed in gold decorated every step of the journey. Abstract depictions of all of the races of Noksonon coming to Demaijos for trade. Tales of heroism. Legends of the Seven Sisters beating back the noktum and protecting the Lux.

Then the Demaijos palace began to change. The white stone darkened to gray, then an ashy black. Silken window dressings transformed to barred windows. Gold-leafed paintings into splatters of dark blood. The pools on either side of the path became mounds of decaying corpses.

Ksara walked through the transformed place with deliberate, quiet steps. The place felt at once familiar and foreboding.

The dead bodies at the edges of the corridor went from bones to dusty corpses to decaying flesh to the freshly dead. She paused at one of these bodies, a Taur-El. The mighty part-bull part-man still gurgled as the blood left a wound in his chest. Just as she knelt to place a hand on the wound to staunch the blood, he coughed and his last breath left him.

Ksara continued on. The next bodies she found cried out to her for help, eyes wide. Some had visible wounds, slashes across their chests, or the punctures of blades through them. Others were half-charred by fire. Yet others twitched and seized with no apparent ailment at all.

But no matter what the wound, nor how much the victim begged for Ksara's help, as soon as she arrived at their sides, they expired.

When she neared the end of the corridor, battle sounds filled her ears. The clang of swords. The cries of the pain. And a laugh, low and visceral. A voice she knew all too well.

Xos.

She crept on the balls of her feet across the flagstones. Her boots were gone. Her Demaijos wrapped tunic gone. All that covered her dark skin was a long, rough spun tunic and a chain around her waist.

She turned back to the corpses behind her.

Each of them wore the same shift and chain. Sometimes the chain attached to their necks or horns. Wrists or ankles. But all wore the chains.

Someone cried out in the room beyond, a squelch of flesh and bone crunching punctuating the sound. Ksara pressed back into the shadows, wishing she were a Shadowvar and could become one with the dark.

Then again, she'd passed more than one dead Shadowvar on her way here. Apparently even they couldn't elude fate.

Placing a hand on the cold stone, Ksara inched herself around the corner to peer into the room.

There she found the feeble remnants of what might have been a rebellion. Led by a Luminent man with shoulder-length golden hair. He clung to a sharpened stick with the fire of justice in his eyes as Xos cleaved the man's chest in two.

Blood oozed up from the wound, but it didn't quell the fight in the Luminent's face. He waved his sharpened stick at the Giant and it looked comically feeble. Even without a three-foot blade in his chest, the only thing the Luminent could have done with that sharp stick was give the fifteen-foot-tall Giant a splinter. And maybe not even that with his clothes crafted in red dragon hide. The head of the dragon forming a breastplate on his chest.

And yet, as the light faded from the man's eyes, watching his blood flee from his body, his resolution didn't fade. And his band of warriors behind him rallied. Some of them had metal staffs, but most carried the same sharp sticks as their leader.

They converged on Xos.

The Giant let them come. He let them take their strikes. Let their weapons clack off his body and break against his might.

And when they'd tired. When their hope wavered, Xos let go of the axe and let the heavy weapon sink the leader to the ground. Then he went about finishing his grisly task. With a gesture of his hand, he petrified one attacker into stone. The next he incinerated in fire. A third he unraveled, skin unwinding off of muscle, muscle off of bone like thread from a spindle.

He finished his work of death in mere moments, laughing a thunderous laugh.

She'd never seen so many die with so little effort.

Xos reached a hand into the dead Luminent's open chest, doused his hand in the blood and smeared it about his already blood-splattered face. Then he turned to Ksara, stared right down at her, and smiled.

Her whole body went rigid at the same moment.

Run! Run, Demaijos!

That wasn't her voice at all. That was the Shadowvar's.

She pivoted on her bare feet and ran.

Xos laughed, the sound so low it shook the stones around her. Then his heavy steps followed her, each footfall sending shivers up her legs as she hurdled over the dead bodies, slipping in pools of blood and clinging to the blood-splattered walls to keep upright.

By the time she made it back to the courtyard, she was covered in blood. Her clothes were still the slave's uniform of the dead and the chain grew heavier and heavier with each step.

Only when she tried to weave around the stone chairs did she realize she was dragging the chain behind her. It had grown much, much longer since she'd last looked down at it. It trailed several feet behind her. The weight of it bit into her sides.

She ran harder and the chain grew heavier and heavier. When she glanced back at it, the chain stretched backward to the corridor she'd fled and Xos held the end of it in his enormous fist.

"No."

His pinched, blood-smeared face squinted into a grisly smile.

CHAPTER SIXTY-FOUR

KSARA

Maybe it was the metal collar around her waist and the chain in the Giant's hand. Maybe it was the way he'd laughed when he'd pulled someone apart like thread. Maybe it was the fact that they were facing off in Ksara's own mind.

Or maybe Ksara was just done running. She'd run from this hulking menace inside of her. From the Dorumai. From her own power.

Right now, with her chain held in this living nightmare's meaty fist, Ksara stretched upright and stood taller than she had in years. Glowering up at the Giant. If she was going to die, she was going to die defiant.

Her legs coiled beneath her and she grabbed hold of the massive chain. Her whole hand could fit in the gap inside each link and its weight seemed to grow as she held it in her palm.

The Giant's face twisted into a cruel smile and he raised his free hand, streaks of purple light crackled across his skin. "Killing mortals amused me once. It is a strange twist of the *kairoi* that I should have need of a mortal at all now."

Go, The Shadowvar whispered in her mind. *Go to a place he doesn't know. A place he cannot follow.*

No. No more running.

Xos flexed his hand and the purple light grew brighter and he placed it on the chain draped between them. She watched the energy rush across the distance, dancing across the links of chain and impacting her stomach.

The blow brought a cry to her lips, but she stifled it in her throat. Her insides grew hotter and hotter as if her very blood would boil her organs and scald her skin from the inside. She let out a small gasp and steam escaped her mouth.

By Grina! What was this magic?

She coughed and straightened her shoulders. Her bones felt wrong. Wobbly. Mushy. She wavered on her feet, but did not fall. She would not fall to Xos.

"Curious," Xos said, his beady eyes bright. "You think yourself strong."

He raised his left hand lazily in the air and spun it to the right.

The air slammed Ksara toward a wall. Xos jerked on the chain at the same time, her neck jerking backward. She landed in a pile at his feet. Her insides still hot from whatever spell he'd sent to her and now her muscles aching, too.

He will kill you, The Shadowvar whispered in her mind. *He can flay your mind right now. Rip your memories, your identity, as easily as a parchment. You have to stop him. Find a way to stop him!*

Her mind raced. She wouldn't hide. She wouldn't run. But she could fight back. This was her mind. It was still her mind.

She had to disorient him.

Focusing on her body, or the body she now saw, she imagined herself growing taller. Larger. With a thick braid of black hair, lighter skin, and violet eyes. As she began to transform, the collar around her waist bit into her skin harder and harder. She kept her focus, keeping her mind on that woman Giant. The one who'd unsettled Xos before.

But the collar kept digging into her flesh. A wound opened up on her sides, weeping blood down her legs.

Xos laughed, that barking cruel laugh. "Paralos doesn't know of this alcove," he said. "She will not find me here."

Pain radiated from her waist and she wrapped her hands around the collar there. It was even tighter now that she'd shifted forms. Even more impossible to slip free of.

Breathing hard, Ksara released the image of herself as the Giantess and immediately her shape returned to herself. But the chain remained just as deeply embedded in her flesh. Just pushing up from the ground sent fresh stabs through her pelvis and legs.

Heavy footsteps crunched stone and rubble as they approached. Ksara struggled on the ground. She would die on her feet. She had to die on her feet. But tried to struggle upward, and slipped in the puddle of her own blood.

He grabbed her by the head and lifted her from the ground. She tried to fight back his hand, but her arms couldn't reach his as he lifted her like a doll from the floor and turned her to look him directly in those pinched, black eyes. The smear of blood dried and cracking on his face.

His grip tightened around her skull and she remembered the way he'd reached his hands into the insides of the dead Luminent.

Hot bile rose up in her throat. She had to disrupt his mind. That was his weakness.

But he'd become more powerful since her first battle with him. He'd twisted the Demaijos palace into some sort of slaughterhouse. Whether it was a memory of his or just a violent flight of whimsy, she had no idea. Did he know her past? Her thoughts? Her experiences?

In a flash she remembered seeing the Shadowvar shot with an arrow. Lying in a forest she'd never seen.

With a curve of her lips, she began changing the Demaijos palace into that forest. She recreated the muted grays of the trees. The stones. The grass. Then she added the Shadowvar on the ground just below her, an arrow through his chest.

Xos laughed and the sound rumbled like thunder from his chest. He bent down, squeezing Ksara's head all the tighter, and snagged the body off the ground holding him around the chest with his massive hand and squeezing the arrow deeper and deeper into the Shadowvar's chest.

"I know you," the Giant said, his thick brow furrowing. "I have felt you before."

The Shadowvar groaned and his eyes flew open. He glanced at Xos for only a moment and then turned his head to Ksara. "You are not alone. Not out there. Not in here."

The warrior stepped out from behind a tree, pulling the enormous sword from his back with a slow scrape. Calm. Steady. With that smile growing on his lips.

The mage followed a step behind, thumbing through a pouch of clay discs on his waist. His eyes burning with curiosity.

The Shadowvar thrashed and kicked, but the Giant's single hand held him high and steady.

"I am your master." Xos's fingers tightened and squeezed. "This is a lesson I teach only once."

"No!" Ksara yelled. The Warrior and the Mage disappeared. The forest began to fade. Vohn's bones crunched beneath the Giant's vice-like fingers.

"No!" She screamed again, grabbing hold of the chain between them and jerking it toward her.

Xos smiled, but his focus remained on the Shadowvar as he squeezed him tighter and tighter. Blood trickled out of Vohn's nose and his breathing became gurgling gasps. "This is your body. Your mind. Your power," the Shadowvar said in a wheeze. "Don't stop fighting. I will find you again."

In an instant, Vohn dissolved into black air and the air shot down a corridor and out of sight. She felt him leave, felt the absence of him in her mind.

Xos looked at his empty hand and then his small, angry eyes found Ksara. The chain between them strengthened, grew heavier even. But Ksara didn't flinch. She stared right up at the Giant's face and smiled.

It was time to introduce this Eldroi to a Demaijos devil.

CHAPTER SIXTY-FIVE

CORONATA

The dingy was gone. The *Falco* was gone. Ksara was gone.

Coronata kept a curve to her lips as she solved one problem at a time.

First was getting what was left of the crew to the Dorumai ship anchored two hundred feet into the bay. All but Ulric and Atlas could swim the distance to the ship. Ulric because of his injuries and Atlas because of his arrogant refusal to take off plate metal armor when in and around an ocean when that same ocean would delight in adding you to its sea floor ornamentation.

She spotted two dead branches on a nearby tree and pointed them out to Merewen. "Use those lovely arms of yours?"

Bless the giantess of a Usaran! She didn't ask any questions. She just received the command with a nod, went to the tree, and used brute strength to crack the low branches off the trunk.

Coronata lashed the two branches together with strips of cloth from Ulric's tattered tunic. Combined the branches formed a ten-inch-wide surface. "Ulric, Atlas, you'll sit on this and we'll get you to the ship."

"And the rest of us?" Genove asked with those bright green eyes that burned with tainted ambition. Ever since Ulric had returned with the Allarune's tooth, the scholar hadn't been more than a step away from the Demaijos at any given time.

"The rest of us swim or stay here and make sandcastles. Your choice."

Genove's gaze lingered on her.

"You first scholar," Coronata commanded. "Merewen, you and I will swim on either side of the logs. Let's get to the ship."

Ulric flashed Coronata a weak smile. "Has anyone told you that you would make a great pirate queen?"

Coronata smiled back.

"You looking to reclaim your treasure?" Genove asked, wading into the surf.

"I am looking to reclaim my friends."

Ulric flashed her a grin and helped pull the logs into the surf and then eased his battered body up onto the makeshift raft. Atlas joined him just behind, steadying him with a hand on his back.

Coronata entered the saltwater and it comforted her. Steadied her. They'd find Ksara. They'd make this right.

She and Merewen guided the raft to the hull of the Dorumai ship. Once there, Genove and Merewen clung to the raft while Coronata grabbed hold of the anchor rope, wrapped her wet legs around it, and climbed up to the deck of the ship.

As soon as her boots touched the planks, a tiny chirp and a flurry of black and white fur barreled at her. In an instant, the creature scrambled up Coronata's legs, making the journey with tiny, sharp claws and ending up wrapped around her neck, its fluffy banded black and white tail coiled around her neck.

She laughed. "Khyven the Unkillable Kapicat. How did you get on *this* ship?"

The kapicat thrummed a happy, throaty sound and rubbed its pointed ears against her cheek. Coronata dodged the black twisted horns and then scratched at the fur between them.

"Shall we get out of here?"

The kapicat flicked the tip of its tail and made a guttural sound.

"Okay. Okay. But let's get the rest of them up here first."

Khyven made a disapproving sound, but Coronata moved about the deck anyways, throwing down a rope ladder to the crew and then busying herself with the sails.

By the time the whole crew was aboard, she'd pulled anchor, had the ship turned toward the canyon, and was surveying the new debris there. The monster that Ksara had led away from the island had made a thirty-foot wide split into the cliff. That path had new hazards, but if the *Falco* had traversed it, then so could they.

"Merewen, man the helm," Coronata said. "Atlas, keep Ulric breathing. We'll catch Ksara by dawn."

"You don't even know where she went," Atlas said as he kneeled beside Ulric and began prodding at the wounds all over the Demaijos' body. "With the *Falco*, she could go to Usara. Taur-El. Anywhere."

"He'll go to the closest noktum," Genove said. "Ksara has no say in it."

Coronata startled a little. The scholar had leaned into the shadows of the ship, staying out of the way so well she'd forgotten he was among them. "Right. To Nokte Murosa, then. Easy enough."

"Easy," Atlas scoffed as he began dressing Ulric's wounds. "There's nothing easy about chasing down a monster and a mage."

"And a Giant," Genove said.

Coronata turned the helm and guided the *Falco* through the new canyon in the cliffs. There were a few hazards—chunks of the cliff that had fallen into the sea, likely after the *Falco* had moved through it—but she saw the eddies of water, felt the flow of it, and got the Dorumai ship through without so much as a scratch.

As soon as they were out on the open ocean, she flipped the helm three times to the right and pointed the ship toward Nokte Murosa.

Some problems were easy to solve. Getting to the ship. Getting the ship out of a treacherous reef and into the open ocean. Even pushing the inferior Dorumai ship to its limits to speed across the water to Nokte Murosa was a problem she was equal to.

But as they sped through the night toward Ksara, she thought about shadows and Giants. Magic and possession. Relics and monsters.

And she wondered if anyone on this ship, Genove included, could help Ksara at all.

Chapter Sixty-six

JUNLI

Junli carried an armful of lumber and walked it down the dock. He made it all of three steps before he tripped over a seabird scuttling across the wood planks. Catching himself just before he pitched into the cold sea, he growled a curse at the bird and kicked at it.

The animal dodged the blow and launched into the sky with a screech. More screeches echoed around him. The petulant birds were out in force today. They peppered the sky, screaming and circling the air. Only landing to apparently tangle in Junli's feet.

He hadn't been able to sleep since he'd drugged Coronata. So he spent the early morning hours mending the dock. Letting the simple work overtake his guilt. The movement of the sea beneath him. The sound of it pushing against the land and pulling away. Again and again.

Junli dropped the load of lumber at the edge of the broken dock. Dockmaster Gid should have had these repairs done days ago, but no one had seen him since the Night of the Soul. And few of his sailors remained. Some deserted Nokte Murosa for the sea and the others kept to the taverns and *shkazat* tents.

More seabirds screamed, a grating cacophony. The majority of the birds swooped and circled in the lightening sky like a nest of bees all stirred up with nowhere to go. A few unwise birds tried to fly over the east noktum and the black air caught them up with a tentacle and pulled them in.

Junli eased himself down to his knees and began positioning the first few planks in the gap. Three pieces would do the trick. He pulled a hammer from his belt and a handful of nails from the pouch beside. Dumping the nails on the first new plank, he took one of them, positioned it against the crossbeam, poised his hammer—

And two seabirds landed on the plank. They gave him a dull-eyed perusal then one of them pecked at the pile of nails.

He swung the hammer at the feathered pests. "Get on with you!"

The birds squawked and pecked at his knuckles. He swiped at them again, but they sidestepped the blow and three more birds joined the first.

"What in Grina's sly smile is this!"

The birds shook out their feathers and glanced all about them. Shifting their feet and swiveling their heads about when an applause burst through the air.

Junli got to his feet then, looking about the dock for the source of the strange noise only to find, not humans, but fish clapping against the surface of the water, flailing. And, as he watched, the fish began flinging themselves from the water and toward the rocky shore, slapping against the sharp rocks and falling back into the waves bloodied only to try it again.

The birds pecked at the fish trying to take up space among them. They could have eaten their fill of fish just now, but none of them feasted on the strange meal and instead fought for their little oasis on the boards.

Junli gaped at the unnatural scene. Fish slapping his shins as they fought to flee the very water they called home. Birds stirring about in the air, pinned against the noktum.

He hadn't believed much in curses. But now, looking at all this strangeness, he wondered if Coronata had uttered some incantation. A final punishment for his betrayal.

He kicked his way across the dock, making his way around fish and bird back toward the dock house, when all the birds quieted in the same moment. The fish on the docks around him stilled. All of the chaos paused for a single moment.

The hairs on Junli's neck rose and he adjusted the grip on his hammer. He felt more than heard the thing approaching the bay. Like his own animal senses, much duller than the seabirds and the fishes', finally attuned to the threat pressing toward them.

When he gathered his wits enough to look across the bay, all he saw was the *Falco* cresting the morning waves at its usual breakneck speeds.

Coronata had returned.

His mouth dried. What powers did the woman have over the sea?

And how long would she make him suffer before he died?

Dark waves rose up on either side of the *Falco*, stretching higher and higher into the air. He realized that these weren't waves, but some kind of creature breaching out of the water. Two angular, dragon-like heads pushed out of the water on long, black necks. The heads swiveled in the air, taking in Nokte Murosa with eyes that glowed orange as coals and mouths that exhaled smoke.

One of the heads tilted up into the air and bellowed a roar, the sound so tremendous it might have rent the sky. But it certainly shook Junli from his surprise. And the birds and fish from their stupor.

All of them animated at once. The birds leaping into the sky, flying away from the monster and into the noktums in droves. The fish bashing their own heads into the sharp coast until they floated lifeless and bloody on the waves.

And Junli tried to run. But as soon as he pivoted, his foot slipped on the wet dock and he crashed against the planks. The platform swayed and creaked. The fish clunked their heads against it in a grisly rhythm. And the water swelled beneath the dock, lifting it up as the monster approached.

Junli lay flat on his back as a third head rose from the waves.

And so did the thing's body.

Water dripped from its wide, flat serpent body, falling like rain all around Junli. The thing loomed thirty feet above him. Its heads snapping at the unlucky fowl still in the air and eating them by the mouthful and its body demolishing anything that got in its way. Anchored ships cracked and sank. The platform buckled and split. And the dock house crumbled to dust.

All the while, the planks Junli lay upon bucked and twisted in the wake of the destruction. He spread his arms wide and clung to it with his fingertips. The monster was close enough he could see it panting, its enormous, flat chest inflating and deflating and one of the heads pulling the *Falco* by its anchor through the debris bobbing in the waves and up onto the shore.

The keel scraped against stone, undoing all of Junli's repairs and then some, and the ship tipped sideways against a warehouse, but it kept upright.

Junli dared to raise his head from the platform an inch to see the two figures exit the *Falco*. The first was a Dorumai scrambling down the side for the ship in full robes. And the second was a woman, carried by a plume of shadow from the deck of the ship to the cobblestone street.

That was the Demaijos Mage. The one who'd escaped the Guildmaster's custody. She was back.

Maybe it wasn't just Junli that had been cursed. Maybe it was all of Nokte Murosa.

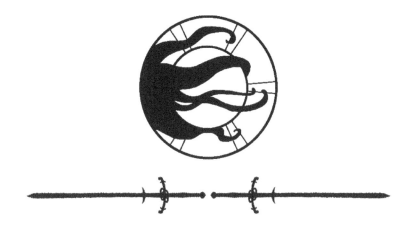

CHAPTER SIXTY-SEVEN

KSARA

os grabbed Ksara by the hair and ripped her backward. She fell a step or two, but she beckoned the shadow to her now. She let it enter in and it tingled through her spine.

The shadow complied, lapping eagerly at her feet.

This was her mind. Her body. And her fight.

She thrust her hands up, envisioned a pillar of black air all around her and the next moment, her thought became reality and the shadow tore Xos's grip from her hair.

She spun around to face him.

The Giant panted, his five-foot-wide shoulders heaving. He squinted his black eyes down at her.

He was not at all accustomed to losing. He dealt blows. He played with mortals, squishing their organs as a diverting pastime.

Ksara lowered into a crouch and spread her hands wide, letting the purple vein inside the shadows brush past her fingertips and tingle her skin with its chill.

Xos bellowed at her, spittle flying from his mouth, "You are mine!"

He raised his arms above his head and the shadows peeled away from Ksara. She felt their loss like her own skin tearing from muscle and sinew. She screamed the pain back in the Giant's face, flexed her hands toward the shadow, and fought for the shadow.

CHAPTER SIXTY-EIGHT

EZELL

 zell Lamar knelt in an aisle of the Nokte Murosan library wearing a cowl up and over her head and lowering her face into the hood's shadow whenever a student walked by.

She wasn't supposed to be in the library. Or on Nokte Murosan Academy property at all.

No one could prove that she was Dorumai. She had an unblemished record as a librarian for the academy. Nothing but begrudgingly kind reviews of her work by the masters there. She'd been efficient. She hadn't bothered much with pleasantries. And she'd kept the library and its collections in pristine condition.

Not that they'd noticed the last one much.

She'd learned early on in her tenure here that as long as the masters could access the predictable texts at their whim—and not have to waste words on her while they did—they'd leave her alone to do what she would with the collection of leather-bound tomes and fragile parchment scrolls.

But her absence during the Night of the Soul hadn't gone unnoticed. She hadn't made it to the Western Plaza in time for the actual ambush, but the Guildmaster suspected her as complicit with the attack. And the end of her career had come on the lips of the Guildmaster's own guards as she'd been escorted off the premises and to the Assembly Hall for questioning.

The interrogation had been feeble at best. She was a woman of little importance. Unconnected in the academy. Friendless on the streets. They'd levied the expected questions and she'd returned the expected answers.

And when she'd returned to her attic above a mill, she'd found her straw mattress gutted and spread across the floor. Her desk had been overturned and the jar of ink there toppled and staining the wood like ichorous blood.

She'd righted the desk, swept up the straw, mopped up the ink, dawned her robe and an empty satchel, and come to the library to gather up her true possessions.

These books. This knowledge. This was the only thing she cared for. It was to preserve these collections, this history, that she had gotten involved with the Dorumai at all.

The Orator had spoken of history with a passion that harmonized with her own. And he'd given her a place. A purpose. A way of preserving history and forging a new future void of the bickering, small minds of masters and students alike.

Glancing up and down the aisle, Ezell pulled two texts from the shelf and tucked them into the satchel at her feet. That filled the satchel to all but bursting. Any more and she wouldn't be able to heft her prize across the library, never mind through the halls and courtyards between her and the academy gate.

Slipping the satchel over her shoulder, Ezell straightened her robe over the bag and strode right at the replacement librarian. The man looked like he'd been shooed out of a dusty closet for the position; he kept twirling about in place, scratching his tufts of red hair and mumbling to himself. She kept her head ducked low and walked right at him.

"Excuse me, Master," she said.

The replacement librarian startled at her presence and stumbled with his reply. "I am no master. Just a keeper of texts.

So many texts. Do you know where the texts on sea faring trade routes circa 2988 would be?"

Ezell clasped her hands together to keep from pointing and shook her head. "Master," she said again. "I don't want to trouble you, but two students are toying with a lamp by the tables and one burned himself. Do you have an ointment?"

The replacement librarian stiffened as if he'd been slapped across his balding head. "Burned? Were there texts nearby?"

Ezell hid a smile. She liked her replacement after all. "One, yes, master. But it was only scorched a little."

"A little!"

The librarian pushed Ezell aside and ran to the back tables. "Attention! Under no condition are we to remove the lamps from their sconces! These texts are one-of-a-kind!"

Four students made their way to the door right away. Nothing cleared out the library like a yelling librarian eager to dish out letters to headmasters. Ezell slipped out just behind the group, following them out of the main hall, passing several Masters, and into the courtyard where there was enough of a commotion, even at this early hour, to make her movement inconspicuous.

Only then did she let herself smile. The replacement librarian would have to catalogue the entire library, find her predecessor's inventory notes, and compare the two to know what she had taken. If he was worth his mettle, he'd catalogue the collections right away, but he wouldn't finish this year. And, even if he did discover the theft and suspect her of it, she'd be halfway across Noksonon by then.

Besides, no one really knew the value of these texts besides her. And this was Nokte Murosa! Where villainy was commonplace. A few stolen texts wasn't going to get more than a passing glance from the Guildmaster. As long as it didn't happen now when the Guildmaster was eager to root out and punish any suspected Dorumai, of course.

Birds screamed in the air above them. A few of the students paused their comings and goings to point up at them. Ezell gave them a casual glance but kept her course to the front gate.

Her heart thumped faster when she saw the iron door. It was not her last obstacle to the new life she'd planned, but it was a significant one. Once out on the streets, she could drop the student charade, lean on a few unsavory academy contacts, and be on the next ship to Nokte Shaddark by midday.

Just feet from the door, the guard locked eyes with her. "Permissions?" Her voice equal parts frosty and disinterested.

"Master Obray," Ezell offered quickly.

The guard frowned and the gesture accentuated the dark bags beneath the woman's eyes. "Again?"

"He only just remembered the rest of the list."

The guard shrugged at that and reached for the door. Master Obray had a reputation of being both infinitely demanding and seemingly random. It had become an accepted quirk of his genius.

Just as she inserted her key into the door, a banging sounded from the other side. The guard stiffened, holding the key still. "What business have you?"

"The Dorumai!" The other voice yelled. "They've returned! With a monster! I must tell the Guildmaster!"

Ezell's mouth parted and words left her. Her whole body flushed with emotion. She was in the middle of history after all. Witness and participant to a new age.

The guard finished unlocking the door and opened it a crack. Ezell pushed the guard aside, ripped the door open, and ran through. Shouts followed her from both the guard and the messenger, but Ezell didn't even hear their words. She ran. Ran to the alley where she'd cached her mask. There she stashed the books, put on the white mask of the Dorumai, and entered the streets anew.

CHAPTER SIXTY-NINE

KSARA

Xos won the shadow to his side, flexing his fingers in the indigo air.

But even as the dark swirled around his fist, Ksara felt its hesitation. It obeyed him, but not completely.

He charged at Ksara, pummeling her head with his fist. She would have dodged the blow—he forecasted the strike and as strong as the Giant was, he wasn't agile—but the shadow caught hold of her neck and head and kept her there. Betraying her. Pain exploded through her skull and her vision blurred.

The strike should have sent her flying. But here, too, the shadow betrayed her, holding her still while the Giant brought another fist down on her face.

Red burst across her vision. She couldn't be sure if it was blood in her eyes or if she'd just been hit so hard she'd gone blind in an instant.

She spat blood from her mouth and smiled her own grisly smile. She didn't need to see to fight Xos. She could feel the shadow now.

Xos growled again. She felt the next blow coming. Felt the shadows resist him. They didn't want to hurt her.

She reached out to that shadow and enveloped it with her mind. It livened at her touch, it wanted to come to her. But she bade it stay by Xos and feign allegiance to the Giant. Then, when Xos's hand was inches from her face, she willed the shadows to pull her head away and smash his fist into the flagstones instead.

The Giant bellowed his rage, his voice shaking the courtyard: "This is my power!"

Ksara blinked open her swollen eye. "Not anymore."

CHAPTER SEVENTY

ARISTON

G uildmaster Ariston sat on a wooden chair at the center of the Assembly Hall's dais. He was the first Guildmaster in recorded history to sit while taking audience with the citizens of the town. But ever since Eshe's death, standing had felt wrong.

The grief had changed him, curled him in on himself so that he stooped, even now, sitting in the chair. Standing upright with his shoulders back and his eyes alight—that version of Ariston had died alongside his only son.

His aides and allies had compromised and allowed him to sit. Anything to resume the comings and goings of the city. The people needed some consistency now. Some sense of normal returning, after the outright attack by the Dorumai and the mage's murders.

His eyes flicked from the citizen who was talking. He'd stopped listening a few minutes ago, picking up the occasional word. Something about fishing infringements by another fishing guild member. Instead Ariston's eyes moved to the pillar where he'd chained the Demaijos mage until they could build the platform and let her hang.

She'd escaped those chains. Thwarted justice. And Ariston had had to bury Eshe and the others the next day. He hadn't spoken a word at their services. It would dishonor the dead to lie to them. To promise more justice that he had failed so miserably at before.

He felt the urge to return to Eshe's graveside. It was an itch that overwhelmed him. He jerked upright in his chair and the fisherman before him flinched.

The fisherman stared at Ariston, the man's whiskered lips frozen.

"Go on," Ariston said, his voice hoarse from hours of weeping.

"The Deep Sea Guild are aware of their violations," the fisherman said, rubbing at his unkempt beard. "They will not stop until compelled to do so."

Ariston tried to focus on the man. His earnestness, the steely gray eyes. The smell of the sea that clung to him. This was who Ariston was here to serve. This man and dozens more like him, sitting in the benches of the Assembly Hall waiting for their chance at audience with him. Waiting for their problems to be heard and a decisive solution to be offered.

But the itch returned, spreading from the back of Ariston's neck and tickling across his shoulders and chest, down his stomach and to his thighs then up and down the back of his legs. He had to get out of this chair. Leave this room. He had to return to Eshe. To be there for his son in death as though that could pay the debt.

A murmur began in the farthest reaches of the Assembly Hall. Already Ariston's advisors warned that the people thought him broken. Ineffective. And many attended these meetings to see it with their own eyes.

Ariston rose to his feet and the itch circled the tops of his feet. He fidgeted in his boots and his eyes moved to the door. He could throw off his boots and scratch at his skin until it bled, but the urge would not wane. The only salve was sitting at Eshe's graveside.

"I will—I will speak," Ariston began, his voice cracking. "I will speak to the Deep Sea Guild."

The fisherman jabbed a finger at a group of sailors on the front row of the Assembly Hall, not twelve feet away from where Ariston stood. "There they sit, Guildmaster. Have at it."

Ariston's mouth parted and he chewed on air. Calling the sailors sitting in the front row representatives of the Deep Sea Guild was a generous label. They'd once been sailors and they still carried the frame of men and women who'd tested their muscle against wind and wave. But that had been another lifetime. Now they were well known goons for the Guthra gang with their gang leader, Mu'Hall, sitting at their center, her crimson lips twisted into a sneer.

In true Nokte Murosan fashion, this wasn't just a simple dispute between two sea-faring guilds. This was the beginnings of another gang war.

Another version of Ariston would have rose to the challenge implied in the fisherman's words, in Mu'Hall's smile.

But Ariston barely knew that version of himself. This version twitched and scratched at the back of his neck and gazed at the door again.

"Master," Omri said.

Ariston startled as his longtime personal guard pulled from the shadows and pressed close to his side.

"We stand with you," he said. "Whatever you decide."

Decide. That was the word Omri emphasized. They didn't care if Ariston made a poor choice. They just wanted him to act. To do something more than fade away and linger beside a fresh grave.

Ariston scratched the tops of his hands and glanced back at the door. Eshe had been alone now for hours. Three hours.

His legs trembled. The murmurs grew in the room.

"Master?"

Ariston took a step toward the door and his legs shook again, nearly pitching him to the floor.

More cries sounded out around the hall.

He pushed himself upright.

Omri was at his side in an instant.

"I'm fine. I'm fine."

"That wasn't you," he said.

Ariston focused on the other Shadowvar's face, willing his wandering mind to steady, if only for a moment.

Omri looked nearly as exhausted as Ariston felt. Heavy lines hung beneath the Shadowvar's eyes. Lines that hadn't been there a week ago. And his thick brows dipped low.

"I have to go," Ariston said. "I can't be here. I can't be this."

"The ground is shaking, Ariston," Omri said. "Something's wrong."

The stone groaned all around them. A crack splintered through the dais and Ariston teetered off of it, spilling into the first row on his hands and knees.

A scream cut through the crowd and a stampede of feet chorused all around him. A boot caught his shoulder and knocked him to the ground. Another foot caught him on the leg.

Then Omri's quick, sure grip had Ariston by the nape of his coat and up on his feet. Three more guards moved in around them. All of them had their weapons drawn and they pressed through the panicked crowd, pushing human and Shadowvar away in equal turns as they escorted Ariston out of the shuddering building and onto the steps outside.

The mayhem there was no less contained.

Two-story houses swayed back and forth like tall grass in a storm. People spilled out of the structures and milled about in the streets. Some running for the docks and others running for the Assembly Hall, only to see the exodus there and pivot around.

He stared at the mayhem in a satisfied sort of haze. The turmoil, the panic, the sudden shock of reality being turned on its head, echoed the grief throbbing inside him. Now they understood.

And, for a moment, he didn't even care what had brought

them that understanding. Just knowing he wasn't alone was enough.

Then the street itself began to rend in two. The crowds fled up the streets, gathering on the steps beneath Ariston.

Two figures divided the chaos. One was a Dorumai in full robes and mask who strode with vigor and shouted over the din of panic. "The Lords of the Dark return! Nokte Murosa will be an example of fealty or it will be finished."

Beside the Dorumai staggered a woman. She jolted forward a few steps and then stopped short, her body locking up in a stiff line. Then she moved forward again and stopped.

The woman's strange gait distracted Ariston, but only for a moment. Then his heart raced as he recognized the Demaijos Devil.

He rushed forward only for the ground to shudder and pitch him sideways into Omri. The guard caught Ariston and kept him on his feet as the crack in the street split wider and wider. And a huge, black serpentine head pushed out of the chasm.

Screams rose up from the crowd. Omri's grip on Ariston's arm tightened.

A second head rose up beside the first. The crowd fumbled backward. People falling and getting trodden on as every instinct told them to get away.

Omri shoved Ariston behind him and against the Assembly Hall's door, pulling a dagger from his belt so that each hand held a weapon.

When the monster's third head exited the now gaping hole in the ground, silence overcame the crowd. All of them stilled, frozen in horror at the things towering over the houses and staring down at them with smoking, glowing eyes.

The Demaijos Devil jolted forward again, stumbling forward like a puppet on a string. Then she stopped and her arms twitched.

"Run," she said, the words coming out as a hoarse whisper that would never have been heard, if even one in the throng dared to breathe. "Run!" She said louder that time.

And the people obeyed fleeing out and around the Assembly

Hall just as the monster lowered one of its heads and breathed out a black mist at the ground.

"We have to go!" Omri said, ripping Ariston away from the door and toward the eastern face of the Assembly Hall. They made it a dozen steps before the mist caught up to the first fleeing citizens.

A new scream split the air, coming from the citizens caught by the mist. A man froze, arrested by the mist, and screamed. When he finished with the terrible sound, black subsumed his eyes. And he attacked the woman holding his hand, tearing into her with nails and teeth like an animal.

Even Omri hesitated for a moment, watching the phenomenon. The monster breathed out more mist, sending more of the poison out into the crowd. In seconds the fleeing crowd began to change into undaunted predators. Citizens fell. People screamed. Blood coated cobblestone.

Ariston pushed Omri now. "Run!"

CHAPTER SEVENTY-ONE

ULRIC

They arrived at Nokte Murosa in time to see the monster, the Worldbreaker, haul the *Falco* up onto the shore and then burrow its body into the street, cutting through the earth and dividing it asunder, then submerging into rock and cobblestone like a crab in sand.

The ground protested with bone-shivering rumbles. The ocean carried the tumult in tall, cascading waves out from the bay in swells so steep that they threatened to capsize the Dorumai vessel.

Under anyone's hand, save Coronata, and the waves would have.

A bandaged, haggard Ulric clutched the ship's railing and stared at the horror unfolding in front of his eyes. He'd thought he'd been prepared for it. He'd tried to prepare for it. Ever since Genove had said that Ksara was coming here. That she was leading the Worldbreaker here.

Even as he picked out the form of Ksara on the *Falco*, even as he watched her alight to the ground with a plume of shadow and stride side-by-side with what looked like a Dorumai, his mind still rebelled at the thought of Ksara being here. Bringing the Worldbreaker here—to the place she'd so vehemently wanted to bring justice to. And that she'd finally lost that fight inside herself. That her power really was a curse and she'd finally succumbed to it.

He pulled his bloodless fingers from the banister and moved one hand to grip the Allarune tusk strapped across the front of his chest. He'd retrieved the thing to give Ksara a choice.

Now, as he watched a thirty-foot-tall monster burrow into Nokte Murosa and split the ground in two as it rushed on—as he watched Ksara point her hand and shoot shadow toward the city center and the monster obeyed, burrowing that direction—he knew she didn't get a choice anymore.

He was going to have to stab Ksara with the Allarune tooth himself.

Genove had made a case for being the one to guide the tusk. Ulric had listened to the arguments until fatigue took him into slumber, but when he woke, hours later, the argument was still on-going. And he'd stopped it definitively by strapping the tooth to his chest without a word.

He clung to it now as Coronata barreled the ship right at the coast.

"I'm not doing another Lotura's Luck," Atlas yelled over his shoulder.

"Lotura's Luck requires an intact dock," Coronata called back.

"Then what is this?"

Coronata laughed into the chaos. "I suppose this will be called a Nokte Murosa!"

"Damn crazy Sandrunner."

Coronata whooped into the wind.

Merewen manned the sails with Atlas begrudgingly helping alongside. Ulric waited at the bow, where Coronata had told him to stand, with Genove lurking behind. Genove hadn't been more than two steps away from Ulric since he'd retrieved the Allarune tusk. Not even the threat of a beating last night had dissuaded him.

"You ready to jump?" Coronata yelled.

Ulric glanced down at his legs. Atlas had splinted his bad leg securely and dumped a cocktail of elixirs down his throat. He could walk and almost run, but jumping seemed like a tall ask. He flashed a smile back at the pirate queen. "I'm ready."

"Hold on!"

The rocky coastline rushed up to meet them with no sign of Coronata throwing anchor or turning the sails. Ulric's heart thumped faster the surf transformed to stone and the Dorumai ship collided, bow-first, with the land.

"Now!"

Somehow, in the midst of the shock, Ulric still heard Coronata's voice. And, even more remarkably, he listened to it.

He leapt on his sore legs up and over the railing just as the ship collided with rock and the buckling planks shot him higher and farther, up over the jagged stone to crash onto a pile of debris that used to be the dock house.

Splintered wood jabbed into Ulric as he lay coughing and blinking in the rubble. His hand checked first for the Allarune and then his injured leg. When both seemed well in order, he rolled to his feet and coughed more dust from his lungs.

The Dorumai ship was in pieces, busted against the rocks. The aft was sinking fast. He heard voices from the ship and he wanted to go to them, but forced himself toward the city center. Toward Ksara. That had been the goal of this foolhardy maneuver. If he went back to help them now, it would all be for naught.

CHAPTER SEVENTY-TWO

KSARA

K sara ripped the shadow away from Xos with both hands and the dark fled him. He bellowed his rage, flexing his own hands toward Ksara and bringing the swirling vortex of black between them.

Widening her stance, Ksara beckoned the power to her. She felt its yearning for her.

She heard screaming somewhere outside this courtyard, outside her mind. Her pulse quickened. She needed control of her body now. She needed the power to be her own.

She wanted the power to be one with her.

This fight had been harrowing, horrifying, but it also had been the first time she'd felt whole. This piece of her, this magic, completed her. Like breathing with both lungs for the first time, she reveled in the wholeness of it. The steadiness she felt. All of the spaces that had once been full of worry and shame could now be filled with something more.

She felt the chill of the shadows and she beckoned it in. Let the cold calm her.

The battle had changed Xos as well. He looked several feet shorter than before. Haggard.

Ksara smiled up at the Giant and wrenched the shadow to her. The Dark fled the Giant and he growled his rage, flexing his hands out and willing the shadow back to him.

She let the shadow return, but not before she willed it into a dozen spears.

Xos beckoned his own defeat to him, skewering himself with the shadow spears. Blood gurgled up out of the wounds and the Giant fell to his knees. "I cannot die. I will live on in the Dark."

"I am the master here," she said, gesturing for the shadow spears to plunge deeper into the Giant's chest. "That is a lesson I only teach once."

The Giant gasped, growled a curse, then his form slowly dissolved into the air. When he was gone, the courtyard began to change, too. Black and gray stones shifted back to white. The bloodstains gone.

Ksara took one look at the palace restored. Glanced into the faces of the Seven Sisters and spotted smiles on their lips. She returned the smile with one of her own and opened her eyes.

The mayhem there obliterated her calm.

She was standing at the foot of the Assembly Hall, nearly in the same place her hanging would have taken place. But the citizens were doing their own executions, tearing into each other with savage ferocity. And the Worldbreaker's three heads breathed more tainted air into the city and gulped the dead down several bodies at a time.

There were at least fifty people killing each other right in front of her. Men, women, and children. All of them ripping at each other's throats with a staggering ferocity.

Ksara reached out, saw the faint indigo in the black of their eyes, and she pulled on it. Her hands flexed wide as she expanded her reach to all the citizens and began inching the tainted dark back out of their noses and mouths.

She'd nearly pulled the air out of the closest dozen citizens, the thread of black was just visible out of their mouths, when something stabbed into Ksara's shoulder from behind.

Pain exploded in her body and the cold withdrew from her, faster and faster, it left her body. She gasped. Her hands went slack. The tainted air returned to the citizens and they tore at each other with renewed vigor.

The strength left her legs. And the cold, the cold was gone. A searing heat replacing it.

Hands caught her. Eased her down to the ground as the heat robbed her breath. Why couldn't she breathe? And where was the cold? Where was the shadow?

"I'm so sorry."

That was Ulric's voice. She searched for his face and only then realized her vision was blurry. She blinked back the sweat. "Ul …" Her mouth stopped the word and just wheezed in air.

"I'm sorry, 'Sar. I'm so sorry."

CHAPTER SEVENTY-THREE

ULRIC

 lric held Ksara as she crumbled into his arms. His heart ached as her panicked eyes found him. They searched for relief, wide with pain and shock.

"I had to," he said, holding the tooth in her back. Black seeped into the tooth, overtaking the white, smooth surface and staining it.

Ksara shook her head and her lips tried to form words.

"It's going to be okay," he said, but he didn't believe his own words.

He didn't know how long to hold it in her shoulder. He didn't know how much the tooth needed to take to bring his sister back or how much it would take of her life force if it remained.

Glancing around, he suddenly wished one of the crew was here. Someone to advise him. Someone to watch the color drain from Ksara's face and to tell him when he'd taken enough.

Instead he saw the throng of humans and Shadowvar tearing into each other with their bare hands and the enormous, sleek black heads of the Worldbreaker hovering fifteen feet above the chaos. The monster's pulsing orange eyes on Ulric and Ksara.

He leaned over his sister, trying to shield her from the monster's view.

One head lowered to the ground, mere feet from where Ksara lay. Ulric called down his magic from his chest to his fingertips, the tingling heat a pitiful defense against the massive skeletal black dragon head with a pulsing orange glow inside of it.

The Worldbreaker opened its mouth and the stench of decay overwhelmed Ulric. He fully expected to be eaten the next moment. The thing had swallowed six humans in a single mouthful.

But the monster opened its mouth again and made a choking sound.

Ksara's eyes moved about wildly. She saw the Worldbreaker and formed a whisper of words: "It's ... waiting ... for ... orders."

Ulric kept his left hand on the tooth in Ksara's back, but freed his left hand and snapped his fingers. A burst of light exploded around them and all three heads turned to the sky and screamed. The sound rang in his ears. The ground trembled all around him. Houses swayed. Glass shattered in the Assembly Hall and rained down on him. He leaned over Ksara again, shielding her from it all. Hoping that if he couldn't protect her from death, at least he could die first.

A thundering crash rumbled around them and he dared to look up from Ksara long enough to watch the Worldbreaker barrel through the city toward the Western Noktum.

Relief flooded through him, but it lasted only a few seconds before a Nokte Murosan citizen with swirling black for eyes, tackled Ulric to the ground, knocking him off of Ksara and breaking his grip with the Allarune tusk.

A portly man scrambled on top of Ulric, scratching at his face and biting his arm. Ulric yelled and kicked the man off of him with his good leg. But before he could get to his feet, the man was atop him again, this time on his back and gnawing on Ulric's shoulder.

"Senji's thighs! Get off!"

Ulric struggled with the man a moment before catching hold

of both of his arms twisting them above his head and throwing the man over top him to land flat on his back in front of Ulric. The man was covered in Ulric's blood. And he should have stayed down. The fall should have taken the fight right out of him. He turned on his side, got his knees beneath him, and then his feet.

And his eyes, filled with that ever-moving black, found Ulric again.

Ulric got to his feet grabbed a chunk of the cobblestone street and threw it at the man's head. Stone collided with bone with a sickening crunch and the man fell to the ground, twitching.

When Ulric turned back around, Ksara was lying on her side. Blood pouring out of a gaping hole in her back.

And the Allarune tusk was gone.

CHAPTER SEVENTY-FOUR

GENOVE

Genove clutched the Allarune tusk with both hands, the thing still wet with the Demaijos blood and humming with her power. With the treasure in his hand, he almost froze right there, standing over Ksara as her blood wept out the hole in her back and pooled around her. She grabbed his ankle, her lips forming words that her lungs could not fulfill.

He broke the grip of her feeble fingers without effort and stole toward the shadows and away from the humans turned feral beasts, the crack in the ground, and the raucous roar of the retreating Worldbreaker.

Within his hands was the thing that would elevate him from middling predator to apex. No more hallucinations. No more mind games. Their fear would be real and it was all at his fingertips.

His power on its own wasn't weak—it was incomplete. And now he could have everything he'd dreamed of.

Crouching in the debris of two houses knocked into each other, Genove turned his right hand over and pressed the needle-sharp tip of the Allarune into the back of his hand. Pain bit at his skin, but he hit the vein with precision. Then he turned the Allarune tooth left and right until he saw his vein darken. Then he held the tooth there another excruciating moment as heat joined the pain and his skin began to blacken.

The ink spread out from his vein and blackened the skin. His hand trembled. Perspiration dribbled down his chin. The heat radiated down to his fingertips and then up to his elbow and shoulder. When the heat began stabbing into his ribcage, he pulled the Allarune tooth out of his flesh. The fossil was altered in the exchange, the tip lightened from obsidian black to a light gray two inches up from the tip.

That brought a momentary frown to Genove's face. A single draw from the relic shouldn't have noticeably depleted it. It was possible the Allarune tooth wasn't the perfect holding vessel for the power, but the perfect extractor.

But that was a worry for another time. Now he flexed the fingers of his blackened hand, working the soreness out of them.

Then he swirled his finger in the air and the shadows all around him hurried to his hand. A wide grin spread across his face and he began making larger, longer strokes and the shadow remained in place for a moment, hanging in the air in front of him. In moments, he finished a rough outline of a Kyolar.

And the Kyolar made of shadow grew taller and wider. Shadow joined with the basic lines and filled in the muscles and claws. Teeth and mane. When the creation was done, it turned its thick neck and snapped its jaw at Genove, missing his shoulder by inches.

Genove held his blackened hand out to the shadow Kyolar and the creature bared its teeth, wagging its head back and forth.

"I am your creator."

The Shadow Kyolar sniffed at Genove's transformed hand and whined.

"I am your master."

The Kyolar bowed its head and whined again. Exhilaration lanced through Genove like lightning. He'd done it! He could draw any of the monsters he'd seen or read about. Even the ones that lived only in his twisted imagination. And they would become living shadows under his control.

Now he could leave Nokte Murosa. No Guildmaster or Academy council could sway his fate now. Not even the other creatures of the noktum could harm him with this shadow Kyolar and more of its kind guarding his every step.

He imagined leaving this cesspool of a town and returning to Nokte Shaddark. Entering the library there with its elite masters—and conjuring monsters to rip their throats out.

A yell distracted Genove. Behind the Shadow Kyolar the brother Demaijos was fighting off one of the citizens who was trying to rip his throat out with bare hands.

Nokte Murosa finally had the anarchy it deserved. Its filth had risen to the surface for all to see.

Guildmaster Ariston arose in Genove's mind and he turned back to his creation. He had but one task to oversee before he would leave Nokte Murosa to its cancerous decay. "Kill Guildmaster Ariston," he commanded.

The Kyolar turned its head away from Genove, snuffed the air, and loped silently away. Its feet hovering inches off the ground and passing through overturned carts and debris only to reappear on the other side.

Genove tucked the Allarune tooth into his belt, stood from the rubble and darted after his creation. He'd seen Ariston cower to the shadows of his own mind. What would he do now when they could bite and tear and claw at him?

CHAPTER SEVENTY-FIVE

ATLAS

hen the Dorumai's ship collided with the coast, Atlas had just enough time to see Ulric leap with the collision before he, too, was thrown.

He'd been thrown from his share of horses. This gave him a similar sensation where the momentum shifted and thrusted him in a new direction and, as he flew through the air, time slowed down. He caught a glimpse of the rocks where he would land. He had but a fraction of a second to adjust his body before it cracked against the sharp rocks breaking the surf.

He hit back-first. His armor clanged and the impact knocked the breath right out of him. Rocks jabbed at him between the gaps in his armor. Sea water lapped at his legs and Atlas took inventory of his body. Nothing was broken. Well, nothing inside the armor was broken. He'd certainly caused fractures in the metal. This was a punishment most armor would succumb to.

In between the roar of the waves, he heard someone shout his name. Growling a curse, he pushed up to his elbows to find Merewen bobbing in the ocean near the sinking ship. Too near the sinking ship. As the thing fell into the water depths, it would create its own current and pull whatever was closest to it down to the same depths.

"Atlas!" Merewen yelled again. "Coronata! She's caught in the sails!"

Atlas cursed again. Loud enough that the sea and sky heard it.

He'd told the Sandrunner this was a foolish plan. That it provided Ulric a quick passage at the risk of all of their lives.

Before he knew what he was doing, he began unbuckling his breastplate. Then his back plate. His arm bracers and leg greaves. All of it until he was only wearing a stained tunic and trousers that barely covered three inches of his thighs.

He dropped his Imprevari armor on the rocks and dove into the sea, fighting waves and the sensation that he'd just left the last of his homeland on the rocks behind him. Kicking through the water, he surfaced beside Merewen.

"She's going to need both of us," the Usaran gasped.

Atlas nodded and they both ducked their heads beneath the surface, kicking through the cold, dark water.

Clouds of bubbles marked the Dorumai's ship's descent and they followed the stream of air to where the mast jerked back and forth.

The mast had cracked and fallen backwards, catching the Sandrunner like a fish in a net. And she'd been underwater this whole time, holding her breath, and struggling to find the surface.

He and Merewen caught hold of the mast at the same time. Merewen wriggled her fingers into a small hole in the mast and Atlas did the same. Each of them pulled in opposite directions and the fabric gave way inch-by-inch. The movement within the mast slowed to occasional jerks and spasms.

Even the pirate queen couldn't survive much longer.

Atlas ripped the canvas with all his strength and caught a glimpse of Coronata's arm floating within. He gave the thing one final heave, opening it a foot and a half wide. Snatching Coronata's arm, Atlas pulled her free of the mast and began kicking hard to the surface. Merewen caught hold of Coronata's other arm and helped drag the listless pirate along.

When they broke the surface, Atlas gasped air into his burning lungs, but Coronata made no sound. Atlas pulled her away from the sinking ship and to the treacherous shore where he found a bit of intact dock, only seven feet long, and climbed atop it, yanking her up from the water to the planks. Merewen helped from the ocean and then climbed up to join him.

He spent the next few breathless seconds listening for Coronata's breathing and feeling for her pulse. He found the faintest bit of blood flow. "She's alive. She's still alive."

He opened her mouth and turned it sideways. In an instant her eyes flashed opened. And she coughed, sputtering water right into Atlas's face.

Holding her head to the side so she didn't choke on the water, he waited until she'd taken a few unencumbered breaths before letting go of her head. She smiled up at him.

"Am I dead or did Atlas lose his anchor armor?"

"I didn't lose it," he said.

"You took it off," she said. "Now you're a lost soldier."

Atlas shrugged and felt suddenly naked. "Not lost."

Coronata smiled wide and shut her eyes, riding the waves of the tumultuous sea on their fragment of dock. "Careful there," she said. "You could be making friends with a Sandrunner."

"I just saved her life," he said with another tight shrug. "She'd better be my friend."

She laughed, the sound was so free and joyful. Even almost dying didn't disturb the woman for long. Nothing did.

"The Worldbreaker is going faster," Merewen said. Atlas turned around to look at Nokte Murosa for the first time since crashing. The *Falco* sat on the shore, docked awkwardly between the few standing houses. Beside it was a thirty-foot hole and a fissure that ran from the pit up the city streets and toward the Assembly Hall. Near the spires of the Assembly Hall the Worldbreaker's three heads shot up into the air. Screams filtered through the air.

Suddenly getting caught in a shipwreck seemed like the easiest part of their day.

"They'll need our help," Merewen said.

Coronata rolled to her side and then got up to her knees. Water dripped from her long black hair. "We should find some weapons."

Atlas glanced about the dock and his eyes narrowed. "And Genove."

The two women looked about the dock for a moment.

"Did he drown?" Merewen asked.

"He was beside Ulric," Coronata said. "He should have been thrown forward not back."

Atlas made the first leap to another floating hunk of dock. Then on to the next. Four more jumps and he was scrambling up the rocky shore. The maneuver had been markedly easier without the full armor, though he figured he'd miss the regalia soon enough when the battling began.

They ran through the city, stopping only to gather two axes from an overturned cart and a busted wheel spoke that served as a formidable club in Merewen's hands.

As they approached the Assembly Hall, the Worldbreaker screamed with all three of its heads in the air and then rushed forward. The ground thundered and buckled beneath them. The houses shuddered on their foundations. Glass shattering. Wood beams groaning and splintering. It felt as though the whole of Nokte Murosa might crumble around them any moment.

They hurried on. Several collapsed houses diverted their course northeast and when they arrived in the Assembly Hall's square they were confronted with a strange scene.

The Worldbreaker was gone, its black heads bobbing over the houses as it rushed toward the Western Noktum. The Assembly Hall was split right in half, the western side of the building reduced to rubble. Hunkered down in the shadow of the still-standing half of the Assembly Hall was a smattering of Shadowvar, a dozen Dorumai, and some kind of translucent Kyolar.

Behind the Kyolar stood a disheveled, and rather overjoyed, Genove.

Dead and dying lie strewn across the courtyard. He couldn't see Ksara and Ulric among them, but he'd have to get closer to be sure.

"That's Guildmaster Ariston," Merewen said pointing at the Shadowvar pressed against the rubble of the Assembly Hall, a few of his guard standing between him and two enemies. "We have to help him."

"No, we don't," Atlas said. "He's an ass."

Merewen pushed past Coronata and Atlas and charged at the nearest Dorumai. They barely had time to register the new attacker before the first masked cultist was clubbed in the head.

"Senji's crooked nose," Atlas muttered. "Why do I follow you?"

Coronata grinned at him. "I get to take out the scholar."

"Grina's ass you do!"

Coronata laughed and dashed across the clearing and added her axe to Merewen's fight. Atlas smiled a little, then hurried to do the same.

CHAPTER SEVENTY-SIX

ULRIC

Ulric's insides wrenched and bile choked up his mouth. The Allarune's tooth was gone and blood rushed out of Ksara's wound in a steady stream. He ripped off the sleeve of his tunic and darted to his sister, tying the makeshift bandage around her.

As he lifted her, she was limp and heavy, but her eyes were open. Focused even.

He tied the bandage tight, staunching the blood and looked into her face. "I'm so sorry, 'Sar."

Ksara's lips twitched into a smile and shadows rushed toward her, slipping out from beneath rubble and away from houses, they slid toward her. Even as she lay dying, the shadows would not give her peace.

Ulric swore and beckoned his own power burning to his fingertips.

But Ksara's hand shot up and caught hold of Ulric's. He hesitated and the shadow pressed through Ksara's skin and entered in. And she smiled wider.

Releasing Ulric's arm, she rose to her feet and another wave of shadow shrouded her. Her legs trembled a little under her weight, but the dark air whipped about her waist and steadied her.

Ulric's mouth parted but no words came. Was she still possessed by the Giant? Had the Allarune failed all together?

"Let's go, brother."

"Ksara?" The word managed to leave Ulric's tongue.

"It's me," she said with a smile.

He glanced at the shadow encircling her legs, holding her steady. Some of the shadow even filled the hole in her back, slowing the blood loss. "How?"

"We'll swap mage secrets later. Now I have a battle to win. And a Worldbreaker to stop."

He eyed her up and down, shrouded in shadow and standing tall. This is who he'd always seen her as. This powerful and confident and certain. And now she was all of those things, while wielding her magic, too. His throat tightened. He wanted to shout his excitement and cry all at the same time.

He'd almost taken this away from her. He'd stabbed her with the Allarune's tusk and almost made this impossible. Guilt robbed the joy until Ksara smiled wider and he couldn't help but smile back. This new Ksara was beaming. Bright while encircled by shadow.

Ulric got to his feet. "After you, Captain."

CHAPTER SEVENTY-SEVEN

KSARA

sara put a hand her brother's shoulder and drank in the joy she saw there for the briefest moments. He saw her. The way she was now. Unafraid and standing in her own power.

The way he'd always said she could be.

But the day wasn't won, yet. And, while she had the energy to stand, to wield the dark, she knew her own reserves were low. When the Allarune tooth pulled the power from her, it pulled her own vitality, too. The two were linked and if she used too much power now, she'd empty the well and die.

Her only advantage was that she was directing the Dark, not conjuring it. It was a nuance, but it might just be enough.

Lurching into a run, Ksara wove around the bodies strewn about the courtyard. Several looked dead. Others unconscious and in need of a healer. But none would survive the day if the Worldbreaker had a noktum full of shadow to inhale and breathe out into the city. It would be feasting upon all their bodies in minutes.

She rounded the broken corner of Assembly Hall to find a melee already in progress. The Orator and his Dorumai were grappling with a poorly armed Merewen, Coronata, and Atlas. Ariston was pressed with his back against the ruins of the Assembly Hall and his three remaining guards were standing between him, battling a Kyolar made of shadow. A grinning Genove stood behind the apparition, laughing with maniacal delight.

There was a ripple in the fight, a pause as they acknowledged Ksara running into the center of the fray.

Ksara dealt with the Kyolar made of shadow first. The creature was larger than a regular Kyolar, nearly six feet tall with paws bigger than the Shadowvar's head that it was swiping at. The Shadowvar already bore five deep gashes down his chest from the creature making contact with him and he swung a sword at the beast only for the metal to whip right through it. The cat took another strike, catching the Shadowvar by the horns and jerking his head around and down with a sickening crack.

Ksara looked deeper into the shadow and found its indigo shades. Then she touched her mind to them, calming them.

The cat backed away from the dead Shadowvar, its tail hung low. It shouldn't have a sentience. Not this sentience. It pulsed with a red light that didn't quite blend with the indigo.

Ksara raised a hand and the shadow, the true, indigo shadow fled the unnatural form and rallied to her. And, as soon as the shadow left, the red veins of power fizzled and vanished.

"Demaijos bitch!" Genove bellowed. He waved his right hand in wide swaths, summoning shadow from his black fingertips and crafting a new image, this one of a mammoth Sleeth with burning eyes and a jaw full of three-foot long fangs.

Ksara twitched her hand and called that shadow to her, too. "No!"

Spreading her hands wide, she split the new swath of shadow into a dozen arrow-sized spears and shot them at the Dorumai's legs. They fell in an instant, grabbing their bloodied thighs and calves.

Coronata whooped and hit a falling Dorumai with the broken shaft of an axe.

The Shadowvar guards rushed at the scholar now, swords ready to skewer the man. He cowered then, stumbling back, catching the hem of his robe with his heel and falling. He lay sprawled out prone and waiting for death.

"Don't kill him," Ksara said, her voice loud and calm. She turned a smile at Atlas, who'd pulled a sword from a prone Dorumai and was stalking toward the Orator. "Nor him."

Atlas paused and so did the Shadowvar guards. Ksara brought her hands back to her side and the shadow spears settled back into the ground, resuming their normal shapes around the fallen.

"Guildmaster?" Ksara said.

All eyes turned to the Shadowvar still cowering against the fallen stone. He glanced about with wild eyes.

Ksara strode toward him and stopped a dozen paces away. "Guildmaster, we leave the Orator and Genove LeGrande in your hands to stand trial by the people of Nokte Murosa."

"You brought them here," the Guildmaster mumbled. "You brought a monster here."

"Would you put me on trial now?" Ksara said. "Or shall I deal with the monster first?"

The Guildmaster straightened. He looked very little like the regal leader she'd seen just days before. His tattered, dust-crusted clothes matched those of his guards, but his eyes were so sullen, so lifeless, they belonged on a corpse, not a breathing, speaking Shadowvar.

"You should die," The Guildmaster mumbled. "For Eshe. For all of them. For this."

"When the day is done, I will be measured," Ksara said. "Then you can have your justice."

She turned, nodding at Ulric. "Get them all into custody. I'll be back when it's done."

"You're not going to take on that monster alone," Ulric spat the words out all at once. "Not a chance."

Ksara cocked a brow at him. "Handle this. Then come find me."

He sighed and he almost argued with her again. Right here. But he swallowed it. "You got it, Captain."

She smiled and jogged toward the noktum.

CHAPTER SEVENTY-EIGHT

KSARA

sara ran until her legs began to buckle and tremble, then she let herself walk. She'd need all her energy, and maybe more, for the task before her.

Morning crested on the city and the people who hadn't been swept up in the initial panic of the Worldbreaker's arrival lingered in doorways until they caught sight of Ksara and then they fled within the houses and shops. The muffled sounds of doors being locked and barricaded rippled around her in a chorus.

Then again, two of the times Ksara had made a public appearance in Nokte Murosa she'd destroyed it. Most recently with a thirty-foot-tall noktum nightmare of a monster.

A dark mist spilled down an adjacent street, clinging low to the ground but moving quickly. Screams began anew in the city.

The Worldbreaker had reached the noktum, had breathed in the shadow, and now was expelling its poison into the city. Preparing its next meal.

Suddenly glad that all who saw her were shutting their doors and windows, Ksara hurried into the Western Plaza with its demolished wall and cracked altar. The blood stains from the dead citizens still marred the flagstones. She'd lost control to Xos here. It had seemed so dire, but it had only been a hiccup compared to what had come next.

Noktum tentacles reached out for her and her pulse quickened, excitement and wonder blending with the old fears at the supernatural air. She looked deeper at the tentacle and found that indigo hue in it and marveled all over again at its beauty. Then she stepped toward the searching tentacle, let it wrap itself around her and pull her into the noktum.

There her senses came alive. That indigo hue brightened and swirled all around her. She felt it as much as saw it and it harmonized with her presence.

"Take me to the Worldbreaker," she said into the noktum, to the Dark.

The indigo light bobbed around her and then flashed brighter to her left. She followed it in a jog.

There were trees, boulders, and even bits of ruins in the noktum. She'd encountered a few of them the last time she'd rushed into the darkness. But this time that violet-blue light burst a little brighter and showed the outline of the obstacles in her way, and she darted around them.

Her legs ached and her vision blurred, but she ran on. The distant cries from Nokte Murosa spurred her faster.

In an instant, the indigo lights darted upward and out, zigzagging across the wide chest of the Worldbreaker and then up and down each of its three long necks and heads.

One of the long necks bowed down from its significant height and lowered to look at Ksara. Even without her connection to the Dark, she would have been able to see the creature's eyes as they pulsed that eerie orange.

For a moment she wondered if she could communicate with the creature. Negotiate somehow for it to leave Nokte Murosa alone.

But this noktum bordered Nokte Shaddark. Could she protect that city, too? Even if she could sail to Nokte-Shaddark the moment the Worldbreaker decided to turn its gaze upon it, the monster moved faster than the ship could and it would breathe its poison into the city and have most of its citizens devoured before Ksara even got near enough to stop it.

And what if the Worldbreaker tired of this cage and moved to the Great Noktum? Could it pass from one to the next without a mage like Ksara guiding it with shadow?

The Worldbreaker cocked its head and snapped at her. The attack was fast, a blur of indigo and those orange eyes. If she'd tried to dodge the attack with her body, she wouldn't have managed the maneuver—not with all of her training in the guardhouse or with a body that didn't feel like it was nearing collapse. But she didn't lean on her body to dodge—she reached for the Dark instead.

And the shadow replied, knocking the monster's jaw up. A gust of air passed over Ksara's head where the Worldbreaker's mouth clamped down on empty air.

Not empty air. Shadow.

Ksara accessed the shadow inside the monster's mouth, felt it as easily as she felt her own fingers. And she beckoned that air around the Worldbreaker's head to wrap tighter and tighter. The head screamed and thrashed; the sound muffled.

The other heads took notice then.

Attacks came at Ksara faster than she could see them. Gusts of air pushed Ksara in every direction as the remaining mouths nearly caught her but were deflected by the shadow.

She wrapped the second mouth in shadow, then the third. But the fight never left the creature. It breathed in some of the shadow, peeked its heads out of the noktum and sent more of that poison mist out into the Nokte Murosan streets.

Enough was enough.

Ksara pulled all of the strength she dared from her body and connected with all of the shadow around the Worldbreaker and jerked her hand upward. The shadow responded with a strength that brought a quirk of a smile to her sweat-riddled face. A plume of dark shot the Worldbreaker a hundred feet into the air. She gritted her teeth and brought her other hand above her head, calling on more shadow and heaving the Worldbreaker over the noktum and screeching with all three heads flailing.

Metal flavored her mouth, and she realized it was blood. Her nose was bleeding. She swallowed the taste down and ignored the apprehension it brought.

She walked toward the edge of the noktum, both hands raised as the shadow carried the screaming, writhing Worldbreaker two hundred feet over her head.

When she exited the noktum, there was mayhem in the streets. A group of citizens possessed with the black mist chased a family yet unaffected by the poison. She let one hand lower, just long enough to sweep it in front of her and pull the shadow from the attacking citizens. The Worldbreaker plummeted, its belly pulverizing the tops of three houses before she could push her free hand back upward and will the pillar of shadow to carry the enormous monster higher.

The citizens took in the astonishing sight of Ksara and the Worldbreaker in a wordless, breathless moment, and then fled from before her. More panicked now than they had been when being chased by each other.

Ksara's right leg buckled, the strength leaving it and she listed heavily. The Worldbreaker teetered in the air and almost crashed into the ground two blocks from where she stood.

Willing her body to obey as completely as the shadow, she moved one trembling step at a time toward the sea. Her vision blurred. She barely saw streets at all, but different smears of color before her. She smelled the ocean, though, and followed the salt in the air and the pull of her feet downhill.

With her whole body shaking from the exertion, Ksara arrived at the sea's edge. Her ship sat on the street a hundred feet from her, anchored between houses. What was left of the docks bobbed up and down on the waves.

Pushing her hands forward she sent the Worldbreaker out over the ocean. It breathed in some of the shadow and exhaled it toward Ksara. She batted the blast of poison away with a shake of her head.

Then she curled her fingers, imagining the shadow wrapping around each one of the Worldbreaker's necks. And, when the shadow complied, she jerked her hands outward and ripped the Worldbreaker into three hunks of flesh.

Its final screams rumbled the earth beneath her boots and brought her to her knees. Her hands fell to her sides and the chunks of monster splattered across the bay in a torrent of gore.

Blood flecked Ksara. Even on her knees she swayed back and forth, her head heavy. More blood dripping from her nose and flavoring the back of her throat.

Screams turned Ksara's head.

A bloodied sailor leapt atop a woman who had been fleeing down the street. Ksara didn't need to see the man's eyes to know they were black.

The Worldbreaker was dead, but its poison hadn't died with it. And that black mist alone could leave Nokte Murosa devastated.

Ksara leaned forward to push herself to her feet and vomited instead. The bitter taste brought some clarity to her for a moment, woke her from the haze of fatigue, and she stood on uncertain legs then pulled the black poison air from the sailor and used the same to push the man off the woman. The push sent him flying a dozen feet to crash into a pile of overturned barrels. He sat there blinking away his stupor when Ksara walked by.

Terror still trembled through the city, a rumble of thunder in the clear morning air. She couldn't chase down every poisoned citizen, as she had with the sailor. She barely had enough strength to keep on her feet at all.

She needed to be done with the poison in one final pull, banishing the tainted air into the noktum where the monsters may have at it and tear each other apart.

So she traveled one more time back to the noktum. Each step riddled with agony and hope and grief and satisfaction. She would end this. She had the power to end this.

Stopping just outside the noktum, she closed her eyes and stood in that Demaijos palace one more time. Glancing at the

Seven Sisters, giving them one last smile, she reached for the remnants of her strength and felt for the tendrils of tainted shadow all across the city. In a flash of clarity she felt them like a web just in front of her face. Reaching forward, she caught hold of the web, and ripped it toward her.

Air gushed around her. Her legs buckled and the Demaijos palace in her mind crumbled and fell. The pieces crashing down on her. In an instant, she was buried beneath it all. Her heart slowing. Air coming into her in rasps.

She'd robbed death once in Nokte Murosa. She didn't have any hope of doing it twice.

CHAPTER SEVENTY-NINE

ULRIC

Ulric punched a merchant with those supernatural black eyes. The blow should have knocked the stocky man back a pace or two, at the very least. Instead, he just turned his head to the side and lunged, throwing Ulric back against a wall.

The man snapped his teeth at Ulric's neck and dug his nails into his face. Ulric dodged the teeth and bore the nails, wrestling the man away from the black mist curling closer to their boots.

Citizens gone savage Ulric could deal with. Breathing in the poison air, he could not.

The merchant clawed at Ulric's eyes, and he growled with pain and threw the man toward the wall, headfirst.

The man impacted hard but bounced back to his feet, blood trickling down his head. Unwilling to stay down.

Ever since they'd restrained the Dorumai and Genove, Ulric been on his way to find Ksara. But the streets were filled with either the black mist or those affected by it. And it had been one skirmish after the next on his way to his sister.

Ulric rallied his strength. Whatever mixture of elixirs Atlas had given him on the trip over here was starting to wear off. He didn't know how many more lunatics he could battle and win.

The black-eyed merchant snarled and started at Ulric, only to freeze mid-step, his eyes and mouth wrenched open wide and the black air seeping out of his nose and throat in a long cloud of black. The poisoned air hovered for a moment and then shot toward the west, fast as a bird in flight. The dark mist on the ground did the same, rolling toward the Western Noktum in a tidal wave.

The merchant crumbled to his knees and Ulric sagged against the wall, catching his breath in gulps. "Thank you, 'Sar," he said between pants.

"Who are you?" the merchant asked, his eyes still wide. "What happened? Where is Adora? Where is my Adora!" He caught sight of his blood-stained hands and began to weep. "No. No. No."

Ulric waited against the wall for a few moments, expecting his sister to come walking triumphantly down one of the streets. They'd all seen the Worldbreaker lifted above the city and torn apart in the sea. But that wasn't enough for Ksara, she'd also saved the lives of every single person still breathing in the monster's residual poison.

She should be here. Walking along the streets. Accepting the accolades of a hero.

That's when a chill worked through Ulric. Something between a premonition and utter dread.

Pushing off the wall, he ran toward the Western Noktum.

He found her in the Western Plaza, a crumpled body on the soiled flagstones.

The cry that left his mouth then couldn't be contained. It wasn't a word, but anguish come alive in sound.

He sprinted to her. Picked her up in his bloodied, dusty arms, and held her to him. "No, no, no, no. Not you. It was supposed to be me. It was supposed to be me!"

He put his hands on her lifeless face. Wiped away the splattered blood there. Remembered the glow she'd had to her eyes last he'd looked upon them. The quirk of her smile when she'd commanded the shadow.

She couldn't be gone now. Not now.

Atlas, Coronata, and Merewen rushed toward him. Coronata and Atlas pulled at his arms and set Ksara on the ground. They said words, but Ulric didn't hear them. Atlas checked Ksara's body with practiced fingers and then put his ear to her mouth to listen.

Then the noktum started reaching for her. Pawing at her. As if the Dark hadn't had enough of her, now it wanted her body.

He summoned his power and unleashed burst after burst of light, growling at the dark. Daring it to come closer to his sister, even as his strength waned and he wobbled on his feet.

Merewen grabbed hold of Ulric's shoulders and turned him toward her, he swung a punch and she caught the weak blow with her palm, stopping it inches from her blue tattooed jaw. "She's still alive. Barely. We need to take her away. Now."

Ulric looked past Merewen. Atlas had Ksara in his arms and was standing looking at the noktum. Coronata was at his side. Two noktum tentacles touched the ground, the shadow reforming into feet, legs, then merging into a body, chest, shoulders, and head. Thick ropes of black hair and a staff at her back.

"Ksara," Ulric breathed.

Then the shadow version of his sister turned and walked into the noktum, pausing once to look back at them, then entering the wall of black.

None of them spoke for a long moment.

Then Atlas took a step toward the noktum. Ulric was between him and the wall in an instant. "No. We have to save her. We have to."

Atlas met Ulric's gaze and found sorrow and steel there. "This is what she wants."

"That wasn't her! That was … that was IT!"

"She doesn't have much time."

Ulric wanted to scream and weep and find a sailor to wallop his fists into. Instead he saw the shadows licking at Atlas's boots, swirling up his legs and reaching for Ksara.

"We need to trust her now," Atlas said. "Do you trust her?"

He knew the answer, it crashed inside his chest as soon as he heard the words. Of course he trusted her. But this was the dark. This wasn't her. This was—

"I'll take her," he said, his voice barely a whisper.

Atlas nodded and eased Ksara's limp body into Ulric's arms. Ulric turned, faced the black, menacing wall of air, and walked into it. His friends a step behind.

As soon as they were all within the black, the shadow pulled her from his arms and set her on the ground. He knelt beside her, resisting every urge to clap light into the world and chase the dark away.

"Keep fighting, 'Sar. Please, keep fighting. One more time."

Chapter Eighty

VOHN

Vohn felt Ksara's heartbeat grow slower and slower. Her vitality, her essence pulsed in the Dark. The shadow had always delighted in her. Reveled in her presence. Even now the voices that rumbled through the black argued over her, their voices so low they groaned like the earth.

He'd seen her enter the noktum, command the shadow, and defeat the Worldbreaker. He'd felt the calm within her. She'd beat back Xos. She'd taken control of her power just as he'd hoped she would.

And now she lie on the floor of the noktum with death looming as her final reward.

He couldn't even put his hands on her shoulders and tell her that she'd won. That she'd saved the city and beat foes few could imagine.

Senji's boots! He wasn't going to watch her die. Not like this.

Leaning into the noktum he traveled hundreds of miles in an instant, feeling for the anchor of the noktum cloak and alighting onto it like a raven on a perch.

Lorelle.

"Vohn?"

I need your help. Get your herbs. Get Slayter. I will show you where to go.

"Slayter is gone," she said. She paused. "Vohn, what's wrong?"

It's not me. It's another.

"Another?"

Her name is Ksara. She saved Nokte Murosa. She's dying, Lorelle. She used all her power to save them and now she's dying.

Lorelle didn't speak for a long moment. He could almost picture the twist of her lips as she considered Vohn's request.

We saw them all die, Lorelle. All of the Nox. I couldn't ... we couldn't save them ... This time we can. For one person we can make a difference.

"I'm writing a note. Slayter will find it."

Khyven's not going to like that.

"Do we have time to convince Khyven?"

No.

"Then he'll have to trust us," she said. *Now go.*

The final words sounded in Vohn's mind as she joined with the Dark alongside him. The nearness of her settled him. He wasn't alone. She was here. She could help.

In a whirlwind, Vohn dragged Lorelle through the noktums and across the hundreds of miles back to Ksara. The journey took longer with Lorelle in tow. Having no corporeal body had its advantages, few as they may be.

❦   ❦   ❦

Lorelle stepped out of the noktum cloak, her stomach lurching a little from the flight. Before she could look about the new noktum, a flash of light caught her off guard. She spun and leapt, blindly fleeing the ambush, when a dagger grazed her side.

She landed the flip and her own long daggers were in her hands.

Stop! Vohn shouted in her ear. *Tell them you're Ksara's friend.*

Lorelle crouched in the dark, assessing the danger in an instant. Four people stood at alert in the noktum, all four of them glancing wildly about. None of them had Amulets of Noksonon. One with wild black hair held another dagger ready to throw at the next sound. A woman as tall as Senji herself brandished a crude club. One of the men held a short sword and the other stood protectively over a woman on the ground, his arms spread wide and a faint glow about his fingers. A mage. The source of the light.

Lorelle sidestepped behind one of the short, gnarled trees, her Luminent feet not even making a whisper of sound. She'd already gained one grazing cut and she wasn't going to chance another. "I'm here to help Ksara."

"Who are you?"

Lorelle hesitated.

We don't have time for introductions! She's dying!

"I'm here to help Ksara," Lorelle said. "If you want me to explain more, she'll die before I'm done."

The man with the sword lowered it and put a hand on the other man's shoulder. "We trust her."

"We don't know who she is!"

"We trust Ksara."

The mage moved a step away from Ksara, but only a step. The women lowered their weapons and Lorelle silently sheathed her own. With long, graceful strides, Lorelle moved to Ksara's side, knelt down beside her. The woman was a Demaijos, dressed in tattered remnants of their garb and her skin was cold. Too cold.

Placing a finger to the woman's neck, she felt the impossible—the woman still had a pulse. Her lungs weren't moving. Her limbs were heavy and lifeless. But somehow the woman's heart was still pumping.

"I don't know how she's still alive," Lorelle said.

It's the Dark, Vohn said. *It ... it has branches inside her chest. It's pumping her heart. It's keeping her alive.*

"That's ..."

Impossible? Vohn finished. *We deal out impossible all the time.*

Lorelle pulled the Avanon herb mixture from her belt and placed them under the woman's tongue. She'd seen Slayter use a version of this mixture to revive his own magic and vitality, but that had been when he was staggering with fatigue. Not defying death by some trick of the Dark. Adjustments were needed.

Placing a hand on the woman's chest, Lorelle felt for the Dark there. Sure enough, she sensed the push and pull of it inside her. Felt it holding the woman together long enough for something else to happen.

There had to be more she could do.

Digging in her pouch, her hand clasped around a polished stick. She withdrew it just as Vohn groaned.

No. That will kill her.

"Her heart needs help," Lorelle said. "Herbs won't be enough. And Slayter isn't here."

He made it for defense. Not medicine.

"You asked me to try," she said. "This is what I have."

She aimed the wand at Ksara's heart.

Hit the rock beside her!

Lorelle adjusted her aim, flicked her thumb across the smooth wood and lightning crackled into the rock, forking over to Ksara. The light flashed. A boom rang all around them.

Watch out!

Ksara's friends converged on the sound and light, weapons back in their hands, but Lorelle leapt backwards, launching herself in a backflip and catching hold of a tree branch, hauling herself to safety before any of them could even slash a sword or swing a club.

Ksara coughed. She wheezed. Her friends fell to their knees around her.

You did it, Vohn said. *She's alive. She's going to live.*

The Dark kept her alive. It kept her heart beating.

The Dark, Lorelle. It can keep me alive. That's what Slayter's missing!

Lorelle flashed a grin and wrapped herself in the noktum cloak. *Time to bring you home, Vohn.*

CHAPTER EIGHTY-ONE

KSARA

sara lie on cream-colored flagstones in an open-air courtyard. A bright sun illuminated the space and seven statues of women peered down at her.

All of them smiling.

"You live," a rumbling voice said. "Curious."

Ksara pushed up on her elbows and even her imagined persona winced in pain. If she was alive, it was fitfully so. "Curious?"

Xos stood in the shadows of a corridor that fed into the courtyard. His expression neutral. "Mortals. You help each other survive in the most curious ways."

Ksara put a hand to her chest. The ache radiating out from there took her breath away. "Giants don't help each other?"

"An Eldroi stands strongest alone," he said.

"No one stands stronger alone," Ksara said between gritted teeth. "Mortal or no."

Xos turned from Ksara and disappeared down the dark corridor, his heavy footsteps matching the thumps of her heart in her chest.

When he was gone, Ksara noticed movement in the opposite corridor. A fifteen-foot-tall woman with indigo eyes, a black gown, and a dark braid of hair trailing down her shoulder. Behind her, deep in the corridor, the shadow pulsed closer and closer. The plume of black formed around two eyes, the pupils an icy-blue.

The woman Giant gave Ksara a quiet smile, turned and strode into the billowing black and the cold, blue eyes closed.

When Ksara blinked her eyes open, she was lying on the healer's workbench. Most of the elixirs were puddles and shards of glass on the shelves, but a few lucky potions remained. Atlas leaned over her and applied a salve to her collarbone, the ointment immediately easing the searing pain there.

Atlas paused his ministrations when he noticed her awake. He smiled down at her, the expression entirely foreign on his face and somehow perfectly suited to it.

"You're alive," he said in the barest of whisper. "What kind of mage are you, Captain?"

She tried a laugh and the heat stabbed into her ribcage, so she gave a weak cough instead. "You were right," she said. Her voice was hoarse, barely strong enough to make words.

"I was right. And very, very wrong." He turned his head to the left and raised is voice, "She's awake!"

Ulric trampled to her side first. He beamed at her, laughing and crying and trying to pick her up from the table only to be chided by Atlas. Coronata stroked her kapicat and leaned against the table. "Never a dull moment with a Demaijos," she said, grinning.

Merewen found Ksara's hand and gave it a squeeze.

"You were always the stronger one," Ulric said when he could finally form words.

Ksara grinned at him. She'd argue, but her voice wouldn't cooperate. Not yet.

"Now that you're awake," Atlas said. "Would you mind telling your shadows to give me some space? It's creeping me out."

Ksara noticed the black air dancing along the walls for the first time and smiled. Then she reached her hand out toward the indigo air and called it to her.

THE END

Epilogue

KSARA

Ksara walked up the stairs to the Assembly Hall. It had taken weeks to rebuild the structure, but they'd left the line that had divided the new and the old building as a reminder of what had come before. A division in history. A scar to be learned from.

"You don't have to do this," Atlas said, walking to her left.

"I hate to agree with an Imprevari, never mind Atlas," Coronata said. "But the *Falco* is ready to go. Ariston's got no jurisdiction on the sea."

Ksara opened the door to the hall and entered in. "I know."

The anteroom was empty save for cracked murals and broken benches. She crossed the solemn space and Ariston's own captain of the guard waited at the door to the chamber beyond.

The captain of the guard gave her a grim smile. "Ready?"

Ksara nodded.

He escorted Ksara in. Every citizen of Nokte Murosa lined the amphitheater and each turned solemn eyes on her now.

They'd seen her do terrible atrocities. Some of them had even lost loved ones to her magic gone wild.

But they'd also seen her destroy the Worldbreaker and pull the poison from their own lips. And, in the weeks that had followed, she'd rebuilt the very building they sat in. All with that selfsame power. With those very hands.

But it was their choice, and the choice of their leader, whether that was enough. Whether justice could be satisfied.

The guard walked her down the steps toward the dais at the center. There Ariston stood with two other bound prisoners on either side. One was a Shadowvar with sawed off horns. The other a scholar with green eyes that stared dully ahead.

Ksara mounted the stairs to the dais and stood between the Orator and Genove. Ulric and the crew sat in the front row of the amphitheater. Ulric clenched and unclenched his fists. He'd hated this plan. They'd argued about it until the early hours of the morning. But she would not relent.

She could not leave here a criminal. The victims deserved justice. And if she hadn't given them that with her best efforts, then she'd give it to them with her life.

Some debts must be paid.

"On a day such as this, I have no elegant words," Ariston said. "We have come here to decide the fate of three who have changed the history of Nokte Murosa forever."

He walked behind Genove. "All victims of Genove LeGrande, former master of the Nokte Murosan Academy, stand and show your mind."

Two dozen people stood in the amphitheater, each extending their hands palm upward.

Ariston nodded. "You have been judged, Genove LeGrande. Today is your last."

The scholar didn't react. His face didn't even twitch. He just stared at his hands with that blank expression on his face.

Ariston moved to the Orator. "All victims of Rouyen Elvar, Orator of the Dorumai cult, stand and show your mind."

The entire amphitheater stood; the shuffling of their feet echoed throughout the hall. Even Ulric and the crew stood among the citizens. And every person standing showed their palms to the ceiling.

"You have been judged, Orator. Today is your last."

The audience took their seats again. There was barely a sound among the crowd. Not a whisper between neighbors nor a shift in a seat.

Ariston's boots clacked loud on the stone dais as he stood beside Ksara. "All victims of Ksara Sajra, stand and show your mind."

Again the whole crowd got to their feet. Only her crew kept their seat. Ulric stared at Ksara, urgency in his eyes and his hand on the sword at his belt.

With a tight breath, Ksara turned her gaze to the rest of the crowd to see her own fate.

Hundreds of people beheld her now. People who had seen the very worst of her. Who had been hurt by her magic. Had their loved ones killed by her hand.

And not a single one of them raised a palm.

Her heart slammed faster and faster as she looked from face to face, scanning the crowd. Hope building in her chest.

Ariston turned on Ksara and her hope faltered as he raised one hand. If even one person condemned her, she would hang. His hand reached forward and clasped her own, dropping a ring into it. Only then did she notice the hum of the ringlet on her arm. The Ring of Salgimore. Ariston had just put the ring in her hand. "You have been judged, Ksara Sajra. We hold you blameless. Go free."

ABOUT THE AUTHOR

Becca Lee Gardner is an 8-time Honorable Mention Winner from the Writers of the Future contest. She writes novels, comic books, screenplays, and short stories. Her sci-fi horror novella, *Mindstorm*, debuted in December of 2021. If it's science fiction or fantasy with monsters in it, she's all in.

When she's not writing, Becca walks for hours and hours, chasing the sunrise. She also plays intense rounds of Marvel Splendor and Star Wars: Battlefront with her three kids. Her favorite evenings are spent watching Korean zombie shows with her husband who jump-scares quite easily.

Connect with Becca on Facebook:
https://www.facebook.com/beccaleeg

And Instagram:
https://www.instagram.com/beccaleeg/

(Photo cred: Norma Carver)

Author's Note

Worldbreaker is the book that almost broke me.

It all started in February of 2022 when I attended my first Superstars Writing Seminars on a scholarship. There I met Rob Howell and he recruited me into a project called Eldros Legacy—a shared epic fantasy world consisting of five continents, five founders that ran each of the continents, and cohort writers to fill in the world.

That's when I started to dream of twin mages, one who could wield shadow and the other light.

Days after the conference ended, I read *Khyven the Unkillable* by Todd Fahnestock and my trajectory changed immediately. This was the kind of fantasy I'd always wanted to read. All of the magic and world building and deep characters, but none of the slow bits.

A few weeks later, Todd and I were fast friends and Worldbreaker was officially going to be set on Noksonon—Todd's continent in Eldros Legacy.

I drafted the book that summer, figuring the book would release later that year. But just as I finished draft one, Eldros Legacy changed publishers. In the midst of the new changes, I took the opportunity to rewrite the ending of the book. By December of 2022, I handed the manuscript to Todd for feedback.

By March of 2023, I was rewriting the whole book.

Now, to be fair to Todd (who will certainly read this), he did not tell me to rewrite the whole book. He asked me to rewrite chapter one as an experiment.

The experiment was a wild success. I found clarity in the story now. So I rewrote the entire 100,000 word novel from memory.

I almost gave up on the process a hundred different times. I'd never spent so much time on a single project before. I battled daily demons that it would never be good enough. That I didn't have the skill to tell Ksara's story. That I should abandon the project and just move on.

Todd encouraged me, inspired me, and rebuked the demons

in my head. Doug Wagner checked in constantly, smiled at the frustrated messages I sent him at all hours of the day and night, and steadied me. They were my crew as I faced my own darkness of uncertainty, fear, and doubt.

And, just like Ksara, I learned that the darkness is not an enemy. The uncertainty in a creative career is part of the adventure. It means I'm trying to do something great and stretching to reach it.

Worldbreaker is the book that *almost* broke me. Instead it broke me free.

IF YOU LIKED...

Mindstorm

Min the Mighty

The Forest Glows

The Valkyries Initiative — "Surprise"

Of Wizards and Wolves: Tales of Transformation
— "The Punstoppable Catfish Stanley"

Made in the USA
Monee, IL
07 January 2024

50227496R00246